Circle of Spies

ROSEANNA M. WHITE

HARVEST HOUSE PUBLISHERS
EUGENE, OREGON

Scripture quotations are from the King James Version of the Bible.

Cover by Garborg Design Works, Savage, Minnesota

Cover photos © Chris Garborg; Photo DC Inc.

Some of the prayers are taken from *The Valley of Vision: A Collection of Puritan Prayers and Devotions*, published by Banner of Truth, www.banneroftruth.org. Used by permission.

Published in association with the literary agency of The Steve Laube Agency, LLC, 5025 N. Central Ave., #635, Phoenix, Arizona, 85012.

CIRCLE OF SPIES
Copyright © 2014 by Roseanna M. White
Published by Harvest House Publishers
Eugene, Oregon 97402
www.harvesthousepublishers.com

Library of Congress Cataloging-in-Publication Data
   White, Roseanna M.
   Circle of spies / Roseanna M. White.
   pages cm. — (Culper Ring series ; book 3)
   ISBN 978-0-7369-5103-6 (pbk.)
   ISBN 978-0-7369-5104-3 (eBook)
   1. Women spies—Fiction. 2. United States—History—Civil War, 1861-1865—Fiction. 3. Maryland—History—Civil War, 1861-1865—Fiction. I. Title.
   PS3623.H578785C57 2014
   813'.6—dc23

                                      2013026761

Printed in the United States of America

14 15 16 17 18 19 20 21 22 /LB-JH/ 10 9 8 7 6 5 4 3 2 1

*To my brave little princess, Xoë,
and my little ~~prince~~ superspy, Rowyn.
What would a day be without your giggles?*

Acknowledgments

Whenever I try to come up with original plots, "different" often means "risky"—which means I email my editor in complete uncertainty. Thanks, Kim, for encouraging me to write this series as it needed written, and to the whole team at Harvest House, who I adore working with! Thanks too to my agent, Karen Ball, for being an awesome cheerleader and go-getter. You amaze me.

And as it may never have gotten written if not for that perfect weekend writing retreat, enormous smiles of gratitude to Stephanie, for instant brainstorming, lots of laughter, and hours of beautiful quiet. Thanks too to Dina for her amazingly quick turnaround while critiquing!

As always, the love and support of my family, from hubby David and beautiful kiddos to my parents and grandparents and sister and mom-in-law, give me the strength and inspiration I need.

Special thanks to Alyson Dow for naming little Elsie as part of a contest win on Go Teen Writers. Big, huge, grand appreciation to Rachel Wilder, fashion expert extraordinaire, who taught me how ladies of the Victorian era dressed, layer by layer.

And though he's unlikely to ever pick this book up, I also want to thank Dave Cherry, the former coworker who regaled me with stories of his classmate with the perfect memory, who could read books with his eyes closed after merely glancing at the pages. Bet he never knew he'd end up the inspiration for my heroine!

Now the brother shall betray the brother to death…
And ye shall be hated of all men for my name's sake:
but he that shall endure unto the end, the same shall be saved.

Mark 13:12-13

Spies are about everywhere.
The Private Journal and Diary of
John H. Surratt, Conspirator

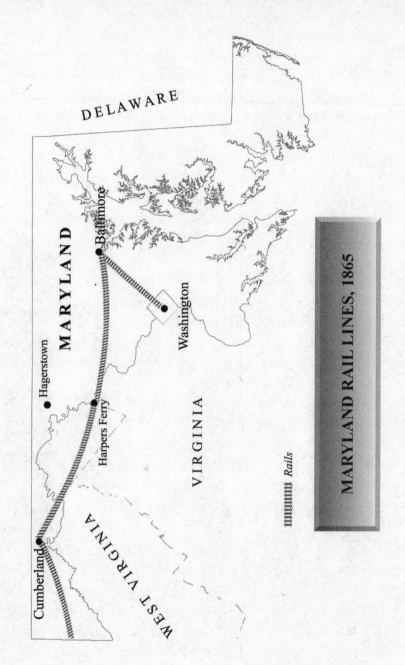

DELAWARE

MARYLAND

Baltimore

Hagerstown

Washington

Harpers Ferry

VIRGINIA

Cumberland

WEST VIRGINIA

|||||||||| Rails

MARYLAND RAIL LINES, 1865

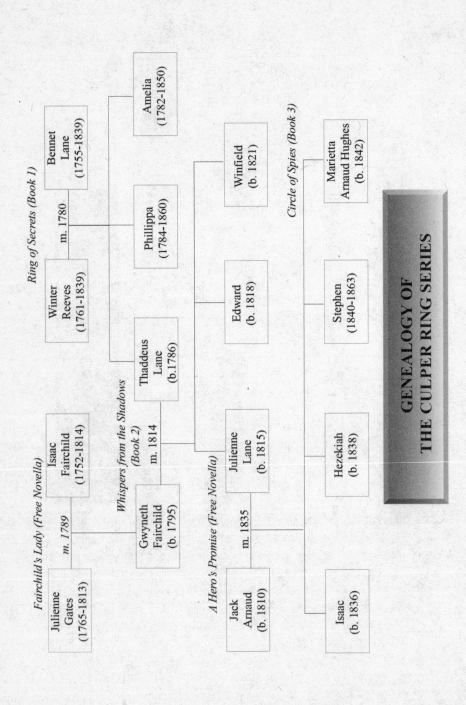

GENEALOGY OF
THE CULPER RING SERIES

Ring of Secrets (Book 1)

Fairchild's Lady (Free Novella)

Whispers from the Shadows (Book 2)

A Hero's Promise (Free Novella)

Circle of Spies (Book 3)

Julienne Gates
(1765-1813)

Isaac Fairchild
(1752-1814)

m. 1789

Bennet Lane
(1755-1839)

m. 1780

Winter Reeves
(1761-1839)

Amelia
(1782-1850)

Phillippa
(1784-1860)

Thaddeus Lane
(b.1786)

Gwyneth Fairchild
(b. 1795)

m. 1814

Winfield
(b. 1821)

Edward
(b. 1818)

Julienne Lane
(b. 1815)

Jack Arnaud
(b. 1810)

m. 1835

Marietta Arnaud Hughes
(b. 1842)

Stephen
(1840-1863)

Hezekiah
(b. 1838)

Isaac
(b. 1836)

One

Baltimore, Maryland
January 16, 1865

Marietta Hughes was the worst widow in the history of mourning. She smoothed a hand down the lavender fabric of her dress and felt the twist in her stomach that shouldn't have been so long absent. The punch to her heart that hadn't made itself known since the first month after Lucien died.

Squeezing her eyes closed, her fingers found the smooth mahogany of the grand staircase railing. Mother Hughes, still weak, her voice feathery, had looked so hopeful when she'd asked Marietta to don the muted colors of half mourning. How could she have refused her? True, it had only been a year and three months since Lucien's death. She had only been three months in second mourning—black relieved only by a white collar—rather than six. But there were so many others with fresh losses to grieve. Her widow's black had made a mockery of them.

Her widow's black had made a mockery of her.

She descended a few steps, but her eyes burned. Her husband was no doubt in heaven begging the Almighty to send a divine bolt to strike her. And not because of the color of her dress.

"I'm sorry, Lucien." The words came out a breath, but still they

9

seemed to taunt her. She should have said those words long before he fell prey to the violent streets of Baltimore. Said them for every thought gone astray, for every too-long look, for every wish she never should have made.

A low whistle made her jump and brought her gaze to her front door, to Lucien's brother. And her stomach twisted again at the object of those stray thoughts. The apple to her Eve.

Upon the wicked he shall rain snares, fire and brimstone, and an horrible tempest: this shall be the portion of their cup.

Marietta's feet pulled her down the stairs, toward where Devereaux Hughes stood with one hand upon the latch. His gaze swept over her, making her cheeks flush even as those words from the Holy Book pounded.

Wicked. Wicked. Wicked.

Sometimes she wished she had never read the Scriptures, so that they couldn't haunt her.

Sometimes she wished she could be, as her parents had advised time and again, *good.*

She swallowed back the regret and guilt—a skill she had mastered nearly six years earlier—and smiled. "Heading home, Dev?"

He leaned into the door, folding his arms so that the fabric of his well-tailored greatcoat strained against his muscles. Glory, but he was a fine-looking man with that charming smirk of his. "I have missed seeing you in color, Mari. Black never suited you."

A fact that shouldn't have bothered her as it did. How vain was she, that she had dwelt on such a truth this past year instead of on the loss that necessitated it?

She smoothed out the wrinkle her fingers had made in the skirt and gave in to the tug that always pulled her closer to Dev, close enough for him to slide an arm around her waist. Given the quiet morning halls, the servants all tending to breakfast or Mother Hughes, she made no objection. Though her heart thudded its accusation.

Wicked.

Her throat tightened. She had never betrayed her husband, not in deed. And who would hold her thoughts against her? Other, of course, than God. And Lucien. She forced a swallow. "Your mother asked me to move into half mourning. I was so glad to see her up and able to speak this morning that I hadn't the heart to argue."

Dev's jaw ticked. "I just saw her. She looks better, but if the doctor is not as hopeful as I expect when he stops in later—"

"I know." Her gaze landed on his cravat. "Dev..."

"Ah, how well I know that look." He bent his head, and when his lips touched her neck, her eyes slid shut. "Hope and regret mixed into perfect beauty. Do you recall when I first saw that expression upon your lovely face?"

As if she could ever forget. "The nineteenth of December, eighteen sixty."

His chuckle sent a pulse of shivers down her spine. "How quick you are with the date."

And usually she would have forced a hesitation. But she needn't with that particular recollection. "It was the day before my wedding."

"The day I met my brother's bride." His chuckle went bitter. "Had I obeyed my father and returned to Baltimore a year earlier, it would have been I you met at that ball. I who would have claimed you. I who—"

"Don't." She pulled away, though his arms granted her only another inch of space. She'd had similar thoughts—much to her shame. "Please, Dev."

Too late. His eyes, blue as July's sky, had already blended in her mind with Lucien's deep green. The parade through her memory had already begun. Each time she had let her thoughts go where they ought not. When she had held Dev's gaze a second too long. Had smiled too warmly.

She was despicable.

"I love you." Vulnerability sparked in his eyes, but his arms were still like iron around her waist. "I have loved you since I first set eyes on you."

The sob came out of nowhere, erupting in a gasp. She covered her mouth, squeezed shut her eyes, and jerked away. Dizziness washed over her when she tried to breathe. Cora had laced her corset too tight when she retied it—that was why the air wouldn't come. Her corset. Just her corset.

Not her conscience. Heaven knew that voice had been muted

most of her life, drowned out by the steady march of meaningless facts through her memory.

"Darling." His fingers closed around her shoulders, so warm against the January chill. "Why does that make you cry? You have known so long how I felt."

Too long. She had known and had held it to her heart, a secret blacker than the gown she had just ordered Cora to pack away. "Tell me I made him happy. Tell me he never knew."

"Mari." He turned her to face him again and tipped her chin up with a gentle touch. What was it about that narrow nose, that tapered chin, those two slashes of dark brows, that made her melt? He thumbed away a tear. "I have pushed you from mourning too fast. Yet I feel as though I have waited forever to claim you."

Her gaze dropped, all the way to the yards of lavender fabric that declared her ready to ease back into society. Why did the declaration make her want to run and hide, when these fifteen months she had struggled so against the confines of black? "I should have better mourned him."

She should have better loved him.

Dev's hand rested on her cheek. "Finish your mourning and take what distance you need, darling. When these final three months are finished, you will be mine."

She didn't know whether to tip her mouth up to invite a forbidden kiss or to pull away. Whether to breathe in his bergamot scent with a smile or let a storm of tears overtake her.

A loud rap on the door saved her the decision and made them both jump. Pulling all those frustrating emotions back in, she waved away the servant who appeared from the kitchen corridor and opened the door herself.

Her smile went from halfhearted to full bloom when she craned her neck up, and up still more to take in her dawn visitor. "Granddad. What are you doing here so early?"

"Your father just made port, and I went to tell him about Fort Fisher's fall yesterday—"

"Fort Fisher? In North Carolina?" Hope surged up, though Marietta settled a hand on her chest to contain it. It would be a mighty blow to the Confederacy, but that did not mean the war was over.

"Hadn't you heard? Then I'm glad I thought to pay a call on my favorite girl while I was out." Thaddeus Lane grinned, tapped a finger to her nose as he had since she was a tot, and strode inside. A blast of icy air came with him, against which she shut the door. When she turned again, his smile had faded to a glower aimed at Dev.

"Mr. Hughes. What are you doing here so early?"

Dev was never one to be flustered, though his smile looked strained. "Mother took a bad turn last night. We feared the worst. She pulled through, praise the Lord, but I couldn't leave until I was sure of it."

Both men sent her a glance. Dev's, full of shared worry and relief and that black secret. Granddad Thad's, full of censure. Marietta opened the door again. One of them at a time was plenty. "Shall I see you at dinner, Dev?"

"Dismissed." He chuckled but obeyed the dictate and made for escape. "You shall. And do send a note to tell me what the doctor says, even if it is good news."

"I will." Her lips pulled of their own will into a soft smile for him. Though after she shut the door, all softness evaporated under the scathing regard drilling into her back. She turned around and looked at her grandfather with arched brows. "Must you treat him that way?"

Granddad's scowl only deepened. "I am your grandfather, young lady. I will treat a man any way I please when I find him in your home at seven in the morning. Now get your cape. You are taking a walk with me."

"I am not. It is freezing out there." But even as she said the words, she reached for the heavy woolen cape on the rack. Granddad never issued orders. Not unless it was of the most vital importance. "You cannot condemn a man for being concerned for his mother."

"If he were so concerned, he would move her into *his* house."

Marietta fastened the toggle and wrenched open the door again. "Must we have this conversation for the ninety-second time?"

"Ninety-two, is it?" Amusement crept its way into his voice. "Is that an approximation or an exact count?"

She glared at him over her shoulder.

He pulled the door shut, and for a long moment held her gaze with glinting amber eyes. "How is it you can know the exact number of times I have said a certain thing, yet cannot see the wisdom in obeying? Go home to your parents, Mari. Or take the money your husband left you and set up house somewhere else. Go to Alain in Connecticut—"

"No. This is *my* house, my home."

He had to have known she would say it, just as she had the other ninety-one times. So why did he look so sorrowful as he offered her his elbow?

She tucked her hand into the crook with an exhalation blustery enough to rival the wind off the Chesapeake. "I am a woman of three and twenty. I am perfectly capable of maintaining my own living, and Mother Hughes needs me."

He sighed, led her down the walk for a few steps, and then turned toward the drive.

Marietta dug in her heels. "You said a walk, Granddad. Why would we need to go to the carriage house?"

"We are walking *to* the carriage house. We need to talk, and that is the safest place."

No, no it wasn't. The carriage house was anything but safe. "We can just keep going down the street—"

"Marietta. *Come.*"

Her throat went dry. He hadn't used her full name in so long...and that spark in his eyes was like a fuse. "What is it? Is something wrong? Grandmama? Mama, Daddy?"

"Something is wrong, but not with them. Please, Mari. For once in your life, stop fighting and do what I ask."

He looked so serious, the lines in his face deepening. She nodded and complied, even though her corset seemed tighter with each step they took.

She had managed to avoid the carriage house and stables for more than a year and would have been happy to make it two. Not that any sour memories were connected to this particular building. It was the similar one at her parents' that made her teeth grind together.

And the arrogant, infuriating man who had once mucked stalls there and now stood in *her* outbuilding, pitchfork in hand. She should have dismissed him years ago. Should have refused her brother's pleading. Should have slapped that patronizing smile from Walker Payne's face the first time he put it on.

"Morning, Walker." Granddad said it with sobriety rather than cheer. Unusual for him.

Walker went still. He used his coat sleeve to wipe his forehead as he turned, a bit of a flush in his pale brown skin, an icy calm in his strange silver-blue eyes. "Mr. Lane." His gaze landed on her. "Princess."

Marietta withdrew her arm from Granddad's so she could fold it with her other over her chest. "Are you still working here? I'd have thought you would have run off by now, looking for the next rush of adventure."

Rather than rising to the bait or mentioning the wife and child that kept him chained to her household, he looked back to Granddad. "Are you sure about this, Mr. Lane?"

Were she a cat, her hackles would have risen. Whatever Granddad wanted to say to her, Walker obviously knew about it.

"It's the only way." Granddad drew in a long breath and caught her gaze. "Mari, I need to know where you stand. On the war."

Of all the... "You question my loyalty? And in front of *him?*"

"Walker is family."

"One's great-grandmother being your housekeeper does not make one family!"

Walker, for some reason known only to the convoluted workings of his self-important mind, smiled. "How sorely I've missed you, Yetta."

A breath of cynical laughter slipped out. He was no doubt as unhappy about his presence here as she was but just as bound by his word to Stephen.

"Could you children stop snapping at each other? We only have a few minutes." Her grandfather led her deeper into the building, where the nauseating scent of hay and horses filled her nose. "Mari, I have no choice but to question you. Baltimore, all of Maryland, is a house divided. You married into a family with firm Southern roots—"

"Really, Granddad. Mother Hughes has been questioned enough on this subject. She may be from New Orleans, but her husband was as solid a Union man as you." Her arms slid down to wrap around her middle. Just an attempt to keep her hands warm, that was all.

"I am asking about *you*, Mari."

Why was she born to live through this blasted war? All she had wanted was to go to the theater, to entertain her friends, to dance until her feet ached. A world that seemed so far removed now. "My brother gave his life for the Union. How can you question where I stand?"

"Your cousin gave his life for the Confederacy in the very same battle. How can I help but question?"

Again tears stung...though tears for Stephen seemed somehow different than those born of regrets for Lucien. "Stephen was my best friend." Her only friend, when it came down to it.

Granddad slid closer. "Does that mean his cause is your cause? One you believe in enough to fight for? To risk dying for?"

Her arms went limp, and icy air nipped at her fingers. "You are scaring me."

"I mean to. Walker?"

Her brother's friend nodded and motioned them to follow him. "This way."

A draft of vicious wind whistled through the building, making a chill skitter up her spine. "Where are we going?"

Granddad rested a hand against the small of her back. To lend comfort or to spur her onward if her feet faltered? "What do you know about the Knights of the Golden Circle?"

"The KGC?" The wind seemed colder. "That they're a Copperhead group. A Southern-sympathizing social club that boasts hundreds of thousands of members."

"Social club?" Granddad's short laugh sounded dry. "Perhaps for many of those hundreds of thousands, but not for the high-level members. It is a very serious organization, one with a very dangerous agenda."

"Promoting slavery. I know."

Walker came to such an abrupt halt that she nearly ran into his back. His eyes shot shards of ice at her. "You want to say that a little more flippantly next time, princess?"

She dimpled and batted her lashes. "Perhaps I could try if you could be more sensitive to the subject."

"Enough." Her grandfather's tone sounded mournful, bringing her gaze back to his face. "This is serious, Mari. A matter of murder and treason, of the deliberate destruction of the Union—and of which Lucien had a part, and Devereaux too."

"Nonsense. They both pledged their loyalty to the Union." Words that came so easily.

But Granddad shook his head, no hint of a jest in his eyes. "Only in words. Think of that unexplained delay in reopening the rail lines last year. Their ties to the land in Louisiana."

Conversations between the Hugheses buzzed in her ears, images flashed. If she were to look at them in that light…but no, it couldn't be. She shook it off. "Half the city likely belongs to the KGC."

The two men exchanged a glance that made her want to grit her teeth again. Granddad nodded, and Walker moved onward, his pace quick.

Marietta held her cape closed and wished she had taken the time to grab gloves or a muff. Her fingers were at the painful place between chilled and numb. "What does this have to do with me?"

"You will see soon enough. First, answer me this. What color dress were you wearing on the fifteenth of May in eighteen fifty?"

Of all the random… "Yellow, but I don't see what—"

"What is the first word on the third line on the second page of the fifth book upon the shelf in your room?"

He wanted to play games? Out here in the cold, in the smelly stables with that patronizing man? She lifted her chin. "I haven't read the fifth book."

"The fourth then."

She shook her head and stared at Walker's back when he stopped in the last stall and fooled with the hay. "It's 'yesterday,' but I—"

"What was the eighth word I spoke to you the last time we had dinner?"

"'This,' though I can hardly think what—"

"Well, it's time to think, Mari." Granddad's gaze combined sorrow with determination. "Time to use that mind of yours for something other than drawing room repartee. Your memory is *perfect*."

Walker knelt down and slid aside a board.

Marietta waved a hand at Granddad's words. "A parlor trick."

"A gift of God." He gripped her arm, a silent bid for her to look at him. Though when she saw the furor in his eyes, she wished she hadn't. "You have perfect recall, beyond even your grandmother's. Perhaps she can draw anything she sees, but you—your recollection extends to what you've heard, what you've done, when things happened. Do you not realize how rare that is? How special you are?"

Walker's scoffing laugh gave her the urge to place her half boot upon his back and give him a nice little kick into... "What is that hole?" Her voice felt strangled, frozen.

"Come see." Walker held out his hands, as if they were still children. As if she could trust him.

She took a step back. "If you think for even a moment that I will descend into some dank pit—"

"We have a very small window of time, Mari. Go." Granddad's hand on her back urged her onward.

But it was the glint of challenge in Walker's eyes that made her huff over to him. She tamped down the shudder when he lowered her into the black, yawning space. Followed him with chin held high when Granddad handed down a lantern and brought up the rear.

A tunnel. They were in a tunnel that stretched toward her house. "What is this?"

"I didn't want to bring you into this business, Mari." Her grandfather's voice echoed strangely off the timber walls. "When my parents passed the mantle of the Culpers to me, and then when I shared it with your father and uncles and Walker and Hez, there was always an understanding that we would shield the family who wanted no part of it. You. Ize. Most of your cousins. But we have no choice now."

Each word fell like a hammer upon a chisel, etching themselves into her mind. Yet with more force than normal words, with finality. "Culpers?"

Granddad prodded her onward. "The Culper Ring started in the Revolution. My mother was a spy in British-held New York, passing information through a collection of friends until it reached General Washington."

"Great-Grandmama Winter—a spy?" Impossible. Her portrait made her look like such a normal woman.

"When I took over during the next war with the British—"

"You?" The world tipped. Her laugh did nothing to right it. "Granddad, you are not a spy."

"Here we are." Walker set down the lantern and put his shoulder to a break in the timbers. "It will open only a foot, but it's enough to get a glimpse. It's a Knights' castle, no question."

A castle, one of their secret lairs? Here, between her home and her carriage house? It could not be. And to prove it could not be, she grabbed the lantern, thrust it through the opening, and stuck her head in after it.

The walls were papered with charts and maps, lines drawn over them helter-skelter. Some of the North, with stars upon the major cities, some of the South, stretching all the way to Texas. One of the entire hemisphere, with a circle drawn around Havana as a center. Papers pinned with what looked like gibberish upon them. And there, nearly out of the dim circle of light, one of Lincoln's election posters. But with "King" scrawled above his name, and a cruel-looking X drawn through his face in an ink more red-brown than lampblack, something nearly the color of...

"Oh, God in heaven." Blood, it was blood. She stumbled back and would have dropped the light had Walker not rescued it. Would have fallen had her grandfather not caught her.

He held her fast. "That had better be a genuine beseeching of the Almighty, Mari, because we need to fall to our knees before Him. They are going to harm the president if we don't stop them. And we've done all we can from the outside."

"Not Dev. Please, not Dev."

Walker eased the opening shut and watched her closely in the golden light. "He's the captain of this castle, Yetta. He took over after Lucien died."

No. She squeezed shut her eyes, but that did nothing to blur the implications. If Granddad spoke rightly, then both of them had lied to her. Had told her she was the most important thing in the world but had undermined all her family stood for. Had made a fool of her. Had they been *using* her, her family's connections?

If it were true... "What is it you want from me?"

Granddad gave her a squeeze. "Allan Pinkerton is sending in a man. He has been in communication with Dev and ought to be arriving in town any day. You cannot let either of them know you realize what they are about, but you have to protect him where you can, Mari. Make sure he has the opportunities he needs to find information."

"His name's Slade Osborne. A New Yorker by birth, but more recently of Chicago. He's part of Pinkerton's Intelligence Service." Walker reached out and took her hand in his. Audacious, yes.

Inappropriate too. And oh, how it reminded her of happier days. "Can you do this, Yetta?"

She saw again that red-brown slash upon the yellowed poster. Shivered at the hatred that must have inspired the defacing. Had the same hand that so recently cupped her cheek marked the president's image for destruction? Had the lips that had kissed her sworn treason?

She didn't know. And the not-knowing made her knees want to buckle. For the first time in too many years, she turned her mind to prayer.

Oh, God, if it's true...What have I done?

Two

Slade Osborne planted his feet on the wooden platform at Camden Station and waited for the locomotive's steam to clear. In the bleak January sunshine, Baltimore looked as he had come to expect—gray, dreary, frayed. A city on the edge of chaos. Hence the many Union uniforms milling about with dour-faced soldiers inside them.

He scanned the buildings, the muddy streets. Even never having seen Devereaux Hughes, he would know him. He would be well dressed, have a charming smile, and eyes as hard as the rails that paved his way to fortune. He'd no doubt send that skitter of warning up Slade's spine. The self-same one that had made him spin around a second before his brother meant to put a sledge to his skull.

His jaw clenched, he hooked a finger in his waistcoat pocket and stepped away from the stream of pedestrians. His train car was being hitched to horses for the trip through the city to President Street Station, but he wouldn't be joining his fellow passengers.

He spotted a few men who matched Hughes's general description. Mid-thirties, dark hair, blue eyes. But he'd place his bets on the one striding from the building far behind the depot. The man was too far away to see eye color, and a top hat covered his hair, but Slade knew authority.

He leaned against a lamppost, though it was likely to earn him soot marks on his worsted wool suit. Despite the gnawing inside that made him want to hurry, he would wait. Pinkerton had trained him well in how to assume a role, and the biggest trick was never to overplay one's hand.

Even when the role one was assuming was one's own.

Of their own volition, his fingers found the silver chain of his borrowed watch fob. The metal was warm against the bitter air, warm as a long-gone memory. Odd how aware it made him of the price of war, the soul-breaking cost of betrayal. Of how his chance to set it all to rights was ticking away.

What an ugly time they lived in.

He released the fob and folded his arms, expelling a long puff of white breath. The passers-by hurried along, mothers adjusting their children's coats as they stepped out of doors, gentlemen pulling hats down. The man he had been watching drew nearer, near enough to spot Slade in their agreed-upon location. He knew he, too, matched the description Hughes would have been given. A shade taller than average, hair nearly black under his bowler, lean. A description that fit any number of men milling about.

That had fit one too many before.

He waited for the man's gaze to wander his way and then lifted his right hand to rub his forefinger above his lip. Recognition kindled in the other set of eyes, and the answering left hand came up, thumb and forefinger taking hold of his left ear.

Slade pushed away from the lamppost and let his coat fall into place around his knees while the man closed the distance between them, hand extended. He knew the Knights' grip—that he must press his thumb against the knuckle while they shook—but it felt odd.

"Mr. Osborne, I presume. I'm Devereaux Hughes."

Slade nodded and reclaimed his hand. "Good of you to come meet me, Mr. Hughes."

"Good of you to travel to Baltimore." Calculation sharpened the blue of his eyes, though his smile was the epitome of Southern charm. "You spent several years in Washington City before this, correct?"

It took all his willpower not to curl his hand into a fist. Several years nearly undone by the last three months in the field. "That's right."

Hughes waited, but Slade offered no more. Words, he had learned long ago, could hang one as quickly as a rope. After a moment's pause, the other man smiled and motioned to his right. "Shall we go? I have sent a note to my mother and sister-in-law that we would have a guest for dinner tonight."

"Certainly." And that was the part of this business he was not looking forward to—socializing. But at least, with the war having washed all the color out of this gray, drab world, no one would expect him to be jovial.

After giving instruction to a stevedore to take care of his trunk, he followed Hughes toward a waiting carriage. Neither spoke until the door closed upon them, the thunk of the trunk sounded on the roof, and the driver's "Yah!" prompted a lurch into motion.

Then Hughes's eyes went sharp, and he leaned against the cushion. "I admit, Mr. Osborne, that your letter of introduction piqued my curiosity. You say you have not been officially inducted?"

Slade made himself comfortable. "Not in Washington. Too many old friends watching."

Those sharp eyes sparked. "Indeed. Though I am curious as to why someone so...dedicated, shall we say, to one cause should turn so suddenly to the opposite view."

A question he had pondered long and hard himself. Only one conclusion presented itself. "I suppose it wasn't so sudden."

"Hmm." The man regarded him for a long moment and made no attempt to hide his perusal.

Let him look his fill. Slade knew well what he would see. The picture Ross had crafted for him—hard shell, empty insides. A picture easily donned again when he realized how deep his brother's hatred had run.

At length, Hughes nodded and relaxed. His acceptance couldn't possibly be so easily won, but Slade was happy to forego an interrogation here and now. He'd had enough of those for a while.

The man adjusted his gloves and offered a smile. "I understand you are from New York City. Are you related to the Osbornes of Fifth Avenue?"

He nearly snorted. "My father is a minister in Brooklyn."

Hughes's eyes dimmed. No doubt if Slade didn't have the information he so wanted, he would have booted him to the cobblestones with a kick to his poor Yankee posterior. Rich, powerful Northerners were of the utmost interest to the Knights. But common ones?

His host studied the fine wool of Slade's coat. "You seem to have risen above such humble origins."

How many years had he wasted trying to do just that? Rise above what didn't need leaving? But the Slade Osborne this man needed to know hadn't realized the error of his ways. He kept his face neutral. "I've done well enough."

Hughes smiled full and bright. "Well, I hope you enjoy your tenure in our city. Have you found lodging yet?"

"I was hoping you could direct me to a boardinghouse."

Hughes waved that off. "Nonsense. I have rooms aplenty. You are welcome to stay with me."

Southern hospitality? Slade suspected not. He knew that particular shade of smile, and it was self-serving. This, despite his confidence and charm, was a desperate man. There was no way the captain of the Baltimore castle of the KGC would invite a stranger into his home otherwise.

Slade's blood quickened. Did he want to spend every hour in Hughes's company? No. But then, if he were staying in the man's house, he would be more likely to find time to poke around. He forced a smile. "Thank you."

"Excellent." Hughes's fingers tapped on his knee. "There is a meeting tonight. If you are earnest about joining—"

"I am."

A corner of Hughes's mouth turned up. Something about his expression reminded Slade of his sister's husband. The way he could charm a crowd with a few well-delivered sentences. Make whomever he was speaking to believe they were the only one in the world who mattered.

Slap a woman till she saw stars and convince her it was her fault.

"I appreciate your eagerness. But let me make something clear." Without so much as a shift in his countenance, Hughes's welcome throbbed with threat. "I will induct no more rabble interested only in the allure of a secret society. The time for society has ended. And when—if—I swear you in, it will be with the understanding that we both mean each and every word of the oath."

For a moment, Slade held his gaze. No urge to flinch, no second-guessing. How could he, at this point? He had already lost everything but his life, and that phrase his father had taught him echoed constantly these days.

To live is Christ, and to die is gain.

Not that he was ready to give himself to eternity quite yet. "I would love to reassure you, Hughes, but given that I don't know what the oath is..."

Amusement joined hands with the threat. "Let's just say you'll be swearing to act solely in the interest of the order—or to never act again."

Death. The word crept its way into the carriage, despite the half smile and vague words. Slade had known when he signed on for this mission that the stakes could be no higher. Maybe it was the former gambler in him that had made him exchange that silent, irrevocable nod with Pinkerton. To be willing to risk it all for a chance to bring down the beast.

Or maybe it was because that gambler was gone. He had changed. And now he saw the world needed changing too.

Into the face of that silent echo, he pursed his lips and nodded. Sure, if this man knew the truth about him, he would draw that pistol from under his fashionable coat in a heartbeat. Nothing new. Slade had spent the last three months surrounded by thousands of men who would have done the same.

"The war has taken its toll." Hughes trained his gaze out the window, so Slade followed suit. Weary buildings, brick covered in soot and wood desperate for whitewashing. "Crime abounds, so step carefully and be ready at all times to defend yourself. My neighborhood is one of the safest, but even so..."

"Mobtown. I know." Baltimore's reputation for murder and assault put even New York City to shame. "Ever think of leaving?"

"I did a decade ago. I should not have. When I returned, my brother had been handed everything." He looked to Slade again. No reminiscence clouded his eyes, no regret. Just that same cold charm. "Have you any brothers, Mr. Osborne?"

And his father had said his hours at the poker table would avail nothing but trouble. If only he knew how schooling his features could now save his life. He kept watching the muted cityscape roll by. "I had one."

A pause. Hughes cleared his throat. "The war?"

"The war." Indirectly.

"I'm sorry. Losing a brother is never easy. Mine fell to muggers some fifteen months ago."

Slade already knew that, and a sketch of information about the Hughes family besides. But because he wouldn't have, had Pinkerton not provided him with a file, he looked back at his host as if surprised. Made sure his eyes softened, as if it created some kind of bond. As if his own loss weren't so much fresher. And so much crueler. "My condolences."

"Thank you."

Silence held for a minute, and then Hughes turned to the latest news from the front. Slade seldom added a word. It was enough to grow accustomed to the cadence of the man's voice. To learn the way his eyes shifted. To note each street they passed.

At last they turned into Monument Square, without question one of the wealthiest sectors of the city. Here the effects of the war were less obvious. The grounds looked tended. A black woman—slave or employed?—pushed a pram down the walk. A gaggle of ladies sashayed along as if they hadn't a care in the world.

Scarlet curls peeking from one of the bonnets caught his gaze, and the face they framed held him captive. An appreciative noise slipped out. He may have reformed his ways, but a man still had to give credit to the Lord's craftsmanship.

Hughes chuckled. "I see you have spotted our neighbors. Though several of those ladies are married, so do be careful who earns those hums of approval, Osborne."

She was middling in height. Her fashionable coat probably provided little warmth, but neither did it hide her figure. And an admirable figure it was. "The redhead?" Not that he could afford divided attention, but a man had to know these things.

He felt Hughes stiffen before he glanced over and saw his smile freeze. Ice snapped in his eyes. "My brother's widow. She is still in mourning, you understand."

"Ah." Yes, he understood. He understood she was wearing lavender, though she ought to be still in second mourning. He understood the possessive gleam in Devereaux Hughes's eyes.

He understood his one little sound of admiration had just labeled him as someone to be watched. Blast it to pieces. His mother had been right. Nothing good ever came of letting one's eyes wander.

Glancing out the window again, he chose another young lady at random. "What about the blonde there?"

Perhaps Hughes relaxed a degree. Or perhaps it was wishful thinking. "Miss Lynn. She had a sweetheart at the start of the war, but..."

"Miss Lynn." He put a grin in his voice as he tested the name.

Mrs. Hughes glanced their way as they rumbled past and smiled. No innocent greeting of her brother-in-law, that smile. No, there was something far more in her cat-green eyes. Something that contained both recognition and question. Both passion and...anger?

Dangerous woman.

The carriage turned into a drive, and Slade's host barely waited for the door to open before jumping down. "Come. I'll show you to a room. We have half an hour before we must repair across the street. My mother is a stickler for promptness, even though she has been bound to her rooms this past month." His face finally softened, a light in his smile.

Slade slid on the old, carefree grin he hadn't worn in so long. "Mine is the same way."

But when he stood in the silence of a guest bedroom a few minutes later, he didn't rush for the basin of water. He didn't loosen the cravat he wanted to take off altogether or poke around the room's elegant appointments. He strode to the window and leaned against the frame. He closed his eyes and, for the first time since he boarded the train in Washington earlier, dared to draw in a long breath. To be the man he was rather than the man he had once been.

Father God. Another deep breath, to clear his mind and cleanse his heart. *Father God, here I am. Where You sent me. Keep my heart focused on You.*

Any further prayer was cut off by the entrance of the manservant who had driven the carriage, Slade's trunk bowing his back. Though he nearly stepped forward to help, he stopped himself. He even let a second man fuss over wrinkles and cuff links. And then he went down, twenty minutes later, to find his host waiting by the door.

Hughes nodded at his appearance and led him outside, across the street to an edifice even larger than his. "The family home," the man said, motioning at it. "I was fortunate to find a house so near when I moved back to Baltimore four years ago."

Had Lucien willed it to the missus despite her giving him no heir, or did Devereaux let her continue living there with his mother out of the goodness of his heart? Or out of *something*, anyway.

A black man in livery opened the door for them before Hughes could even knock. "Evenin', Mr. Dev. Sir. Come right on in outta that cold, now."

His host made some reply, but Slade couldn't have said what. He'd no sooner taken off his hat and handed it over with his overcoat than he spotted her. First the deep flame of her hair, and then the swish of her pale purple skirt. She came their way from somewhere down the hall, gliding forward with that grace Southern mamas seemed to instill in their daughters from birth.

"Good evening, Dev." Her voice was what he'd imagined it would be. A warm alto, thick with honey.

He recognized the tug in his gut for what it was. She was beautiful. Too beautiful, the kind that knew well the power it gave her over the male half of the species. And if he read that calm control in her eyes aright, the kind that used it like an overseer would a whip. Still, recognizing it didn't stop the tug from repeating when she turned those pale green eyes his way.

"And this must be Mr. Osborne." Her smile was all rehearsed charm as she held out a hand, wrist limp. "So good of you to join us."

He took the hand because propriety said he must and bowed over it, but he stopped shy of pressing his lips to her knuckles. She would call it bad manners—he called it survival instincts. "Good of you to have me."

Hughes stepped to her side and cupped her elbow. The curl of his fingers looked like a shackle. "Allow me to make proper introductions. This is Slade Osborne of New York, a security agent trained by Allan Pinkerton. I'm considering hiring him, what with all the sabotage to the rails. Mr. Osborne, my sister-in-law, Marietta Arnaud Hughes."

"Arnaud." It took him a second, but likely only because of how distracting it was when she arched those fiery brows. "Any relation to Commodore Arnaud of the USS *Marguerite?*"

Her smile went warm. "My father."

Her father was one of the Union's most vital naval commanders? He didn't dare look at Hughes, but he had to wonder. Did that fact gall him, he with his Confederate sympathies? Or was it, in fact, a mark in her favor?

He supposed he would find out if he did his job well.

Another man may have commented on Commodore Arnaud's legendary bravery. But because she obviously knew the stories better than he, Slade simply nodded again. And, when she motioned to his right, turned.

"Do make yourselves comfortable, gentlemen. I just need to check in with Tandy in the kitchen."

His gaze snagged on Hughes's, and his host jerked his head toward that room to the right—a library—while he pulled Mrs. Hughes to the left. "You get settled, Osborne. I need a word with our hostess."

Seeing no reason to argue, Slade strode into the library, taking in the fine furniture with a slow turn and sweeping glance...which made its way back to the hallway just as Hughes pulled the lady close, wrapped his arms around her, and kissed her like there was no tomorrow.

Subtle. With a snort, Slade turned away. About as subtle as Ross's sledgehammer.

Three

How Marietta wished the boning in her corset would allow her spine to sag. She perched upon the edge of the settee and willed the evening to be over. Her head pounded, her neck ached. All she wanted was to shut herself in her room, curl up on her bed, and try to convince the questions to stop whirling. The doubts to stop nagging. Her heart to stop twisting.

It was all too much for one day. Far, far too much. Each new fact hovered before her gaze, images forever scored into her mind. What would it be like to forget? Perhaps if she could get lost in a book...or fall into the oblivion of sleep...

But Dev and Mr. Osborne had come in right behind her after dinner, eliminating all chances of escape. Though rather than sit, Dev just flashed that charming smile. Her stomach knotted, but not quite like it had this morning, before Granddad had dumped the wretched questions upon her. He was wrong. Mistaken. Dev could have no part of any dark secrets.

Yet Thaddeus Lane had never been mistaken about anything so important, not in her recollection. And he never would have come to her about it unless he had been entirely certain.

Which facts, then, to believe?

Dev's eyes looked as soft as ever when he gazed at her. The love and desire still gleamed. Just as Lucien's always had. How could they both pretend to be one sort of man in her company, and then crawl underground like a serpent and plot destruction?

Well. She squared her shoulders and made herself smile. She would discover the truth somehow. And if he had lied to her for four years, then she would return the favor. Convince him she was the same woman she'd always been, even if she hadn't a clue who she might be when she shut her eyes tonight. Was she Dev's love, or a...a Culper?

"I had better go sit with Mother for a while." Dev smiled at her and then glanced at Mr. Osborne. "I trust you can entertain our guest for a few minutes, darling?"

"Of course." She kept her smile neutral, though her chest tightened as he left the room. They all knew their guest had witnessed that kiss an hour and a half earlier, but she could hardly pull away and slap Dev the way she had wanted to do. Not when she had welcomed his kiss too often this past year. If Granddad *was* right, she had best obey his insistence that Dev remain oblivious to her knowledge of his loyalties. And if she could prove him wrong, then why take it out on Dev?

Though she had hissed at him about making such a move in plain view of the man across the hall.

Over dinner, she had paid their guest no more attention than she would any other guest. Hadn't looked at him overlong, hadn't let herself wonder.

Now, though, with Dev gone, she turned her gaze his way and watched him. He still stood, looking perfectly at ease and showing no inclination to sit. Which suited him, somehow. He wasn't all that tall—at least three inches shorter than both of the Hughes brothers—but his limbs seemed to have a fluidity to them, like a wild animal perfectly content to stand and watch...until it pounced.

A panther, maybe. Or a wolf, rangy and alone. One with eyes so deep a brown they were nearly black, much like his hair. He wore a goatee, neatly trimmed, and a fine suit of clothes in charcoal. The look in his eyes said he thought he understood everything perfectly.

Unlikely.

He motioned toward the bookshelves lining the westward wall. "May I?"

"Certainly." She toyed with one of the curls Cora had arranged over her shoulder as he slid toward the books. "I confess you didn't strike me as the studious type, Mr. Osborne."

"Guess it depends on with whom I'm being compared." He turned to peruse the shelves.

An odd man to send to infiltrate the KGC. One who harbored a secret that could get him killed, yet whose cover was, in fact, that he was one of Pinkerton's agents. Foolish or brilliant. She would reserve judgment as to which.

He pulled a book from the shelf and paged through it. Rather than replace it again, he stood there and read.

Marietta frowned. "Well, I am surprised. Sermons?"

He turned toward her, the book still in his hand and a question lining his forehead. "My father is a minister. And you must have fine eyesight to have seen the title from there."

"Must I?" A smile bade for leave to touch her lips, and she allowed it. She couldn't make out so much as a word of the title, but he had pulled down the twelfth book, the one with the blue spine. The sermons of John Wesley.

He ran a finger down the edge of the book, more thoughtfully than he would from simple reminiscence—more like a man who valued the words inside. Then he snapped it shut and lifted his chin. Studied her.

A wolf, without doubt.

"I was sorry to hear about your husband." Yet no apology softened the gaze that dropped from her face to the lavender silk. "Though I know my condolences are belated. How long has it been?"

Four hundred fifty-eight days and—she glanced at the mantel clock—twenty-two hours and sixteen minutes.

But that was surely not the answer he was looking for. No, he sought no answer at all. No question burned in his gaze. But censure gleamed where it ought to have been. She let the hair wind around her finger. None of her friends at the Ladies' Aid meeting had been anything but supportive—to her face, anyway. But this stranger would stand in her house and judge her? She pulled the curl tight before dropping her hand and letting it bounce free. He couldn't know how fully she deserved the condemnation.

Still, she kept her smile in place. "Not long enough to be out of second mourning. Mother Hughes requested the change, though, and her health has been so fragile. If something so simple can help buoy her, who am I to refuse?"

Perfectly honest, yet he studied her as if trying to unravel truth from lie. "Kind of you. To care so for her when most would leave her to her other son."

Marietta reached for the basket of bandages waiting to be rolled. Something useful ought to come of this conversation. "I could hardly ask her to leave the only home she has known since her marriage."

"Of course not," he said. Yet when she glanced up, his eyes said *that* was the answer he had sought.

She found the end of one strip and began to roll. Why had he wanted to know who in the family owned the house? It could be of no...

She granted herself only a moment's pause as the realization struck. The castle. It was on her land. Lucien's father had willed it to him, and he had willed it to her. If she sold the house...if she chose to marry someone other than Dev...

The ache expanded until it took over her heart too. Yet another question to pile on the day.

For now, she fastened on her most charming smile. It might be a bit rusty after these months at home in mourning, but it would suffice to parry Mr. Osborne's unfelt compliment about caring for her mother-in-law. "Well, sir, I am only striving for Christian perfection."

She was guessing, of course, as to which sermon he had landed on when he flipped the book open. But if his father had educated him in Wesley's works, then he would be familiar with it.

He glanced down at the tome and then looked at her again, those wolf eyes smirking. "Now I am the one surprised. You have read Wesley?"

Had his shock not been well deserved, it might have offended her. As it was, she chuckled. "My parents hoped to fill my mind with all things high and good."

Amusement twitched his lips. "Did it work?"

She straightened the length of cloth before winding it more and then sent him a laughing gaze. "What do you think?"

"That you gave your parents many a headache."

Remembering all the times they had threatened to cart her off to

Connecticut to Grandpapa Alain and Grandmère Adèle, Marietta grinned. "An understatement. And you, Mr. Osborne with a penchant for Methodist sermons? Were you the perfect child?"

He walked over to a chair and eased into it, but the action did nothing to banish the thunderheads in his eyes. "I left the perfection to my brother."

"Hmm." Such an easy excuse to make for oneself, that one's parents already had children who fulfilled all their expectations, so that left one free for...anything. She tilted her head to the side. "Let me guess. You left home too young and proceeded to make a career of carousing, engaging in all that sport we ladies of breeding cannot mention. At which you must have enjoyed enough success to continue for a fair number of years, but eventually you realized it was not as fulfilling as you'd hoped, so you settled—somewhat—to a real career. With Allan Pinkerton, it would seem."

Had his gaze been a knife, it would have sliced her to ribbons. "Mr. Hughes told you about me?"

She would have snorted had it not been so unseemly. Instead, she turned it into an echo of a laugh. "No. But I know your type."

A single flame of anger flickered through his glare before he banked it. Ah, her guest did not like to be labeled. Poor thing. Perhaps, then, he should not apply them so freely to her.

The acidic thought ate away at her as she finished that roll, put the bandage back into the basket, and pulled out the next strip.

Her chest went tight and heavy. This was why she had silenced her conscience long ago. It was dashed uncomfortable. And yet the thought of shushing it again made the tightness worse, made panic steal into her lungs and wring the air from them.

Made her acutely aware that if she really were on the tightrope Granddad had said, and if she had only herself to rely on, her wits would not keep her alive. The danger he described was not a backbiting social circle or a catty rival. This was not dangling one suitor before another's nose.

This was a matter of treason.

She let her eyes fall shut for a moment. Just one. One moment to wonder why, of all her siblings and cousins and aunts and uncles, this task had fallen to her. She was no spy. She was no Culper, whatever a

Culper really was. She was no Patriot. A Union sympathizer, yes, but believing in it enough to make it her cause?

She'd never had a cause. Not beyond her own.

Her eyes opened again. Again she saw the agent seated across from her. She nodded toward the book he still clutched against the arm of the chair. "Would you read to me, Mr. Osborne?"

His facial muscles didn't so much as twitch, but incredulity came off him in waves. "From this?"

Her attempt at a smile felt sorrowful. "My perfect brother was in divinity school before the war. That was his book. So yes, please."

He opened the cover, probably perusing the table of contents, but then went still before shooting her a probing look. "Which brother?"

He knew she had several, which proved he had done his research. Her throat ached. "The youngest of them, though they are all elder. Stephen."

The mantel clock ticked. Tocked. Ticked again. "The one who fell at Gettysburg? I remember hearing that Commodore Arnaud lost a son in the battle."

All she could manage was a nod. In some ways, the older loss was fresher than Lucien's. Maybe because she had loved Stephen longer. Maybe because he had understood her better.

Mr. Osborne flipped the pages, landing close to where he had been before. "'"Not as though I had already attained, either were already perfect." Philippians 3:12.'" He paused, cleared his throat. "'There is scarce any expression in Holy Writ which has given more offence than this. The word *perfect* is what many cannot bear. The very sound of it is an abomination to them. And whosoever preaches perfection (as the phrase is,) that is, asserts that it is attainable in this life, runs great hazard of being accounted by them worse than a heathen man or a publican.'"

Funny how it could make her smile. How often had she tossed that word in scorn at Stephen? Resented him for his seeming perfection? Yet he had only to say the first words of this sermon, and the rest would come rushing back.

Her guest kept reading, his voice deeper than Stephen's had been but using the same intonations. The same reflection. She could almost, almost believe that her brother would have sounded this way had he made it through the war, back to school, and stood someday in a pulpit. She could almost—*almost*—imagine Mr. Osborne in the same position. Though he would have to put some emotion upon his face to be believed as a clergyman.

"'Even Christians, therefore, are not so perfect as to be free either from ignorance or erring—'"

"Error." The correction slipped out, as if he were Stephen reciting, as if she had been charged with making sure he got each syllable correct. *Fool.* When she glanced up from her growing stack of bandages, it was into his frigid stare.

"You have the entire sermon memorized?"

Memorized—laughable. That would imply some effort had been put into the remembrance. Marietta smiled and wound another strip. "Of course not, Mr. Osborne. I just have *very* good eyesight."

Devereaux put the spoon down on the tray and reached for the fine linen napkin. When his mother took it from his hand and dabbed at her own lip, he smiled. Still, it felt tight around the edges. "You gave us such a fright last night."

Lucille Fortier Hughes could look scolding even with the lines in her face telling the tale of illness. "I will recover. I have said from the start I would."

A sigh worked its way up, but he halted it. There had been a day not so long ago when that word would have been enough. For even the Almighty Himself, it seemed, obeyed the dictates of his mother. But lately? Nothing had gone right. Nothing. All their plans, all their goals, all their careful work…stymied again and again.

He summoned another smile. "Of course you will, and I am glad to see the proof of that."

Reprimand still gleaming in her eyes, Mother smoothed down the blanket over her lap and then fussed with the lace of her collar. "Mari said you have a guest tonight."

Surprised she hadn't asked the moment Devereaux stepped foot in her chamber, he nodded and leaned back against his chair. "Slade Osborne."

"The Pinkerton agent." Thought raced through her summer-sky eyes. "What were your impressions? Do you trust him?"

The very question made his blood hum. Did he dare to trust? Did he dare not to? "He is a hard man to read. Very cold, very closed off. Which is what we need, but..." He shrugged. "I will induct him tonight, but he will have to earn full trust."

"He'd better do so quickly." Though she obviously tried to keep her features schooled, weakness asserted itself in the lines of sorrow around her mouth and eyes. "From what Mari read to me from the papers..."

"I know." He took her hand and gently rubbed it. "But we haven't been defeated yet. That's what matters. And you well know the Union has an iron grip on the papers. They cannot always report the truth."

He read the worry in her gaze but felt the determination in the fingers that gripped his. "Well, let us pray this Mr. Osborne can give you the aid you need. And in the meantime, we must tend our own house." She shot him a stern look. "I trust you noticed that Marietta has entered half mourning."

At that, Devereaux couldn't hold back a smile. It felt as though he had waited forever to see her out of black. When she had come down the stairs that morning in lavender, he had thought his heart would stop. And now, just three more months until he could claim her as his own. "Yes, I noticed."

"Shameful." Mother tugged her hand free and turned her face toward the window. Darkness had fallen, but she set her gaze upon the glow from the street light. "And so unfair to Lucien."

Unfair to Lucien? He bit back a retort. His brother had had it all. *All.* The house, the business—and Marietta too. He had lorded it over him in life, but heaven help him if he would grant any rights to his brother's ghost. "You are the one who encouraged her to transition early, Mother."

"Because we haven't the luxury of time." She snapped it out, snapped her frustrated gaze back to him. "A man should always be mourned properly, but your brother lost his right to that when he left this house to *her.*"

"Watch your tone." He stood, his own frustration surging.

She held his gaze with pursed lips. One moment, two, and then she shook her head, sending her blond curls bouncing. "What is it about that girl that so enthralled you both?"

He folded his arms over his chest.

She sniffed. "Well. The important thing is that you marry her as quickly as you can, before she decides to sell or wed another. Though I would like to say again that I am sorry Lucien has forced you to this. You ought to have had the freedom to choose your own wife, one from an upstanding Southern family, rather than being relegated to his widow."

He saw no need to tell his mother that he would be happy to wed Marietta even if she were the daughter of Lincoln himself. There was no point—she always did exactly what she had now, going from questioning her allure to denying it in virtually the same breath. And then, of course, acting as though Marietta were the daughter of which she had always dreamed when they were in the same room.

Rather than argue, he leaned down to press a kiss to her forehead. Her skin still felt papery and thin. "Rest, Mother. You have a long road of recovery ahead of you."

She waved that away, but weariness lined her face.

He was glad to see mere weariness. This time yesterday, she had been thrashing about with a scorching fever, her breathing shallow and sparse. And yes, he had feared. Feared that before the night was over, the Hugheses would suffer yet another loss.

But the fever had broken, and now look at her. She was nearly herself again. He sent her a smile. "I had better get back to my guest. If you need anything—"

"I will ring for Jess. You've enough to worry with tonight." She produced a smile for him and picked up the *Godey's Lady's Book* from her bedside table.

It was several months out of date, but Mother hadn't felt up to even flipping through a magazine in too long. "All right. Enjoy your evening, and I shall see you tomorrow." He slipped into the hall and closed his eyes, taking a moment to switch tracks. He put aside thoughts of his mother and focused on the meeting ahead.

If all went according to plan, it could be an important one. Several Knights had arrived back in Baltimore over the past few days from

Washington and points north. Devereaux hoped they came with some helpful observations that would lead to a new plan. So many, too many plans had been foiled over the years. But enough smaller ones had been a success that all the Union knew who they were. They knew to fear the KGC.

From the direction of the stairs came an echo of laughter. Marietta's, which drew his feet her way. His blood warmed, but not entirely pleasantly. He had left her alone with Osborne—a necessity, but still. What could the newcomer, whose bad attitude rolled off him in waves, possibly have said to make her laugh?

Another trickle of it made its way to his ears when he reached the staircase, and this time it relaxed him. Sterling but empty—her society laugh. Good. Marietta had an inability to be in male company and restrain herself from flirting, but he took no issue with it so long as it remained distant.

He kept his tread quiet as he descended, careful to keep out of sight of the library door. It was Marietta's favorite room, though he was not sure why, as he scarcely ever saw her with a book in her hands. More often she would be sitting in her chair with her eyes closed if she weren't busying her hands with mending or bandages.

He stopped and leaned against the wall where he had a view of her, but where Osborne remained out of sight. She was as he had expected, in her favorite seat with a basket of cloth strips beside her, her scarlet hair hanging in perfect curls over her shoulders, and her flawless face still lit with a mask of a smile. A breath hummed out as his gaze lingered on the figure finally back on display and not hidden beneath yards of black crepe.

How clearly he remembered the first time he saw her, across the crowded ballroom in this very house, the day before she and Lucien wed. He had come back from New York City that morning and had rolled his eyes as his younger brother went on *ad nauseum* about the beauty of his bride. When he had come down to the dinner party, he hadn't realized that the woman who caught his gaze so quickly was the same one Lucien had claimed.

It had been too late, then, to change anything. All he could do was maneuver her away from the crowds for a few minutes, under the guise of brotherly interest. Small consolation as it had been, she had felt as quick a connection as he had. He had seen it in her eyes and had known, all these years, that her heart was his more than Lucien's.

And now, finally, *she* was too.

Perhaps she sensed his gaze. She glanced up and looked out the door. Grinning, Devereaux crooked a finger.

Her hesitation lasted only a moment, no doubt that perfect hostess breeding rearing up and telling her she oughtn't to leave a guest alone. But then she set down her roll of bandage and rose. "Will you excuse me a moment, Mr. Osborne?"

His pulse speeding, Devereaux straightened as she exited the library, her skirts swaying. He backed into the parlor. The only light was the soft golden glow from the lamp in the hallway, touching but a few feet of the Turkish rug. He paused on its edge, hand extended.

Her fingers fit in his like the pieces of a puzzle, and he used them to pull her near. She came to an abrupt halt with a foot still between them, her eyes flinty.

A grin teased the corners of his mouth. "Are you that afraid of my kissing you again?"

"'Afraid' is hardly the word for it." But she tugged against his fingers and increased the distance separating them. Had it been rebuke in her eyes, or teasing, he would have pressed closer.

But it was remorse.

He drew in a long breath, mentally cursing himself. If he had pushed her away, had made her retreat...no. She just needed time. He rubbed his thumb over her fingers and let the breath out again. "I promised I wouldn't push you, Mari. And I won't."

She stopped trying to free her fingers, but the expression on her face was pure exasperation. "A strange thing to say after embracing me for our guest to see not two hours ago."

He loved to hear her say *our*. How was he not to smile? "That was entirely for your benefit, my dear."

Her features wore incredulity well, her light-green eyes going calm and her lips just parting. "My benefit? How, pray tell?"

He nodded toward the library and its occupant. "Osborne was ogling you on the street. I thought to save you from having to rebuff his advances by making it clear where things stood. Kind of me, wasn't it?"

For a moment, she made no reaction whatsoever. Then the glaciers thawed in her eyes and a low, soft laugh sounded in her throat, tying him in knots. "Oh, Dev." She eased close again, going so far as to rest her forehead against his chest. Though he hadn't even the chance to put his arms around her before she retreated once more.

Was it only the shadows cloaking the room that made the circles under her eyes so deep? He cupped her cheek and swept a thumb under the offending bruises. "You look tired."

"I had a long night."

"Long, but well spent." He leaned down, thinking only to press his lips to her forehead, but she jerked away. And might as well have plunged a knife into his gut. "Mari, please. I said I will give you what space you need, but do not retreat entirely. I need you."

"Do you?" She turned halfway toward the faded rectangle of lamplight.

"Do you doubt it?" He clasped her shoulder and would have pressed his lips to the pulse under her ear on another day. "I would do anything for you."

"Really." Her face turned toward him, muted mischief in her smile. "What if I were to ask you to...to run away with me? Leave all this behind and go someplace new. Someplace the war hasn't touched."

Devereaux chuckled. "If I thought for a moment that would make you happy, then we would be on the first train."

"Everyone is so sure they know what I want." Weariness colored the words—strange. Had Lucien made such assumptions? Her parents? Possibly. But none of them knew her as he did. And well he knew that she appreciated the fine things in life.

He gave her delicate shoulders a light squeeze. "Do you know what you need?"

"No." The word sounded so heavy. So worn.

"Rest." He let his hands fall away. "You have worn yourself thin caring for Mother. Osborne and I will take our leave so you can retire."

Were those tears in her eyes? Between her blink and the shadows, he couldn't tell. But given her smile, sincere if not as bright as usual, he decided it must have been a trick of the light.

"A wise idea. I think tomorrow I shall try to catch Daddy before he leaves port. I missed him today."

To that, he could only hum. Jack Arnaud was likable enough—if only the man weren't such a Unionist. "All the more reason for us to leave you to your repose." He took a step toward the door.

"Dev?"

He paused, frowning at the plaintive note in her voice, one he had never heard in it before. One that lit an ember of worry. "Yes?"

Rather than turn into the light, she faced the darkness again. But she took his hand. "Do you love me?"

"Oh, darling." He lifted her hand, pressed his lips to her knuckles, and held them there a long moment. "You know I do. More than anything. Anything."

She said no more, merely nodding and turning with him back to the door, keeping her face partially averted.

Feminine insecurities were not her usual trade...but it had been a trying few days. No doubt tomorrow she would be herself again, all fire and laughter.

And in the meantime, he had another fire to tend. One that was no laughing matter at all.

Four

Darkness pressed on all sides. Slade said nothing, made no move, but the familiar dread settled into his stomach. The one that said this kind of darkness hid monsters. Not the fanged, hairy kind boys created in their stories, but the ones of true terror—men with hidden hatred.

"Halt." The voice snaked through the black.

Given the feel of cold steel against his face, Slade happily obliged.

"Those who would pass here must face fire and steel."

His guide shifted beside him, someone Hughes had introduced as Surratt before he disappeared. "We are willing to face both—for liberty," the man said.

Liberty, was it? Slade made no move.

The blade lifted. "It shall be ours. Pass!"

A gloved hand gripped his and pulled Slade farther and farther until he wondered if they knew his true identity and were going to take him into a dank basement and leave him there to die like a victim of an Edgar Allan Poe story.

A question that only grew stronger when another set of hands collided with his chest. Someone jerked off his coat, and his wrists were wrenched behind him. Cloth, soft but thick, came over his eyes.

Then a rip, and the sudden influx of wintry air against his chest. Slade clenched his jaw against any reaction as they tore his waist-coat and shirt. If this were to be his last moment, then he would face it with dignity.

He was shoved onward.

Doors opened and closed, but he could detect no light, no warmth. Nothing but the icy darkness and the smell of...earth? A basement lair, then. They must be under Mrs. Hughes's house. Knowledge that would do little good if that steel bit him.

His guide halted him. A rap upon wood, and then a returning one from the other side.

"Who comes here?"

The man beside him cleared his throat. "One who is true to our cause."

"How is he known to be true?"

Under the blindfold, Slade squeezed his eyes shut. How indeed.

"By the recommendation of a tried Knight."

"He can then be trusted?"

His muscles wanted to tense, wanted to coil. But he held himself perfectly still. No tells.

"Such is our belief."

"Should he fail and betray us, he will learn the penalty soon enough. Advance."

The door creaked on its hinges, a sound eerie enough to fit into this untold story of Poe. A few steps, and the blade touched him again, bringing him to a quick stop.

"Those who would pass here must face both fire and steel." A new voice, and he sensed movement from beyond its owner.

"Are you willing to do so?" Hughes now, his voice pitched low.

Slade's shoulders bunched—a normal reaction, surely. For this must be their usual induction into the circle, and this his last chance to change his mind. If only he had such a luxury. If only his brother hadn't forced him here, with this one chance to make right all the wrongs committed in his name.

"I am willing." *Father God, help me.*

"Advance."

The blade retreated again, the hands pushed him forward, and

Hughes ordered him to kneel. His knees met the icy earth. His right hand was loosed, lifted, and settled on the pages of an open book.

His fingers flexed. Thin paper, smooth and even. A Bible? Despite the freezing air that made his muscles quake, he felt a warmth within. Even here, He was there.

"You must remember every word you have uttered and will yet utter here tonight. And you must forever bar your lips against repeating them to any but a fellow Knight. If you betray us, the penalty is—"

"Death!" It came as a chant from all directions, resonant as a thundering cannon. "Death! Death! Death!"

"You will disclose no names, or you will taste—"

"Death!"

"You will always aid a brother Knight, even unto—"

"Death!"

"You will abide by all orders, carry out all objects, bear witness, and even swear falsely in order to save a brother's life or liberty."

Slade forced a swallow. *A brother's life or liberty.* Admirable...if only those bonds meant anything. If only he had a brother, a true one, left in this life.

"The business of this new body will be preeminent before all. Before religion. Before political feeling. Before familial duty. It must be first and foremost in everything, at daylight or midnight, at home or abroad, before the law of the land or the affection of wife, mother, or child. It must be all and everything."

All and everything—he had One of those already.

"Are you willing to abide by this obligation?"

He had nothing left to lose. "I am."

"Brother Knights! Recall to the mind of him who now kneels here the penalty of betrayal, either by sign, word, or deed!"

Countless blades sang from their sheathes and clanged one to another. Countless voices murmured, groaned, or whispered, "Death! Death! *Death!*"

Chilling as the pronouncement was, worse was the silence that followed. It seemed Slade could hear his own pulse in his ears, his blood rushing to the point where the blade still rested, threatening.

"Death." Hughes's voice rang in a final blow. "Show him all."

The blindfold was removed, and Slade blinked against the sudden light. Lanterns were placed at intervals along the wood planked walls. They shone on a dozen swords—all of them pointed directly at his chest, a breath away from touching. His gaze followed the blades up to the men holding them, dressed in chain mail and armor, feather-crested helmets obscuring their faces.

A glance to his side proved that the book on which he had sworn was indeed the Bible. Comforting, and yet the irony of it pierced where the swords stopped short. How could these men put their hand upon the Good Book and swear to uphold their brotherhood above its statutes?

"Rise."

He rose, once the swords all returned to their sheaths, and accepted the shirt someone handed him, and then his frock coat. His gaze fixed upon the central Knight as he lifted his visor.

Hughes. He nodded and made a motion to the men who had led Slade in.

Surratt stepped forward and indicated a door to the left. "Through here for the meeting. It'll start as soon as the officers take off their armor."

Slade finished buttoning the shirt. Hopefully they hadn't ruined his waistcoat—Ross had only commissioned him that one for evening wear. The warmth of the frock coat was as welcome as sunshine. He followed Surratt through the door and then into a chamber with dozens of men jammed within and papers tacked to the walls. A defaced poster of Lincoln drew his eye.

"Here." Surratt held out a mug.

He had no idea what was in it, but it steamed, so he took it. "Thanks." He sipped—coffee—and noted the men milling about.

That dread in his stomach churned. Too many were familiar. Cabinet members. Congressmen. Judges. Actors and editors and...

"Osborne, isn't it?" Surratt drank from his own mug, his gaze darting about the room before landing on Slade again. "We were all surprised to hear Hughes was bringing someone in. He hasn't nominated anyone since the start of the war. Something about too much rabble who are not dedicated to the Cause."

Slade merely took another drink.

Surratt—a shrewd-looking fellow, with a beard only upon his chin that gave him a rather pointed face—shifted from one foot to the other. "He must know you very well."

Another man sidled toward them with a grin. He looked familiar... an actor, wasn't he? Name started with a B. Or was it a P?

"Ah, Booth." Surratt greeted him with a smile just warm enough to speak of friendship and just small enough to speak of one too familiar to need formality. "Come to meet our newest brother?"

Booth, right. John something-or-another Booth. He held out a hand, spurring Slade to switch his mug to his left hand and hold out his right.

The actor pumped it. "Is it true? You were a member of Pinkerton's security for King Abraham?"

Surratt froze with his mug halfway to his lips.

Slade reclaimed his fingers. They wouldn't say such things if they actually knew the man. If they saw his daily struggles, the way he sorrowed at the divide in the nation he loved.

But they saw only their own side. A side he must convince them was now his. "I was."

"Then you know his routine. You know the weak spots in his security. You know—"

"I know what they were three months ago, before I left." Slade took another drink and another glance around the room. According to the information Pinkerton had put together, most of the men were already suspected Southern sympathizers. But a few had fooled them.

Surratt and Booth exchanged a glance, dark hope in both sets of eyes. "Well," Surratt said, "I suppose it's no wonder, then, that Hughes recommended you. What convinced you to join us?"

He knew what he had to say. Still, the words tasted like bile.

Ross's words. Ross's sympathies. Ross's betrayal.

"When one is that close to the tyrant for that long, it's hard to ignore his failings." *Sorry, Mr. President.*

Surratt smiled. "Well, we welcome you eagerly to the ranks. Are you staying here in Baltimore or going back to Washington? My mother runs a boardinghouse there if you are in need of new rooms."

He certainly hadn't gone back to his old ones, not since that night. "Hughes invited me to be his guest for a while."

Another look between the two. Serious and sober, but then Booth grinned. "Lucky you. You will get to spend time in the company of his lady, then. Have you seen her?"

Surratt sent his gaze to the ceiling. "Forgive him. He has a weakness for anything in a skirt."

"And you a prejudice against them."

"Because," Surratt said in an even tone, "they are faithless, fickle, and false."

Booth shook his head, exaggerated disappointment upon his countenance. "You are too determined to remain unattached, John. How you can be unmoved when a pretty girl bats her lashes at you I will never understand."

"You would do well to try, as often as they have led you into trouble. And as for Hughes's molly…" he turned back to Slade and used his mug to point at him. "Steer clear. He has killed men before over her."

Booth grunted. "Too true."

Slade gazed first at one John and then at the other. "How long have they had an understanding?"

Surratt snorted. "Since the day Lucien died, he has made it quite clear she was his. Makes one wonder if she had been all along, and the poor sap of a brother just didn't know it."

Lucien Hughes, from what Slade had gleaned, had been no sap. "I've heard about the late Mr. Hughes."

"He was a strong leader, a good captain. We were all sorry when he fell to the streets." Booth edged a bit closer. "But Devereaux has a sharper approach that we need now. We have had too many failures."

"Just don't anger him," Surratt said. "A quicker man to issue a challenge I have never met, nor a better shot."

Slade took another sip of coffee. "Why does anyone accept his challenges then? Or choose pistols?"

"He knows how to put a man's pride against the wall." Surratt leaned against the planking behind him. "And he's as proficient with a blade as a gun. At this point, everyone knows it and does their best to remain on his good side. Which means, to circle back to the point, avoid anything more than polite flirtation with the widowed-and-soon-to-be-anew Mrs. Hughes."

Advice Slade certainly didn't require. Marietta Hughes may be beautiful and charming—and perhaps mysterious—but Hughes had no more than to crook a finger to bring her flying to him.

Did she know what he was? Part of him wanted to think not, given the Unionist family from which she hailed, the brother she had lost at Gettysburg. But how could she not, if she were as close to him as she seemed?

And how dangerous did that make her, if she did? The daughter of a commodore in league with the captain of a KGC castle. One alluring enough that she could no doubt smile at many a man and get whatever information from him Hughes wanted.

A cunning enemy indeed. He took another drink of his coffee and held his tongue. But the rust-red gash across the printed face of Lincoln said plenty.

These were men out for blood. And very little stood between them and it.

Marietta eased the door closed, silent but for the faintest of clicks. Behind her, the soft glow of the banked fire lit her chamber, its warmth scarcely making a dent in the January chill.

But that was nothing. Nothing compared to the chill in her core.

Her hand still touching the place where door and jamb met, she rested her forehead against the solid wood. Tears burned.

She shouldn't have gone. Shouldn't have crept from her room after she dismissed Cora for the night, shouldn't have snuck out the back door and over to the carriage house. She shouldn't have returned to that tunnel of nightmares and shattered dreams.

Shouldn't have pressed her ear to the wall nor followed the sounds farther down than they had gone earlier.

She shouldn't have listened. Because now the words would never leave her. They would forever echo in her mind, another memory to chain her down. To rattle around and rise to the fore when she least wanted it.

...preeminent before all...before the affection of wife, mother, or child.

Her tears felt scalding upon her cheek. *Before all.* Her hand slid down, and she let it dangle there between her and the door, with nothing but frigid air to hold it. No warm fingers around it, no lips upon its knuckles. No love.

If Dev could issue that oath, he had sworn it himself. As had Lucien. The two men who had claimed to cherish her above all. Both had turned around and sworn to put these *brothers* above her. Was she anything to them? Was it love they felt or, as Stephen had insisted when she announced her engagement, something baser?

Maybe it was. Maybe that was all any man could ever feel for her. Maybe she was nothing but a fool to ever think she could find something real, some genuine affection to carry her through life.

A fool. A wicked, selfish fool who had done nothing but chase her own desires, and who had nothing to show for it but a stone heart crushed to pieces.

She ought to have learned her lesson the first time, when she stood in the summer-warm stable and saw her dreams stomped to dust. She ought to have turned around right then and sworn off men.

Or the second time, when that bolt of attraction to Dev proved false her feelings for Lucien. She should have canceled the wedding and...and joined a nunnery. Or at the very least, taken the train to Connecticut and let Grandpapa Alain hold her tight to his chest and whisper French assurances into her ear.

And now here she was again. Her memory etched with the proof that nothing was what she thought it.

She turned, put her back to the door, and slid down. Maybe if she were lucky, her bones would turn into nothing but a mound of dust on the floor, to be swept away.

The hand of the Lord was upon me, and carried me out in the spirit of the Lord, and set me down in the midst of the valley which was full of bones...

The floor was like ice against her legs. Perhaps that was what Hades really was, ice rather than fire. For she had tasted fire, had let it consume her—and this was worse. This was the punishment. Not an inferno of feeling, but a total lack of it.

And caused me to pass by them round about: and, behold, there were very many in the open valley; and, lo, they were very dry.

The time had come to learn. That was what Stephen had said to her when he confessed he had enlisted. "You can list every mistake you ever made, Mari, but at some point you have to learn from them. You have to recognize them for what they are. You have to take consequences into account."

Her own voice echoed back through her head, tinged with anger— anger at him for saying the words, and more, for leaving her alone to hear them again and again. "You can't understand, Stephen. You speak of consequences as if the future matters, but if you had these bells of memory forever clanging in your head, you would understand why I only want *now*."

"If you gave more thought to the future, maybe the past wouldn't hurt so much." Oh, how those words echoed. He had spoken them with such disappointment. As if he had known she would never listen. As if he mourned for her long before she had mourned for him.

And he said unto me, Son of man, can these bones live?

A shiver coursed through her and stole any energy she had left. Her eyes focused on the red-orange glow of coals, she drew in a quavering breath. The tears had already given up. She was empty inside. Dry. Dust. Bone.

Her eyes slid shut. "'And I answered, O Lord God, thou knowest.'"

Five

Walker tossed fresh hay into the stall and smiled at the nicker of the horse. "You're welcome, Bay. Now, you need anything else before I go get my Elsie?"

The mare whinnied and bumped his arm with her nose, eliciting a chuckle. He obliged her with a rub. If only the other females in his life were so easy to please. He checked her feed and water, glanced down the line of other horses, and then stepped away.

And frowned. The mound of hay in the last stall wasn't as he had left it yesterday morning after showing Mr. Lane and Marietta the tunnel. He had arranged it very deliberately so he would know if it were disturbed.

It was disturbed.

"Blast it, Yetta." He planted his hands on his hips and scowled. She must have come out here after she dismissed Cora. Hadn't he found it strange that his wife had come so early to their apartment?

He should have known she would come back alone. That she would ignore the risk and focus only on what *she* wanted, what *she* needed. In this case, proof. Shaken as she had been when they explained the situation, he had seen in her eyes that she wanted desperately to believe they were wrong.

Well, if she had timed it right, she would have heard an earful. Maybe that was what she needed to rouse her from her stupor, proof that her precious Dev wasn't the kind of Knight she wanted him to be. Proof that she had let a brood of snakes, of Copperheads no less, into her family.

But dash it, she shouldn't have had to witness that alone.

He hadn't seen Marietta yet today, which was the usual way of things. She had called for a carriage, but Pat had taken it to the front of the house. If Walker could find a subtle way to accomplish it, he would ask Cora how she seemed. Surely she would notice if something were amiss. Though what would he do about it? Stephen may have made him swear to stick close and keep an eye out for her, but there was precious little he could do when it came down to it.

Shaking his head, he put the pitchfork away and slapped the dust from his trousers as he closed the stable door behind him. The sun shone today, but it was winter weak. The air had a bite to it as he circled the building to his rickety stairs, making him glad to step into the warm main room of their small quarters. His mother bustled from fireplace to table, humming a hymn.

"Morning, Mama."

The older woman glanced up when he came in and gave him her usual smile, big and beaming. "Hey there, Walk." She nodded toward the corner, where Elsie sat with the little rag doll Cora had stitched so carefully for her for Christmas. His little girl made the toy dance, rag feet jumping and leaping upon Elsie's chubby toddler legs.

He had to wonder what music it was dancing to.

The little one didn't look up, so he moved into her line of vision a little more, waving his hand. That got her attention, and Elsie surged up with the light of pure love upon her beautiful little face.

"There's my girl." He crouched down and held out his arms for her to run into, and then he gathered her close when she did. She wouldn't hear him, he knew that. But still he had to talk to her. Maybe she would feel the rumble in his chest as she snuggled in. Maybe that would tell her she was loved. He pressed a kiss to her curls and stood with her on his hip. "Ready for lunch, precious?"

She looked up at him, her hazel eyes content and bright but questioning. He patted her tummy. "Hungry?"

Her grin always made his heart light. She patted her belly too and nodded.

Walker turned to his mother. "Has Cora been in yet?"

"Not yet, no. But I have a few errands to run while you're here, so I'll see you in about an hour."

Errands. Knowing his mother, they would be the dangerous kind that involved sneaking runaway slaves northward. Work she would never give up, no matter all it had cost her. Yet work she put aside to help out with Elsie.

He picked up his mother's cloak and handed it to her with a smile. "Thanks, Mama."

She waved away his gratitude as she always did, and let herself out.

Cora's stew sure smelled good, and Walker's stomach rumbled its agreement as he put Elsie in her favorite spot, atop the table. She kicked her legs and giggled—a sound he wished he could bottle and pull out whenever he needed a smile throughout the day.

He could go ahead and serve them, he knew, but he would rather give Cora a few minutes to join them. He had some time to spare before he had to start his afternoon chores. He picked up the only book Elsie ever showed any interest in, the nonsense verse with illustrations. He held it where she could see it, and she clapped her agreement and reached for him.

Smiling, Walker scooped her up again and settled in his chair by the stove with her on his lap. He opened the book to a random page. "Humpty Dumpty sat on a wall..."

He finished reading it, though Elsie made no shift when he stopped. Her finger was tracing the drawing of the man-egg, touching his boots, his hands, the ink bricks. What did she wonder?

For the millionth time since they realized their angel couldn't hear them, he wished for some way to know. They had their method of communicating, to be sure. And at two, she was still so young that even if she could hear and talk, they would probably scarcely understand her. But what about the future?

The door opened, and Cora came in with the wind. Her rosebud mouth smiled. "You could have started."

"This was better."

Her smile stayed put until she unfastened the cast-off cloak

Marietta had given her last year. But when she reached to hang it up, she winced and put a hand to her back.

Walker stood, Elsie and all, and moved to her. "That pain again?"

She rubbed at it and nodded. "I reckon I oughta be used to it by now, but—"

"Go lie down for a minute and stretch it out." He handed the reaching tot to her mama and put a hand on Cora's rounded abdomen. His babe within kicked. Smiling, he leaned down to greet his wife properly.

She kissed him back, but her look afterward was rebuking. "You know I don't have time to rest, Walk."

"Yetta won't care if you're ten minutes late sweeping the hall." Only when her gaze went hard and cold did he realize his slip. Usually he called her Miss Mari like the rest of the servants, but sometimes he just forgot. She had been Yetta all his life until he came here.

A reminder Cora never much appreciated. "*Yetta* ain't the one I worry 'bout."

He said nothing. He just leaned against the solid table while she, with Elsie on her hip, pulled out three bowls and spoons. The way he saw it, old Mrs. Hughes oughtn't to evoke much fear. The house was Marietta's, even if the servants still belonged to the older woman.

But then, Tandy and Norris, Norris's uncle Pat, Jess, and her late husband had come with her from Louisiana. Cora had been born here to Jess, a slave too. And so Elsie was, legally, because her mama was. No matter that Walker was free.

No matter that the South's slaves were free. The Emancipation Proclamation hadn't covered them here in Maryland, hadn't freed them. Far as he could tell, the politicians hadn't wanted to shake things up with the border states. If Maryland seceded, Washington would be completely surrounded by the Confederacy. The politicians had tried to strike a balance.

And in doing so, had left his wife's family in chains.

Elsie tugged on a tight spiral of Cora's hair. Cora chuckled as she pulled the lid off the stew pot, sending aromatic steam wafting upward.

"Cora." He kept his gaze on their little one, watching her eyes and wondering. Just wondering. "Have you thought more about it? Teaching her signs?"

She sighed and put the girl upon the table so she could reach for the bowls. "What good would it do, Walker?"

"What good? We could talk to her. Know what she's thinking. She could talk to *us* and know what *we're* thinking."

"We do well enough with our own gestures. And it ain't like no one else will be able to talk to her, even if we teach her these signs."

"Sure they will, some of them. I asked Mr. Lane about it. He said there's a school in Connecticut—"

"You wanna send her away?" Cora spun around, nearly sloshing the bowl of stew she held. "Send away our baby? As if they'd even let a slave girl in?"

"No, that's not…I don't want to send her anywhere." He pulled out his chair and sat, sucking in a deep breath. "I just meant to tell you that they have developed a universal system of signs there. They call it American Sign Language. They're trying to get all the deaf folks in the country to use it so they can all talk to each other. It's pretty close, I understand, to what Mr. Lane learned from his mother. They've got a book. We could get it, learn it. Teach it to her."

"A book." Her tone said it all.

Walker sighed. "With drawings, I bet, of the motions."

She slid his bowl onto the table and urged Elsie into her chair. "A book."

He picked up his spoon. "We could do it."

"Walker." With a shake of her head, she turned back to the pot and ladled up a small portion. "Blow on this for her."

He took it, blew and stirred.

Cora rubbed at the pain in her back, the same spot that always hurt her after a morning of cleaning. The one that often got so bad by night that she hobbled up the stairs to their rooms, whimpering in pain.

"I just don't see the point. I know you wanna talk to her, but we can do that on our own, with our own ways. Don't need no *book* to show us how. Not with me who can't read and you who say yourself you don't learn well from paper and ink. You need visuals. Ain't that what you said?"

It was, and he did. But wasn't it worth trying? "Mr. Lane would help."

"Mr. Lane's got his own life, his own family. How much time could he give us? An hour here and there? Wouldn't do no good, honey."

He had the Culper business too, and the weight of the fractured nation upon his shoulders. But Walker couldn't mention that to Cora, and wouldn't anyway, as it hardly helped his point. "He taught it to his kids. Miss Julie taught it to us. I don't remember much, but..."

But Marietta would. She'd remember every gesture, every meaning. Every single lesson. She'd be able to glance at one of those books once, and it would be in her head forever.

Cora turned back to him slowly, obviously knowing the direction of his thoughts. She plunked her bowl onto the table and eased into her chair, eyes glinting. "Don't even suggest it."

"She could help."

"I ain't asking that woman for nothing—*nothing*. You understand? Maybe you could, you who don't have to serve her each day, empty her slops, obey her every command, but I'm tellin' you I *won't*. And you better not neither." She picked up her spoon and stabbed her stew with it.

Walker tested Elsie's and, finding it cool enough, slid it over to her with a smile. "But if she could help Elsie—"

"It wouldn't help. And I won't go beggin'."

"It wouldn't be begging. It would be..." He let his voice fade as pain burst through her eyes again, screwed up her face, and made her back arch. Maybe he should let it drop. The last thing Cora needed was more distress. That couldn't be good for her or the baby. "You all right, honey?"

"Mm-hmm." She stretched, and the discomfort eased from her face. She took another bite. "I doubt she'd help anyway, even if you did ask. That woman never does nothing unless it's for herself."

At that, Walker grunted and chewed one of the few pieces of meat in his bowl. She hadn't always been that way. When they were children, Marietta had been as bright and cheerful as Elsie. Always laughing and shrieking at the four boys—him and her brothers, Stephen and Hez and Isaac—when they played pranks on her.

Surely that Yetta was still inside somewhere. And maybe, if he prayed hard for her, this shake to her foundation would set her loose.

Cora rubbed her abdomen. "Did Mr. Lane say anything more about the amendment nonsense when he was here yesterday?"

"The House is still debating or whatever they do. But they'll pass it. If it passed in the Senate, it'll surely pass in the House. You'll be free soon."

She kept on rubbing and gazed at Elsie, who happily spooned up a potato chunk. "What if it ain't soon enough? I don't want this new baby to be born a slave, Walk."

He didn't either, but what could they do? "He won't be. And even if he is, it won't be but for a few months. They're going to grow up in a whole new world. A world with no more slavery, where they can be anything they want."

Hopeful idealism. He knew it even as he said it. He had been born free, after all, and that didn't open any doors for him. There might be white men aplenty who had a moral objection to owning another man, but there were few indeed who thought blacks equal to them. The Lanes and Arnauds were the only ones he'd ever met he could say that about.

Obviously it hadn't been true of his father, whoever he was. His mother never spoke of the attack, but he had gleaned enough over the years to know she had roused the suspicion of a runaway's master and he'd found her one night. Punished her. Left her with a son on the way and no man to be a father.

"Maybe we should just leave. Surely with the amendment coming, they wouldn't hunt us down if we ran."

She had made the suggestion once before, when it was Elsie growing inside her. He reached across the table and took her hand. "We're not running, Cora. You're not going to be a fugitive."

Though she turned her hand so she could squeeze his fingers, sorrow blanketed her face. "We both know that ain't why you refuse to go."

Little fingers landed on his other hand, and he grinned at Elsie, who was trying to reach for her mother too.

Cora slid the bowl out of the little one's way and clasped her fingers, but her smile was still sad. "He's long gone, Walker. I know you miss him. I know he was your best friend, but he ain't here no more to hold you to your promise."

"That was the point of it, honey. He knew he might never come home to watch over her again." He held her hand another moment and then tightened his grip on it. "And I never would have met you if I hadn't come here like Stephen asked."

She released their hands and went back to her stew. "I gotta get away from this family before it gets worse. My mama will understand. She won't leave, but she won't mind my goin'."

"It won't get worse."

"It will. When Miss Mari marries Mr. Dev, it *will*."

"She's not gonna marry him." Funny how he said it with such certainty, when two days before he would have said the opposite and felt just as sure. But he'd seen the look in her eyes when she caught sight of that poster. The horror, the realization.

And this being Marietta, it wasn't something she could forget. Not to say she hadn't done a fine job of ignoring things in the past, but this was different.

Cora, however, had no reason to believe him. She shot him a look of utter incredulity and set about finishing her meal.

He let her. And he sent up a silent prayer that Marietta would make her way back to the stables soon to demand answers of him. Because he had a few questions to put to her too.

How long could one stay numb? Marietta moved the teacup from saucer to mouth and back down again and felt as though she were merely watching a play. Nothing that day had penetrated the fog inside her. From the time she'd pulled herself from the floor at dawn, a cloud had descended over her vision. Of all the memories branded into her, yesterday's would remain the most vivid.

She had betrayed Lucien.

Dev was a monster.

Her grandfather was a spy.

And she had been charged with protecting a wolf. Though she was none too sure he wouldn't turn around and snap at her if she tried.

Mama chatted on about the aid meeting yesterday, about the next one planned, about how sorry Daddy had been to miss her visit. Words, nothing but words.

"Marietta, sweetheart, are you feeling ill? You seem so distracted."

"I'm sorry, Mama. I suppose I'm still a bit tired." She dredged up a smile. "How long is Daddy here, do you know?"

"Just until tomorrow. More tea?"

She shook her head and cast her gaze out the window. If her father weren't due back any minute, she would make her excuses and go home. Curl up on her bed and try to forget. If only she could pull a blanket over her mind. Obscure the past for just a moment.

"It's good to see you out of second mourning already." Her mother sipped and then lowered her cup. A dance of graceful movements. Yet her delicate brows were drawn. "Though I do hope you'll not rush into another marriage. I know you are...fond...of Dev, but—"

"You needn't worry about that. I think I..." Her mother's gaze pierced. Too intent, too interested. Marietta set her saucer upon the table and toyed with the edge of the linen napkin. "I should have listened to you. I never should have had anything to do with Lucien."

Mama chuckled and selected a piece of cake. As if all was right with the world. As if they hadn't had fifty-seven different arguments about Lucien Hughes before she married him. "You were in love. Reason had no effect on you."

"No, I wasn't." She had wanted to believe she was...but then, why hadn't she ever been able to say the words to him? Part of her had known all along she wasn't. "Was it just his money? His looks? Why was I so convinced I had to marry him?"

Her mother scooted her chair closer to Marietta's, concern etching lines into her face. "Has something happened?"

She shrugged. "I never really mourned him, and now...now, when I decided to try, I wonder why I made the decisions I did. Decisions that sealed my future. And now with Dev..."

"You've no obligation to marry him, much as he may wish it." Her mother's fingers, familiar and warm, brushed away a curl from Marietta's temple. "Do you want to come home? We can have your room ready in minutes. I would love it if you would. We could keep each other company. Worry for your father and uncles together."

For the first time, that oft-repeated suggestion sounded tempting. If she didn't have to face Dev every day, perhaps her heart would stop twisting. Perhaps the disgust and the echo of desire would stop waging war. She could break free. Start again as someone else, anyone else.

Except she couldn't. She had promised Granddad she would help. And she owed it to him, to Stephen's memory, to her whole family. Who knew what damage had been done through her, the Hugheses using her connections against the Union? All because of her choices.

Now, it seemed, she would pay for them. "Perhaps I will soon." How long could Mr. Osborne possibly continue his charade? He would find whatever he needed, and he would make his escape. Then she could leave too.

As if distance would change anything. Dev still expected to marry her. And with the house and its secrets at stake, no doubt he wouldn't accept no for an answer. Especially given the fact that months ago she had agreed to his whispered proposal. Perhaps she had drawn away a degree yesterday morning, before she discovered the truth. But it wouldn't have been enough to mean a break. Not if Granddad hadn't put the chisel into that crack and slammed it wider.

"I do hope so. I know you are loath to leave Lucille alone, but Dev can care for her, and she has her servants. She would be fine."

Did Mother Hughes have any idea in what her sons were involved? Marietta smoothed the napkin flat again and let the images run through her mind. None gave her decisive answers. She had always defended her mother-in-law's loyalties, but really, why would the woman be loyal to anything *but* the society she had been born and raised a part of? All the rest of the Fortiers were fighting for the Confederacy.

"Mari!"

Her father's voice brought her head up and a smile to her lips. She stood and rushed to meet him. "Daddy! I've missed you."

His arms closed around her as he chuckled. "And I you. How has my little girl been?"

"Well enough." She pulled back to take his measure. He was thinner than when last she saw him, with new lines around his mouth. But still he was the same Jack Arnaud she had always equated with solidity. "When will this war be over so you can come home?"

Weariness saturated his exhale. "Soon, I think. I hope. Though we were only putting in for supplies and repairs, and then back out we must go to our place in the blockade. Sorry I missed you yesterday."

"I would have stayed longer, but we had that aid meeting—"

"I understand." He clasped her shoulders before planting a resounding kiss on her forehead. "But you will join us for dinner this evening, won't you?"

"Of course." It would give her an excuse to miss sharing a meal with Dev and Mr. Osborne.

"Good." He looked past her, to Mama, and his smile shifted as it always did when he saw his wife.

As she had thought Lucien's did for her. Thought Dev's did too. But it wasn't quite the same, was it? Daddy's had something more...and something less. Crucial somethings.

"I need to go see your father for a few minutes, Lenna. Would you care for a walk?" Daddy was the only one to ever call her that. Most everyone else called her Julie, except for Grandmama, who called her Julienne. But when Marietta heard her talking to herself, Daddy's nickname was the name she chose. *Come now, Lenna,* she would say. *Where did you put it?*

Evidence of the kind of love they shared. That even in that, they identified.

Mama smiled but made no move to rise. "I shall stay inside where it's warm, but perhaps Marietta would enjoy the exercise."

"I would indeed." More, she hoped she might get her grandfather alone for a few minutes, so she could ask him if he knew how long Slade Osborne would be invading her world.

"Well, so long as I have at least *one* beautiful girl to accompany me." He winked and went over to his wife, no doubt to exchange a kiss or quiet word. Marietta smiled as she stepped out in search of her cape and bonnet.

A few minutes later, she and her father were out in the crisp air, her hand secure in the crook of his elbow. Neither spoke until they reached the corner, at which point he looked down at her with somber eyes.

"Your granddad said he paid you a visit yesterday. A rather startling one."

She sucked in a breath. "He told you?"

"I should think so. I am as much involved in the family trade as he is himself, and as my father."

Granddad had said as much yesterday morning, but those words had been lost amidst the others. Now they reemerged. Her father, her uncles, who were spread all about the country now, Hez, and even Grandpapa Alain. "It is so difficult to believe we even have such a thing as the Culpers."

He hummed and led her around the corner, heading for the house Thaddeus Lane had called home for more than fifty years. "I'm sorry we had to involve you. We wanted to avoid it if we could. But given the Hugheses's affiliations..."

Her hand tightened around his arm. "Did you know, Daddy? Before I married him?"

He patted her fingers. "Thad found it out the day of your wedding. A bit late to step in. Especially," he added, grinning down at her, "given your stubborn refusal to listen to any of our concerns."

"I'm so sorry. For so much." So much he didn't even know about.

"As are we. We have been trying these four years to put a stop to the war, and to the so-called 'fifth column,' without your needing to know. But the times are dire, Mari."

"I know." They had been dire for years. And while much of the reality of war had become routine, some parts never did.

Like the casualty report that said *Stephen Arnaud.*

"Still, we'll not ask much of you. Just distract Dev when you can. That ought to suffice. Let this young man poke about wherever he might need to. If you call to mind something that might be useful for him, perhaps leave it where he can find it."

An exasperated breath eked past her lips. "But he is not one of...of us." *Us.* "How is it you trust him to handle this?"

"We will make sure he does what he ought with the information. But we must be certain to otherwise stay out of sight. The last thing the Culpers need is the attention of either the KGC or Pinkerton's detectives. We operate successfully because we operate anonymously. Even the president does not know we exist. None has since Washington himself."

A chill swept up her spine. From the wind or the talk? "What if I hear something or find something? Do I tell Granddad? Mr. Osborne?"

He glanced around the street. Few pedestrians were out, though carriages rumbled by now and then. "Your granddad can advise you on whatever you find. If it is something he feels Osborne should know about, he will direct you on how to get it into his hands. And while we are there today, we will..." He paused, drew in a deep breath, and pulled her closer. "There is a code and vials of invisible ink. If ever you need to get a written message to him, you must use those."

Codes, invisible ink, spies, secret societies. They belonged in the pages of a Gothic novel, not in her life. "Did Stephen know?"

He made no hesitation as he shook his head. "Nor did Walker until Stephen sent him to your house. Knowing what we did by that time, we thought it wise to educate him. Mari." He paused, thereby making her pause with him, and looked down into her eyes. "You mustn't seek anything out. You mustn't put yourself in undue danger. We've already lost Stephen."

"I will be safe." Even if Dev somehow found out, he wouldn't harm her. She didn't think so, anyway. He wasn't a violent man.

But he would be hurt when she broke things off, not to mention if he found out she was aiding someone against him. Would he feel the same heartbreak that held her immobile on the floor last night? The same suffocating weight of the one you thought you loved proving to be someone else entirely?

Part of her hoped he would. He deserved to hurt, deserved to learn what it felt like to be lied to. Deserved to be told he was the most important thing and then find it wasn't so.

That is the beauty of grace. Stephen's words, spoken so many long years ago, echoed. He'd been reclining on their parents' couch, his Bible on his lap. Gray trousers, crisp white shirt, his frock coat long abandoned. She could still see the wave of his dark hair, just like Daddy's, the gleam of his warm brown eyes, and ink stains on his left middle finger. *We all deserve punishment, but He gives us instead forgiveness. Redemption.*

She hadn't wanted redemption. She knew too well what it meant. If the Lord redeemed her, He would pay for her, buy her, and she would be His. A slave to Him, bound to do His will above her own. And she had liked her own far better.

Today redemption sounded very different. Today she didn't much like where her will had taken her. Today she had slaves under her roof when she'd been taught all her life slavery was a vile practice.

Who was she? Yetta, the girl without a lifetime of memories to plague her? Mari, the young lady who could charm any man she set her sights on? Marietta, the rich widow who had too many ghosts rattling around in her head?

I don't want to be any of those anymore, Lord. Maybe…maybe it's time to see who You would make me. Redeem me, Father. Purchase me from this life of which I've made such a mess. Make me someone new.

"I've lost you." Daddy's smile had a sad note as he led her onward. "To the past?"

"Is there anything *but* the past?" She matched her step to his so she could lean over and, just for a moment, touch her head to his shoulder.

"There is. There is a whole future ahead of us. One that can be as bright as we're willing to make it."

Or as dark as they let it be.

Six

Slade stepped on stocking feet into the hallway and paused, listening. From below came distant kitchen noises, and a muted humming sounded from down the hall. He hadn't the time to waste trying to pinpoint it. He had already been trapped here half an hour talking to a reminiscing servant. Satisfied no one was about, he headed down the stairs.

Five days in Baltimore already, and this was the first time he had been left alone in Devereaux Hughes's house. Every other day he had been expected to go to the rail office and play the part of detective out to ensure the security of the rails.

Under normal circumstances, it would have been a fine job. But it was a cover story on top of a cover story, and it had kept him from what he was really here to do.

The evenings had been spent across the street. The elder Mrs. Hughes had made it downstairs for dinner twice now, apparently the first time in months, and a big to-do had been made over her. Slade had barely managed to be polite, knowing as he did that she was the one who had raised her sons to be snakes.

But tonight he and Hughes would dine in, so he had gone now to visit his mother—and his molly, if that's what the younger Mrs.

Hughes was. Didn't much matter to Slade. Whether accomplice or ignorant of his dealings, she was still Hughes's woman. She still set Slade's nerves to twitching, and she still unsettled him with that feline gaze of hers. He'd been quite happy to stay here this afternoon.

He crept down the hallway as if headed for the library, satisfied no one was nearby. A few days ago he'd seen his host leaving the corner room, locking it behind him, so he assumed that was the one he wanted. A study, he would bet.

It was, of course, still locked. Hence the pick in his pocket. He inserted the tool into the keyhole, his watchful gaze on the hallway and ears on alert. But the only sound he heard was the faint *click* of the tumbler. A moment later he eased open the door, slipped in, and shut it behind him.

Twilight possessed the room. This window overlooked the street at the Hughes family home, which meant he would see when the man was returning, but there was little light left to shine upon the mahogany desk and matching shelves, and he certainly wasn't daft enough to bring in a lamp.

He would just have to be quick, before the last of the day faded away.

Not that he knew what he was looking for. Given their desperation in bringing him into the circle, they likely had no firm plans. But they would try something sometime, as they had before. Surratt and Booth had regaled him the other night with the tale of their first botched attempt to kidnap Lincoln on his way to his inauguration.

Kidnap. Pinkerton had thought it an assassination plan and had recommended Mr. Lincoln separate from the rest of his group, that he go through Baltimore under cover of darkness and in disguise rather than risk the triumphant arrival he had planned.

And so when the two Johns and their compatriots arrived at President Street Station, waiting for "King Abraham" to debark from the train and board a carriage to take him to the next one at Camden Station, they found only Mrs. Lincoln and her entourage.

Slade had managed to hide his smirk in his coffee, but it had been close. The papers had lambasted Lincoln for his so-called cowardice, apparently convinced there had been no attempt on his life because, well, there had been no attempt on his life.

They didn't seem to realize that was an indicator of a job well done on the part of Slade and his colleagues.

Now to do the same again. Ideally he would find something here to indicate future plans.

The desk seemed the most logical place for anything of interest to reside, so he headed there first. The top was cleared of all but a single sheet of paper with a list of railroad employees. He sat in Hughes's chair and reached for the bottom drawer.

Unlocked—not a good sign. He pulled it open anyway, but a growl formed in his throat. More railroad documents. Employee records, complaints that had been filed, ledgers. "Blast."

He scrubbed a hand over his face and made himself pause. *God, You sent men into the Promised Land to scout it out, right? And You sent me here. So please, if You could help me find what I need…please.*

He rolled the kink out of his shoulders and surveyed the dim room. Where to look next?

Bookshelves lined one wall. Not filled, but enough tomes took up residence that the thought of paging through each and every one made his pulse keep time to the clock. Seeing nothing else in the room of promise, though, he headed for them. His breath whooshed out when three letters on one of the spines caught his eye. *An Authentic Exposition of the KGC.*

They had a book. What kind of secret society actually had a book? Slade pulled it out and flipped to the first page. Four years old, and who knew how accurate. It could have been produced by the group to put out misinformation. Still, it was worth looking through.

Movement out the window caught his eye, and he flattened himself against the shelf. Hughes was on the opposite sidewalk, strolling arm-in-arm with his brother's widow as if it were a fine summer's day and not a frosty winter's eve. They paused where the walkway to her door intersected their path, and it seemed from the angle of his body that he would bid her farewell and cross the street.

Blast it to pieces. Even if he hurried, there was no way he could make his room again before Hughes gained the door. He could duck into another room down here, but his host was the type who would notice his lack of shoes and wonder about it. And tearing through the house wouldn't escape the servants' notice.

He had to try something, though. He moved but then froze again when Mrs. Hughes looked past her companion. To his house. At the very window Slade stood beside. Had his movement caught her eye? Was she even now readying to point him out to Hughes? Maybe she assumed it a servant. *Please, Lord. Please.*

Or maybe she hadn't seen him at all, for she smiled up at Hughes and motioned toward her own house as she tugged on his arm.

Slade took a breath, aware only then that he had been holding it. Hughes was walking with her toward her front door.

Thank You, Lord. He replaced the book—a good thing he hadn't darted out of the room with that still in his hand—and made for the door.

Two minutes later he was back in the relative safety of his own chamber. As close calls went, that hadn't been too bad. There had been no weapons aimed at his head, no enemy a mere hair's breadth away. But it had still been a close call.

And he still didn't like them.

Fool man. Marietta stood at her bedroom window on Saturday morning and watched the carriage roll away from Dev's house with him and Mr. Osborne inside. He wouldn't work long today, but that just meant he would likely spend the afternoon here, and his guest with him.

The guest who would have gotten caught in Dev's study last night if she hadn't urged Dev back into her house.

Why had Mr. Osborne waited to search? He'd surely known Dev wouldn't be long gone.

Though she had her doubts he had found anything there. If Dev were now the captain of the castle under her house, he had only assumed the role after Lucien's death. Which meant that if there were any documentation pertaining to the group, it would have originated with Lucien. Would have been, if anywhere accessible, in his study.

Her fingers slid down the edge of the velvet drape. She hadn't even ventured into that room since the funeral. It still shouted *Lucien* in its every appointment, and she hadn't wanted the reminder of him while his brother secretly courted her. The household accounts were already in her small desk, and she had asked Norris, the aging butler, to fetch the bank ledgers for her. She knew there had been business records there too, which were obviously Dev's domain now.

But he hadn't moved them, at least not many of them. She had offered to have it all crated up and sent across the street, but he had just taken her hand and said he would rather have the excuse to visit.

No doubt he wanted to keep his roots firmly planted within these walls that meant so much to him.

If those were still here, though, what else was?

She turned when the door opened and Cora slipped in. Perfect. She would dress and do a little investigating of her own.

"Morning, Miss Mari." Cora eased the door shut behind her and headed toward the boudoir, though she paused beside the bed.

Marietta frowned. The woman had been moving slower of late. Not just from her changing shape, but in a way that bespoke distress. "Are you well?"

Cora's startled gaze flew her way and then darted back to where it had been—the Bible on her bedside table. "I'm fine, ma'am. You want the lavender or the gray this morning?"

"Gray." And was it that unthinkable that she would have a Bible out? Granted, it had been on her shelf all these years. But she had still read it regularly, more or less. The pages had merely been in her mind rather than before her physical eyes.

She sighed and sank down onto the edge of her feather-filled mattress. Perhaps it *was* unthinkable. Which spoke to her need for it. Hence why she had fetched it last night. She had wanted the feel of leather. The weight of pages.

She had wanted it to be real. Not just memory. Not just words.

"Here we are." Cora reemerged, her arms full of fabric. As she set the layers on the floor—hoop, petticoat, bum roll, more petticoats, and finally the dress itself—Marietta shrugged out of her dressing gown and positioned her corset over her chemise, hooking it up the front.

The laces remained well tied, so she slipped the corset cover overtop and turned back to Cora.

The woman still knelt on the floor straightening petticoats. Her hair hung in perfect midnight spirals, her complexion smooth and even. She was a pretty girl. A fact Marietta had noted upon joining the family, yes, but had then pushed from her mind. She hadn't wanted to consider that her husband owned a beautiful young slave girl. The worry had been somewhat put to rest when Walker strode back into her world and married Cora within a fortnight, the first baby following directly.

Were they happy, her childhood friend and this woman who now straightened and rubbed a hand at the small of her back? She had never paused to wonder. Certainly never asked.

Her heart tightened within her chest. Who in the world had she become these last few years, that she never looked past her own nose?

Cora emptied her countenance of the pain pinching it and held out a hand. Marietta put hers into it and stepped over her skirts into the center of the hoop. "Is your back paining you, Cora? My sister-in-law complained of terrible back pain when she was expecting."

Cora withdrew her fingers so fast, Marietta wobbled. "Nothin' to worry about, ma'am. Just a twinge is all."

Twinge? Images flashed through her mind's eye. "You are always hobbling by nightfall. Would it help to stretch out midday? Laura said it eased her discomfort."

Cora moved behind her and pulled up the mass of skirts, tying the hoop tight around her waist. "Can't, ma'am. You's shorthanded, and there be cleanin' to do."

"Your health is more important than the furniture getting dusted every day." The words felt right on her lips, in her heart. And yet foreign. Which made her stomach churn.

The first, thin petticoat fell into place, and Cora went to work positioning the bum roll. "Miss Lucy's mighty particular, ma'am."

"I can handle Mother Hughes. Consider this an order, Cora. I want you to rest after your midday meal for an hour."

The only indication the girl heard her was a momentary pause. Then she fastened the heavier petticoats over the roll.

Marietta pressed a hand to her fluttering middle before slipping her arms through her sleeves. Why was it so unsettling to be having an actual conversation with her servant? As a child, those who worked

for them had been family. Walker and her brothers had been insepara-
ble, their mothers best friends.

Yet she didn't even know if Cora loved Walker. Hadn't seen their
daughter since she was a babe. They kept her in the carriage house all
the time, a place Marietta had always avoided. "How is..." the name
sprang to mind, yet had she ever even said it? "Elsie?"

The tug upon her waist felt angry. "Good." She might as well have
screamed, *Why are you asking?*

Marietta squeezed her eyes shut. "Have you and Walker made any
decisions about what you will do after the amendment passes? I know
your mother will stay, but..."

But she couldn't, suddenly, imagine Cora remaining here. Not now
that she enumerated the many times resentment had sparked in her
eyes.

"Don't know. But don't you worry, I'm sure you'll find other black
folks to clean your house and muck out your stalls if we leave."

She deserved that. Still, it stung. "Well. If you need references, do
let me know." Paltry, but she could hardly undo four years of ignoring
the girl in one conversation.

Her bodice felt smooth against her chest, telling her the last of the
buttons had been fastened. Cora stepped away. "I'll go tell Tandy to
ready your breakfast."

"Not yet. I need to do some sorting first. I shall be in Lucien's study
if anyone needs me."

Cora froze, discarded dressing gown dangling from her fingers. "His
study?"

Marietta moved to the mirror and the combs and snoods strewn
over her vanity top. "Is there a problem?"

"Mr. Dev said ain't no one to go in there, even to clean."

"He didn't mean me, I daresay." Her first instinct had been to slip
in unnoticed, but why? She picked up a comb and turned back to the
girl. "And what business is it of his if I do?"

Cora pressed her lips together and straightened the rest of the way.
"I sure ain't gonna tell him."

"Well, then." She rolled her hair back, secured it with the combs
and lace, and then headed downstairs.

Cigar smoke clung to the study. From Lucien, or had Dev been enjoying his brother's collection of Cubans? A thick layer of dust covered the shelves, motes danced in the air.

Her eyes slid shut, but she still saw the room. Only now Lucien sat behind the solid mahogany desk, sunlight catching on his burnished blond hair and twining around the tendrils of smoke from his cigar. How many times had she come in here and found him in almost exactly the same position?

Three hundred twenty-two.

And each time he had looked up and shot her the grin that had made her determine to marry him. The one that said she was all he wanted, all he needed.

How she had wanted that to be true, at first. And then feared it when she realized her heart was not so steady. Not so faithful.

But then, had his been either? He had a mistress, as did Dev—their beloved KGC.

She opened her eyes again and moved into the chamber, letting her fingers trail through the dust on a shelf. His desk, at least, looked clean. Dev wouldn't want to soil his clothing.

The bottom drawer on the left-hand side of the desk. That was where she had seen them both slipping things when she came to the door. Sometimes they would leave their work out—railroad papers. What, then, did they put away?

The drawer would be locked. She had asked Lucien about that once, early in their marriage, and he had smiled, pulled her onto his knee, and said their company had enemies who weren't above bribing servants, which was why he kept his important documents locked away.

But it wasn't company files in that drawer. So then. The key.

She sat in his chair, reaching as she had seen him reach under the desktop. His arm had moved like so...but his was longer. His hands larger, so if she stretched hers out...

Cool metal brushed her fingertips. Clever—a little shelf had been built for it, a thin veneer of wood that the tip of the key hung over. She slid it out and turned it over in her palm as she retracted her arm.

Dusty. Dev must use the other key that Lucien had kept on his ring, the one she had handed over the day of the funeral, knowing most of the keys opened doors at the rail office.

Perfect. She could keep this one to herself. She unlocked the drawer and then took off her necklace, sliding the key down the gold chain until it settled against the cameo.

The clock in the corner hadn't been wound, so she glanced at the sun outside the window. Still several hours until Dev's carriage should rumble back over the cobblestones, but she wasn't about to be caught by surprise like the wolf. She opened the drawer and studied its contents.

Files hung, unlabeled. Ever-organized Lucien would have had everything in a very particular order. And more-organized Devereaux would know exactly what that order was.

He could discover she was in this room, and she could talk her way out of it without any trouble. But if he found her in a locked drawer where he kept sensitive information...that could get dangerous. She would keep things in their proper places, down to that single sheet raised a sixteenth of an inch higher than the others, and the file in the back that looked as though it had been rifled through.

She pulled out the first file, flipped it open, and drew in a deep breath.

She needn't read anything now. Instead she opted for speed, flipping page after page, glancing at each only a second.

A second was all she needed. Each paper's image seared itself into her mind's eye.

One file finished, she moved to the next. Then the next and the next, until she had looked at every sheet within the drawer and had replaced them all. She compared the image before her to the one within her mind of how it had been forty minutes prior. Adjusted the height of this, the angle of that. Then she closed the drawer again and relocked it.

Now what? She could keep poking through the room, but her twitching nerves dissuaded her. She would retire to her own desk, where she usually spent her mornings seeing to correspondence, and examine all she had just found at her leisure.

On her way out, she grabbed a few books from the shelf. She would move them into the main library and claim, if Dev asked, that she had gone in for that express purpose.

Her second-floor drawing room faced east, where morning sunlight filtered through the lightweight curtains and gilded the chamber in gold. She had redone the appointments in pale greens and blues when she moved into the house after her wedding, and now its familiarity wrapped around her. She settled at the delicately carved desk and opened the first letter awaiting her.

But she didn't read the missive from her aunt. She read instead the first sheet she had looked at in Lucien's study.

Names. Members of their castle? Assuredly. Lucien's took the first position, with *Captain* written beside it—and then crossed out.

The page was filled, front and back, Lucien's hand mixed with Dev's. Some of the names she recognized, some were unfamiliar. Some surprising, some not.

And several more crossed out. A few with a note—*fell at Shiloh, fell at Carthage, fell at Gettysburg*. Many had stars beside them and notes as to which regiments they belonged to.

Northern ones, most of them. Sorrow pinged. This was why the president had made mention of the group being another arm of the military, because they had invaded his own forces and were undermining his troops.

She focused her mental eye upon one of the names. He had died at Gettysburg. And was a member of the V Corp.

Stephen's corp.

Her brother had likely been fighting side by side with a traitor. Someone who had joined the Union army with the sole purpose of betraying it.

Marietta drew out a fresh sheet of paper, her personal stationery, and her pen and ink. *Dear Granddad...*

The note was benign, inviting him and Grandmama Gwyn to dine with her on Tuesday. But then she stood and went to the door. After glancing down the hall, she eased it shut and flipped the key in the lock.

She had stashed the invisible ink he had given her with the small vials of perfume she kept in her desk. She often dabbed their sweet scents on her correspondence as an added personal touch. If any of the servants happened across the bottles of straw-colored stain, they would think it her lilac water.

Granddad Thad had shown her how to use it, how to develop it with the counter liquor. He had also pulled out the code book he and her uncles and father and brother used. Flipping through the pages and then putting it away, he had smiled. Because, he'd said, he didn't have to make another copy and didn't have to fear it falling into an enemy's hands.

Finally, a valid use for her perfect recall.

She extracted the vial and a new quill pen from the drawer, and then dipped. Between the lines of the note itself she penned her encoded message, careful to keep the invisible ink from passing over the black, lest it run. She kept it concise, merely explaining what she had found and where, and saying she would put the list of names on the back of the paper. After waiting for it to dry into nothingness, she flipped the page over and got down to work.

Names were difficult to encode, having to do so letter by letter and using a dictionary as key. Granddad had said it was unnecessary in any-thing she would send him, that the ink itself was insurance enough. So she just wrote. And wrote, until her hand cramped. Each and every name on the list.

Some he no doubt already knew, but some he might not. She crossed out the ones that had been crossed out, starred the ones that had been starred. Wrote until what she assumed was the entire castle filled her page.

While it dried, she unlocked her door. Mother Hughes would likely wonder where she had gotten to this morning, and Dev would be back soon.

She folded the page, put it inside an envelope, and warmed her wax. A glance at her clock told her time was running short. No mat-ter. She would run the message out to Walker in the stable, and then she would go about her day.

Her first action as a spy. A Culper. Maybe eventually it would stop making her sick to her stomach.

Seven

Walker gave Elsie a playful toss into the mound of hay and smiled at her giggles. She was a happy child, but questions kept filling his head. What did she dream about? Were they soundless pictures? Could she tell his voice from her mother's by touch? What did that little flutter of her fingers mean? Was she trying to tell him something or simply playing with the hay?

He wanted to talk to his little girl. He wanted to hear her call him Daddy. And if that would never happen, he wanted to *see* it.

"Walker?"

He turned at the voice, once so familiar but now so out of place. Marietta stood in the center aisle, too pristine for her surroundings, and looking about as comfortable as he would feel in her fancy parlor. "Princess. You need something?"

Irritation flickered through her eyes, and his conscience reared up. They were on the same side now, again. They should be friends. Again. Which meant they should stop trying to goad each other. "I'm sorry." He shifted so that he filled the stall door. Instinct, that. Cora always tried to shield Elsie from anyone in the big house, so he had followed suit. "Old habits."

The irritation gave way to amusement. "I know what you mean."

She waved an envelope. "For Granddad. Usually I would send it round with Pat, but..."

He stepped forward even as he bit his tongue against the warning that had leapt to the tip of it. "Yetta."

That was all he said. Not a word about unnecessary risk or how they had specifically told her never to seek information. But she would remember what censure sounded like in his tone.

It didn't get her dander up this time, though. It made her sigh. "I was careful. But I think it could be useful."

Walker hummed in his throat and stepped forward. "I'll take it over when I finish mucking."

Something flitted across her face. He would have thought it regret, had that not been an emotion she had sworn off years ago.

Then her gaze went down, a moment before he felt Elsie's little hands take hold of his trouser leg. He swallowed, watching her face carefully.

Recognition weighted her eyes. She swallowed and offered his girl a tight smile. "I haven't seen her since she was a baby."

"You never come out here. Cora doesn't take her to the house."

"I can see why." Her eyes slid shut. No doubt comparing pictures in her head. Elsie's flaxen locks, which didn't bear a resemblance to Cora's black ones, nor to his middling brown. He had more white in him than black, and Cora had some in her too, but a blond-haired child between them still wasn't likely.

She might be able to make excuses for the coloring if Elsie didn't have the Hughes nose. And chin. And smile.

For a moment, he thought she would ask. Just come out and demand to know who his daughter's father was. Then he would have to figure out what to tell her, and how to make it clear that no matter her blood, she was *his*.

But her mouth stayed shut tight. Breeding wouldn't permit such a conversation, and she had that by the bushel.

He cleared his throat. "I've been hoping you'd come out. I have a couple things I want to talk to you about. First is Cora."

Her eyes opened again, and her shoulders edged back. "She's in pain. I told her this morning I want her to rest an hour each afternoon. You may have to help me enforce that."

Well now, that was interesting. He slid the letter into his coat pocket and then rested his hand atop Elsie's head. "I didn't think you'd notice."

"I hadn't. And I'm sorry for that." She cleared her throat and studied the beam that traveled from stall to ceiling. "I'm sorry for a lot of things."

That last part was so low he scarcely heard it over the nickering of the horses. And so unexpected it took a long moment to sink in. He smoothed down a wild golden curl on Elsie's head. "I'm sorry for a lot of things too. But it all turned out as it should have."

"Did it?"

Maybe it didn't seem that way to her. She was learning a lot of ugly about her world right now, after all. But the Lord had led them here. "Other thing's Elsie."

Her gaze went back to his girl. She said nothing.

Walker lifted the tot into his arms and kissed her cheek. "She's deaf. It took a while to figure it out, but there's no question."

"Will you teach her signs?" She asked it matter-of-factly, as if that were the obvious and immediate answer.

Something inside unknotted. "I would, but I don't remember much. Your granddad said he could get me a book on that version they came up with at the school in Connecticut. But..."

She grinned. It was the first he had seen her grin in so many years, he nearly stumbled backward. "You and a book? Walker Payne, are you trying to pull the wool over my eyes?"

"I know." He smiled too. He couldn't help it. "Makes me wish I hadn't always asked Stephen to summarize them. I'm afraid I'll mess it up. And Cora, she can't..."

Marietta went still. Just watching them, him and Elsie, watching and waiting. As though she didn't know exactly what he was getting at. Then she swallowed. "What are you asking?"

He repositioned Elsie in his arms. "I need your help, Yetta, in making a life for my little girl. Cora didn't want to ask you, but I don't know another way. It would take me hours to learn what you could in a second." He paused, watching her face. Looking for signs of capitulation, of softening, of some warm feeling. All he could see was the same pretty mask she'd been wearing since she caught him saddling up one of her daddy's horses six years before, ready to take off and never look back. "Please."

She stood like a statue so long he feared she'd turned into one. She would refuse. Make her excuses. Claim, reasonably, that with all Mr. Lane had just pushed upon her, she didn't have the wherewithal to handle anything else. Especially an "else" that wasn't her problem, wasn't her responsibility, had nothing to do with her.

Then she turned her gaze toward Elsie, smiled that sun-bright smile of hers, and made a few quick motions. Pointed at the girl, waved a hand in front of her face. "You're a beautiful girl, Elsie. We're going to make this your name." She curled her fingertips down, thumb in. "This is an *E. E* for Elsie." Then she went around her face again, in the sign he now remembered meant *beautiful*. "Elsie." She pointed at the girl, repeated the sign, and said her name again.

Elsie hooked a finger in her mouth and smiled around it.

Walker's throat felt so dry, he wondered if he'd ever be able to swallow again. "You'll help?"

"I already have the book. I only flipped through the first few pages to see how similar it was to my family's signs, but I'll get it out. We can... we'll have to find a time when you and Cora can both join me. It will hardly do any good if you don't all know it."

Somehow he didn't think Cora would be too fond of that plan. But it was for their girl. She would put her dislike aside for Elsie. "I doubt evenings would work, then. You usually have...company. Maybe afternoons?"

"Maybe. Probably. I—"

A throat cleared, cutting her off. They both spun to the door. For a second he was sure it would be Hughes, but the silhouette that stood against the sunshine wasn't built quite right. He was too rangy, and stood with too much patience. Must be the newcomer.

Walker didn't know if that was better or worse.

Slade let his eyes adjust to the dim light, not sure how to interpret what he knew he'd see. He'd recognized Marietta's voice. And it wasn't, he supposed, odd to find her in her own stable. Maybe she liked to ride. Maybe she was making changes to the way things were run. Maybe that was why she was setting up a daily tryst with a servant.

Maybe.

But when another blink helped his vision focus, his gut twitched. The man standing in the empty stall had features that bespoke Negro blood. His skin, however, was no darker than Slade's after a few weeks out of doors in the summer, his eyes a strange blue-gray.

And the little girl in his arms was as blond as...well, as the elder Mrs. Hughes.

Some story waited here, he had no doubt. The only question was whether it had any bearing on his business. For now, he saw no reason to pry. Especially since a Negro woman bustled in from the rear door, full of energy and exclamation.

"Lands, but it's cold out there today! I—" She halted when she looked up from her shawl, her gaze darting from the lady to him. "Mari."

Marietta's smile looked tight. "Morning, Freeda."

The man cleared his throat. "Mama." When the child in his arms wriggled and clapped, he held her out to the woman.

She gathered the little one close, smiling. "There's my precious. Grammy has a treat for you." When she moved her gaze to Marietta, her expression remained indulgent. "You might want one too. Gingersnaps. Your mama and I just pulled them from the oven. That's why I'm late."

Slade blinked again and let the pieces slide into place. He'd done a bit of asking about the Arnauds, so it only took a moment to place this woman as Freeda Payne, a free black who had been working for Julie Lane Arnaud since...always. As her aging parents still did for Thaddeus Lane. Her father, Henry Payne, was apparently one of the most renowned pilots Baltimore had ever seen.

Gossip had mentioned that she'd never married despite having a son, but it had failed to inform him that the son in question worked here. He'd be free because she was. This man before him might be an ally-in-waiting. Or he might be something else entirely.

The mistress of the house chuckled but made no other response about the cookies. She instead turned to Slade. "Did you need assistance, Mr. Osborne?"

How cool she sounded. All polite inquiry, not so much as a residual gleam of unease in her eyes over being interrupted with her stable hand. Maybe that meant it had been innocent.

Maybe.

He pulled out as much of a smile as he figured the situation warranted, which was about half. "I was hoping I might borrow a mount. Hughes said he doesn't have riding stock, but you do."

"Hmm. Walker can help you with that." She sashayed his way while Freeda bustled toward the opposite door with the girl.

Slade forced his gaze from his hostess and fastened it on the man, who regarded him as though he were a predator on the prowl. "I would appreciate it."

Walker nodded but made no move to fetch a horse. Slade knew when he was being assessed. He held his ground as he held the man's gaze...at least until Marietta's skirt swished within a few inches of him. He figured then it was only natural to take her in. Perhaps most men would have moved out of her way, but she could get by. The doors were wide. "You're looking well this morning, Mrs. Hughes."

He suspected she'd practiced that smile in the mirror to find the perfect balance of saucy and demure. "Thank you, Mr. Osborne. I put another book beside your chair in the library." She swept her lashes down and then back up. Artistic flirtation that barely covered challenge. "Surely if you enjoy Wesley, you will equally enjoy Jonathan Edwards."

The other half of the smile threatened to stake its claim on his lips. "One of my father's favorites. Especially 'Sinners in the Hands of an Angry God.' Care to recite it for me?"

"Don't think I couldn't." She swept past him before he could tell whether she smiled as she said it.

His smirk faded when he faced forward again and slammed into a warning glare from Walker.

The man strode past Slade and yanked a saddle from its shelf on the wall. "Don't."

"Pardon?"

"Don't look at her like that."

Interesting. Slade trailed behind him as he fumed down the center aisle. "Like what?"

"You know very well like what. Like every other man, like the Hughes brothers. You don't wanna be like them."

Slade's gait hitched but then evened out. "What does it matter to you?"

Walker slung the saddle over a stall door and shot Slade another glare. "I promised her brother I would look after her. Keep her out of trouble."

The snort of cynical laughter escaped before Slade could bottle it. "You haven't done the best job of that, have you?"

He regretted the jab when Walker spun on him, not stopping until they were toe to toe. No doubt with his fingers curled into a fist, though Slade wasn't about to look down to see. He just waited. One tick, two.

Walker snarled. "You ever try talking sense into a woman like her?"

"Yep. Never worked."

Just like that, amusement took the place of anger, and Walker backed off with a soft laugh. "Then you know. Ain't no keeping her out of trouble. Best I can do is make sure she survives it."

Something about the way he said it indicated he understood the danger that was synonymous with Hughes. And if Walker hated it as much as Slade did, maybe he could be trusted. He cast a glance over his shoulder, sent a prayer winging heavenward. *Do I dare, Lord God? And how much?*

Peace filtered in through the crevices of the wall inside him, slow and seeping like a midnight fog. Cooling the embers of frustration. He let it soothe as he drew in a breath. "I'm not like them."

Walker opened the stall and rubbed the horse's nose. "You're trying not to be, anyway. I can appreciate that. But you wear your past like an ill-fitting coat, mister."

He didn't know whether to be insulted or flattered. "You ever try to change who you are?"

"Sure did." Peace rang in the words. And a far sight more of it than Slade could boast.

"How did you manage it?"

Walker chuckled and went about saddling the mare. "It helped that my best friend was all but a saint."

"Stephen Arnaud?" He seemed to run into the man's name everywhere he turned.

"That's right. You got someone like that?"

His father's face filled his vision. So many years he had run from him, from the expectation he thought came with his affection. He hadn't realized how exactly he fulfilled the story of the prodigal son until he'd woken up in a gutter one morning and realized what he'd become. Until he tossed his old ways aside and came home. Until his father embraced him.

Until he saw the resentment burning in Ross's eyes when he did.

He cleared the memory from his throat. "Yeah. I have someone like that. Just nowhere nearby."

"Hmm." Walker put the saddle on over the blanket and reached under the horse for the billet strap. "I guess it's a good thing the Lord ain't just where that somebody is, then."

"Guess so." What a strange conversation to be having in Marietta Hughes's stable. With Devereaux Hughes even now inside with his mother, knowing well the KGC castle was all but under his feet. "Guess so."

Walker cinched tight the loop. "Do what you gotta do and get outta here. You need help with something, come to me. But keep away from Marietta, and don't let Devereaux catch you looking at her like she's a lamb to your wolf."

Slade's every muscle turned to stone. It was one thing to wonder if he could trust, could share a morsel here and there, and quite another to have some random man in his enemy's stable all but shout that he knew Slade's business.

And Marietta Hughes was no lamb.

He said nothing.

Walker finished his task and handed him the reins. Met and held his gaze. "Are we clear?"

Slade took the straps of leather. That made four men now who had warned him away from her. For different reasons, but the same point.

She was trouble. A smart man would never so much as glance at her out of turn.

He jerked a nod and led the horse out of her stall. And he wished he were a little smarter than he knew himself to be.

Eight

Devereaux read the invitation through twice. Nothing out of the ordinary, a small dinner party among old friends. He knew what he found interesting—that it had been addressed to Mrs. Lucien Hughes and Mr. Devereaux Hughes, together.

But he wasn't entirely certain what had garnered Marietta's attention. He looked up as he handed it back. "Why would you not accept, darling?"

Marietta stiffened, as she did every time he used an endearment in the presence of anyone but Mother. She darted a glance to the other end of the room, but Osborne still sat with a book of sermons and a scowl, as he had most evenings for the week he had been with them. Why he read the things if they bothered him so, Devereaux couldn't say.

"It would be my first social appearance." She smoothed the pearl gray silk of her evening gown, a movement that was graceful, elegant, and shouted her nerves.

"And a fine time to ease back into such things. Do you not agree, Mother?"

His mother had been brought down an hour earlier, and though she had not moved from her chaise, her color was still good. Now she looked up with that sweet-as-molasses smile she always gave Marietta. "The Ellicotts are a fine family. I'm certain whatever invitation you decide to accept as your first appearance will be the perfect choice, Mari dear."

More like whichever decision she made, Mother would scoff over it the moment Marietta left the room.

But if ever she detected her mother-in-law's insincerity, Marietta hid the realization so well even Devereaux couldn't find it. She sent a warm, unclouded smile to the chaise. "I would feel better about accepting any invitation if you were well enough to join me, Mother Hughes. I hate the thought of leaving you on your own for a whole evening."

"Ah, *c'est la vie*. You mustn't put your life on hold for me, dear. I shall be just fine."

"You have French roots, do you not, Mrs. Hughes?" This came from the corner, though Osborne didn't glance up from his page. Nor did he bother to keep his posture upright. He slouched in the chair like a university student amongst his peers—or like the common stock he was.

Both Mother and Marietta looked at him, both opened their mouths, both paused.

Now their guest looked up, his eyes keen despite his apologetic smile. "I'm sorry. I meant the elder Mrs. Hughes."

"It does get a bit confusing, doesn't it?" Mother simpered and smoothed down her skirt too, though her gown hung on her after all the weight she had lost in recent months. "Perhaps you ought to call my dear daughter by her given name, like the rest of us, Mr. Osborne."

Marietta pressed her lips tight. And because she obviously wanted to withhold her permission, Devereaux could smile and grant it. "You might as well. Though the answer to your question would be the same, whichever of them you asked."

"That's right." Mother went back to her embroidery. She was working on a Union sash, though he knew it galled her. "My family is from French Louisiana, just outside New Orleans. My brother now owns the plantation on which I was raised. The Fortiers are known far and wide for the best sugar in the South."

"And Marietta has French on both sides of her family." Devereaux took a draw from his cigar and picked up the paper he had yet to read today. "Right, darling?"

She had a book by her side, though she hadn't opened the cover. At his prod, she sent him a look that said she was perfectly capable of carrying on a conversation without his guidance. He grinned back.

Though she refrained from rolling her eyes, he had a feeling it took effort. Effort which she channeled into the smile she sent Mr. Osborne. "That's right." She drew the book into her lap. "My father's father was French aristocracy. He fled to America with his parents in the face of the French Revolution. And my grandmother on my mother's side is half-French as well, with a similar story. Except that Great-Grandmama Julienne ended up in England with my Great-Grandpapa Isaac."

Osborne glanced between the two ladies. "I imagine that shared heritage bound the two of you together."

The ladies were quick to agree, but Devereaux narrowed his eyes. Osborne obviously knew their loyalties were different, but something about the slant of his brows made Devereaux think he suspected more of Mother's sentiments than he should have.

A detective *ought* to have keen powers of observation, he supposed. But still. He had no business using them to find the cracks in the foundation of the Hughes house.

Perhaps Mother felt it too. She shifted, refreshed her smile, and directed it to Marietta. "Entertain us, Mari. Recite something." To Osborne she added, "Our Mari has an amazing ability to recall the written word."

"Does she?" Osborne sat up a bit straighter. "Fascinating. Do you take requests, Mrs.—I mean, Marietta?"

Devereaux shifted. He didn't much like hearing her name trip off his tongue after all, though it was a little late to rescind the invitation.

Running the tip of her finger along the edge of her book, she smiled. "That is one way to play the game, Mr. Osborne. But it is more fun if *you* recite a snippet of something, and I try to finish it and give you the reference."

Always entertaining, assuming she was in company that enjoyed the same things she did. Though boredom snuck in fast if a bunch of pretentious gentlemen were present who insisted on tossing out Greek or Latin references, or the religious texts she so despised. The moment they ventured into those, she would demure and claim ignorance.

"All right." Osborne sat straighter still, his nearly black eyes going narrow in thought. He glanced to Devereaux. "Why don't you start us off, Hughes, while I think?"

"Very well." He thought for a moment as he took another puff of his cigar. "Ah. 'There were a king with a large jaw and a queen with a plain face, on the throne of England.'"

How he loved the way the smile curled just the corners of her mouth. Every time he saw it, he wanted to kiss those corners until the smile bloomed full. "Really, Dev, that is hardly even sporting. You might as well have begun with 'It was the best of times, it was the worst of times.' The next line is 'There were a king with a large jaw and a queen with a fair face, on the throne of France,' and the book is *A Tale of Two Cities* by Charles Dickens. Mother Hughes, do show your son how to make this game challenging."

Mother laughed, though no doubt later she would huff about Marietta's audacity in insulting him before a guest. "All right. Hmm. Oh. 'There was no possibility of taking a walk that day.'"

Marietta made a show of considering, though she wouldn't have had to. Mother only ever quoted from three different books, and even Devereaux knew which one that line opened. She had used it in this game half a dozen times before.

She tapped her chin and tilted her head. "I do believe...no...is it—oh! Of course, your favorite, Mother Hughes. *Jane Eyre.* 'We had been wandering, indeed, in the leafless shrubbery an hour in the morning.'"

Mother clapped. "Your turn, Mr. Osborne."

Osborne snapped his book shut. "'But then, though we all hope to go to heaven when we die, yet, if we may judge by people's lives, and our Lord says, "that by their fruits we may know them..."'"

Marietta didn't so much as blink. "'I am afraid it will be found, that thousands, and ten thousands, who hope to go to this blessed place after death, are not now in the way to it while they live.' Whitfield, 'Marks of a True Conversion.'"

Devereaux ground out his cigar in the bronze ashtray beside him.

Osborne lifted a brow. "'Down she came and found a boat/Beneath a willow left afloat—'"

"'And round about the prow she wrote/*The Lady of Shalott.*' Which is your answer, sir. Tennyson."

Devereaux frowned. Marietta didn't like poetry.

Their guest leaned forward, challenge making his eyes hard as onyx. "'The analytical power should not be confounded with ample ingenuity...'"

"'...for while the analyst is necessarily ingenious, the ingenious man is often remarkably incapable of analysis.'" She lifted her chin and stared Osborne down. "Edgar Allan Poe. 'The Murders in the Rue Morgue.'"

Enough. Devereaux laughed and clapped along with his mother, ready to end whatever *that* had been. "When have you read Poe, darling? I cannot imagine it would suit your sensibilities."

It took a long moment for her to look away from Osborne. And when she did, ice filled her eyes. Cold and hard and unyielding. Even when she smiled, it glinted like frost. "A lady must have her secrets, Dev."

So long as they were a stash of sweets or a tawdry novel. The Poe he certainly didn't care about. But that glint...that wouldn't do.

"Oh, my." Mother fussed with the lace of her shawl and pushed herself up. "I do believe I had better retire. Mari, dear, will you ring for Norris and Jess?"

Though her features thawed, it was a bit too late for Dev's peace of mind. "Of course."

Osborne stood, his movements languid but shoulders tense. "I think I will adjourn to the library if you will excuse me. That exhausted my literary acumen."

Devereaux waited for Osborne to leave. For the slaves to get his mother from the room. For Marietta to meet the gaze he kept on her face for a solid two minutes during the exodus. And he was only marginally mollified when rather than just look to him, she joined him on the settee.

He let her settle at his side, let her send him her usual smile. Then he took her hand and held it fast. "You need to be more careful with him, darling."

At least it was genuine bafflement in her pale green eyes. "Whatever do you mean, Dev? I never even speak to him but when you bring him here."

True as that may be, it didn't negate his concerns. He glanced to where Osborne had been sitting. "Explain that little exchange to me."

Her cheeks flushed, her gaze fell to their hands, her fingers tightened around his. "I am sorry. I know such competitiveness isn't becoming, and usually I curb it in company, but having grown up with three brothers…he looked just like Isaac, tossing out those obscure references."

Devereaux studied her face, glanced at the flutter of the pulse in her neck, and noted the pressure she put upon his fingers. Nothing gave him any clue that she spoke amiss. That it was any more or any less than that. Still. "Just promise you will tread with care in his company. I cannot forget the look in his eye when he first spotted you."

She was too savvy a flirt not to recognize jealousy. Too skilled a beauty not to know what it did to him when she looked at him like that, from under her lashes. When she traced a finger along the ridge of his knuckles, he wanted to lean over and kiss her, promises be hanged. "You needn't worry, darling. He doesn't even like me."

"I find that infinitely hard to believe."

Yet her smile was genuine, with just a touch of conspiracy. "Because you like me so well. But trust me, I know how to read men. He may like my face well enough, but that is where it ends."

Was it? He knew how to read men too, and he was none too sure. But then, his expertise was not in that particular measure of them. "And what are your thoughts on him? I have yet to hear them."

She shrugged, her shoulder gleaming alabaster in the light from the grate. Yes, he was glad to see her out of the suffocating styles of mourning. "I confess I fail to see why you are keeping him so close. Perhaps he is an able guard or detective or whatever he is, but he is hardly your usual choice of houseguest."

How true. And how glad he was to hear her say it. "He hadn't any other place to stay in Baltimore. It seemed logical."

She sent him the look that had bound his heart to hers those four years ago. Tease, spice, wit, all joined together inside the most fetching form he had ever beheld. "And you, being ever so generous, took the poor soul in. A veritable hero."

"And all yours." He wanted to pull her closer, to hold her tight and remind her of how well suited they were. And he would have, if not for that blasted promise he had made her. "I suppose I should gather my unusual houseguest and leave you in peace."

But she stayed him with a hand to his chest. "Not quite yet." Her mischievous smile fading to a more yearning one, she leaned into his side and rested her head on his shoulder. "Give me a few moments first."

Well. He was really in no hurry to go home.

She'd given him half an hour. So far as Marietta knew, Slade had actually spent it in the library—which would be foolish—but she was at least doing her part. Keeping Dev away while the servants were busy tending Mother Hughes.

A better time to search she couldn't possibly have handed him. But more than half an hour would be pushing the boundaries. She had done her best to keep Dev relaxed and at ease, reminiscing with him about inconsequential things. Trailing a finger along the V of his waistcoat.

Wondering if the Lord would judge her for using her charms in such a way. Jael had acted similarly in Judges to kill the enemy king, Sisera, though. Perhaps not going so far as to snuggle to his side and thereby hold him immobile, but given the variance in their circumstances it surely wasn't so different, was it? Jael had taken in the enemy, had given him milk when he asked for water, had invited him to lie down and rest.

And then she had plunged a tent stake through his head.

A shudder worked through her. She had tried to tell her mother the Bible was too gruesome a book for her to read, but Mama had just sent her one of those looks that had kept three boys in line and tapped another page.

Dev trailed a finger down her arm. "Are you chilled, darling? You have misplaced your wrap again."

She knew that tone, warm and thick as syrup. Knew that in another moment, he would forget his promise and kiss her until she forgot too. Or if not forgot, at least pushed it aside. She had become skilled at the one over the years, since she could never accomplish the other.

And that, now, would not do.

"I suppose I should find it and bid you good night." She pulled away, making sure her blink was heavy, tired.

She feared he would refuse to relinquish her, but with distance came reason. He let go with a sigh. "I suppose that is a wise idea."

"Hmm." She meandered over to the chair she had occupied before, picked up her shawl, and wrapped it around her. The hallways would be cold. "I'll see you out."

His arms closed around her from behind, though she hadn't noticed him rise. "Soon enough you won't have to. I am counting the days, my darling."

Lord, give me strength. Praying still felt like moving a rusty gate— but one desperately needing to be opened. Heaven help her, but part of her still yearned for the feel of his arms. Her strength was not sufficient. Could not see her through this.

But His was made perfect through her weakness. If only she could remember to cling to that as easily as she recalled the words themselves.

"I am counting them too." And there were only eighty-two. Eighty-two days until he would at the least announce his intentions, and at the most insist on a small, private ceremony that would bind them together for all time.

When she stepped toward the door, he followed. She glanced at Lucien's study as they passed but saw no evidence of anyone having gone inside. Not that she knew what she expected to see.

Mr. Osborne, however, was as she had come to expect him. Perusing her shelves, though she still could not reconcile the figure he presented with the thought that he was an avid reader. He didn't look the part, didn't act the part. Even while he did it, he looked as though he would as soon toss the tomes into the fire as turn another page.

He had found Stephen's books again. His sermons, his Bible, his beloved novels.

His photograph that fluttered to the floor when Mr. Osborne opened the cover of Kierkegaard's *Frygt og Bæven. Fear and Trembling.* Stephen had worked for months trying to get enough of a handle on the Danish to read it.

"Sorry." Mr. Osborne crouched down to retrieve the photograph, though rather than replace it, he studied it. "Pretty girl. A relation of yours, Marietta?"

She nearly shivered again when he said her name. Somehow it didn't seem to belong on his lips. She moved forward, her hand outstretched. "I didn't realize there was a photograph in there."

Why could the man not just glance at her, or anything else, casually? It felt as though he were measuring the whole world, that he took note of everything. Every pulse, every shift, every breath.

He held out the thick paper, and she braved a half-second catch of his gaze before dropping hers to the photo.

Dev looked at it over her shoulder. "Isn't that Miss Gregory?"

"Yes." She nearly ripped the likeness in two. Might have, had she not been so closely watched. Glancing up at the question on Mr. Osborne's face, she said, "Just someone my brother briefly courted."

Someone. The one someone, other than Lucien, on whom they had ever disagreed. She had won that battle, had convinced him that Barbara Gregory was after nothing but his name and means.

Though if she had won, why did he have a photograph of a girl too poor to have afforded one on her own?

She was too tired for that question. And really, what did it matter? Stephen was gone.

Handing the paper back to Mr. Osborne, she let her gaze drop to the book. "Do you read Danish, sir?"

"Maybe."

Her gaze flew to his face, where a grin hid in the corner of his mouth.

He shrugged and closed the cover over the photograph. "Maybe not. Do you?"

"No. But I could if I wanted." Stupid, stupid thing to say. It may have earned a quick, gruff laugh from Slade Osborne, but that in turn earned her a scowl from Dev.

Marietta backed away and folded her arms over her middle. The Lord's strength was having plenty of opportunity to be perfected in her tonight.

Nine

Slade needed some favor. Since their evening at the family home on Monday, Hughes had barely spoken to him. The silent treatment from one's enemy. One would think it wouldn't be a bad thing, but three days later...he released a puff of frosty breath and dug his hands into his pockets.

The rail yard yawned quiet around him, black as tar. Vandals had struck the other night, covering the tracks with sand and cutting telegraph wires. Hughes had put up a big fuss about it publicly and had seen to repairs within hours the next day. But his private scowls had been testier than Slade had expected. The rails were targeted often, so what had been different the other night?

Slade hunched against the wind and stared down the track heading to Washington City. Because he was forced to hang around the place anyway, Hughes had put him to work on trying to determine who was responsible. Slade figured neither of them really expected answers, but it was something to do. So he had done it.

Maybe a little better than his "boss" had anticipated.

He'd determined pretty easily what had been different about the particular shipment that had been thrown off schedule because of the vandalism, and the message waiting in the queue at the telegraph office. And in the determining had realized it was no wonder Hughes had seemed genuinely upset. The telegraph cutting had interrupted a series of messages between John Surratt and John Booth, and it was a safe assumption that the interruption had caused some trouble for the KGC.

And the next shipment supposed to head out at first light on the rails had been Union rations gone rancid. Thanks to the holdup, someone had come along to inspect it again and had noticed.

At a faint scuffling sound, Slade slid in behind a stack of crates. The perpetrators had no doubt been overeager Southern sympathizers who didn't realize they were interfering with Hughes's plan. In which case, Slade had no problem whatsoever finding their names and hauling them before his host. It would earn him some respect from the man who seemed to like him less and less, and it wouldn't hurt his own cause any.

They hadn't struck again in the last few nights, whoever they were, but another of Hughes's disguised shipments was going out tomorrow, so this was a good night to play the shadow. If they didn't come, he could claim to have scared them off. If they did, he would catch them in the act.

The scuffling grew louder, though still faint by normal standards.

Slade's spine coiled and his muscles bunched. His fingers tightened around the pistol at his hip.

Three men slunk into view, barely discernible in the unrelenting black of night. The one in the lead had to be every bit as tall as Lincoln, if not a fraction taller. The other two were of more average builds, but something about the middle one caught his eye. Something familiar. Something...

He muttered a curse and stepped out, drawing his gun from his holster, though he kept it pointed at the ground. As much favor as this particular capture would win him, he couldn't do it. Not when it would mean losing a potential ally. "Walker Payne, you mind telling me what you're doing slinking around here in the dead of night?"

The trio came to an abrupt halt, silence echoing for long seconds as Walker no doubt tried to place him. At length, the man hissed out a breath. "Osborne? What are you doing here?"

"My job, as far as Hughes is concerned. Was it you the other night?"

The clouds meandered away from in front of the moon, and its silver light angled down across their faces. He was surprised to see that the tall man was old enough to be his grandfather, and the other one obviously a relative. Their faces were all but identical, though the younger man couldn't be more than thirty. Son? Grandson?

Walker shifted. "You really want to stop us?"

Slade gripped his pistol tighter, just to give himself something to hold to while he considered.

The tall old man stepped forward, his hands out in a placating gesture. "Easy now, Mr. Osborne. We don't intend to get in your way, and we would appreciate it if you would stay out of ours."

Ours? Who were they? Did Pinkerton have more detectives in Baltimore he hadn't mentioned?

No. His boss would have told him if he were sending him under the very nose of another detective, but something in his gut told him he had to trust a little here. He slid his pistol into its holster. "Educate me. And if it isn't too much to ask, don't do whatever it was you were going to. If I can claim to have scared off the vandals, it'll go far with Hughes."

The trio exchanged a glance, the tall one nodding to his whatever-he-was. "Fall back to B. Go on, Hez."

Hez. Why did that sound familiar? He tried to place the name, but it wasn't anyone he had met before. And even as he considered it, Hez melted into the night, not making so much as a sound on the gravel in the lot.

The old man turned next to Walker. "Go home to Cora, son."

Walker stared up at his companion. "Come again?"

"Go on. I've been wanting to talk to Mr. Osborne anyway."

Slade shifted his weight to his other foot, still on alert but more curious than wary. Walker met his gaze and held it for a second. And managed, in that brief span, to pack a wallop of warning. Then he turned and followed after the mysterious Hez.

"Consider the vagrants scared off." Amusement laced the old man's tone, though Slade felt miles away from laughing. "How about a cup of coffee, Mr. Osborne? Do you drink coffee?"

Coffee. Coffee at midnight with an old man he'd caught sneaking onto railroad property, who didn't show so much as a whisper of unease. "Yeah. Mr...?"

"'Mister' will do just fine." The gent's grin both put him at ease and made him twitchy. "At least until you figure it out for yourself. Come along. I imagine my wife is still up."

Maybe he had fallen asleep when he sat down on his bed two hours ago. Maybe this was all some bizarre dream. Saying nothing, he followed *Mister* to the street. A block down, the man climbed into a carriage and indicated he should join him inside.

Slade hesitated only a moment. In for a penny... He settled onto one side while his companion made himself comfortable across from him and tapped the roof. Though Slade hadn't noted the driver, one must have been waiting. The carriage rolled forward.

Clouds covered the moon again, and the drawn curtains kept out any lamplight they may have passed, but he still noted a few things. Like the quality of the upholstery under him, the thick padding upon the bench. The scent of flowers that indicated a lady usually rode within.

"So. How have you found Baltimore thus far, Mr. Osborne?"

Slade folded his arms across his chest. "Dirty, mean, and divided."

The old man sighed. "Sad but true. It was different in my day."

"When was that?"

A laugh rumbled in the darkness. "Many years ago. You should have seen her during the last war. Everyone came together to save her from the British. It was an inspiration to behold."

The last war...in 1812? Slade pinched the bridge of his nose. Surely a dream. "What do you know about me?"

"Enough. Enough to trust you to do your job. Enough to know you're smart enough to accept help when it's offered. You can trust Walker. He's a good boy."

"And who is he to *you*?" As if he would answer.

No, the low chuckle was more what he expected. "Do your research, Detective. You will figure that out soon enough."

He would love to figure it out *now* and was hoping for a clue when the carriage rocked to a halt a few minutes later. But the neighborhood he stepped out into looked like many another in the intermittent moonlight. He didn't catch a glimpse of a street name or house number.

The old man led him from the carriage house to the back door. A light burned in a window, and when they stepped into the dark kitchen, that was the direction they headed.

Heat welcomed them in the room the man ducked into, along with golden light that showed him more of Mister's face. Movement then stole his attention, and he looked over to find a grandmotherly woman turning from her chair at a small desk.

She smiled, as if it were perfectly normal for her husband to bring home strangers in the middle of the night.

"Sweet, this is Slade Osborne." The old man made a few strange motions with his hands and headed for the fireplace. A tin percolator sat in the coals. "Oz, the missus to my mister."

Oz? They were all of a sudden on such friendly terms that he got a nickname?

The missus apparently thought nothing of it. She stood with that same serene smile and came forward with her hands extended, leaving him little choice but to take them. "So good to meet you, Mr. Osborne. You may call me Grandmama."

He heard England in her voice. A strange thing, given her husband's talk of fighting off the British in the War of 1812. But he wasn't about to say anything about that, not when her silk-soft fingers slid into his and gripped his hands tight. Welcome and acceptance shone from her eyes.

"Grandmama." Yet the word sounded cynical on his lips. His mother would slap him upside the head for such a tone. He made an effort to soften it. "Good to meet you. You can call me Slade."

The mister held out a mug of steaming coffee from the percolator. The missus let go of his hands so he could reach for it.

"Have a seat, son."

Seeing no other worthwhile alternative, he sidled to the chaise and sat, taking in every detail he could find in the hopes that it would help him discover, later, where and with whom he was. The fabric of the chaise was worn soft, its pattern decidedly Turkish.

Overtop the fireplace a painting caught his eye, one of a ship with *Masquerade* on the hull tossing upon the waves. A storm was coming up behind it, but the captain who stood with spyglass in hand showed no signs of concern. And he looked more than a little like the gent before him. Imagination or truth that he had sailed?

The missus turned back to her desk and what looked to be drawing rather than writing. She adjusted her hoop as she sat, the three pearls of her necklace swaying with the motion and then coming to a rest against her collar.

Slade took a sip of his coffee and focused on the man. The silence spun out. The old man folded himself into a chair and just stared at him. After a snapping two minutes, Slade cleared his throat and set his cup on the table beside the chaise. "Well? You said you wanted to talk with me."

The old man gave him half a smile. "I *did* talk with you."

"We exchanged three sentences."

From the desk, the woman laughed. "Rest easy, Slade dear. If you hadn't measured up, he wouldn't have brought you here."

This night just kept getting stranger. "So..."

The mister chuckled and pushed out of his chair again. "Would you hand me the prayer book, sweet?"

Grandmama bent down with a happy bounce, as if she had been waiting for just that request, and pulled open a drawer. After withdrawing a crude leather book that looked old as Methuselah, she closed it again.

Her husband took it from her and rested a hand on her shoulder. Just for a moment, no longer than their eyes met. But Slade saw the communication in that quick exchange. A touch of sorrow, a shade of hope.

For what?

Slade stood when the man turned toward him and saw little recourse but to take the book he held out. He turned the cover carefully, the pages brittle under his fingers. Within, the faded words were handwritten. "What is this?"

"Puritan prayers. My grandfather transcribed them well before the Revolution. Take it. Read them."

"No." He let the cover fall shut and held it back out. A book like this was too precious. "I can't take a family treasure."

But the old man leaned against his wife's desk and folded his hands. "We've made other copies at this point, and everyone has theirs."

"Even so." He held it out still, though curiosity nipped at him. Puritan prayers. His father would love that.

"Take it." The man's voice had shifted. It was soft now, and sure, and reminded him of his father's when he stood in the pulpit. Filled with that something that had once grated and then comforted. Authority. "I've been waiting a lot of years to hear the Spirit's whisper telling me to whom to give it."

Well. Slade lowered his hand, the aged leather still clasped within it. He had learned the hard way not to argue with the Spirit. "Then... thanks."

The old man nodded and straightened again. "I'll see you out. Henry will take you home. And when you figure out who I am, feel free to come back for another visit."

Slade couldn't think of a single thing to say to that. So he buttoned his lips and followed the man back into the night while the woman bent over her paper.

Ten

Marietta pushed away from the table, never so happy to hear the chime of noon. Her gaze flew to the tall case clock in the corner, the one she recognized from her childhood. It had been Granddad and Grandmama's before they found a new one and passed this one along, apparently, to Walker and Cora.

Cora stood up just as fast, wincing. No doubt her servant liked Marietta's presence in her home about as well as Marietta did. The word *strained* hardly covered it.

But the lessons couldn't be done in the big house, where Mother Hughes or Dev himself could come upon them. Nor did weather permit an outdoor meeting this time of year. So here they were. Above the carriage house, in one of two rooms that Marietta had never even glimpsed before today.

Cora and Walker had managed to make the close space a cozy home, but Marietta clearly didn't belong in it.

She dug up a smile, though, waved to the wee one, and made the sign for her name. "Bye-bye, Elsie."

Her grin made every nerve inside Marietta go taut. Because she knew it too well, when she scarcely knew the child at all. Elsie waved back, backwards, and then earned a gasp from her mother by making the sign for *thank you*, even adding the one they had made for Marietta's name.

"See." Walker, beaming, tousled his daughter's hair and pulled his wife in for a sideways hug. "She'll pick it up fast."

"*She* might." At least Cora smiled as she said it. Marietta knew well that Walker had had a battle on his hands, getting his wife to agree to this at all. Hence why it was the fourth of February, and they were only now having their initial lesson. "Come on, baby. Let's you and me take our nap."

That too had been a battle hard won, one fought with Mother Hughes as well as Cora herself. And oh, the glint in Mother Hughes's eyes. A glint Marietta knew well, though she usually chose to ignore it. The one that said that the woman might have a sugarcoating, but that's all it was. A coating. Still, she was Lucien and Dev's mother. She deserved respect. But sometimes Marietta had to put her foot down, as she had done with this.

"I'll walk you down, Yetta."

She merely nodded and swung her cape over her shoulders, careful to keep her back to the little family as Walker bade them a temporary farewell. Just as she was careful to keep her gaze locked on the rickety stairs as she descended.

Once their feet were on solid ground, Walker halted her with a hand on her elbow. "Thank you, Yetta. I can't say it enough. Thank you."

She opened her mouth, but words wouldn't come. Or rather, appropriate words wouldn't. The ones that vied for a place on her tongue were impolite, risky, and...and so very important that they would not remain unsaid another day. She strode away, into the stable where the whinny of horses would give them some semblance of privacy. And then she turned.

He was only a step behind her, the muscle ticking in his strong jaw. The gratitude was gone from his smoke-blue eyes. "Go ahead. Ask."

"I don't want to. I don't, Walk. But I have to know." She squeezed her eyes shut, willing the images away. Elsie, with her familiar hair, familiar smile, familiar face. And Marietta's husband, the one who made them familiar. "Is she Lucien's?"

Walker's breath eased out as one of his beloved horses craned over the stall door and gave him a welcoming nudge. He stroked the brown nose, but his gaze stayed glued to Marietta's face. He swallowed. "No."

"No?" Relief should have welled. She should have been happy to think that her husband had not been unfaithful, had not been dallying with his slaves.

Instead, her knees gave out, and she sank down against the half-door behind her. "Dev." Of course it was Dev. The memories came in rapid succession now, a quick calculation thrusting her back to the right time. Three years ago. One too-long look, one too-wrong wish. His sizzling gaze, and the anger that pulsed through it when Lucien had happily declared it time to retire and had pulled her from the room.

The scream that had echoed through the halls a half hour later. She had sat up in bed, had been ready to go investigate. But her husband had pulled her back down and held her close, muttering something about a clumsy servant bumping into something.

Cora's cry. She'd known it even then. But when she did indeed see a bruise on the girl's arm the next day, she assumed Lucien's suggestion had been right.

But no. She had been attacked. And it was all Marietta's fault.

Her breath coming in heaving gasps, she lowered her forehead to her raised knees. "No. No. I'm sorry. I should have…I never even…you came two days later. You married so soon. I never thought to question."

"No one expected you to. You weren't raised to ask those kinds of questions." Why, then, did his tone sound so incredulous? Probably for the same reason he spat out her grandfather's favorite exclamation of "Thunder and turf!" and did a quick pivot away and then back. "How couldn't you know, Yetta? How could you not know what they were like? How could you even marry a family that owned slaves, knowing well how so many of them are treated?"

Her hands shook. Maybe it was the cold. Or maybe she couldn't stop trying to lie to herself even now. Fingers fisting in her gray skirt, she looked up into the accusation. He had aged in the last six years, of course. But as he towered over her now, he looked like he had then, as he flung the world's problems at her like they were her fault.

And in this particular case, maybe he was right. She swallowed back the bile that rose up on the heels of truth. "I didn't care. You'd left me, and I just didn't care."

She expected an explosion. A curse. Maybe even for him to storm off. Instead, his shoulders sagged and he leaned into the door beside her, propping his elbows on the top of it. "It was the only thing I could do. You know that. Surely by now you can understand."

She had understood then. But that hadn't made it hurt any less. "You crushed me. I loved you, and you walked away."

"There was no other choice. What kind of life would we have had? Me, a quadroon who would never rise above a trade worker, and you the rich daughter of an important white family?"

It hadn't stopped him from giving her her first kiss in her daddy's stable when she was sixteen. Hadn't stopped his lips against all those promises of love and dreams, each one etched in her mind forever. All of them dust. "I would have gone with you."

"You would have been miserable."

"You can't know that!" She averted her face, knowing her voice had been too loud. "You never gave me the chance to prove my mettle. You ran."

"Yeah. I ran." And he obviously wasn't about to apologize for it. She stared at the stall across from her, at the swishing tail of the horse that watched her warily. Walker toed the wood on which she leaned. "I wasn't going to. Stephen said I had to."

Stephen? No. "He didn't even..." She halted when she felt the weight of his gaze. "You told him."

"I couldn't run off with my best friend's sister and not even tell him I loved her."

Yet he could run away from the woman he claimed to love without a word. If she hadn't seen the light and gone to investigate, she never would have known he was leaving.

She had. They fought. He ran.

She had spun into the social world with a gusto born of wrath.

And she had proven her mettle. Proven it to be not of gold but of the cheapest alloy. Pushing herself up, she leaned beside him, still facing the opposite stall. "You saved her. Cora, I mean. By marrying her."

"Easiest decision I ever made. She's a good woman, Yetta. She's made my life complete, her and Elsie. I love them both more than I thought I could love anyone." He nudged her with his elbow, and when she glanced up, she saw his handsome, happy smile. "You'll find that yet."

Marietta shook her head and looked away again. "I squandered my chance, Walk. I've made decisions I can't undo."

"Don't talk like that." He pushed away from the stall door and stepped in front of her, his brows knit. "You're young yet. And as bleak as things look right now, they'll change. They always do. The war will end, the Knights will fall, the dust will settle. You'll be able to get away from these people and start over."

"It's not that easy." Saying it pierced through all those optimistic dreams about going home and breaking things off with Dev. Yet it brought relief too. Because for the first time, she was being honest with herself about how completely she had messed up. "Dev isn't going to let me go."

"He can't stop you."

"Can't he?" Tears gathered, but she must hold them off. Just a few more minutes. "We'd been planning to marry as soon as it was acceptable."

"Yetta." He shifted and reached for her hand. As it had when he'd taken it that morning two weeks ago, it gave comfort, even if it shouldn't. "I know this is a bad thing to say given the conversation just past, but promises can be broken. Sometimes they have to be."

And comfort could evaporate like a drop of water on a summer-hot cobblestone in the face of one's own shame. She tugged her fingers free and looked down to the hay-strewn floor. "I gave him more than a promise."

Even the horses went silent. She didn't want to glance up again, didn't want to see the revulsion on his face. But the quiet was too heavy.

Though they looked nothing alike, he reminded her of Stephen in that moment. The way his expression combined sorrow with pain for her. "Tell me you don't mean what I think you do."

The tears pressed harder. "I'm not proud of myself. I never thought I would...but I was weak. Weak and lonely. I thought I was in love, and I had no idea he was...the monster he is."

"Don't cry, Yetta." He said it now the way he'd done dozens of times as they grew up. Desperately, with an edge of panic. And it did no more to urge the tears away now than it ever had. "We all have those struggles, even Stephen with Barbara. It's natural. And sometimes we make mistakes. But you can get away. You have to. You can't stay with him."

"He might as well own me, don't you see that?" She slid past him, knowing he wouldn't thank her for it if she let the tears come. But she couldn't hold them back any longer. "He won't let me go."

"It's not his choice. You're not his. You're God's."

By the time he spoke the last word, she had gained the door, her feet flying toward the back of the house. The world had gone blurry through the lens of her tears, but she didn't need to see. She knew every rock, every root, every bump in the ground. Knew it was three stairs to the kitchen door, and then a quick dart around the thick slab of a table.

"Miss Mari, what in the world? You a'ight?"

Knew Tandy wouldn't follow her if she just moved fast enough.

"You need Mr. Dev, honey? He's up with his mama."

No! She might have screamed it if a sob hadn't choked her. Scurrying down the back hall, she pressed a hand to her mouth. She couldn't go upstairs to the sanctuary of her chamber if he were up there.

You're God's.

The words pounded with each footfall as she ran into the main hall, battered her mind as she pushed into the library. Stephen, at least, could be found there. His books on the shelves, his wisdom hovering around them.

You're God's. God's. Yes. He had bought her. Redeemed her. Purchased her from the man to whom her sins had bound her.

Ye were not redeemed with corruptible things, as silver and gold... But with the precious blood of Christ, as of a lamb without blemish and without spot.

Without blemish—not her. She was tarnished. Ruined.

Her face in her hands, she bypassed the chairs, the couch. She didn't want to be comforted by soft cushions and velvet. She wanted to disappear. And so she headed for the far corner and the little alcove that was a mere quirk of the architecture and arrangement of shelves. One little rectangle tucked away, just big enough for her to curl up in on the floor.

Why could God not undo the past? If she could go back, if she could resist him one more day, then she never would have made such a stupid mistake. It had seemed bad enough that morning, when she realized how she had betrayed her husband's memory.

How much worse an hour later down in that tunnel.

And now, knowing what he had done to Cora...

For ye are bought with a price: therefore glorify God in your body, and in your spirit, which are God's.

The wave hit so hard it forced her down still more, until she felt the cold floor against her cheek and could hear her strangled cry reverberate in the planking. She splayed her fingers over the honey-colored wood, wishing she could press hard enough to go through it. To sink down until she disappeared altogether, vanished from her wreck of a life.

...glorify God in your body, and in your spirit, which are God's.

She pressed her lips together, tried to hold back the sob, to keep it from drawing anyone in. But a whimper slipped through. *How can You love me, God? When I have not glorified You in my body, when I have ignored You in my spirit?* Much as she squeezed her eyes shut, she couldn't erase the images flashing forever before her eyes. All her sins, all her failings, all the times she cared only for herself.

God commendeth his love toward us, in that, while we were yet sinners, Christ died for us.

A shudder coursed through her. Why did the words come so quickly, so easily? Yet never in her life had she felt them the way Stephen said he could. Never had it been solid, like a touch upon her heart, like an embrace from her parents. Never had it warmed her when the winter winds closed in.

If You are there, Lord God, then please be real to me. Please come. Please show me You are real.

A flutter against her hair made her breath catch and then quaver its way out. She squeezed her eyes shut tight and listened to her brother's voice in her head, saw his earnest face. *You can never be more stubborn than He is loving. You can never be so far from Him that He cannot touch you.*

The flutter turned to a stroke, soft and tentative as if she were mist, and then settled, light as a snowflake.

She had fallen too far. Her world had turned dark, all because of her poor choices. With no one to blame but herself for the pieces that lay about her. Destroyed. And yet He promised to pay the price for her.

She couldn't forget her sins. But He could forgive them. He could wash them white as snow.

When the torrent slowed, when the shudders eased, she opened her eyes again. Her ribs hurt from where her corset pressed in, her neck from the strange angle, her knuckles from pushing so hard against the floor. And her eyes ached as they traveled down wool-clad legs and fastened upon the scuffed black shoes stretched out against the wall.

A hand was still resting—or perhaps hovering—on her head. And she was too drained to even be mortified. Gathering together what tatters of strength remained, she pushed herself up.

How very strange. Never in all her lifetime would she have thought that when she prayed for the Lord's touch, He would choose to use Slade Osborne's hand.

He shifted as she sat up but only to accommodate her, not to move altogether. He didn't look at her in question or as though she were made of glass and might break with one wrong move. No, he just pulled out a crisp white handkerchief and, black eyes steady on hers, dabbed at the tear tracks on her cheeks.

For the first time since she watched Walker disappear into the night, she didn't know how to respond to a man. So she sat still, refusing to look away, and let him soothe. Her eyes felt swollen, but they were clear enough that she had to wonder where the wolf had gone from his. He looked, as he moved to her other cheek, like a...friend.

The thud of footsteps sounded in the hall. "Mari? Are you in here?"

Dev. Panic replaced the hard-won peace, and she shrank back against the wall, pulling her skirts in with her.

Slade's eyes went sharp again. He pressed the handkerchief into her hands, sprang to his feet, and strode to the door. He must have stepped into the hall because his voice sounded distant. "I saw her go upstairs."

She leaned her head against the wall and prayed blessings, heaping blessings, upon Slade Osborne's head.

"I must not have heard her slip up. Well, we had better head back to the station. Are you ready?"

"Sure. Go on out. I'll just grab my book."

Though it took effort, she eased silently to her feet, holding her breath until she heard Dev's familiar tread move away and then the door open and shut.

Slade strode back into the library and headed straight for her, pausing when he was a foot away.

She would have attempted a smile, but her lips wouldn't cooperate. All she could manage was to hold out his handkerchief.

He took, not the square of white cotton, but her fingers. Her breath caught in her throat. He had ignored even that common greeting since their first introduction. Curling her fingers around the fabric, he lifted her hand to his mouth.

The touch of his lips was as featherlight as that of his hand had been upon her hair. Certainly no more than polite if one went by pressure, duration, or any other measurable quality.

But Slade Osborne was not polite. He was not measurable. And his obsidian eyes seemed to have no bottom as he held her gaze through the two-second exchange.

Then the wolf sprang again, and he turned and left, grabbing the book from the arm of his usual chair on his way out.

Marietta stared at the crumpled white cloth clutched in her hands and decided she would never again trust her judgment when it came to a man. Thus far, she had been wrong about each and every one of them.

Eleven

Devereaux tapped his pen on the blotter as he read the telegram, drawing in a breath that felt hot and smoky. The words didn't change.

The end was upon them.

For a long moment he stared at the words as their meaning festered. President Davis's peace talks with Lincoln and Seward had failed. They would not relent, and the South had no more resources. The Canadian government had signed a bill to prevent raids across the border, and no help was to come from any other side.

He shoved a hand through his hair. When Fort Fisher fell on the fifteenth, he should have known the South wouldn't, couldn't recover, but he had been more concerned that day with his own house. With Mother, and with seizing the chance to make Marietta his when she came to his room to tell him the fever had broken.

He should have been out that very night, communicating with the other captains, and with Richmond. He ought to have set in motion that very hour plans to save all they fought for.

Balling up the telegram, he shoved to his feet and tossed it in the wastebasket. Lincoln would pay for what he had done to their country. If he hadn't stepped foot in office, this war never would have started.

They could have found a peaceable solution. They would have convinced the Yankee-livered politicians to grant the Southern states their rights, the rights the Constitution had granted them.

But no. King Abraham had taken over, had seized power never meant to rest in the hands of the president, and had sent them all to their deaths. And for what? To end a way of life centuries old, one with its roots in the rich soil of the South, one that had seen the entire nation to prosperity.

Devereaux braced his arm against the window frame and looked out at the crowds bustling about his depot. Most of them no doubt felt exactly as he did, but few would dare to say so at this point. Not with Maryland in the grip of martial law. Women couldn't even mourn for their fallen Confederate relatives without the authorities seizing them and carting them over the river into Virginia.

And the tyrant dared to call it a fight for unification. Dictatorship, that's what it was.

He pushed away and snatched up his greatcoat, charging out into the frigid, damp air. His last communication with Davis had laid it all out very clearly. Peace, the president claimed, must be bought at any cost, before the last resistance the South could offer was broken.

Peace, it seemed, was not of interest to Lincoln. And so, the plan would proceed. Lincoln would pay. They would topple him from his throne, and when he found himself in a small, dark room in one of the towns his precious Sherman had burned to the ground, with a gag in his mouth and a hundred hate-filled eyes staring him down from behind armored helmets, then they would see how tall he stood.

"Osborne!"

Osborne straightened from where he had been crouched, examining something beside a stevedore. As usual, the man couldn't be put upon to say anything, he just arched a brow and stepped toward him.

Which suited Devereaux fine. He didn't need a man of words; he needed a man of action. One who knew what in blazes he was doing. One who would spend a cold night in the pitch-dark to scare away a few anonymous vagrants.

Devereaux didn't pause, just strode past him, motioning him to fall in alongside. "I'm calling in the brothers. It may take a few days for them to assemble, but in the meantime we need to make plans.

Contact your old friends on the security detail. Try to get a feel for how this next inauguration will be run. If we can seize him beforehand, we must."

The crunch of their boots on the gravel disappeared under the whistle of an incoming train. Osborne made no reply until they had climbed up into the carriage.

Then the man sat back with pursed lips and hard eyes. "It won't be easy. They know that is the most likely time for you to target him, so there will be guards everywhere and spies out."

Devereaux felt himself glower. "I don't need to hear why it will *not* work, Osborne. I need to be given a way to ensure that it *will*."

Osborne folded his arms. "Ready to trust me, then?"

"I haven't the leisure not to." When he realized the carriage had yet to move, he pounded upon the roof. "Able! Go."

His driver bounded onto the box with enough energy to shake the whole carriage—energy he should have spent keeping an eye out for their approach and already being in his position. Blasted, lazy slaves who thought the promise of freedom meant they could stop working.

Feeling his companion's gaze steady upon him, he nearly growled. "What?"

Osborne tapped one finger against his opposite arm. "You realize that if you pull this off, you'll be an outlaw, you and every man who takes part."

That was assuming his part was known, something he would work at all costs to avoid. "I know the risks."

A snort spilled from Osborne's lips. "Do your women?"

Devereaux bit back the words that wanted to snap out and borrowed his new friend's usual silence for a few beats. Paired with his own glare, it must have done the job.

The man shrugged. "Just observing. It's what I do. Your mother's health is still fragile. And Marietta...well, are you planning on taking her with you?"

He sure as thunder wasn't leaving her behind. "Don't worry yourself about my personal business. Just talk to your friends. And be ready to make plans."

Osborne held his hands up in surrender.

Good. About time something worked in his favor.

Slade left the parlor without so much as a glance over his shoulder, but he kept his ears strained. Marietta's laughter covered Hughes's response to Slade's declaration that he would, yet again, be in the library. The servants were helping Mrs. Hughes back up the stairs.

And if it worked this time as it had before when this situation presented itself, it meant he had at least half an hour to do some snooping.

Because the old butler and his wife and Mrs. Hughes were still on the stairs, he went into the room he said he'd be in. He pulled out a book at random, opened it, and set it on his chair. The household had come to anticipate him enough that the fire had already been stirred, a lamp already lit.

When he peeked out the partially opened door, he saw no movement. Perfect. Easing through it, he darted across the hall toward the one room he'd yet to search. He'd managed to peek into it once, but someone had come before he could do more. A study, it had looked like, which meant Lucien's.

His blood rushed with promise.

He pressed tight to the door to blend in as he tried the handle. Unlocked, praise be to the Lord.

From the parlor door came a swish of pale color and Marietta's, "I'll get it for you, darling."

Blast. Quick as he could without making a noise, he jumped into the study and closed the door, praying she hadn't seen him.

In case she checked the room, he sprinted around the desk and crouched behind it. That *darling* rang in his ears like a taunt. On Saturday pure fear had flashed through her eyes when she heard Hughes, and now, on Monday, she called him *darling*?

Maybe she had just been afraid of him seeing her with puffy eyes, her scarlet hair out of place.

She moved too quietly on her slippered feet for him to know where she had gone, so he stayed still and let his eyes adjust to the unlit room. No fire had been laid today, and he could see his breath in the moonlight that speared its way through the drawn curtains.

A soft click, and then a shaft of golden light from the hallway.

He pressed his lips together against a telltale plume of white air and willed his heart to slow. It was dark. He was hidden behind the desk. The massive, solid mahogany desk that looked exactly like the one in Hughes's study. His eyes fell to the drawer in the same location, which had a matching keyhole.

Marietta's hum filled the room. A hymn—"Rock of Ages."

Slade eased closer to the wood, kept his head bowed.

And so he saw the lavender silk swish into view even as the humming went from song to simple *hmm*. Letting out the breath, he looked up and saw her leaning against the side of the desk, fiddling with the chain of her necklace while she gave him a charming smirk. "Looking for something, Mr. Osborne?"

Even knowing full well he would never pull it off, he went for casual and smirked back. "Yeah. Dropped my cuff link."

"Ah. Of course. And no doubt kicked it in here under the door, around the desk, and...into the drawer, perhaps?" She twisted the chain around her finger, the round top of a pendant peeking up from her modest neckline.

Maybe she mocked him, but she sounded so dashed pleasant...and she hadn't yet called for Hughes. "You know, I was just thinking it must have bounced in there."

"Wily things, those cuff links." She made a show of peeking over the side of the desk. "Unfortunately, I believe my dear late husband kept that particular drawer locked. And equally unfortunately, my charming brother-in-law is now in possession of all Lucien's keys."

And of his wife—how would ol' Lu have felt about that? "Is he now? Well. By pure coincidence..." He reached into his pocket and pulled out his pick. "I never need a key."

Though her brows went up in obvious surprise, she didn't miss a beat. She clucked her tongue and twisted the chain again around her finger. "I invite you to notice, my friend, that everything in here is showing its neglect, other than the top of the desk. Even the lock has a film on it, and if you go scratching at it with that...*tool*, you could very well leave a mark. And Devereaux does detest seeing marks upon his things."

He sighed and paused with his pick an inch from the lock. When he angled another glance up, he found her leaning closer, finger extended.

And from its tip dangled the necklace she must have pulled over her head when he looked down.

The necklace with a key at its apex. He looked from that metallic answer to prayer back into her cat eyes. It didn't feel like a trap. Didn't smell like one. No tingles of warning shot up his spine. And yet it couldn't be as simple as that. "Why?"

She turned her finger, let the gold slither down. He caught it by instinct but kept his gaze locked on hers. And so he saw the bravado fade and watched her go from charming socialite to the vulnerable woman from the floor two days earlier. "I didn't know who they were when I joined this family. Now I do."

He closed his fist around the key, held it until he felt its indentation in his palm, and then flipped it into the lock and turned. "And you love him anyway."

Did something flicker in her eyes, or was it a trick of the moonlight? She stood and picked up the pipe lying cold and dormant in the middle of the desk. Apparently where her *darling* had left it. "He'll know if you move anything."

"Can't be avoided." He pulled it open and hissed out a breath at the reams of paper within.

Marietta tapped the pipe against her palm. "Don't take anything. And relock it when you're through."

Because it was wise advice, he nodded. Even as he wished he could put a few sheets into his pocket. Like this one with a full list of area Knights.

The light turned to shadow, and he looked up to see her in the doorway, one hand upon the post. "Slade...thank you." She glanced at the library.

Forcing his fingers to resist the instinct to curl around the paper, he nodded again.

She tapped the doorframe once and then disappeared into the hall. He heard her voice, laughing its way back to Hughes. "I declare, Dev, I about got lost in the mountain of dust in there. I'm telling Jess to clean it tomorrow, and I'll not hear a word of argument."

She'd left the door open, which meant some light for him, if a greater risk of being seen. He settled on the floor, held that first sheet in front of him. And glanced into the hall instead of at the paper.

Was that all this had been? A thanks for being nice the other day? Favor for a favor. Tip for tap.

He had no better explanation. Even if she disapproved of what her husband and brother-in-law did, she'd made no move to separate herself. From all he'd seen, Marietta Arnaud Hughes answered first and last to her own desires. And for whatever reason, those desires now focused on Devereaux Hughes.

Maybe that wasn't a generous view of her, but it explained everything. All but his own slip Saturday, when he'd seen a hurting girl and forgotten to be the Slade that Ross had made him. When he'd just wanted to help and couldn't resist that tug inside that said *Go. Be My hands.*

He gave himself a moment to shut his eyes and refocus. He could be that softer Slade when this was all over, when his brother's betrayal had been redeemed. For now, he had work to do. And it didn't involve wondering about what had sent Marietta into the library sobbing.

Twelve

Marietta looked from Walker's back to the dismal clapboard house in front of which he had stopped. She twisted her necklace around her finger once and then tucked it beneath her collar lest playing with it turn into a habit. It wouldn't do to pull out the key when Dev was around.

She had thought Slade would keep it and was happy to let him—she needed it no longer. But last night he had taken her hand upon leaving as he had in the library. And pressed the key back into her fingers instead of the handkerchief with *S.O.* embroidered in the corner.

Tapping her foot against the floor of her barouche, she willed the vision before her to change. Maybe Walker had the wrong address. Or maybe she'd misread that look in his eyes when she'd cornered him in the stable that morning and demanded to know *how* her brother could have struggled in certain unmentionable ways with Barbara Gregory when their relationship had not lasted a fortnight.

Walker turned on his seat to send her a look. "End of the line."

Had it been old Pat driving her as usual, she would have told him she'd changed her mind. But she had asked Walker to come. "I don't think I want to."

"Then it must be the right thing to do. Out. Now." He jumped down and held up a hand to assist her.

"Tyrant."

"Princess."

She put her hand in his and climbed down. Then took a moment to straighten her skirts. "I'm glad we're back to being friends, Walker. It makes me feel...level again."

"Me too. Now level something else that's been sorely out of plane for years." He nodded toward the house.

A shack, really, no doubt held up more by the buildings that shared its walls than its own integrity. Not that its neighbors looked any sturdier.

"Yetta."

"I'm going." She took a step to prove it, and then another. Up the sagging stair to the sagging stoop, she invited a litany of prayers to run through her mind. Yet the only one that appeared was a snippet from her grandparents' book of them: *Holy Lord, I have sinned times without number, and been guilty of pride and unbelief...*

She knocked before Walker could follow and do it for her. The door creaked open too soon.

Barbara. She had changed a great deal since the last Marietta had seen her, but dull hair and a loss of weight couldn't disguise the woman's beautiful brown eyes. Nor, apparently, could it dim her broad, guileless smile. "Marietta! What a pleasant surprise. Come in, please."

She did, but the warmth of the greeting made her feel all the more chilled. "Hello, Barbara. I...I'm sorry to drop in unannounced."

Again she smiled, bright and full, as if Marietta had been her dearest friend and not her enemy. It made a marked contrast to the dull, unrelieved black of her dress. "You're welcome anytime, Mari. Anytime. Can I get you tea?"

A refusal was on the tip of her tongue. From the looks of the threadbare rug and the peeling walls, this woman had nothing to spare. But she couldn't be rude. Not now. "I would like that. Thank you. But perhaps not yet."

"You've come with a purpose." She motioned Marietta to follow her into a sitting room no bigger than a speck and indicated the couch, which looked slightly less worn than the chair. "I was so sorry to hear about your husband. I sent a card, but..."

"I received it. Thank you." She should have replied. She had to all the other notes of condolence, even those from near strangers, but that one she had tossed directly into the wastebasket. Sitting gingerly upon the couch, she focused her gaze upon her hostess's dress, absent so much as a white collar. "I had not heard of your loss. It must have been recent. Your uncle?" A safe guess, as her uncle was her only living relative.

Barbara's smile went weak. "Several years ago. But the mourning is for my husband. He fell at Gettysburg."

"So did—" But of course she'd know that, if she knew when Lucien had died.

Barbara sat in an uncomfortable-looking chair and studied the hands she folded in her lap.

The photograph. Walker's words. The fact that he knew where she lived. Marietta sucked in a quick breath. "He married you."

For a moment the woman made no response. No doubt she feared that if she dared to, Marietta would go from polite to spiteful in the blink of an eye. But there was not so much as a thread of dishonesty in Barbara—with a wary glance, she nodded.

Marietta's lungs refused to work. "When? He was at college, and then the war—he never said a word."

Tears gleamed in the eyes Barbara turned toward the wall. Her hands twisted, fretted with the frayed ends of her shawl. "Forgive us, Mari. I asked him not to tell anyone. I knew what you thought of me and could hardly blame you for it, so we wed in secret. Before he signed up."

He wed in secret. Her brother, her dearest friend, and he...she had forced him to lie about something this important. "Did you tell my parents? Grandparents?"

Her voice must have conveyed more amazement than censure, for Barbara met her gaze again. She shook her head. "We told no one. Walker found out after Stephen died, somehow. He and his dear Cora have been a tremendous blessing, always making sure I have enough. But no one else."

For a long moment, Marietta could only stare. This woman was her sister, every bit as much as Hez's and Isaac's wives, yet she lived in squalor and had to take handouts from servants. "But *why*? My parents would have welcomed you with open arms if Stephen loved you enough to marry you. Surely you know that."

Barbara smoothed the shawl's tassel. "They were always very kind to me."

"But I wasn't." It burned, seared, one more transgression on the ever-growing stack. "You didn't tell them because I didn't approve."

"Your reasons were valid, Mari. And your opinion meant so much to Stephen." How was it, when she glanced up, that her eyes held only sorrow and goodwill and not so much as a stitch of blame? "I always wanted us to be friends, but I knew we couldn't be, so long as I was poor and your brother rich. Even though we both loved him so."

He hadn't been rich, not compared to families like the Hugheses. Just compared to folks like the Gregorys. But yes, the difference had been marked enough that she had pointed it out. Repeatedly.

Marietta didn't know what to do with her hands, folded under her cape. She didn't know what to do with this woman, who said such things so calmly. "You're still in full mourning. It has been almost two years."

The word *beatific* sprang to mind at the smile that emerged on Barbara's lips. "Can one ever stop mourning Stephen?"

"No. Never. He was the best of men." And Marietta had taken all his books, the things he treasured most. What had he left for his wife? "Did he not set up a living for you?"

"He sent me his pay from the army while he was alive, but I would not let him do more. I did not want—"

"Me to find out and judge you." Which, yes, she would have done even a month ago had she discovered that Barbara had wed him in secret and now lived on Arnaud money. And she would have been utterly wrong. "But Barbara, this is ridiculous. My family will provide for you. You are one of us."

For a moment, Barbara's luminous eyes went wide as a doe's, her lips parted. Then she shook her head vehemently enough to send a strand of honey-brown hair fluttering against her cheek. "I cannot accept such generosity, Mari. Family I would gladly take, but I have no right to your parents' money. The baby died before she drew breath, and I—"

"There was a baby?" A little girl, half her brother? Her eyes slid shut. What if it were these wretched living conditions that made it turn out so terribly? Another loss, her fault. "I am so sorry. So very sorry for every mean thought, for every word I spoke against you. For everything."

A rustle of stiff fabric, the sinking of the cushion, and Barbara's cool, delicate fingers brushed over hers. "Loss is as much a part of life as joy, Marietta. And without it, the other would not be so sweet."

Was it? Then why, having lost so much, did she feel so lifeless?

Barbara touched her cheek, a silent command to open her eyes. Though Marietta felt like a penitent at the feet of a priest, she obeyed.

The woman let her hand fall back to the cushion between them. "You have changed. He would be so glad to see that light in your eyes."

"Light?" Surely she was mistaken. All Marietta felt inside was the certainty that she could never undo all the wrongs she had committed.

"You finally believe." Barbara wove their fingers together and squeezed. "He prayed every day you would, and asked me to pray every day as well. I have been faithful in that."

They had prayed for her. As cruel as she had been, as stubborn and petty, and they had prayed. She shook her head. "I know all the words. But...forgiveness may wash me clean, but it cannot change what I have been. It does not negate the consequences of my actions."

"No, it doesn't. But it gives you the strength to face them." It was so easy to understand, now, why Stephen had fallen in love with this girl who volunteered beside him at the hospital. How had Marietta never seen the heart that all but radiated from her? It was nearly like having her brother with her again.

She squeezed the slender fingers back. "You need to come with me to see my mother. Please."

"Sweet Mari." *Sweet?* An appellation no one had ever applied to her, even when she was a child. But Barbara looked utterly sincere. "It has been too long. I cannot intrude upon your family now—"

"Would you deny me a friend, a sister, when I need one most?" She gripped her other hand too, certain this was one time she must achieve her goal. If she left her brother's widow in this house, this rough neighborhood, without a family, she might as well be turning her back on Stephen himself.

But Barbara's eyes went soft with refusal. "You have never needed anyone, Marietta. It was one of the things I always admired about you, how you knew exactly who you were."

"You thought that?" She sat back with a shake of her head. "Why?"

Barbara pulled a hand away and gestured, as if to say, *Look at you.* The fine silk, the fine house, the fine life she had purchased through wile and simmering smiles.

Look, indeed, where it had gotten her.

"I would trade it all. Every last stitch and gem for just one more chance to see Stephen and apologize."

Her hostess went still. She sat there and studied Marietta's eyes, the fingers of one hand still caught within hers. Marietta held steady and prayed she saw whatever she needed to see. That the Lord would grant her this chance to make just one thing right.

At length, Barbara's shoulders relaxed. "I would be honored to be your sister and friend."

"Then come." She admired her determination? Then she would taste it in full. Marietta surged to her feet and pulled Barbara with her, out of the minuscule room and back toward the rickety door. "Grab your wrap. Mama will be at Grandmama's this morning, as it is Tuesday, so we can catch them both together."

"Oh, I..."

"Ah, I see your bonnet." She snatched it from the half-broken rack by the door and turned to put it on the woman for her. "The sun is doing a fair imitation of spring today, so I brought an open carriage. This should suffice nicely." She swung the thin cape from the same wobbly rack and whipped it around Barbara's shoulders. "There. Pretty as a picture."

True, even if the words were meant more to overwhelm than bolster. Barbara might not have the kind of cultivated beauty Marietta had so carefully created, but she had never wondered why the girl had caught Stephen's eye. Something about her open face and that wide, honest smile...

She opened the door and pulled her sister-in-law, agape, into the sunshine.

Walker had been lounging in his seat, no doubt enjoying the touch of early spring upon his face, but turned and greeted their appearance with a grin. "Miss Barbara. Do I get the joy of driving you somewhere today?"

"We're going to Grandmama's." Marietta pulled her to the carriage as Walker jumped down. She delivered Barbara's hand into his, but when she just stood there looking dazed, he lifted her in. Marietta met his smile when he turned back to help her. "Thank you, Walk."

He chuckled. "That's my Yetta. 'Bout time she showed back up."

Barbara turned back toward escape. "I really don't think—"

"One thing that still holds true about me, my dear Barbara." Marietta used Walker's hand to vault up and settled on her seat with a *whoosh* of skirts and petticoats, leaving her guest little choice but to follow suit. She grinned. "I never lose an argument."

Marietta loosed what might have been her first sigh of pure contentment as she watched Mama and Barbara cry and embrace, amidst laughter and reminiscing. There had been, in Marietta's mind, no question how her brother's widow would be received. If the Lanes and Arnauds did one thing well, without fail, it was loving.

And, apparently, clandestinely working to keep the country united. Though that one seemed to be giving them a few headaches just now.

Needing a respite from the emotions saturating the parlor, Marietta wandered out into the familiar hall of the Lane home, past all the paintings her grandmother had hung upon the walls. Generations of family, places they had visited aboard the *Masquerade*, the wilds they had seen through fifty years of marriage.

Fifty years. She paused just inside the drawing room and stared at what she knew was the first painting Grandmama had done for Granddad Thad, before they married. Granddad's ship, with him at the helm.

Her fingers stroked over the lavender of her day dress. Perhaps she would soon be out of mourning, but no fifty years of marriage waited in her future. No husband who would know her every thought just by looking into her eyes. Who would love her, despite her every failing.

No one who would ever love her above all else save the Lord.

A familiar arm slid around her waist, and Grandmama Gwyn leaned into her. "You did a wonderful thing, my precious girl, bringing her here."

"I was due for a wonderful thing, I suppose." She turned to smile at her grandmother, but it froze on her lips when she caught sight of the canvas half-covered in paint. He had no shoulder yet, no waist, the fireplace behind him was but a sketch. But the face was all but finished, and far too startling in this room. "Grandmama, when did you see Slade Osborne?"

"Oh." Undisturbed by her alarm, her grandmother turned toward the painting and tilted her head to one side. "Your grandfather brought him home one night, briefly. Must be nearly two weeks ago now. He apparently caught Thad and Hez and Walker trying to...interrupt one of Dev's shipments."

Marietta could only stare. At the painting, and at the woman who delivered that news so calmly. Calmly! As if it were all old hat to her.

Maybe it was, given those fifty years with Thaddeus Lane.

But still. "He caught...Granddad was...Grandmama! He is eighty years old! He has no business prowling around in the middle of the night with his grandson." And would she ever give her brother an earful when she next saw him...

But her grandmother laughed, light and free. "He chafes so against being always at a desk that I haven't the heart to remind him of his decades." She patted Marietta's waist and pulled her closer to the painting. "The risk was small, as risks go. He knew well he could bypass what security Devereaux might post, as he has done often enough before. Though he had not counted on young Mr. Osborne."

It all swirled too quickly for her to make sense of it. "You know."

"About the Ring? I have known since the last war, when my uncle was its greatest enemy."

And now Marietta's would-be betrothed took that role. A thought she wished she could forget. "What did he tell Slade?"

"Slade, is it?" Her grandmother lifted a brow, her blue-green eyes twinkling. "Not much. He was feeling rather mysterious that night, apparently, and said his name was 'Mister.' He instructed me in signs not to use names. Though Mr. Osborne will figure it out soon, I imagine. Who we are, if not our roles."

Marietta had no response to that.

Grandmama apparently didn't need one. She studied her painting again with a smile. "I daresay it's no hardship to see that face at your table every night, hmm?"

That at least teased a laugh from Marietta's throat, which in turn eased the discomfort balled up in her chest. What in the world was Granddad doing, after making it clear Slade should not know about the Culpers? She had helped him overtly, yes, but he would think it nothing but a returned favor. Her grandfather, though...

Well, there was no arguing with him. Especially once a thing was already done.

"I wanted to give you something." Her grandmother withdrew her arm from Marietta's waist and reached up for the gold necklace clasped, as always, around her neck.

"Grandmama, no." Marietta stepped back, hands up. She couldn't remember a time the three pearls had not hung around her grandmother's neck. And much as she might treasure the gift, there were others more deserving. "I cannot take the necklace Granddad gave you on your wedding day."

"Of course you can." She fumbled with the clasp a moment before undoing it. "It is part of the Culper legacy. And you are the first woman to be involved in it since me. Therefore..." She reached around Marietta and fastened it, a smile upon her face. "Perfect."

Marietta rested her fingertips on the warm, iridescent spheres. "There is so much to live up to."

"And if anyone can do it, it is you." Grandmama rested her hand against Marietta's cheek, her eyes as deep as the Caribbean waters. "You are our miracle, Marietta. Endowed with a gift beyond what any of us could have dreamed possible."

Strange how small those lofty words made her feel. "I am a selfish fool. I have squandered it, often hated it." She covered the aging fingers with her own. "So many times I just wished I could forget."

"I understand that. I know what it is to have images locked forever in your memory. But the Lord gave you this mind for a purpose, my precious child. Yours is to discover what that might be."

Marietta let her gaze fall to the multicolored rug as the words tumbled through her mind. Recent events indicated that her purpose lay in undermining the man she had let into her heart. Which seemed such a cruel, painful thing to call one's destiny.

Yet even as she looked on that possibility, memories crowded. All the times her family had tried to steer her away from the Hughes family. All the times her conscience had niggled. All the times she had silenced any voice that did not offer what she wanted.

If that now caused her pain, it was pain she had chosen through disobedience. She never should have given herself the chance to fall in love with Dev. So being forced to accept the truth about him and change it—that was perfect justice.

"Mari." Her grandmother's voice pulled her back to the present, even as those of Mama and Barbara drew nearer. "Embrace what the Lord has made you."

She could only nod before the other two women entered and then turn her gaze on the happy, tearful faces.

They would have been a part of each other's lives for years already had Marietta not interfered.

"Stephen would not have wanted you there, though, Barbara. You know it as well as I." Mama glanced from Barbara to Marietta, who had been sure to whisper to her about the living issue some twenty minutes ago. "Your uncle always provided as best he could, but you needn't remain there from pride. Please. With so many of our men away at war, we women must cling together. Come stay with me. Or with Mari. She has empty rooms aplenty."

Panic rose fast, like a storm surge in a hurricane. First the old, familiar objections, the ones that slid into her mind without thought, without reason. That she would not be impressed upon, that she had no obligation to take a veritable stranger into her home. That it was not what she wanted.

But then, just like a surge emptying back into the bay, those acidic thoughts were pulled from her heart and replaced with pure fear.

She could not expose Barbara—pure, tenderhearted Barbara—to the Hugheses. They would crush her. They would destroy her. This young woman was not made for that kind of family, the kind that hated where they should have loved. Too much darkness saturated that home. They would...

And the darkness comprehended it not.

Marietta relaxed as she drew in a long breath and remembered all Barbara had already survived. If she could withstand the mean streets of Mobtown with a smile, if she could withstand the loss of Stephen, of their child, then the Hugheses could do nothing to her.

Perhaps they were darkness. But darkness could never overcome light. And a beacon might be exactly what Marietta needed within her home.

Only a beat having passed beneath the rapid wings of thought, Marietta smiled and stepped forward to take Barbara's other hand. "With me, Barbara, please. We can finally get to know one another."

Barbara searched her eyes for a long moment, no doubt looking for hidden motives, for some sign that obligation spurred the request. Marietta held her gaze as firmly as her fingers.

Perhaps she still had plenty to hide. But not, for the first time, her heart.

Thirteen

Devereaux spread out the pages on his brother's desk, side by side until they covered the entire expanse upside down. The muscle in his jaw ticked, he clenched his teeth so tightly.

The telegram weighed heavy in his pocket. Defeat was certain. President Davis had authorized their worst-case-scenario plan.

And Devereaux had been charged with two vital tasks: rallying the men for the second rising sometime in the murky future, and burying a portion of the South's hope. Gold. Rations. Weapons. Gunpowder. Medical supplies.

First, the physical. He braced himself on the edge of the desk and scowled at the papers. Though the fronts were covered in type, the backs hid the real information: a faint outline on each that would look like nothing but a mistaken mark of a pencil if taken individually. But together, they showed Maryland. The Southern state held by force in the Union, where those loyal to their roots couldn't breathe a word of it lest they be seized. Maryland, with its thriving city of Baltimore and its western territories still largely wild.

Maryland—his domain. His to use as a hiding place for the stock-piled goods. All these years they had known it was a possibility, and so they had been readying the codes to guide future Knights to the caches.

To hide them, he would utilize architecture by engraving symbols into stone and referencing landmarks. Structures unlikely to change in the next few years.

He glanced briefly into the empty space where Pennsylvania, Virginia, Delaware, and the so-dubbed *West* Virginia lay. If necessary, he could venture into those areas. He might need to do so to plant the symbols. But for the treasure itself...

His eyes fell again on that narrow strip of western Maryland. The mountains would provide the perfect hiding places. There were still enough uncivilized places that they could get in and out without drawing attention, places where only the rails went. Whole valleys still untouched, protected by the natural barriers of the Appalachians.

A better hiding place he could not have designed.

Best of all, he knew the area well. Railroad business took him frequently to Cumberland, a town that had sprung up primarily to accommodate the passage west.

Noise from the hall caught his attention. Jess, if the tone of grumbling could be trusted, and her heavy tread. His gaze went to the clock, now free of dust. Much as he appreciated that Marietta accepted his presence enough to want the space clean for him, he still despised the thought of others, especially the slaves, treading so close to plans so vital. Lucien had trusted them, at least enough to carry the Knights' secrets on under their noses.

The fool.

Devereaux shuffled his papers together and toed shut the drawer from which they had come. He was not usually away from the rail offices so early in the day, and he had no desire to fend off questions from the stupid, over-inquisitive slave of his mother's. He crept to the paneling beside the curio cabinet, reached to the hidden latch behind the massive piece of furniture, and pressed. The click signaled the release of the lock, allowing him to open the panel like a door.

An icy draft radiated up the hidden stairwell. He grabbed a lantern from the cabinet, struck a match to light it, and stepped into the cold.

Fifteen steep steps later, golden light touched all corners of a small room. It didn't hold much at first glance. An old table, a single chair, a few crates. Nothing upon the dirt walls shored up with wooden beams, nothing to attract attention.

Which was the point. If anyone ever stumbled upon this chamber, with any luck they would think it naught but an abandoned cellar connected to the oldest part of the house. Hence why first Lucien and now Devereaux used it to store the most vital and sensitive of the Copperhead documents.

He spread his papers out again on the table and set the lamp near them, pausing afterward to grab the wool coat shoved into one of the boxes. Warm enough then, he fished out a more complete map to put alongside the sketch and turned back to his perusal.

Caves—he needed caves. They were in short supply on the eastern side of the state, but in Allegany and Washington counties it was a different story. Years ago, he and Lucien and Father had explored the areas around which their rails were being run, and they had wandered through the countryside.

More than wandered, a few times. His gaze fell on the detailed map, the mountains between Hagerstown and Cumberland. That was where they had been when he and Lucien had ventured far into a cave and then stumbled across a vast cavern buried deep in the hills. He had been but a boy, no more than ten or eleven, but such a cavern could not be forgotten.

A cavern big enough to hold all the gold he had stockpiled. All the gunpowder barrels. Weapons, even cannons. It was big enough to hide anything that would fit through its mouth. And yet no one knew about it—the locals claimed they had no caves.

Pulling out paper and pencil from the box, he sat on the uncomfortable chair and got down to business. First a list of all the items he would be responsible for storing, most of which had not been sent to him yet. But as they arrived he would load them into his private train cars, ready for a trip into the mountains...

First, though, he must take a trip himself, and better sooner than later. A week from now, perhaps, after a few important meetings. A fortnight at the outside.

And while he collected the goods, Booth and Surratt and Osborne and whoever else they brought in could be taking care of the King Abe nonsense. He would do well to separate himself from that, if President Davis expected him to remain in good standing with both North and South to effect the next uprising.

He pulled out his pocket watch. Another hour until those gentle-men were scheduled to join him in the more accessible part of the base-ment lair. That would give him plenty of time to complete his lists and update the membership based on the latest casualty reports.

A creak from above jarred him half an hour later, and Devereaux straightened on his chair. Perhaps Marietta had returned from wher-ever she had gone—likely her grandmother's house, given that it was Tuesday. The thought was incentive enough to put his work and coat away and climb the steep stairs again. If he could steal a few minutes alone with her, perhaps he could charm her into his arms.

Distance didn't suit him at all. Not when she was forever a few feet away, looking so dashed alluring. The mere sight of her heated his blood. And if he thought of her kisses...

Devereaux replaced the lantern, eased around the desk and to the door that opened into the garden. Warm sunshine touched his face when he stepped outside, a welcome reprieve from the icy cellar. He headed for the carriage house to see if she had returned.

He was nearly to it when movement caught his eyes. A swishing skirt, to be sure, but not the one he wanted.

Had she continued on her path, or retreated into the shadows as she usually did when he passed by, Devereaux would have said nothing. Cora might have been an entertaining diversion for a night, but a taste was all he had needed to assure himself she didn't satisfy him for long.

But the way she halted, her eyes wide with terror. The way she reached behind her...

He too came to a lazy stop a good stone's throw away and arched his brows.

She swallowed and backed up half a step, her hand still behind her. "You need somethin', Mr. Dev?"

"Well, now." For the pure pleasure of watching her quake, he swept his gaze down her. She was breeding again, apparently—and appar-ently had been for a while, though he hadn't looked at her long enough to notice. "Kind as it is of you to offer, I prefer my women with a waist."

The way her face twisted nearly made him laugh. Though his atten-tion was snagged by a little blond head that peeked from behind her skirt. Her brat. Lucien's, from the looks of her, though his brother had always sworn he needed no concubine after marrying Marietta.

His gaze went back to Cora's petrified face. "What are you doing out here this time of day? Don't you have cleaning to do?"

"Yes, sir. I just...Miss Mari said...yes, sir."

Miss Mari said *what*? He nearly asked, but what did it matter? "Speaking of Miss Mari—is she back yet?"

"No, sir. Not yet."

No point in continuing to the carriage house, then. He dismissed the slave with a flick of the wrist and headed instead to the side of the house they so rarely used, especially in the past fifteen months. Much of it was taken up by the ballroom—a chamber that had been draped all this time in the silence of mourning. The rest were guest rooms also not needed recently.

The hedges had been let to grow around this side of the house, which allowed the Knights to slip in as they pleased without being seen. Once in the darkened room locked from the rest of the house, he followed the usual path. Through the concealed door, down the stairs, and along the long tunnel.

No light burned in the meeting room. He must still be a few minutes ahead of the others. No matter. He lit a lamp, laid the fire, and prepared the coffee.

They had plans to make.

"No. That is unacceptable. It must be before the inauguration."

Slade leaned back against the wall beside the fireplace, his arms folded as he watched Booth pace the room. He knew well his line was a thin one to walk. He had to appear every bit as frustrated as they, encourage them, and yet speak reason. "We can try. But you wanted the truth."

Surratt tapped his pen against the table, his gaze flickering from the pacing Booth to the brooding Hughes. "Osborne is no doubt right, Booth. It is when they will expect us to move. Lincoln will be too closely guarded."

"I was the first to insist that Osborne find us a way, but in reality this second inauguration changes nothing." Hughes pushed himself up and dumped the dregs of his coffee into the fire. "We may simply not be able to act beforehand."

"Still, we must try. Think of all the soldiers we could get released with him as ransom."

Slade swallowed. No doubt they were right about that. But they might be surprised by Lincoln himself if they succeeded in capturing him. The president underwent trial each and every day of his life, and he stood tall under it. And not just because of his height.

Their three gazes fell on him, as if awaiting a response. What did they want? His opinion on how many soldiers they could get in exchange for Lincoln? He had no way of knowing, so he had no reason to opine. He unfolded his arms and meandered to a map tacked to the wall. "Escape route?"

"Ah." Booth leapt to his side, eyes alight. "I have been working on one for months. Assuming we take him in Washington, we will make first for the Mudd plantation twenty-five miles out. Mudd is a doctor, so if we need any medical aid, he will no doubt give it."

Slade glanced at Hughes and tried to recall if he had seen the name on the list of KGC members. He didn't think so, but he couldn't be sure. He needed a copy of that list. "Is he one of us?"

Hughes shook his head. "He is a slave owner, though, who has been hit hard by the prospect of losing his labor force. Booth feels certain he can be swayed."

His noncommittal grunt was drowned out by the rattling of a carriage directly over them. Though not so much as a pebble tumbled down, it still made his shoulders tense.

Surratt inclined his head toward Hughes. "It sounds as though the missus is home."

"Time to adjourn." Their host went about extinguishing the fire. "Osborne, try to sound out your friends for a weak spot in their protection before the inauguration. But if there simply is none, look for one afterward."

Booth took his hat from the table and tapped it into place, taking a moment to smooth his pomaded curls around it afterward. "I will keep you updated as to where I am staying. Or you can always reach Surratt at his mother's boarding house."

Hughes shooed them toward the exit. "You fellows and those you trust must see to this. I will be out of town on other Confederacy business soon."

They all fell into a line to leave, Surratt saying something that sounded like agreement but which was interrupted by Booth's mumble about the imbecility of the Confederacy. Hughes ignored them both and waved them all into the dark stairwell, shutting the door to the meeting room behind him.

No doubt their host was eager to greet his would-be missus.

Slade let the past hour spin through his mind as they took the shadowed journey up the stairs and into the never-used ballroom with its outside entrance. They apparently already had a location in mind for where they would hold Lincoln if they managed to kidnap him, but they hadn't named it. Just kept referring to it as "the hideout." Still too soon, he supposed, to have their complete trust.

The men filed into the ballroom one by one. Hughes closed the paneled door behind them and then peeked out the one into the hedge. He waved Booth and Surratt out. No one said a word as they slipped into the evergreen shroud and from there into the open. Booth and Surratt vanished down the alley. A few moments later, Hughes led Slade to the front door.

No one opened it for them, which was no doubt why the man's face contorted into a hard scowl. He pushed the heavy wood open himself, but then he stopped so abruptly that Slade nearly ran into his back.

No surprise, given the picture within. All of the servants dashed about, Walker and Norris and old Pat carrying trunks, the women bandboxes and wrapped packages. Headed, not for the main stairs, but the ones leading to the side of the house from which Slade and Hughes had just come.

Mrs. Hughes stood at the base of the steps, pale and seeming in shock, while her redheaded minx of a daughter-in-law laughed with a woman Slade had never seen before. Though there was something vaguely familiar about her... He frowned at the frayed black dress the guest wore, the threadbare shawl.

Not Marietta Hughes's usual company. Which stirred up all sorts of questions.

"Mari?" Hughes moved another step into the chaos, sidestepping a box full of...photographs? When the women looked his way, he went still again, and stiff as ice. Slade slid off to his side and closed the door behind him. Hughes smiled, but it looked about as friendly as a rattlesnake's tail. "Miss Gregory, isn't it?"

"It used to be." Marietta's grin, if Slade weren't mistaken, contained a hint of smugness. Which was odd, given her reaction to the photograph he now remembered to be where he'd first seen the woman. "Though for some years now it has apparently been Barbara Arnaud. Gentlemen, allow me to introduce my sister-in-law, Stephen's widow. Barbara, you no doubt remember Devereaux Hughes, and this is his guest, Slade Osborne."

"Ma'am." Slade stepped up when Hughes remained still, took her hand, kissed it. And knew with one glance into Barbara Arnaud's serene face that he would like this woman. That peace in her eyes called his mother to mind. And it didn't hurt any that Hughes was obviously less than thrilled with her presence.

"How good to meet you, Mr. Osborne." Her voice was soft, both in volume and texture. She turned from him to Hughes. "So good to see you again, Mr. Hughes."

Hughes took her hand, but too slowly. Bowed over it, but didn't kiss her knuckles.

Slade shot a glance to Marietta, who smirked back at him.

She stepped nearer, and light from the window angled over her. It lit the flame of her hair and set to glowing the pearls around her neck.

Familiar pearls. Three of them on a thin strand of gold. Slade frowned. The very same three pearls he had seen that bizarre night on the wife of the tall old man. He hadn't had time to slip away and discover who they were. All he had managed to verify was that a ship still bobbed in the harbor with *Masquerade* painted on her hull.

"From the looks of it," Hughes said to Mrs. Arnaud, "you will be visiting for a while."

"Indefinitely." Marietta looped her arm through her guest's and pulled her a step away from Hughes. "I'm afraid that since she and Stephen married in secret, she has been living all this time in a part of town of which my brother would disapprove. We are going to remedy that and welcome her to the family properly."

Though Hughes's smile stretched, it looked no more welcoming. "How good of you." His gaze tracked the servants disappearing up the side staircase. "Where have you put her?"

"The suite of rooms on the third floor, above the ballroom. They will be most to her liking and provide her the privacy to which she is accustomed." Marietta, unlike her suitor, beamed with pleasure at the prospect.

Odd indeed. Slade had seen her flock of friends several times now, and they were all the same. Women of means, of important families. Women who arranged their faces in masks and whose eyes always snapped with calculation. Like Marietta's so often did.

This one was different. The kind of different that made him wonder not just about Barbara Arnaud, but about Marietta. Because had anyone asked, he would have said she never would have invited someone like this sister-in-law of hers into her house. Not for an hour, much less indefinitely. And she sure wouldn't have looked so pleased about it.

Curious indeed.

Hughes found it more distasteful than intriguing, given that glint in his eye. Perhaps he didn't like the idea of someone living right above the entrance to his castle. "How lovely. Why don't you let Mother show her to her rooms, darling? It has been too long since she had the pleasure of welcoming a guest properly."

Because he kept his gaze on the women, Slade saw the shift. Calculation reentered Marietta's eyes, and questions sprang to life in Mrs. Arnaud's at that *darling*. Questions colored with shadows. Sorrow, perhaps. Suspicion. Maybe a splash of disappointment.

Mrs. Arnaud, it would appear, was no fonder of Devereaux Hughes than he was of her.

Well. This ought to make things interesting in the Hughes house.

Mrs. Hughes took her cue to come down the last step, her sugary smile pasted into place. Marietta slowly released her friend's arm. "Of course. Barbara dear, I'll be right up to help you settle in."

The guest's smile wavered around the edges. "All right." Obviously too polite to argue, Mrs. Arnaud turned to Hughes's mother.

The son took Marietta by the arm. "A word, darling."

Slade's fingers curled into his palm. Not at the endearment, which he had grown used to hearing—mostly—but at the tone. And the grip. It mollified him only slightly when Marietta's chin came up. When her lips turned in a flinty smile.

She glanced at Slade over her shoulder as Hughes pulled her toward the parlor. "I put a new book out for you, Mr. Osborne."

"Thanks." But he made no move toward the library. Not with Hughes's face blurring in his mind with his own brother-in-law's. Marietta and his sister didn't seem like the same type of woman. He wanted to think this one before him now wouldn't suffer a man striking her.

But then, he hadn't thought Jane would either.

Neither noticed him trailing behind them, pausing outside the parlor door.

Marietta pulled her arm free of Hughes's grip the moment they were inside. "Is something the matter, Dev?"

Planting his hands on his hips, he glared at her. "What is going on with you, Marietta? You despise her, you always have. Yet now you invite her to share your home?"

Her chin went up another notch, her eyes glinting more. She shifted away from the door. If he didn't know better, Slade would have thought for sure she was drawing Hughes's attention toward the opposite direction, away from him. Nonsense, of course.

"Stephen loved her enough to marry her. Enough to marry her in *secret*, which would have been a hard decision for him. If he loved her so much, then obviously I misjudged her."

"Mari, you know your brother..."

Her eyes narrowed to slits. Cat eyes, no question. "I know my brother *what?*"

Hughes's hands came up in surrender. Apparently Stephen Arnaud was sacred ground that even he respected. "Nothing. But you are not one to change your mind once you have made it. I don't understand—"

"I don't expect you to understand. I just expect you to be civil."

Hughes folded his arms across his chest. "I don't like her. And I don't want her in my house."

Those cat eyes threw sparks. Slade half expected her to hiss and bare her claws. "She isn't in *your* house, Devereaux. She's in *mine*."

He took a step closer to her. Did it look as menacing from her angle as it did from the hall? Perhaps not, given that she didn't so much as flinch.

"There is very little difference, darling. And there will be none in a few short months when you are my wife."

She sashayed a step nearer to him too, charm coming off her in waves as her eyes went from slitted to hooded and her lips quirked. Her fingers walked up his chest. "And until then, darling...she stays."

His growl didn't scare her off. She didn't pull away when he slid an arm around her waist. "It is a foolish move, one you will soon regret. And Mother didn't like her when your brother introduced them."

Her head tilted, scarlet curls cascading. "Nor did she like me. But she gets on well enough pretending. I'm sure she can do the same with Barbara."

Slade pressed his lips together against a laugh and slid to his left to remain out of sight when Hughes jerked away a step. "Whatever are you talking about, Mari?"

She sent her eyes heavenward. "Do you think me such a fool I cannot tell when another woman dislikes me?"

"Hmm." Apparently seeing no reason to continue the charade, he slid close again. "Yet you have never been less than kind to her."

"She is my mother-in-law." Her voice changed as she said that. Went from insistent, even seductive to...warm. Sincere. As if that bond were enough for her, enough to create what affection had not.

A testament, in Slade's mind, to the family from which she came, to have given her such respect for the institution.

As Hughes pulled her to him, she wrapped her arms around him. And then settled her gaze on Slade with such calm that he retreated a step. She had obviously been aware of his presence the whole time. And now she looked at him, not with censure for eavesdropping, but with warning. The kind that seemed sympathetic rather than threatening.

A flick of her fingers, a darting of her eyes toward the library, and over Hughes's shoulder she mouthed the word Go.

Good advice. Hughes didn't seem likely to strike her at this point, but he would have no compunction about leveling a fist at Slade's nose if he caught him there. A fate she wished him spared? Or did she just not want him watching anymore?

Either way, the twist of his gut as he watched Hughes hold her tight convinced him to obey. He turned and crept to the library. Then hissed out a breath at his own stupidity. What was he doing? His gut had no business twisting, not over them. Over her. She was nothing to him. Nothing but Hughes's puppet, his future bride.

So what if she had helped him once or twice? Probably just to keep her darling Dev happy like a good little woman. Keep him from finding out something that would upset him and thereby spoil their evening.

He rubbed a hand over his face and realized he still wore his bowler. Sweeping it off, he slung it toward his usual chair and paced to the table beside it. He had no business liking her, not when he disliked Hughes so much, and they were so obviously similar. In love. Marietta Arnaud Hughes might recognize that her beau was a monster, but it never stopped her from falling happily into his arms.

He scooped up the book sitting out on the table. So he found her beautiful. He was a healthy man. That ranked as "obviously." Maybe her peculiar wit made him smile. Also no great surprise. That didn't mean he had to let a simple attraction have any effect on him. He would do what he could to make sure Hughes didn't hurt her, but when his business here was done, she would have to answer to her own allegiances.

And they were poor ones, so she had better steel herself for the consequences.

His gaze fell to the book in his hands. And his lips pulled up. *The Confessions of Saint Augustine*. Nice. As if she knew well he was judging her and was trying to tell him anyone could change.

More likely, just a book she had spotted that fit with the others she had seen him reading.

Seeing a slip of paper sticking out, he opened it to the marked page. A passage was underlined in faint pencil. By Marietta or her brother? He scanned it and sighed. Augustine's conversion. He shifted the book, moving the spine enough that the slip of paper tilted to the other side, revealing three words written upon it, in a script undeniably feminine. *Under the cushion.*

First his eyes went back to the page. A note on the text?

No. He looked instead at the chair in which he always sat. The very one he had been in the other day when she burst in upon him and hadn't even seen him through her tears.

Surely not. Surely this was just some note randomly placed here years before. A reminder of...to...what? No answers sprang to mind. But it couldn't be for him.

Still, what was he to do but lower the book and reach for the cushion?

When he spotted the key to the desk drawer, he forgot to breathe. A measure of peace settled upon him as he picked it up and put the cushion back. But why would she give it to him?

"Have you read that one yet, Mr. Osborne?"

He spun at her voice. "Too long ago to remember much."

"Then a revisit should suit you." She moved toward him in that way she had—smooth, graceful, but not like some of the other women he'd seen, who could balance books upon their head. Her grace was more...liquid. Feline, to match her eyes. She halted a foot shy of her skirt brushing him. "You could have kept it."

Then she could have told him so at the time. He shrugged, tilted his head, and focused his gaze on those pearls. "Nice necklace. New?"

"Old. Very old." Her eyes lit with a mischievous smile as she touched the gems. "My grandmother just gave it to me. It has been in our family since the days of the Revolution."

"Your grandmother." Gwyneth Lane then, as her other grandmother lived somewhere in New England. Which meant that "Mister" was Thaddeus Lane. He should have known. Merchant, soldier, father-in-law of Commodore Jack Arnaud, and, from what he had gathered when researching Marietta's family, loved by most everyone he knew—and he knew everyone.

Somehow, having the name didn't answer any of his questions.

"Keep it." She nodded toward the hand that still held the key.

Because she looked ready to pivot and leave, he moved. And wished he hadn't when his fingers enclosed her wrist and awareness hit like lightning. The way she paused, he wondered at first if she felt it too.

But no, it no doubt just reminded her of the way Hughes had grabbed her minutes earlier. She looked from his hand to his eyes, her gaze going hard.

Still, he didn't let go. Not yet. "Marietta." He tried to keep his tone even. He failed. It came out quiet and strained. "Be careful. This is no game."

"One might turn that warning right around on you." Her voice matched his. Then her eyes thawed, and the mischief returned to them. "You ought to pay my grandparents another visit, Slade. Grandmama has begun a very nice painting of you."

"Of me?" His hand fell away from her wrist. In part because she obviously knew about his midnight visit there if she saw such a thing. In part because of the painting itself. "She barely saw me."

Her lips turned up to match her eyes. "A glimpse is all she ever requires." She took a step toward the door. "Do put that item somewhere safe, won't you?"

He slid it into his pocket, the safest place he had at the moment. "Aren't you curious?"

She paused again and lifted her brows.

He had to appreciate a woman who could speak without words. "About what's in there."

Tilting her head, she smiled again. "You're assuming I didn't look."

True. But surely if she had, she wouldn't sit idly back. Would she? "Did you?"

"Briefly." She turned to the door again.

"Briefly." What did that mean? What had she seen? Enough to know that she made her bed in a den of Copperheads, or just enough to know she didn't want to look any further?

Halfway to the door, she glanced at him over her shoulder. Her smile still lingered, but the mischief had abandoned it. "That's all I require, Slade. Just a glimpse."

Fourteen

Walker looked up at the sound of footsteps on the outside stairs. He put a stray ribbon in the book of signs to mark his place, which was still woefully near the beginning. He tried to learn on his own, but it made little sense until someone showed it to him. With Barbara's arrival that afternoon, there had been no time for another lesson, so...

He darted a glance at the little cot where Elsie slept, a chubby arm curled around her rag doll. An image to make him smile. And the smile just kept on going when the door opened and Cora stepped in with a gust of cold air. He pushed himself up to greet her properly.

She returned his smile and his kiss, and nestled into his arms...but tension rode her shoulders and knotted her back, more than it had any other night since Marietta insisted on her resting every day. "Something wrong, honey?"

Cora gave him a squeeze and pressed her face to his chest. "No. Not really." But she held him tighter still. "I ran into Mr. Dev today is all, and it shook me up some. I had Elsie with me."

His breath eased out. They both knew it was unavoidable, but they had done all they could to keep their girl away from him. Keep her out here, far from the places he usually went. But Elsie wouldn't long be contained to their rooms as she grew. "Did he touch you? If he touched you, I swear I'll—"

"No. Nothin' like that. Just made a nasty comment and told me to get back to work." Though her lips said *just*, the eyes she turned up to him were misty. "Walker, I need you to promise me. If she marries him, if he takes over this house, we have to leave. Freed or not, I can't stay here then. Or if his mama dies and I go to him—"

"Shh." He buried his hand in her hair and held her close, close enough that he could feel his babe's happy kick. "It won't come to that. She won't marry him." Though it still made him sick to consider what she'd told him three days ago. Marietta was right. He wouldn't let her go, not if he had such a claim on her. "And Miss Lucy is on the mend."

She gripped his shirt. "Promise me, Walk."

Looking down into her beautiful eyes, her precious face, he sighed. "I promise you, honey. You'll never be his." He pressed his lips to her forehead to seal the oath. "Now come rest. I bet you had a busy evening with Miss Barbara."

"Busy on top of busy. But the good kind." She pulled away and untied her apron, draping it over her chair while she reached for the cup of water he had waiting for her. "I still can't believe Miss Mari brought her here."

Walker turned to pull out the bread and meat he'd kept warm by the fire. "I really think you're gonna see a different side of Yetta now."

Cora sank down onto her chair with a weary exhale. "The side you used to be in love with? Don't know that I want to see that."

"Stop." He slid the plate in front of her and took up his position behind, where he could rub her shoulders. "You know I love you more than I ever loved anyone. Except maybe Elsie, but that can hardly be compared."

She let out a puff of laughter and tilted her head forward. "Miss Mari's taken to thanking me these past couple of days. Every time I help her with something. It's…"

"Encouraging? Refreshing?"

"Discombobulatin'."

He laughed, quietly enough that he had no trouble hearing the tap on the door. His hands went still.

"Hez, you think?" Cora toyed with her bread.

He eased away. "Hope not. I kinda fancy an evenin' at home with my best girl."

"Your girl would like that too."

A few steps took him to the door, but when he opened it and saw Slade Osborne on the other side, he had all he could do to keep his countenance clear.

Osborne, a dim outline in the moonlight, nodded. "Do you have a minute?"

In answer, Walker grabbed his coat from the peg and said, "Be just a second," to his wife. Then he shut the door quietly behind him and indicated the stairs back down. "You need to arrange for a horse for tomorrow?"

Once back on solid ground, the detective turned on him with hands planted firmly on his hips. "What in blazes are you up to?"

"Pardon?"

Osborne stepped closer and raised a hand with one finger lifted. "You." Another finger rose. "Thaddeus Lane." A third. "Hezekiah Arnaud."

Half a smile wormed its way to the surface. "Figured it out, did ya?"

"Not enough."

Good. He shrugged. "Just three loyal Americans doing what they can, Mr. Osborne, when opportunity presents itself."

Spinning away, Osborne muttered something unintelligible before pivoting back to him. "Look, Payne. My gut says we're on the same side, and I've learned to trust it. But I can't have you, some spoiled rich boy, and a doddering old man interfering with my plans. It's too dangerous."

Walker let out a low, laughing whistle. "Doddering? He could probably outrun you, even at eighty."

"Really not the point here."

"And Hez, he ain't no spoiled rich boy. He's a scholar, just like his great-granddad. A chemist."

Osborne blinked, heavily. "Irrelevant."

No, but Osborne didn't really need to know about the nice little formulas Hez came up with to aid in their family business. Walker shrugged.

With a shake of his head, the man drew in a long breath. "Let me start again. You know what Hughes is about?"

Walker put his hands in his pockets to fend off the cold night air. "More or less."

"Even 'less' ought to be enough. When he goes down, those around him could get hurt." He leaned a little closer, and moonlight sparked in his eyes. "Tell Lane and his grandson to stop playing at being heroes. Focus on clearing the innocents out of the way—assuming there are any."

Walker drew in a long, careful breath. "What are you afraid of, Osborne? That she's gonna get hurt, or that she's gonna do the hurting?"

Without another word, the detective strode away, shaking his head. It didn't take long for the night to swallow him up. Walker took just a minute to let it all settle, to look at where he'd been. Then he turned and went back up to the warmth of his kitchen.

Marietta flexed her cramping hand and straightened her spine. Sleep had eluded her these past three hours, so she had put her time to good use. Now, of course, with sunlight streaming in and a stack of pages before her, her eyes felt gritty and heavy.

But at least she had something to show for her exhaustion. Stretching her arms above her head, she took account of the pages she had transcribed. The list of names—again—the other pages she had already sent to Granddad. And then what seemed the most critical of the rest from the drawer. Two copies of each. One for the Culpers.

And one for Slade Osborne. She shuffled his into a stack and stared at them with pursed lips. Getting them into his hands would be a simple matter of slipping them into a theological text in the library.

She could leave said book out for him, or direct him to it on the shelf casually enough. Either way, he would know they came from her. Which would prove she had spent time in the drawer, and he would assume it hours. Would assume she had copied directly from the page. Which she could certainly do more easily than he could, it being her house, but...

Tired, she slumped against her chair and squeezed her eyes shut. He was already suspicious of her. He may be concerned for her safety, he may be grateful for the aid she had given, but he couldn't make it any clearer that he didn't trust her. Would he even accept these copies as accurate or think she fed him false information?

Well. She could do nothing about his perceptions. All she could do was put the documentation into his hands.

At the jiggle of her doorknob, she folded the stacks of paper and set her Bible on top of them. Cora couldn't read to know what they were, but still. She would secure them in her desk as soon as possible.

"Mornin', Miss Mari. You're up early."

She turned on her chair with a smile she hoped covered the shadows under her eyes. "One of those nights."

The woman grunted a laugh and rubbed at her back. "I know all about them." She looked over. Frowned. "Lawsy, ma'am, you look fit to fall over. Hop back into bed. I'll bring you up a tray."

So much for covering the shadows. She stood. "Nonsense. I only need a stiff cup of coffee. I can't leave Barbara to fend off Mother Hughes's veiled insults alone."

Cora folded her arms and held her ground—something she wouldn't have done a fortnight ago. "Miss Barbara can take care of herself."

"I know. But that doesn't mean she should have to."

Apparently that point won her a bit of favor. Her maid loosed a hum and strode into her boudoir. "Lavender or gray?"

"Whichever you think."

That brought Cora to an abrupt halt. "You ain't never left it to me, even mornings you were tired as this after a night o' dancin'."

Nights of dancing—how far away those seemed. "There are many things I've never done that I should have. Nearly as many as the things I shouldn't have that I did anyway. And I'm sorry for them all." She wrapped her arms around her middle and resisted the urge to sink down into the feather mattress of her bed. "I am trying, Cora. Trying to change."

Cora merely disappeared into the room full of gowns and hoops and petticoats, reemerging a moment later with a day dress of lavender. She glanced at Marietta only once while she laid it all out. "Elsie told me 'good morning' today using the signs. And she's been using 'Mama.' When we realized, I thought I'd never hear her say 'Mama.' Feels like she has now."

Marietta smiled and shrugged out of her dressing gown and then into her corset. "I'm so glad, Cora. She's a darling child." She hooked the corset before slipping the cover into place.

Hand outstretched to help her step into the circle in the middle of the skirts, resignation settled on Cora's face before she moved to the rear to hoist up the fabric. "Walker said he told you. About who..."

A knot formed in her throat. Somehow she hadn't thought Cora would ever speak to her about it. Marietta needed a moment, a nod, to be able to speak. "He did. And I am so, so very sorry."

"Ain't your doin'. But if there's one thing I've learned in this house, it's that sin has consequences. Just a funny thing that sometimes them consequences be borne by someone other than the sinner."

Sin has consequences. She splayed a hand over her abdomen under the guise of smoothing the layers. Was it wrong of her to pray, pray with every fiber of her being, that her particular sin would not result in the same consequences Cora had suffered?

Fear gnawed. She had done wrong. Had betrayed her morals, her late husband, the God she had too long ignored by indulging in a moment of weakness that night. She had sold herself short, seizing one stolen moment rather than waiting for forever. And she would pay for it.

Perhaps the Lord had forgiven, washed her scarlet sins white. But her own words, an echo of so many she had heard from behind the pulpit over the years, clanged in her head.

Forgiveness does not negate consequences.

She squeezed her eyes shut. *Please, Lord. Please have mercy on me. If I am with child, I see no escape from him. I will have to marry him. I would have no other option, not unless I wanted to resign my offspring to life as an outcast.*

Compared to the other women in her family, she had never felt particularly maternal. She had experienced only occasional pangs at having never conceived, not the agony Hez's wife, Paulina, had gone through before little Ezra came along. But the thought of finally having a babe and ruining his life before he was even born...nausea roiled.

"If you are too tired for the lesson this afternoon, Miss Mari—"

"We'll be there." If she were tired enough to require a midday rest, she could take it before or after the signing lessons. And heaven knew

Barbara never seemed to tire, though she insisted on continuing her volunteering at the hospital three days a week and came with Marietta to the carriage house when she was at home.

Her maid said no more as she buttoned the back of the dress and then coiled Marietta's hair at the base of her neck and secured it with a lacy snood. Though she felt as though she should follow up this thawing between them, Marietta couldn't think what to do other than smile and thank her. She added a silent prayer for Cora and her babe, for Elsie and Walker, but she wasn't Barbara. She didn't yet feel comfortable talking about faith at every turn.

Once she was alone again, she fastened Grandmama's necklace around her neck and scooted her Bible off the stacks of papers. Taking them in hand, she headed down to the second floor. A minute later she stashed them with the invisible ink in her drawing room.

Her hand hovered over the drawer. Or rather, over that white square of fabric she had looped around the vials. The S.O. initials peeked up from the handkerchief's corner. She should have it washed. Return it. Something. Something other than leaving it there, encircling her secrets.

She closed the drawer, turned the lock, and hurried into the breakfast room. Barbara and Mother Hughes were both inside already, and both greeted her with a smile. Funny, though, how the sincerity in her sister-in-law's made the pretense in her mother-in-law's all the more apparent.

"Good morning." Marietta filled a plate, poured herself a cup of coffee sans sugar or cream, and took her usual seat.

Mother Hughes touched her napkin to the corner of her mouth. "How good of you to decide to join us, Mari dear."

"You look tired." Barbara, seated at her side, touched her wrist. Her warm eyes glowed with concern. "Are you well?"

"Fine, thank you." She took a sip of the strong brew and felt marginally better. "I awoke a little after four and couldn't get back to sleep. My mind would not stop spinning."

Barbara's laugh sounded like sunshine. "How well I understand."

Marietta smiled and took another drink. And wished, prayed, that the spinning of her mind were like everyone else's. The pictures sometimes raced by so fast she couldn't grasp hold of one, none of the details that vied for attention had any rhyme or reason. Most of the time she could pull forward what information she needed, but sometimes it was more cacophony than symphony. More thunder than lightning. More a dizzying circle than a line she could follow.

Mother Hughes merely sniffed and took a bite of egg. Her appetite had improved, for which Marietta was thankful, and her cheeks had color again.

Though she could do without the return of the disapproving glint to her eyes.

A glint that shifted into pure adoration when heavy, quick footfalls sounded and Dev strode into the room as if he owned it.

Marietta put down her cup. If he had his way, he would own it soon enough, and her with it. How could a thought that made her blood race in expectation a month earlier now make *her* want to race from the room?

"Devereaux darling." His mother held out a hand and tilted up her face to receive his kiss upon her cheek.

"Good morning, Mother." He smiled, no doubt cataloging her continued improvement just as Marietta had. Then he turned to her.

It wasn't right, the way it all got tangled up inside her. New truths and old, repulsion and attraction, the memory of love and the need to escape him before he devoured her whole. Too tired to wade through the mess, she merely dug up a halfhearted smile and muttered, "Dev."

"Darling." He kissed her cheek as he had his mother's and rested his hand upon her shoulder. Not so much as looking at Barbara, he leaned into the table. "I wanted to stop by before I head to the station. I need to travel to Cumberland. I'll depart on Monday and will be gone a week."

Marietta lowered the fork she had picked up but had yet to use. "A week."

His strong brows arched. "Is there something wrong, darling?"

She shouldn't say anything. Better to be gracious and forgiving and praise the Lord for seven days away from him. And yet she felt her eyebrows move to mirror his. "We were to go to the Ellicotts' that Friday."

He looked genuinely distressed. For a single moment, that is, before determination flashed through his eyes and then softened into regret. "I am sorry, Mari. It slipped my mind. You know I haven't the head for dates you do. Your heart was not set on that particular invitation though, was it? I have a whole slew of others we can attend when I get back."

"Of course. It hardly matters." Except that Lucien had done the exact same thing twenty-seven times. It wasn't the disappointed hopes that bothered her, or the need to write an apology after she'd already written an acceptance. It was the fact that neither of them ever saw fit to explain the situation before announcing it. For being "the most important thing" to them, she got surprisingly little consideration.

Not so surprising, considering they lied through their teeth as adeptly as their mother.

"I'll make it up to you. I promise." Too much heat saturated his words, especially for being spoken in company. He squeezed her shoulder, chuckled—no doubt at the blush she was too tired to restrain—and turned his head back toward his mother. "I dislike the idea of leaving the two of you alone for so long with no able-bodied man about, though. Discontent is too high in the city."

Three of them. Marietta reached for the butter, largely to shake off his hand. "Walker is here and able-bodied."

"And distracted with his breeding wife. And heaven knows Pat and Norris are too old to scare away any miscreant. Not sufficient. I have asked Mr. Osborne to stay behind and keep an eye on things in my absence."

She could only imagine the anticipation that would have surged through Slade upon that request. An entire week to snoop without the fear of Dev coming upon him. If he were the praying man his taste in reading indicated, this was an answer to it.

And why couldn't she put it to use too?

Mother Hughes was making the expected reply, thanking her son for his thoughtful provision. Barbara, on the other hand, focused her curious gaze on Marietta. Seeing what? One never could tell with her.

Dev didn't stay long. No doubt he was eager to get to the rail offices and schedule his trip. Marietta took a bite of the toast she didn't feel like eating and let her gaze go unfocused.

What was he about in western Maryland? Railroad business? Possibly. Yet with the Confederacy's surrender being touted as a surety, she doubted he would leave his precious KGC unless the trip had something to do with their plans.

Images flashed, but they were too quick. Too random. A few lines on the back of a page from the study...she shook them away. Perhaps she *should* take a nap sometime today to clarify her mind.

"The sun is shining again." Barbara's soft voice broke through the clouds of her mind. "Perhaps we could take a walk."

"That sounds lovely for the two of you." Mother Hughes took a delicate sip of her tea. "Bulah and Nadine are coming by to visit this morning, and we old ladies would no doubt bore you young things to tears."

Barbara's smile didn't falter. "Nonsense. But we are happy to grant you time with your friends."

"And so very happy you are well enough to receive them, Mother Hughes." Marietta's smile was no doubt wearier than her friend's, but she could manage no more. She ate enough to sustain her until midday, hurriedly delivered the packet for Granddad to Walker, and tucked the second into a volume of Thomas Aquinas. For now, it would stay on the shelf, where no curious eyes would notice the pages making it bulge. She would direct Slade to it later.

Soon enough, she had pulled her cape on and smiled to see Barbara in the new one she had purchased for her. To be sure, the young woman had refused to abandon her full mourning. But at least she had submitted to sturdy, serviceable fabrics in place of the ones worn to threads.

Marietta liked to think that Stephen smiled down on her. For perhaps the first time.

Barbara linked their arms together as they stepped out into the cool morning. Bright as the sun was, the air was frosty and carried the scents of coal and wood smoke. "You cannot fathom how much this means to me, Mari. Strolling with you as friends. I thought it would never be."

Marietta told herself the stinging in her eyes was naught but the wind. "And I have walked along like this with so many acquaintances, yet none true friends. I have never...I have not been a very nice person. All the women I know are as happy to gossip about me behind my back as they are to welcome me into their parlors."

Barbara chuckled, soft and sympathetic. "From what Stephen told me, you had beaux lining up down the street. That would have left little for the other young ladies."

"Hmm." All those beaux, and she had picked Lucien Hughes. How different it all would have been had she chosen more wisely.

"May I ask you a personal question, Mari? I don't want to pry, but..."

Marietta eased out a smile. "You are my sister. Pry all you please."

Those doe eyes brightened but then went sober. "It is about Mr. Hughes. Devereaux, that is. You two obviously have an understanding."

Obvious indeed, given the way he had been acting. Ignoring Barbara's presence altogether, staking his claim before Slade. Yet in the face of her sister-in-law's unrelieved black, she had little choice but to avert her face.

"I cannot blame him for wanting to move quickly." Barbara patted her arm, drawing her gaze again. "But you seem less than enthusiastic. You are attentive in his company, to be sure, but when he is gone...I believe I detect a reticence."

She focused her gaze straight ahead, along the empty street. "When I agreed to this understanding, there was much I didn't know." Feeling the warmth of acceptance, she looked to her friend again. "I have recently found out that he is not a good man, yet I fear there is no escape from him."

Barbara made no quick assurances. She merely tilted her face toward the sun and drew in a long breath. "My instinct is to say there is always an escape. And yet I know how long it can take and what tragedy can strike in the meantime." She caught Marietta's gaze again, her face serious and lined with concern. "I will be praying for a way that will allow you to extricate yourself without danger."

"I don't think I need to fear him. He is not—" Images cut her off. Cora's face, and little Elsie's. Her throat went dry.

Barbara opened her mouth but then shut it again, turmoil evident in her eyes.

Marietta's frown deepened. "What is it?"

Looking as though she held her breath, Barbara searched her face. "A man came into the hospital last fall. Shot. A soldier, but he had not been in a battle. He'd been in a duel."

The implications were as glaring as the low-hanging winter sun. "It couldn't have been Dev. Had he shot a man, he would have had to flee the law."

"The man wouldn't name him to the law. He said it would do no good, as his opponent had the law in his pocket."

Once again she had to look away as the confounded list of names filled her vision. Judges. Police officers. Lawyers. "I see."

"I'm not sure you do. Mari, he said Mr. Hughes called him out merely for mentioning your beauty and implying he would call on you when your mourning was complete. But that Mr. Hughes so misconstrued it, and in front of all their friends, that he had no choice but to accept the challenge."

Perhaps walking had been a bad idea, given how weak her knees felt. Surely, surely Dev was not so jealous as all that. Why would he be, when he had been the only man in her life since Lucien died? Until that fateful sixteenth day of January, she had never wavered in her determination to marry him as soon as propriety allowed.

But then, her very affection for him was proof of her fickle heart, was it not?

The cold air hurt, she pulled it in so fast. "What happened to him? The other man?"

Barbara merely pressed her lips together.

Marietta let the silence hold as they navigated around the city block. Down the busier thoroughfare of Monument Square, they spoke of Stephen and of the joy Barbara had from finally being able to answer to her married name. Then they turned again, back onto the street that led home. Where the rows of townhouses typical in Baltimore gave way to free-standing edifices like hers.

Barbara focused upon the graystone building nearest the Hughes estate. "Are your neighbors in residence? I have not seen anyone there."

"No. I am afraid the Pinkneys shut up their house at the start of the war."

A frown knit her brow. "I wonder...perhaps there is someone prowling about in their absence. I heard voices outside last night. They sounded as though they were in the alley between your houses."

Marietta's pulse kicked up. "Walker, perhaps? Hez occasionally comes by of an evening."

"At one in the morning?" Barbara shook her head, though given their shenanigans with Marietta's granddad, her dismissal was likely mistaken. "I know their voices. It wasn't them."

"Likely prowlers, as you said, then. I'll be sure and mention it to Walker." Prowlers of the Copperhead variety, no doubt. Her eyes focused on the side of her house nearest the Pinkneys', on the high hedge meant to lend privacy...and perhaps succeeding too well. Was that where the main entrance to the castle was?

She would have to look, though not with Barbara. Her new friend ought not to be drawn into this mess. Marietta would figure it out herself, or perhaps with Walker's help. She would check the perimeter of the house. The cellars. Perhaps even search Lucien's study again for some clue she had missed before.

It was there, obviously, some entrance other than the tunnel they had found, which had likely been built as a secondary escape route from the main lair. She would find it.

Slade Osborne might already be initiated, but there was no reason to entrust it all to him, was there?

Fifteen

Slade eased the study door shut behind him and exhaled slowly. He had begun to think Hughes would never leave this morning, satchel in hand for his trip and trunk strapped to his carriage roof. But the man had finally gone after one more sober warning to keep an eye on Marietta and Mrs. Hughes.

As if Slade intended to let a band of marauders gallop through and steal them away.

Then he had left the detective free to go about his business, praise be to the sovereign and Almighty God. A more perfect answer to prayer he could never have envisioned.

Later today he had to head to Washington, but for now he was determined to find a few answers. And as he'd already discovered there were none to be found at Hughes's house, he had sauntered across the street and snuck in.

The pages that had been in the book of Aquinas were in his inner pocket, as taunting as they were alluring. Marietta's script matched the slip of paper from the Augustine. But though his pulse had kicked up to near euphoria when he clapped his gaze upon that list of names, he had forced it back to rational.

For all he knew, she had deliberately miscopied the information.

How did she even get it to copy if she'd given him the key? That didn't make sense, unless she also had the *other* key, the one Hughes kept on him. Which would mean Hughes had been the one to open the drawer for her and instructed her to feed him false information.

But *that* would mean Hughes was on to him. Possibly, but he didn't think so.

Which left him with one itchy conundrum when it came to Marietta Arnaud Hughes.

He turned to survey the now-clean study, sunlight shafting through the open drapes and pouring its precious illumination onto each surface. He headed straight for the drawer, withdrew the key from its place with the folded papers in his pocket, and crouched to open it.

Making himself comfortable on the floor, he pulled out a handful of leaves from the front of the drawer. And frowned. The list was gone. Hughes could have moved it to another place in the drawer, he supposed, but it was nowhere in this first stack. Or maybe Marietta had taken it.

No, she wouldn't be so stupid. Unless she were trying to set him up to be caught...

Another page caught his eye. One of the ones from the selection she had given him, he was fairly sure. He pulled out his copies and flattened the sheet in question beside the original.

Identical. Other than the handwriting, *exactly* identical. Wherever Hughes had put a note in the margin, the same one appeared in the same place in Marietta's. Each random scratch of ink from a slipping pen, each space, each crowded squeeze of a forgotten word had been duplicated.

For the life of him, he didn't know what to make of it. Not of the information itself, which seemed to be the transcription of an encoded telegram, but of the fact that she had made one for him—an accurate one—and slipped it to him.

His thoughts rampaging like those nonexistent marauders, he returned the drawer to its usual state, relocked it, and set to pacing. He needed to figure out if he could trust her. And with *what* he could trust her. How much she knew and who in blazes the woman really was, beyond the name all of Maryland knew.

Father, I could use Your wisdom here. He passed a hand over his hair.

Show me if she is an ally or an enemy. Show me, please, what I am to do, with her and the whole situation.

He felt a whisper of wind touch his neck, sending a chill down his spine. In part because it felt like an answer, and in part because it was a literal, icy draft. He eased back a step—there. It came from...the wall?

Interesting. Turning to face a massive curio cabinet, he lifted his hands, feeling for that cold touch of air.

The break in the paneling wasn't so much visible as just discernible when he studied it enough. A push against the section in question didn't budge it, though. So he spent five tedious minutes pressing every section, every nearby decorative piece of molding, before finally reaching behind the cabinet.

When he heard the *click* of a lock releasing, a prayer of gratitude swelled through him. Now he could swing the panel open, outward, like a door.

Pitch-black stairs greeted him, heading down. No cobwebs obscured the passage, so Hughes must use this whatever-it-was fairly regularly.

A quick search of the study produced a lantern stashed in another cabinet. He lit it, stepped into the passage, and loosed an exasperated breath when he heard the tap of dainty feet in the hall. Headed straight for the study door, from the sounds of it.

Or perhaps the front door, a definite possibility. As for who it was... it could be Marietta, who wouldn't be surprised to find him here. But it could as easily be Barbara or Mrs. Hughes. And if the latter found him in her precious son's study, it would spell trouble. Not worth the risk. He pulled the hidden door shut, leaving only the tiniest of slivers open. He didn't know how this door worked from the inside and wasn't about to lock himself in.

Marietta sashayed into his slit of vision a moment later and sat at the desk. Slade set his lantern silently down on the step behind him and watched.

For a long moment, she leaned onto the desk, her head in her hand. Her eyes were closed, her lips parted and moving ever so slightly, as if she were praying.

Was she praying? He hadn't thought Marietta Hughes, socialite and siren, the type. But as he studied her profile, he didn't see the woman he'd come to expect. A mask had been peeled off. Absent the flirtation, absent the pleasantries, absent the control, she looked like an entirely different person.

One just as beautiful as the belle, but younger looking. Almost— he could scarcely think to apply the word to her, but it was the only one that fit—vulnerable.

She blinked her eyes open, the breath she drew in catching. Moistening her lips, she shook herself and opened the topmost drawer. It had nothing of note inside, but something gave her pause. She reached in and drew out what looked like a photograph.

Right. A picture of her in a wedding gown. He had glanced at it on his own search last time. She looked at it for a long moment, the press of her lips indicating some emotion he hesitated to label.

Then her head jerked toward the French doors, and she jumped from her seat, dropping the photo back into the drawer and shutting it before rushing to the panes of glass.

His straining ears finally heard what she obviously had—a carriage halting outside the house. He watched her shoulders hunch, her frame coil as if ready to run. "Dev," she muttered, panic making the name a blade. She spun, eyes wide, and took two steps toward the door before apparently hearing what he'd just noticed too—footsteps in the hallway.

In Slade's opinion, whoever was outside the door was a lesser evil than getting caught in this room by Devereaux Hughes, especially since she had every right to be in here in the servants' eyes.

That didn't seem to occur to her. She turned around, obviously looking for a hiding place.

Blast it. Not sure if he was a complete fool or just struck by an unanticipated bout of heroism, he pushed open the door.

Marietta jumped and splayed a hand over her heart. And then went from shocked to exasperated when her gaze fell on him. Well, she could lecture him later. They hadn't the time right now. "Hurry." He waved her in. If Hughes had forgotten something that sent him to her house, chances were it was in this room.

She rushed toward him, grabbing her skirts to pull them out of the way. He swung the door shut, wincing at the click, but he would look for the release later. He had apparently been blocking the view of the steep steps behind him, for Marietta didn't halt quickly enough and tottered on the edge. He slid an arm around her waist to keep her from sending them both tumbling down.

The close call was surely what made his heart pound in his ears. Surely.

A second later, the unmistakable sound of the French doors opening sifted through the panel. His gaze entwined with hers. The pale green of her eyes looked nearly golden in the lantern light that seeped past her voluminous skirts. For once, they held no calculation, no tease, no intrigue. Only fright.

Her hands had landed on his arms, fingers clinging. No doubt to keep her balance on the narrow top step. Slade had little choice but to hold her close, given the tight space of the stairwell. He could only hope the Lord wouldn't blame him for enjoying it.

From the study there came a mutter too low to be intelligible and the sound of a drawer. Slade closed his eyes and prayed with every ounce of his heart and soul that the man would need nothing from down these steps. That he would have no reason to investigate the hidden door.

For an interminable, full minute he heard nothing but his own thudding pulse and Marietta's near-silent breath. The cold pushing up the passage set her to shivering. Not daring to move or rustle enough to take off his greatcoat to share, Slade wrapped his arms and coat around her as best he could without making a noise.

For a moment she remained still, held herself away. Then a crash sounded from the other side. Her shivering quickened, and she nestled into him, going so far as to bury her face in his lapels.

Bad, bad idea. He should have let her flee. Then the scent of lilacs wouldn't be tormenting him, and he wouldn't be infinitely aware of the feel of her back under his hands.

From the exterior, a satisfied, "Ah!" And then, half a minute later, the rattle of the French door as it slammed shut.

Marietta's head came up, her lips parted. Slade shook his head and withdrew one arm from around her so he could touch a warning finger to her lips. "Not yet," he murmured, more air than words. He had long ago learned that in situations like these, patience afforded one much forgiveness.

He had apparently not learned, however, the dangers of touching a woman's petal-soft lips. It certainly didn't help that she looked up at him with an intoxicating mix of trust and question, amusement and relief. No woman had any business being quite so alluring. It ought to be illegal.

And he ought to pull away.

He got so far as moving his finger, but then his rebellious thumb took its place, brushing over her bottom lip as it had absolutely no right to do. And then his jealous mouth demanded its turn, and with only a few inches of space to cover, his mind hadn't the time to halt it. Before he could even call himself a fool, his lips were on hers.

He expected her to push away, slap him into next week, shove him down the stairs, or at the very least blister his ears with her opinion on his forwardness. When she rather held still, he figured he might as well enjoy the single moment. Make it memorable. Push his luck.

What was life without a little risk, anyway? He settled his raised hand against her neck and tilted her head back, used the one still around her waist to press her closer. That put him all in, so from there it was either win, fold, or bust.

Her call, and he had no idea what move she would make, not until her fingers knotted in his waistcoat, her lips moved under his, and she lifted up on her toes to meet him.

A gamble that paid off. Not knowing when or if he'd ever have her in his arms again, he kissed her like there was no tomorrow, until he forgot what in the world he was even doing in this place. Kissed her until his senses swam and he had to shift to compensate.

His foot slipped off the edge of the narrow slab of wood, and it was her turn to catch him. She did so with a laugh, pushing him into the wall at his back to steady them. And with laughter still dancing in her eyes, she didn't seem too resentful. "That was a bad idea."

Trying to move or kissing her? A grin won half of his mouth. Either way. "I know." He glanced down the stairs and then inclined his head. "Curious?"

She glanced toward the door and then crouched down to pick up the lantern, holding it out to him as she straightened. "Lead the way."

The temperature dropped with each step, making him look back at Marietta, two steps above him. She hadn't even a shawl over her gray dress, which surely offered little by way of protection. As soon as he reached the small chamber at the bottom, he set the light upon the rough old table and shrugged out of his greatcoat. "Here."

Marietta paused at the base of the stairs, four steps away. "You needn't make any sacrifices for me, Mr. Osborne."

Stubborn woman. "I still have my frock coat. Take it. It can't be more than forty-five degrees down here."

Still she hesitated, folding her arms around her middle.

Slade sighed, and his gaze caught on a mound of wool in the corner. The way it sat on top of a pile of crates, folded neatly, made him think Hughes kept it here specifically for when he came down. He motioned to it. "What about that one, then?"

Marietta strode to the corner, picked up the coat, and then tossed it back down with stony anger on her face. "I would rather freeze."

"Out of fashion?"

"*His.*"

His. Whether she meant Lucien or Devereaux he didn't know, and it didn't much matter. Heaving another sigh, he moved up behind her, dropped his coat over her shoulders, and held it there. "If I let you freeze, my mother will somehow know and box my ears."

The breath she released sounded amused. She slid her arms through the sleeves. "To appease your mother, then." She turned, quickly enough that he hadn't time to back up to allow the proper distance between them. Which he should do now...but didn't. Her smile small, she gazed first into his left eye and then his right. "I imagine you have questions."

"A few." Dozen.

She spread her arms, which she no doubt meant to illustrate something, but which only served to demonstrate how big his coat was on her. "I daresay we shall never find more privacy than this. Ask— though I cannot guarantee I have answers."

Oh, she had some, if she chose to part with them. He turned to examine the room and allow his senses a respite from her. "What do you know about me?"

"A logical place to start." He heard her skirts rustle, though he didn't turn to see what she was doing. "Let's see. You are one of Pinkerton's detectives. Ostensibly here to join the KGC, but given the many times I have caught you digging into things you ought not, it's a safe assumption that you are rather trying to infiltrate them."

She stepped into his line of vision. He didn't turn away. "Is it?"

The look she sent him was the very one his mother used when making it clear she wasn't fooled by whatever story he came up with to try to wriggle his way out of trouble. "What I can't figure is why Dev is so willing to believe you. What is it you have, Mr. Osborne, that he needs?"

So she knew about the Knights, she had deduced his purpose...he saw no point in hiding what was fairly common knowledge anyway. "I was one of Lincoln's guards until a few months ago."

She tilted her head, sending a single flame of a curl to rest on the shoulder of his jacket. A wonder it didn't burn it. "Why were you reassigned?"

Why indeed. He swallowed and moved back to the crates, the only thing of interest in the room. "Pinkerton had something else for me to do."

"But you told Dev it was because...what? Your loyalties had shifted?" She appeared at his side, reaching into the topmost crate even as he did. "And he believed you?"

He let her pick up the first stack, watched her flip through it methodically, page after page. Yet she never paused to read a single line. "To his view, I was just coming to my senses."

Her snort of derision did nothing to slow her hands. Slade reached out and stilled her with fingers on her wrist. "I need to know whose side you're on."

Marietta went stiff. Every muscle froze, the one in her jaw tight to show the clenching of her teeth. Then she drew in a slow breath, relaxed, and met his gaze. "Yours."

His fingers slipped away from her wrist. The one word shouldn't have struck him like it did.

He cleared his throat and picked up the pile she had already flipped through. "Aren't you going to read these?"

"I will later."

She intended to come back down here, alone? His stomach went tight. If Hughes caught her, even her considerable charms would have little effect if he saw her as a threat to his carefully laid plans.

He very nearly touched her hand again but held himself in check. "Please be careful, Marietta. Better still, leave this to me. I can't have you getting hurt."

"It's a little late for that." She flipped through a few more pages and then paused, frowning. "He has been shifting things around. This is the list of names. Updated, by the looks of it."

He took the page from her, though his gaze moved to the newspaper folded behind it. "Casualty reports." Though he scanned the list, the crossed-out names meant nothing to him. No one he had met, no one they had talked about. Nothing nearly as interesting as the cool detachment on her face. "How long have you known? About their part in this."

If possible, her expression emptied still more. She kept flipping leaves. "Since the day you arrived." Five simple words, yet her tone was rich with meaning. Accusation aimed at herself, disappointment. A sorrow that must have run deep indeed to elicit that note of betrayal.

One he knew all too well. "You never knew about your husband, then." He wasn't sure if that was a blessing or not.

Given her shaky exhale, the correct answer was *not*. "No. And discovering it now makes me revisit every conversation we ever had, makes me wonder what information I told him from my father that I shouldn't have. Makes me wonder if he ever would have looked my way if Daddy were a lawyer or an academic. Anything but a naval authority."

The laugh slipped out before he could stop it. When she turned her sharp, cat eyes on him, he shook his head. "Have you looked in a mirror lately? It wasn't your father that drew his eye."

She tilted her head again. Any moment now she'd either purr or hiss. "Was that a compliment?"

"Maybe."

Now she was the one to laugh, low in her throat and electrifying. Then she shook her head and returned to her task. "My family tried to warn me away from Lucien. They didn't know about his...allegiance. But they saw in his character what I refused to see. And, of course, his family owned slaves. That alone made them object."

He studied another page, though he knew he wouldn't remember much of what he read. He'd have to return alone so he could concentrate. "Are you not the abolitionist the rest of them are?"

Now her wisp of laughter sounded bitter. "I am. But my first cause was always myself. And I so wanted to hurt him."

"Who? Your father?"

"No." She straightened her shoulders and looked at him again. "Dev's even worse than Lucien, isn't he? Barbara said...she said he killed a man in a duel."

"Sounds right." And he didn't even want to consider the torture Hughes would devise for him if he'd seen that kiss. The thought made something go tight in his chest. Not out of fear, not of Hughes. Something deeper.

He flipped another page. Time to change the subject. "You did a good thing, bringing Barbara here."

Her smile, serene for once, made his chest go tighter. "I know. It's what Stephen would have wanted me to do. I so wish...I so wish I hadn't been cruel all those years ago. I deprived them of something precious. I made Stephen hide their love." She shook her head.

And yet the fact that he had... "You and he must have been very close."

She nodded, sniffed, and blinked a few rapid times. Then she pasted on a smile that was strained around the edges. "What about you and your brother? Were you close?"

She might as well have tossed a bucket of icy water over him. Slade kept his gaze on the page before him. Some sort of encrypted telegram, given the length and arrangement. "No. Never."

"What was his name?"

"Ross."

A beat, silent and tense. Marietta lowered the page in her hands. "Were you far apart in age?"

His breath came out short and amused. "Oh, about five minutes."

"Twins?" The incredulity in her tone brought his gaze up. "I thought twins were always close."

He set down the page. It was merely an acknowledgment, a promise from Hughes to do what had been asked of him. "We were more Jacob and Esau."

"Who was who?"

"That would be the question, wouldn't it?"

He glanced up to see the mask of charm reclaim her face. Or maybe her amusement just struck him that way, maybe it wasn't a mask so much as the way her smile tugged at him. His fault, not hers. But oh, the way that grin knotted him up inside...

"I have a theory," she said.

So had Ross.

Her smile faded. "I can see it pains you. I'm sorry. When did you lose him?"

Usually, he would redirect the conversation. Shut it down, extinguish it. But he hadn't even let himself think about Ross's death since that night with Pinkerton and his father. When his boss had laid out the plan and his father, eyes deep and sad, had told him to do it.

He had to clear his throat again. "About six weeks ago."

"So recently?" Her hand settled on his arm. He didn't dare look into her eyes. "I am sorry. The war?"

"Not directly." He put aside the papers and reached into the box for a thin, bound manuscript. Her fingers fell away, and he felt the withdrawal down to his toes. Dangerous woman indeed.

"What, then?"

His lips didn't want to form the words. His chest didn't want to grant him the air. But he forced it through anyway, forced himself to look her in the eye. And said the sentence that had brought him to this path. "I killed him."

Sixteen

Marietta let the words rattle around in her mind. But mingled with them, woven through them, stretched the agony. The way his shoulders balled up said he expected her to recoil in horror. But something about his stance made her inch closer instead. "An accident?"

His Adam's apple bobbed as he tossed a slender, crudely bound book onto the table. "Self-defense. He was waiting for me one night when I got back to my room. I heard someone, felt something swinging toward my head. Ducked. The sledgehammer hit my bureau. When he turned for me again, I shot." His eyes slid closed. "It was dark. I didn't know it was him. I..."

"Slade." No words seemed sufficient. And though he had just pulled away, she didn't know what to do but touch. She clasped his hands between hers. "Do you know why?"

The shrug of his shoulders was filled with what the Germans would call *angst*. "He'd made no secret of his feelings when I went home reformed a year ago. He hated me. Then I returned to Washington from the field and ruined his plans." His obsidian gaze clung to hers. "He was the one who had contacted Devereaux and put this whole thing in motion. He used my name because he knew it would get him in."

Something inside her strained, and her fingers gripped his tighter. "To foil them and take the glory?"

"No. He was Confederate."

Her eyes slid shut. It had been bad enough to have a cousin who had fought against her brother. She couldn't even consider Hez and Isaac and Stephen pitted against one another. "I wouldn't have thought, your being from New York."

"He said it was a matter of states' rights, and he had some valid points. But secession shouldn't have been the answer. You can't fix something from the outside." He gave her hands a returning squeeze and then pulled away, turning back to the crates.

He moved the top one and sorted through the items in the bottom. After a glance inside it to make sure she knew where everything belonged, Marietta stepped toward the table and flipped open the book. She frowned at the columns within. Numbers with dashes and phrases after them. Explanation of gestures. Crude drawings that looked like something a child might do, simple lines and shapes.

She glanced again at Slade's back. "So you assumed the identity he had created for himself, but which used your own name and history. How very convoluted."

"Good word." The smile he shot her may have been shadowed, but it was at least a smile. That was something.

"I think these must be KGC codes." She tapped the booklet.

She expected him to straighten and come see, but apparently he was more intrigued by whatever was in the crate. When he pulled out a wicked-looking knife, she understood why. Backing into the table, she stared at it. Perhaps it was a hunting knife...though neither Lucien nor Dev knew how to hunt. Protection against the violent streets? Perhaps, but both wore pistols for that.

Though it hadn't done Lucien any good that final dark night.

"There's blood on it." Slade held the blade up toward the lantern. "Not much. Looks like it was cleaned pretty well, except where the blade meets the handle."

He no doubt had more experience with weapons than she, though her father had taught her how to handle a gun with reasonable accuracy. "Why would he have that here?"

Slade shrugged. "Protection. Utility. Hunting. Could be an heirloom, given the styling."

"With blood on it?"

"Might be fifty years old for all we know." He put it back as if it didn't matter. As if his eyes weren't as hard as jet as he considered it. Then he straightened and came to look at the booklet. "Hmm."

"Hmm?"

He glanced from the pages to her. "There's a book across the street I'd like to compare this too. Would you mind if I took it? It's easier to transport the smaller one without being seen."

"So long as you have it back before Dev gets home." She folded her arms over her middle and scanned the small room again. She was ready to escape the cellar. It was too cold on the one hand...and too warm on the other, with Slade Osborne taking up all the air. His coat smelled like him, citrus and spice, and filled her with the foolish longing to lean close again. She shrugged out of it. "I'd better return before I am missed."

He nodded and put the coat back on, his breath catching on an inhale, eyes flashing to hers. Then he reached to his inner pocket and tried to slip the booklet in. It apparently wouldn't slide easily, for he pulled another slender tome out.

A familiar slender tome. Ignoring the chill air that surrounded her again, she snatched it from his fingers. "Granddad's book of prayers."

She heard his sharp intake of breath but didn't look up. It had been years since she had last held this treasured volume, with its aged leather binding and yellowed pages. The ink within had long ago faded to reddish brown. "He gave this to you?" It would be just like Granddad, to save something for years and then pass it along on a whim to a near-stranger.

Or, as he would say, at the prodding of the Spirit.

"You can have it if you want." Uncertainty did strange things to his voice, made it lower, so that it thrummed over her nerves.

"No." Much as she loved this book, she didn't need the original—she already carried it inside her mind. She closed her eyes now to flip through the pages as they had been a decade earlier, paused to read a few of the words transcribed by her great-great-grandfather. The words whispered out. "'God of my end, it is my greatest, noblest pleasure to be acquainted with Thee...'"

"I just read that one this morning. The prayers are beautiful."

"Yes." She opened her eyes and let her fingers remember the feel of the cover. It had a scratch that hadn't been there ten years ago. Summoning a soft smile, she handed it back. "He must have seen something special in you to give you that. It has been in my family for a century."

Uncertainty edged toward panic. "Then I shouldn't—"

"He gave it to you. Keep it."

His eyes went still again, the wavering vanished, and that hint of a smile reappeared on his lips as he tucked both books into his pocket. "Interesting family you have, Yetta. What's his story?"

No one but Walker had ever called her Yetta. So why did it sound right coming from Slade's lips? Warm enough to make her aware anew of the cold, familiar enough to tease the smile back to her mouth. "Oh no, Slade. One kiss does not entitle you to that information."

"No?" His hint of a grin grew to a full one, and full of mischief as he slid closer. His hands settled at her waist again, and her foolish heart beat too fast. What was she doing? "What about two? What will that get me?"

Why did she have no desire to fend him off? She rather chuckled and rested her hands on his arms. "Trouble."

"Convenient. It's an old friend." He leaned down, his intent as obvious as it had been in that flash on the steps.

Marietta lifted her face and waited, watched his wolf eyes gleam, flicker...and then shift, as if he heard something. He halted several inches away, inclined his head, and then retreated a step with a scowl. "Blast it."

"What?" She heard nothing. No footsteps, no carriages...

He closed his eyes and shook his head. "Not what I wanted that to be, Lord."

"Pardon?" The cold compounded, and she wrapped her arms around herself again. Still, it seeped all the way to her core.

Slade rubbed a hand over his face and leveled a gaze on her that was...warm. Open. With no hint of the wolf. "My conscience. I'm sorry. I had no right to kiss you, not when you're promised to Hughes."

Now her blood ran as cold as the air. "I'm not going to marry him."

"He doesn't seem to know that." A small glint reentered his eyes.

Her chin lifted a notch. She couldn't stop it. "Do you think it a wise time to send him into a rage?"

Now the flashes she saw race across his face were more of fear. And somehow she suspected they weren't for himself. "No. You can't do that. He would..."

He would what? She didn't want to think he would hurt her, but Cora's scream echoed in her ears. She could almost hear the fire of his dueling pistol, the gasps of a dying man who had done nothing worthy of a fight.

If he could be so violent because of her, what would he do to her if she broke things off? Or what if the duel had been more because of the castle under the house? *Her* house. And if she refused to marry him, what would he do for that? She shivered.

Slade ran a hand down her upper arm and cupped her elbow. "Do you realize what will happen to him if he succeeds in his plans, Marietta? He could hang."

The shiver turned to convulsion. She couldn't love the man he was, the one who had lied to her about the things he valued most highly. But she didn't want to see him executed. "Do your job then, Slade. Stop him."

"I will. But he'll still be arrested and spend the rest of his life in prison."

She would never have to see him again. He could never reach her, but she wouldn't have his death on her hands. She nodded.

"You're sure you're all right with that? To the point you'd be willing to testify in court?"

Testify? She wanted to squeeze her eyes shut, but she forced them open wide. Forced her breathing to steady when it wanted to ball in a scream or a sob. "Is that what this was about?"

Had that always been what it was about? Had she ever been more than a means? A means to her father for Lucien, a means to the house for Devereaux, a means to a witness for Slade.

"This?" He looked baffled for about half a second, and then realization dawned. He squeezed her elbow. "No, *this* was about your being too blasted alluring. The question is because I've been watching the two of you together for almost a month now. You look to be very much his girl."

She didn't pause to examine why the observation made her blood boil. It was enough that it fired through her. Surging up on her toes, she pressed a hand to the back of his head, pulled it down, and caught his mouth in a kiss as searing as the anger in her veins. And then, just as his arms started to come around her, she pulled away. Not to tease, but because the fire turned from anger to shame, and a small voice inside chided her.

No doubt the same voice that had just chided him. She couldn't quite catch her breath when she turned away. "I'm not his girl." Unwilling to look to see if he believed her, she spun for the stairs and charged up them.

The door refused to budge when she pushed, and the circle of light dogged her heels. Giving in now to the urge to close her eyes, she leaned her head against the unyielding wood.

She heard the lantern come to a rest on the step. His hand settled on her back. "I'm sorry. Again." Oh, he had such a voice. So rich. Just the right timbre. It was a shame he so often chose silence. Although he could have chosen it again now, and she wouldn't have minded. "I've made a mess of things where they should have stayed neat and put us both in danger. Worse, I didn't show you the respect you deserve."

As if she deserved any respect. What was wrong with her, that she must always have a man's affections? Her stupid, foolish heart was as fickle as the weather over the bay. From Walker to Lucien to Devereaux, and now would she focus her vain hopes on Slade Osborne?

Willing the idiotic fluttering of her heart to still, she pasted on indifference and made a show of examining the door. "There's no need to dwell on it. We shan't make the same mistake again."

He ran his hand down the opposite side of the door and found the latch within five seconds. Though he paused with his hand upon it. "Thanks for listening. About Ross."

They must have been identical twins for Ross to have tried to take his place as he had. Two of them with the same dark, brooding good looks, the same strong jaw. Had they both had the wolf's eyes? Not that the predator shone through Slade's in his softer moments. Only when he was at work, playing the part his brother had written for him.

The part, perhaps, he had played of his own volition before he went home changed?

She had a feeling the turn of her lips was too small to be called a smile. "Thank you for trusting me enough to share."

With a scant nod of acknowledgment, he pulled on the latch and pushed open the door.

Because she wanted to linger, she swept through the opening without hesitation. And because it hurt so much, she paused in the study, turned, and lifted to her toes to press a kiss to his cheek. Friendly, that's all. A show of appreciation for honesty in a world that seemed to have none.

Yet when she rushed into the hall, her heart twisted, keen and painful. She wanted her mother. Someone to embrace her with no expectations, someone to love her in the truest sense. She would grab her cloak and...no, Mama was spending the day with Paulina and baby Ezra. Marietta would be welcome there, but it wouldn't be the same.

For a moment she stood in the hall with no direction. Then her eyes caught on the side staircase, and her feet aimed that direction. A minute later she knocked on the door to Barbara's sitting room, and her friend opened it with a welcoming smile.

Marietta hastened in. Barbara was about as close to Mama as she could get just now.

"Mari. Are you all right? You look upset."

A quick denial was on her tongue, but she swallowed it and stopped in front of the window. The world outside looked so drab and dreary. "I don't know."

Barbara joined her at the window and took her hands. "You're like ice! Were you outside?"

"No." She gripped Barbara's fingers and closed her eyes, calling up an image of the street with green buds on the trees and flowers blooming. She thought of summer with its waves of humid heat.

But these past years, it had been only oppression. No picnics in the parks or walks along the harbor, nothing but dread of the next casualty report. Everyone knew someone who had fallen. Sometimes it felt as though there had been no life before the war, that there would be none after it.

The image of warmth vanished like smoke in the wind. There

wouldn't be much by way of life after this. Not for her. Her association with Lucien and Devereaux Hughes would ostracize her from the society that mattered. And if she were with child, there would be no sanctuary from wagging tongues.

"Mari?"

She blinked away the haze and focused on Barbara's guileless face. "Slade kissed me."

Barbara's brown eyes went wide with...mirth? "Well, now. I suppose that could render any woman dazed."

Marietta searched her face for censure but found none. Only that soft amusement. "Shouldn't you be shocked? We have only known each other a month."

With a light laugh, Barbara chafed some warmth into Marietta's hands. "I had only known Stephen a week when he first kissed me."

Her brother? Staunch, staid, upright Stephen—kissing a girl he scarcely knew? "Surely you jest."

The dreamy look in Barbara's eyes proved the truth. "I had never thought to gain the attention of a man like him. Aside from my humble means, I have no great beauty, I know—but our love came so quickly. We both knew by then that God had meant us for each other."

At the time Marietta would have scoffed. Now, satisfaction glowed beyond the regret. Perhaps he died too early, but he had lived. "You sell yourself short, Barbara. It is easy to see what Stephen loved, and I am so very glad you found it together. But it is hardly the case here."

Barbara's gaze sharpened. "Did you kiss him back?"

"Well, I am not made of stone." Heat crept up her neck.

Her friend laughed. "Why, then, are you so quick to dismiss all possibility? He is a man with depth of character and conviction; I saw that quickly. And the way he watches you..."

Marietta knew well enough how he watched her. With as much suspicion as attraction. And knowing her loyalties now wouldn't change the reality of her bonds to Dev. Slade would destroy him, and he wouldn't be interested in picking up her pieces when he was through.

More, she shouldn't want him to. Her gaze latched on the windowsill. "I think I ought to remain free of romantic attachments."

Barbara squeezed her fingers before releasing them. "Because you feel you should, or because you have given up hope of finding real love?"

"Because I..." The feelings came again, swamping her, twisting her, making her doubt. "Because I cannot be trusted with these decisions. I am too fickle."

"Oh, Mari." Barbara took her arm and led her away from the panes of glass radiating cold, over to the settee by the snapping fire. They both sat. "Perhaps your emotions have been shifting because they hadn't been aligned with the Lord's will. Seek Him, and you will be able to trust where He leads you, whether that means remaining alone or loving again."

The words sounded so simple, so wise. Yet never in her life had she given her future over to another, even One she knew to be so much bigger than she. But loving *again*...that implied she ever had, which she was none too sure of. Well no, that was unfair—she had loved Walker, as best as she knew how at the time. But when he hurt her...it had been so much easier to focus on more superficial things with Lucien and Dev. The breathless excitement, the glow of attraction, the sparkle of wealth.

The pride of knowing she could snag any man she wanted.

What a fool she was. Perhaps she had snagged them, snagged them both—but now she was caught in her own hooks with little hope of breaking the surface.

Seventeen

Devereaux swung down from the rented horse and tied it to the hitching post, his gaze sweeping over the large white house. The wooden sign planted just ahead said *Appalachian Inn*. Though on the direct road from Hagerstown to Cumberland, the coming of the rails had no doubt hit it hard since there was no stop here, twenty miles outside Cumberland and across the river from the rail line that went through West Virginia.

Perhaps that explained its dire need of a new coat of whitewash and neglected look. He had a very different image of it from his first visit here, with Father and Lucien, when he was a lad of eleven.

Ah, well. Times changed, fortunes rose and fell, and those who did not adapt were trampled.

A bell jangled when he opened the door, the brisk February wind gusting its way in with him. Devereaux cast his gaze around the entry-way as vague recollections stirred. They had passed an entire month here in '42, but most of his memories were linked to what he had done out of doors. All looked well-enough appointed, though, if worn to comfortable.

From deeper within the house came a call of, "Just a moment!" and then the soft tread of a female. He prepared a smile and tried to discern if the woman who emerged from the hall was the same Mrs. Jackson he had met before. Hard to say. Twenty-three years earlier, the proprietress had been a new bride. The woman before him now wore the black of mourning, had streaks of silver in her hair, and bore lines on her pleasant face.

Her smile was tired but welcoming. "Good morning. May I help you, sir?"

"Certainly. I'm Devereaux Hughes. I'd like to book a room for a few nights. Are you Mrs. Jackson?"

She headed around a high desk to where a book lay opened upon it. If she recognized his name, she gave no indication. "I am. Have you stayed with us before?"

"Many years ago when I was a boy. I have fond recollections of exploring the area with my brother. I believe your husband took us fishing one day." He set his bag down by his feet.

Her smile turned wistful. "That sounds like Peter. He always took time for the guests." She trailed a finger with a torn nail down a page in the book. "I will put you in the East Room, shall I? Our best."

"Perfect."

"I'll have my niece ready it for you, and my nephew see to your horse. Please make yourself comfortable in the parlor for a few minutes." She motioned him to the right and then disappeared back the hall once more.

Devereaux meandered into the parlor, his gaze flitting from faded painting to faded rug to faded sofa. Against such a backdrop, the newish-looking photograph displayed upon the mantel stood out. He moved toward it, frowning at the two men pictured in Confederate uniforms.

The one on the right looked somewhat familiar, but only because he expected to see him here. Peter Jackson, proprietor, he was fairly sure. Standing next to a man far more recognizable, though Devereaux had never met him.

Stonewall Jackson.

Interesting. He looked from one bearded man to the other, noting a resemblance. Interesting indeed.

But far more than who might be a relation to whom was the unexpected information that he was staying in a Confederate home. If he had needed encouragement to go about his task, this would have provided it.

The soft rustle of heavy fabric from the hall made him turn as Mrs. Jackson swished her way into the room. She came to a halt, a smile frozen upon her face when her gaze landed on him by the fireplace. Glancing from the photograph to him, she cleared her throat. "Would you care for some refreshment, Mr. Hughes?"

He could understand her hesitation to address the photograph. One never could tell, in their part of the country, where a stranger's loyalties might lie. "Thank you, but I need nothing right now." He motioned toward the picture. "I believe I recognize your husband. Was the esteemed general a relative of his?"

"Cousin." Her shoulders were square, tense, though her face remained clear of shadows. "Are you of the railroading family of Hugheses, sir?"

Ah, she *had* recognized the name. Good. "I am. Though I fear at this point I am all that is left of us."

"I am sorry to hear that. I recall your father being a very amiable gentleman, and you and your brother to be...rather lively boys."

He laughed at that. No doubt she had been none too thrilled to have them tramping through her house covered in the mud they had collected on their adventures. "We were. I hope we didn't cause you too many headaches."

Her smile made soft lines fan out from her mouth and eyes. "It is always a joy to watch happy families."

Happy families. Perhaps they had been, then, when all was so much simpler. Before the war forced them to lie to their father. Before disease stole him from them. Before Lucien took all that should have been Devereaux's. "May I ask, is your husband...?" He sent a pointed look to her black dress.

Mrs. Jackson sighed. "It has been only four months, though he has been away since the war began." She smoothed a hand over the black bombazine of her skirt. "Your family is Unionist, is it not?"

He was accustomed to everyone knowing his assumed position, what with the railroad declaring it for him. He canted his head to one side. "That is our official stance. Though you needn't apologize for Confederate sympathies in my company—with a mother from Louisiana, our house has long been divided."

Her smile reemerged, this time with a note of amusement. "I was not going to apologize." The good humor faded. "Though I hate how this war has divided us. So many nights I have spent on my knees, begging the Lord to knit our nation together. Sometimes I cannot fathom how it will ever be so."

Sometimes *he* wondered how anyone could ever expect it to be. The time for unity had long since passed.

"Aunt Abigail?"

His hostess turned, but Devereaux needed only to lift his gaze to see the young woman standing in the doorway. And Mrs. Jackson's niece caught the eye. She looked decidedly out of place in her simple brown skirt, with the faded backdrop of the inn behind her. With lustrous hair dark as midnight and snapping cobalt eyes, the girl was stunning. And, given the way she shifted her stance upon spotting him, well aware of it.

Devereaux fought back a smile. She could be no more than eighteen or nineteen, and the look in her eye reminded him acutely of Marietta. More specifically, of Marietta when he first met her. Flirtatious and confident, and just reckless enough to spell danger to anyone who didn't know how to handle her.

"There you are, Ruby." Censure laced Mrs. Jackson's tone, which the girl no doubt heard as clearly as he did.

Ruby produced a sultry smile. "Our guest's room is ready, Aunt."

The elder woman turned back to him, her smile strained. "Mr. Hughes, allow me to introduce my niece, Miss Ruby Kent. Her brother, Judah, ought to be in momentarily. And you will no doubt see the youngest of them, little Rose, about the house as well."

Devereaux fixed on a polite smile and nodded at the girl. Well he knew how he must look to her eye—a stranger, obviously well-to-do, from a city just far enough from her rural home to be enticing. Given what was sure to be a shortage of suitable, desirable men for her, he probably looked like a romantic escape in waiting.

She would have to get over that idea, and better sooner than later. The last thing he needed was a would-be debutante dogging his heels. "Good to meet you, Miss Kent."

The light in her gaze didn't so much as dim, and it remained fastened on him as she curtsied. "Likewise, Mr. Hughes. Shall I show our guest to his room, Aunt Abigail?"

Mrs. Jackson pressed a hand to her forehead, lifting away one of her silver curls. "Of course, yes. Mr. Hughes, supper will be at six o'clock. If you need anything beforehand, don't hesitate to ask."

"Thank you, ma'am. Though I intend to spend much of my time exploring the area, so I hope not to be a bother to you." Just as he hoped that, given her recollection of him romping through the woods as a boy, she wouldn't think it odd for him to do so now. Plenty of men escaped the city now and then to adventure through the mountains, after all—though no doubt not many these days.

Mrs. Jackson merely said, "Oh, you could not possibly be a bother," as she shooed her niece out the door.

Devereaux fell in behind the girl, careful to keep his gaze up and raking over the walls so long as he was within sight of the proprietress. Perhaps once he was up the stairs he let his eyes dip to enjoy the exaggerated sway of Ruby's hips, but the stir of desire was more an echo, a strain. A realization that he wanted only Marietta, and he hadn't much longer to wait. Two more months and she would be his. His wife, his to hold every day. No more longing glances, no more sneaking about under cover of mourning.

It was finally his turn to have it all.

They turned at the landing to the second half of the stairs, and Devereaux glanced out the window at the valley beyond. The Potomac slipped along, the hills rose again in West Virginia, and there were the rails, with the puff of a train on its way to Cumberland.

His fingers tightened around the handle of his valise. All his...but the enemy was ready to pounce at one wrong move. He could lose everything. If their plans went awry, if he was caught while undertaking this task, the penalties would be severe. And then where would he be? He could lose the house, his stake in the railroad, and Marietta...?

He clenched his teeth. She was loyal, at least enough to honor her word. Her Yankee-loving father had certainly instilled that in her. Hence why, try as he might to lure her away from Lucien, she had never once crossed any bounds of propriety.

Once she was his wife, she would honor that. Forever, no matter what. If he were arrested, she would wait for him. If his reputation suffered and they had to move to Mother's home in Louisiana, she would go with him.

And so they must wed before he undertook anything too dangerous. Because he would not—*would not*—risk losing her. He must marry
her and get her with child quickly to tie her even tighter to him. Perhaps, with a bit of luck, that night a month ago...but she would have
said something already, if that were so. Wouldn't she have?

"Will your wife be joining you?" Ruby turned to the right at the top
of the stairs, slanting a flirtatious smile at him over her shoulder. Was
the girl a mind reader?

Regardless, subtlety apparently failed to interest her. Or perhaps
she just hadn't yet learned the full art of her chosen trade. Devereaux
let his lips turn up. "I imagine I will bring my intended here sometime
after we have wed, yes. But not this trip."

"Oh, you are engaged?" Rather than looking put off, Ruby's smile
went brighter.

"I am."

"And here we are." Ruby flounced to a halt just inside the door to
a spacious, well-lit room. The flutter of her lashes drew his gaze to her
face, and once there, it lingered on her smile. "I'm certain you'll find
the room comfortable."

"It's perfect." He stepped into the chamber and set his bag down
upon a chair. When he looked her way again, he found her twirling a
midnight curl around her finger.

"If there's anything else you need, Mr. Hughes, anything at all,
please don't hesitate to ask."

Devereaux hooked a thumb in his pocket and measured her. For
the mere fun of it, he eased closer and watched her eyes go sharp. "Oh,
I wouldn't hesitate."

She cleared her throat and slid a step over, to the door. Her smile
didn't falter, but the confidence in her gaze certainly did. Just as he
thought. She was all flirtation with no actual experience.

Ah, well. He didn't need to dally with some pretty bumpkin when
he would have Marietta so soon.

Footsteps thundered up the stairs, and Ruby seized the excuse to
turn around. "Judah?"

The boy who darted down the hall looked the part of her brother, to
be sure. The same black hair, the same blue eyes, the same well-crafted
face. He was probably thirteen or fourteen, and he offered Devereaux

an open, bright smile. "I fed your horse, sir, and gave her a quick once-over. Looks like her back right shoe is coming loose. You want me to walk her down to the smithy?"

The blacksmith was a man he needed to meet anyway. That particular skill could come in handy when it came time to set out the clues for the Knights. He grinned at the boy and tossed him a coin. "If you could just show me the way, I'll walk her myself."

Judah caught the coin with sparkling eyes. "Yes, sir, Mr. Hughes, sir. Whenever you're ready."

"I'm ready now." Focusing then upon the retreating back of the boy, Devereaux strode past the girl and down the stairs.

Within ten minutes, he and the talkative Judah, who kept up a steady monologue on all the neighbors Devereaux had no interest in knowing, arrived at the smithy with his rented mount.

Steel rang on steel somewhere within, and the heat of the forge warmed him the moment he stepped inside. Judah didn't wait to be noticed. He called out, "Mr. Mason!"

The ringing ceased, but the man who emerged from the depths of the building looked none too happy at the interruption. At least until he spotted Devereaux beside his neighbor. Then he managed a nod. "Morning."

Judah grinned. "Morning, Mr. Mason. This is our guest, Mr. Hughes. His horse is gonna need a reshoeing."

Mason let out a puff of air through his lips, all pretense of welcome gone. "It's going to be a while. Been backed up something terrible since that blasted Negro took off on me."

"I'm in no great hurry for the horse." Though that tingle at the base of his neck was interesting. Devereaux waited for the man to look his way again, and then he lifted a hand, rubbing a finger over the top of his lip.

The smithy's eyes snapped. He cleared his throat and gave the answering tug on his ear.

A brother Knight. Finally. *Finally* things were going right.

 Eighteen

Slade might be a friend of silence, but he hated little more than the sudden descending of it on a room just because he entered. Well, not the whole room. But the familiar corner of the tavern in Washington went deathly quiet when his colleagues spotted him. And the ever-present knot in his gut twisted.

The men had been friends not all that long ago. The kind he would give his life for, certain they would do the same for him. Brothers, far more than Ross had ever been. But now they all looked at him with distrust, some with outright hatred. As if they were none too sure it had been his twin who had been buried. As if wondering if the face that had deceived them four months ago were the same one approaching them now.

None of them had been willing to take his father's word as to which Osborne son had come away from that dark boardinghouse room the victor. None but Pinkerton himself.

Slade's fingers curled into his palm as he wove his way around the last crowded table between him and them. Was there anything left in his life Ross hadn't tainted, hadn't ruined?

Yet part of him knew it was his own fault. He forced his fingers to relax, and then forced his face to follow suit into the peaceful lines his brother could never replicate, hadn't understood. Had Slade not taken that assignment, hadn't been the first one to borrow his brother's name, he wouldn't be in this mess.

It hadn't been his idea. He hadn't *wanted* to assume the cover of a soldier in the Confederate army, arriving to take his brother's place after their father begged Ross out of following through on his commitment. Pinkerton had been the one to ask it. Pinkerton had been the one to claim that he could get invaluable information from behind enemy lines.

He stopped at the table of stony, silent detectives and nodded at them. It hadn't been his idea, but he had been so sure it was the right decision. And why? Why had the Lord wanted him there, while his brother ruined his life here? Why had He led him home that day, the day Ross was lying in wait for him? Why, why had He whispered a warning to duck but not stayed his hand when he raised his pistol?

Why did the whole blasted world have to shatter with that one pull of a trigger?

Frederick Herschel, once the closest of his friends, leaned back in his chair and glared at him. "What do you want, Osborne?"

Osborne. He used to call him Slade. Back when he could be sure that's who he was. He drew in a long breath that brought no ease. "I need to talk to you."

The man to his right, Kaplan, pushed away from the table with thunder in his gaze. "You've got nothing to say I wanna hear." He spat on the floor and strode to the bar.

The others followed him, their movements all slow, deliberate, and menacing. As if they would pull their weapons happily. Herschel was the only one who held his seat, but Slade knew it was no favor. He was flipping a coin through his fingers, the way he did when he was working. Measuring, probing, discovering. Ready to pounce. He used his foot to push out a chair. "This ought to be real entertaining."

Slade sank onto the sturdy wood. If any of these men should have known him, recognized *him* behind the face that Ross shared, it was Herschel. "Hersh..." He met his friend's gaze but saw nothing. Nothing. He sighed and leaned close. "Pinkerton said he'd tell you about this new job he has me on. Did he?"

The only indication that Herschel even heard him was the long, lazy blink.

He'd take that as a yes. Leaning even closer, he pitched his voice low. "I'm in. The groundwork Ross laid—" He hated to even say the name, but what choice did he have? "—did its job like Pinkerton hoped. They're starting to trust me."

A snort escaped Herschel's lips, puffed out beneath his long mustache.

It might as well have been a curse. Or a dagger, the way it pierced. Would he ever be able to convince these men he was honest? Or would they think him always just waiting for the right moment to betray them, the way Ross had done?

The words of the prayer he had read on the train here, the faded brown writing on the yellowed page, whispered through his mind. *Let me willingly accept misery, sorrows, temptations, if I can thereby feel sin as the greatest evil, and be delivered from it with gratitude to Thee…*

Slade let the centuries-old thought sink deep and join with the truths his father had taught him all his life. He had been forgiven. He had left the old ways behind. And so what were these pains but a reminder of what he had escaped? Even if his friends never accepted him again, he would know he was living according to the Lord.

He took a moment to swallow down the frustration. "What do I have to do, Hersh? Tell you all about yourself? Spend an hour reminiscing about all our exploits? I can do that. I can—"

"Don't waste my time." The coin flipped again, was caught and clutched. Herschel's mustache twitched. "Even if you are who you say you are, this is your fault. Slade disappeared without so much as a by your leave, and then that—that *usurper* came and undid *months* of our work. Years. We had to reorganize everything. Double our guard on Lincoln. I had to listen to the screeches of Mrs. Lincoln for a week on end, and no apology can undo that."

"I know, but…" His watch felt heavy in his pocket. He didn't need to pull it out to know he hadn't much time here. Why use it on an apology that wouldn't be accepted anyway? "We were right. About the plot before the first inauguration—or close, anyway. They were planning to kidnap him, they say, not to kill him."

Was that a spark of interest in Herschel's eyes? He couldn't be sure. His friend had a poker face as well tuned as Slade's. But he would press on, assuming it was. "They want to try again, now, before the next inauguration. I've told them security will be too tight, but they want me to find a way around it."

The muscle in his friend's jaw pulsed. "And you come here? To me?"

"Not for what you think." Though he wasn't sure exactly what Hersh *did* think. If he were really here to gain information underhandedly, to betray the cause he had sworn his life to, he wouldn't have just admitted it, would he?

The coin flipped again. Herschel looked to be physically biting his tongue, given the mean-looking grimace on his face.

Its reflection settled in Slade's chest. God had forgiven, but his friends might never do so, even if he single-handedly brought down the KGC. And then what? Pinkerton would place him someplace else, on some other assignment with new men, men who didn't know him. But it would never be the same. And that set up an ache not so different from the one that had attacked him each of the two nights he had settled to sleep after that stupid kiss the other day.

The ache of knowing that something was, and maybe *should* be, forever out of reach, no matter how much he might want it.

Resignation edged out the intensity. "They'll plan to kidnap him another time. After the inauguration. I'll know the details, and I'll make sure you do too, so you can strengthen the guard or change what needs changed." Given the next twitch of Herschel's mustache, he splayed a hand against the table. "You have to believe me. Like you did that night at the docks."

Appealing to the shared memory achieved nothing but the crossing of Herschel's arms. "Yeah, the other you knew that one too."

Blast it to pieces. Ross had never seemed to pay attention to all the stories he had told his parents on that trip home a year ago. But he had been, apparently. He had used them all against him, and now here he was. Brotherless, and friendless to boot. He pushed to his feet. "You ought to know me better than this, Hersh. I don't care how good an actor my brother was, you ought to know *me*, now."

He pulled out his watch, unfastened it from the fob he had borrowed from his friend more than a year ago. He tossed the silver chain onto the table. "You won't believe this either, I know. But it's yours, so take it."

Not waiting to see Herschel's reaction, he pivoted and strode back through the crowded tavern. He'd made it two steps out into the cool Washington evening when a hand on his arm stopped him.

Herschel's eyes had changed. The shuttered look was gone, though that just meant the caution shone through. "Ross didn't have your watch. He said he lost it but didn't apologize about losing my fob. That's when I knew something was wrong. That he wasn't...that you weren't yourself. I didn't mention it to him. I assume you never did either."

A corner of Slade's mouth pulled up. "And have my father find out I'd lost the one he gave me?"

His friend exhaled a long breath and let go Slade's arm. "What do you need to know?"

When he got back to Baltimore, back to the safety of his room, he'd fall to his knees and praise the Almighty.

He pulled Herschel into the nearest alley and shared in a low voice the Knights' would-be plans for taking Lincoln before the inauguration. They were all vague, at best—possible places where they could grab him.

To each and every one, Herschel grinned and gave the same reply. "Covered."

"Good." Slade nodded after the last one. "I assumed it would be, but I needed to be able to assure them of it. They'll be watching, and if I say you will be somewhere you're not..."

Herschel nodded and glanced toward the street. "You need them to trust you if you hope to undermine them. But Slade...tread carefully."

Slade. Peace swept through him, despite the warning. "I'll be in touch when they have a plan in place."

"Yeah." His friend straightened, his expression not relaxing any. "I'd better get back in there and assure the others I was just giving you the what-for."

And down his spirits spiraled again. Maybe he should resign himself to being always a pariah with this group of brothers. Maybe he just wasn't meant to have any brothers. "Tell them you punched me in the nose. That'll make them feel better."

At least Herschel laughed. That was something. Enough to spur him on to his next meeting, strange as it felt to head to the National Hotel, where he had made arrangements to change into evening dress in Booth's room. Not that he would have imposed upon Booth, but the man had offered when he had heard Slade was coming in to the city to go to the theater, and it had seemed wise to accept.

Though he still wished he could have found a way out of the theater invitation itself. Maybe had it been Marietta issuing, he could have—largely because she wouldn't have invited him at all. They had avoided each other neatly the past forty-eight hours. But Barbara Arnaud had cornered him, and she'd had help in the towering form of Thaddeus Lane. Why *he* insisted Slade join his family for a play, he couldn't say.

But here he was, knocking on Booth's door en route to Ford's Theater, pretty sure he would look exactly how he felt in formal attire—like a pretender. The only time he had ever bothered with finery in the past was when he was fresh from a win at cards and needing to impress his way into a higher-stake game. That didn't exactly make him a gentleman worthy of passing his evening with some of Baltimore's finest. Not unless they had hired him as protection.

The door swung open, and a smiling John Booth stood in the entrance. "There you are. Cutting it close, don't you think? Hurry. I brushed your coat for you, but only because I was afraid you would mention you knew me and I didn't want to be embarrassed by you."

Slade breathed a laugh and stepped into the nicely appointed hotel room. He knew Booth called no one place home, but he must be doing pretty well to afford to stay here regularly. "Thoughtful of you."

Booth ushered him in and shut the door, motioning to the chair onto which he'd laid out Slade's tail coat, the matching trousers, and a waistcoat he had never seen before. "There is 'no beast so fierce but knows some touch of pity,' as the Bard said."

"Shakespeare?" He measured the waistcoat with pursed lips. His father had never insisted he read Shakespeare as much as the theologians.

"*Richard III*. My favorite role. Is there a problem, Osborne?"

He glanced at his host and motioned toward the waistcoat. "That's not mine."

"Well, of course not. Yours was for day, not evening. You can return it to me when next we meet. I won't miss it." Booth shot a pointed look to the clock set upon a shelf. "You intend to make the start of the show, do you not? Wait much longer, and you'll be barred until intermission."

Why argue? He scooped up the clothes and stepped behind the screen. After discarding his everyday clothes he said, "I was visiting with that friend I told you about, the one still a member of Lincoln's security team."

All went silent in the room. Then Booth let out a quick breath. "And? Did you find anything? Can we take him before the inauguration?"

Evening suit on, Slade slid his arms through the velvet filigree waistcoat and winced. "No. They have already anticipated every option. There won't be any weaknesses, not that day."

The sigh that sounded forth bore an acute resemblance to one of Chicago's gusts of wind. "It was too much to hope, I suppose. You were subtle? He suspected nothing?"

Slade reached for the detestable bow tie. "Does Shakespeare have some quote about giving a fellow a morsel of credit now and then?"

Booth laughed. "No doubt he does. I apologize, Osborne. I am merely frustrated by all the failures. I see you have gaiters, at least. Have you appropriate gloves?"

Gaiters? It took him a moment to realize he had moved back to talk of clothes and meant the shoes that had been in his closet along with the tail coat and top hat. As for gloves? "Ah..."

"No matter. I just purchased a new pair of maroon doeskin ones. You can borrow my old gold pair."

Was the man always so generous? He finished with the tie, shrugged into the coat, and stepped from behind the screen.

Booth surveyed him, making a show of it worthy of his beloved stage. At length, he smiled. "I suppose you can admit to knowing me. So long as you hurry. I can't claim an acquaintance with anyone who arrives late to the theater."

Slade reached for the shoes. "I'm hurrying."

"All the same, I had better show you the quickest route. I need to pick up my mail anyway."

When he straightened from putting on the shoes, he found Booth standing with Slade's greatcoat and top hat and gloves, his own accessories already on. Slade knew his suspicion must be obvious as he took them. "What is it with you, Booth?"

The man chuckled and opened the door. "You need to ask? You are accompanying Marietta Hughes to the theater, with Devereaux clueless in the mountains. This may be one of your last living acts. You ought to look the part."

"Of all the..." He stomped his way into the hall as he put on the coat. "I am not *accompanying* her. I am merely in a party that includes her. And Hughes himself charged me with keeping an eye on her, so—"

Booth's laughter cut him off. "The gentleman doth protest too much, methinks." He gave Slade a friendly elbow and hurried down the stairs. "Make the most of it, I say, because you will pay for it regardless."

They emerged onto the street. The air had cooled more during his brief stint inside, reminding Slade that February still had some teeth left. "It's only a play. With, from the sounds of it, her entire family."

"It is *only* what you make it," Booth said with a smirk in his tone. "If I were you, I would see that it was worth the punishment Hughes is sure to dole out. Enjoy the flirtation she's so good at. Maybe steal a kiss when you see her home. For that matter, steal an extra one for me."

His throat went dry at the mere suggestion. "I would rather live."

Booth laughed again. "Might be a fair trade."

Slade didn't mean to scowl. He just couldn't stop himself. "Aren't you engaged?"

"Hush, man. That is not yet known. And my lady is unsurpassed, to be sure. But Marietta Hughes..." He made an appreciative noise.

Was that what Slade had sounded like to Hughes's ears that first day in the carriage? It was a wonder the man hadn't socked him. "She's his." A fact of which he had reminded himself approximately two thousand times in the last two days—every time his lips wanted to remember the feel of hers. No, he wouldn't be stealing any more kisses, tonight or ever.

Booth loosed an overdramatic harrumph. "Have it your way, though I still say you ought to live a little before he calls you out. Not that *I* will say anything to him, mind you. In my opinion, it's high time someone pulled one over on him, but all of Washington will see you, so he *will* hear."

Slade shoved his hands into his pockets. Yet another bad idea, this.

"He won't call me out." He hoped. "And least not until after this business is concluded."

"Hmm. Maybe. At any rate, you ought to enjoy the play tonight. Laura Keene plays the dowager to perfection..."

All too soon they arrived at Ford's Theater, and Booth left him to go in the front entrance while he took himself around the back to collect his mail. Slade stood on the walk outside for a long minute, watching the well-dressed couples sweep through the doors before him. Women in expensive gowns, men in extravagant coats and hats, more than one gold watch glinting in the lamplight.

All this, while not so far away men were freezing in the trenches.

He nearly turned on his heel and left. But before he could move, familiar laughter tickled his ears, and his head swiveled to his right. There, coming en masse down the street, was his party. Both the elder Lanes, Marietta's mother, Marietta herself laughing with Barbara Arnaud, and two couples besides that he didn't recognize.

No, wait, he knew one of the men—the third man he had caught at the rail yard that night with Lane and Walker.

Before he could even think to evade them, Lane raised an enthusiastic hand in greeting. "Oz, hallo! What perfect timing."

Yeah. Perfect. He mustered the biggest smile he could, not that that was saying much, and tried not to look too closely at the redhead ensconced between her mother and Barbara. "Good evening, Mr. Lane."

"Indeed it is." Lane led the way into the theater, his good humor not faltering. "Have you met Mari's brothers yet? Ize is the elder, Hez the taller—Isaac and Hezekiah, that is."

"No, I—"

"Boys." Lane waved them over as they handed off their outer garments to an attendant. Slade begrudgingly relinquished his hat and coat as well.

He meant to look only at them. But it was hardly his fault Marietta chose that moment to sweep her cape from her shoulders, was it? Nor his fault that the gleaming light from the chandeliers reflected just so off the shoulders bared by her gown, which fit her far too well. And shining in the light, the gray—silk, was it?—turned to silver against her ivory skin.

Her brothers stepped into his line of vision, both giving him a look that convinced him he should have fled when he had the chance.

Their grandfather didn't seem to notice—or perhaps it was that he didn't care. He slapped a friendly hand to Slade's shoulder and grinned. "Boys, this is my and Mari's friend, Slade Osborne. Oz, Julie's boys. Isaac Arnaud, who now runs my shipping ventures, and Hezekiah Arnaud, academic and chemist."

He still wasn't sure when he had become the friend of Thaddeus Lane. And he seriously doubted Marietta would term him such. But he refreshed his tight smile and held out a hand.

The Arnaud brothers seemed bent on breaking rather than shaking it, but he did his best not to grimace. Especially when the Lanes moved off to greet someone else and Marietta swept up halfway through Hez's death grip of a squeeze.

Her cat eyes flashed green sparks. But that didn't quite cover the shadows of pain lurking underneath them.

"Hezekiah!" She all but hissed the name, and moved her hands in some quick series of motions that left Slade scowling every bit as much as the crushing grip.

His confusion only increased when Hez released his hand and made a few motions back to her. Then Isaac jumped into the fray. Slade backed away, glancing down when he felt someone at his side. Barbara, her gaze on the siblings too. Though she smiled.

He glanced from them to her. "Are they...arguing?"

A soothing chuckle came from her throat. "I don't understand much of it, but I caught Mari's initial command to stop."

His scowl deepened still more. "Is it a language?"

"Indeed. Sign language. Was that 'doll'?" Barbara tilted her head to the side. She too wore a more formal gown, though still in unrelieved black. "How very odd. But I'm sure it was. That was one of the first signs she taught Elsie."

"Elsie?"

"Walker and Cora's little girl. She is deaf. Mari has been teaching them signs so they can communicate."

"She..." Marietta Hughes taking the time to teach a new language to her servants? Was that the meeting he'd overheard her and Walker

Payne making when he first arrived? Slade's gaze fell on her again. Maybe a little differently than it ever had before. Maybe. "Interesting."

"Oh, it is. You ought to sit in on a lesson sometime, Mr. Osborne. Mari is a wonder. Never faltering or forgetting a single sign, and always so patient." A tinkle of laughter. "I'm afraid Elsie is picking it up much faster than the rest of us."

A few other gazes swung their way, a fact which apparently didn't escape Marietta. Socially conscious, that was more in keeping with his picture of her. Her face neutral, she made a few more signs, small and discreet. Though whatever they meant, they didn't seem to please her brothers, who looked about to make the argument vocal.

She spun, her gaze locking on Slade, and strode across the steps between them. Fury blazed in her eyes, not unlike the way it had in the cellar the other day as she claimed she wasn't Hughes's. Right before she stretched up and kissed him.

This time she halted at his side and lifted one flame of a brow. "We had better head to our seats, Slade."

She'd used his given name—in public, in front of the brothers who looked as though they would as soon tear him limb from limb as take in the play. Slade did the only thing he could think to do.

He offered her his arm.

Nineteen

Marietta had all she could do to keep her pleasant smile pinned to her face and her hand relaxed against Slade's arm. Anger wanted to push through her fingers, and the pain from a headache contorted her face into a wince as they started up the stairs.

Slade's fingers brushed over hers. She glanced up into his face and saw concern knitting his brows.

"Are you feeling all right?"

The question made her breath catch in her throat. Mama had seen the pain—Mama always did—but no one else had. "Just a little headache."

His frown didn't ease. "Do you want to leave?"

The hopefulness in his tone teased out a smile, but she shook her head—a mistake, that—and then nodded to a passing congressman. "What I want is to enjoy the play my grandparents have been eager to watch, let all of society see that I am through with mourning Lucien and *not* on the arm of Dev, and give my overbearing brothers a few swift kicks to the posterior."

That last part she barely even muttered, but Slade's chuckle said he heard her. "My fault. I think I looked at you wrong."

Why should that make heat sweep over her? She already knew he thought her attractive. And she had commissioned this dress months ago to elicit reactions when she reentered society, having it modeled on a green gown that had left the Hugheses breathless. Though at the time she certainly hadn't imagined wearing this one first to a play in Washington on the arm of a detective rather than Dev.

Perhaps she ought to have left it in the closet with the ill-fated green one she never intended to don again.

"They deserve no excuses to be made for them." She tossed a narrow-eyed glance over her shoulder at her brothers, both of whom still scowled her way, despite their wives' obvious attempts to distract them with conversation. "Those two have always been this way. Virtually ignoring me day in and day out, as if I am nothing but a pretty doll upon a shelf, until I dare to assert some individuality in public, and then they suddenly remember they are older brothers charged with protecting me."

Stephen was the only one of the three who had ever bothered to talk to her. To try to understand why she behaved as she did.

Isaac and Hez just patted her head day to day and then blustered and fumed when she didn't act as they thought she should. Granted, she wouldn't be in this mess if she had met their standards all her life. But tonight she had done nothing wrong. She was, in fact, distancing herself publicly from Dev, which ought to please them.

Slade hummed. "I can understand their protectiveness."

"It isn't protectiveness; it's control. And I am sick to death of all these men in my life thinking they know so much better than I what I need or want." Again, she spoke quietly, fastening a belying smile to her lips for all the passing families she hadn't seen much in the past year.

"Then it's an honor to aid you in convincing them. Although," he added, a smile coloring his voice, "Booth thinks it will be my last living act. When Hughes finds out..."

"Oh." Oh, mercy. She hadn't even paused to consider...The headache pounded, streaked behind her eyes, and lodged in her heart. When would the selfishness recede? What she was doing to Slade with this show hadn't even entered her mind.

She tried to pull her hand away from his arm, but he chuckled and covered her fingers with his again to hold it there. "It's a little late for that, Yetta."

He was right. Too many people had seen them. She had sealed his fate already. Dev would find out that she had made her reentrance into society on the arm of Slade Osborne, and he would be furious.

The pain settled behind her eyes, and another twisted her abdomen. "I'm sorry." Paltry words, but so very true. For so very much.

"Don't be. Didn't you hear your grandfather? We're...friends."

Friends. She motioned toward the row Granddad Thad had rented for the night and tried, in vain, to keep her gaze from Slade's face. He was looking down at her, no evidence of the wolf in his eyes. Still, the kindness that seemed at once out of place and natural in his gaze didn't make that word make any more sense in relation to this man. She wasn't sure she could be a friend to Slade Osborne. He was too...and she wasn't enough...and what with those kisses the other day...

Lord, help me, please. Even now, with watchful eyes on her from every direction as she indicated the seats that were theirs, she had to fight off the urge to lean in to his side. Fight off the longing to feel his arms around her. Fight off the thought that maybe he could make everything right.

He couldn't. She knew that.

Marietta moved into the row first, unwilling to deal with a brother manipulating his way to the other side of her. Barbara or Granddad would help insulate Slade from them, but they wouldn't think she needed the favor.

Usually she wouldn't. Frustrating as they were, she knew how to handle Isaac and Hez. But just now the twisting pain in her abdomen knifed its way to her back, and she sank with gratitude into her chair, willing the ache to ebb and yet knowing she deserved every pulse of it. She had, in fact, been praying so diligently for this discomfort that she could hardly complain about its intensity. She ought to embrace it. Praise the Lord for it.

He had spared her. She was not with child.

Relief ought to dominate every other feeling today. And it did...for a while. Then shame had billowed over her like the sea. Perhaps the rest of the world wouldn't know, now, what she had done. But privacy made it no lesser a sin. Forgiveness did not make it disappear. God's eyes saw no more stain, but there would still be consequences. There were *always* consequences.

And if He had spared her this in His mercy, what did that mean about what else would be coming her way? Was her future so bleak that the Lord wouldn't want to subject an innocent child to it?

Warm fingers touched her arm and then retreated. She glanced over to see that Slade's frown had scored its way deeper. "Are you certain you are well enough for this? I could see you home."

Home sounded like heaven. She could curl up with a hot water bottle, close her eyes, and read.

But this was her grand reentrance, independent and victorious. At *Our American Cousin*, a play Granddad and Grandmama had been wanting to see so badly. With most of the people dearest to her—even if two of them were shooting visual arrows at her even now.

She summoned up a smile. "I'm fine."

The look he gave her was rife with disbelief, but he said no more. He merely pulled out his pocket watch to check the time.

It was Marietta's turn to frown. "What happened to your fob?"

"Pardon?" He replaced the watch.

She waved her hand. "You usually have that on a silver chain. Is it in need of repair?" It was none of her business, granted, but a better topic for conversation than her health.

A lopsided smile settled on Slade's mouth. "No. I had borrowed it from a friend a year ago and finally remembered to give it back today."

Hez, seated on the other side of Slade, snorted. "You borrowed a fob?"

If she could just reach across to smack that derision from his tone... but Slade laughed. "Only after I lost the one my father gave me and didn't want him to find out."

Hez looked about to make reply—though whether it would be amused or cynical she couldn't be sure—but he paused as more people moved to the seats on the other side of Marietta.

She glanced over too and smiled at the couple. Polite greetings sounded from both sides of her, but thankfully servants began dimming the house lights, and the babble in the auditorium quieted. The play would soon begin.

She made it through the first act with no increase to her headache.

Lucien had taken her to New York once to see the original cast, and she always enjoyed watching how productions changed over time, the roles growing and expanding. This set of actors breathed life into the lines.

During the first intermission, all the voices around her started buzzing. Much of the second act she scarcely heard. And when she rose for the second intermission, the pain behind her eyes pierced too quickly for her to control the response.

Her whole family, it seemed, had been waiting to pounce at the end of the row.

"You are ill." Isaac said it like an accusation. "Why did you even come tonight if you are unwell?"

Hez rolled his eyes. "You know how she is when she makes up her mind to do something, but this is absurd, Mari. You must think of your health. Come, I will see you home."

A train ride home with Hez when he had a bee in his bonnet—not a relaxing end to the evening. "I'll be fine. It's nearly over."

Granddad elbowed his grandsons out of the way and tipped up her chin to look into her eyes. "A headache? You need quiet, Mari." He tapped the end of her nose. As always, pure love flowed from the point of contact. "Which you wouldn't get if we all left with you."

"I am ready to go as well." Barbara slipped into the place at her side and wove their arms together. She did look exhausted, no doubt from her hours of volunteering at the hospital that day.

Granddad patted her on the shoulder as he would any of the grandchildren who shared his blood. "Good of you, my dear, but two lovely young women will not be making the trip back to Baltimore on their own. Oz, you'll see they arrive safely, won't you, son?"

Isaac stared at their grandfather as if he had lost his faculties. "Granddad—"

"An elegant solution." Isaac's wife, Laura, tugged him back a step, amusement gleaming in her eyes.

Slade looked none too sorry to be asked to depart. "It would be my pleasure." He crooked both his arms. "Ladies?"

Too miserable to argue, Marietta settled her hand in the curve of his left elbow while Barbara took his right. "Thank you. Goodnight, everyone."

None of them said much as they descended the stairs and waited for their wraps, nor during the hack ride to the train station. And, of course, once they were on the train to Baltimore, it was far too easy to stare into the darkness and let the sway of the car lull her into a half sleep. She scarcely noted the second cab ride home, and she may have trudged up to her room without even the presence of mind to wish Slade a grateful farewell had Barbara not taken the lead.

She halted them all inside the front door by the low-burning lamp and smiled warmly at Slade. "Thank you so much for seeing us home, Mr. Osborne. And Mari dear, for insisting I come. It was a true pleasure. Shall I fetch Cora for you?"

"No." No need to rouse Cora from her bed. Marietta returned Barbara's smile. "I can manage on my own."

"Then I will bid you both good night." She grasped Marietta's hand and gave it a squeeze, dropped a quick curtsy to Slade, and turned toward the stairs.

Marietta watched her disappear and then pivoted slowly toward Slade. His gaze was already on her. Maybe that was why her throat went so dry. "I...thank you, Slade. For seeing me home."

"Sure." His fingers tangled with hers, and she wasn't certain which of them had reached out first. "You looked beautiful tonight, Yetta."

A breath of a laugh eased past her tight throat. The familiar compliment brought no pleasure, just another wave of shame. "I meant to. Probably just to slap at Dev, and it didn't...it didn't occur to me that it would hinder your work here. He's going to be angry, and I'm sorry. I've made things more difficult for you when I wanted to be a help."

His thumb stroked over her knuckles and tied her in knots. "I'm not worried. You have him wrapped around your finger, and I know how to play my hand."

Wonderful. He wasn't worried because he recognized her as what she was—a professional coquette. Tears burned at her own weakness. Even now she would rather curl into his chest than stand on her own feet and face what she had done, what she was.

"Hey, now. What's this?" His fingertips brushed her cheek, making her aware that her tears hadn't just burned; they had slipped through her guard.

For a long moment she could only squeeze her eyes shut and struggle with all her might to keep her breathing even. Once she felt marginally under control, she shook her head. "I'm no good at being good."

His laugh was a low rumble, somehow soothing. "Ah, Yetta. In some ways we are so much alike."

A wobbly smile stole onto her lips. "In all the ways we shouldn't be."

He wiped away another tear. "Don't cry. I don't have another spare handkerchief to lend you."

How could he make her laugh now? More, why did the laughter have to catch and make the burn behind her eyes worse? "I should give that back to you."

Her tone must not have sounded very promising. His hand cupped her cheek. "But?"

"But I don't intend to. And I don't know why." She risked a lift of her eyes and found his face close, intent. And oh so alluring. "That's terrifying."

"I know." In the lamplight, low and golden, his black eyes gleamed like onyx. They stayed locked on hers for a long moment, long enough that she nearly wished for the familiar snap of the wolf within them. At least then she knew how to respond, knew how to keep her distance. But the way he looked at her now...it wasn't like the looks she was used to. It was softer, almost mournful. When his gaze fell to her lips, she felt the familiar pull in her chest, but it lacked the edge she expected.

The breath he drew in shuddered. "Yetta." His voice was a mere exhale, lower even than a murmur. He rested his forehead against hers. "I want to kiss you."

"I know." Her fingers tightened around his of their own volition, and her free hand settled on his chest. "I would let you."

"I know." He pulled away and caught her gaze again. His eyes looked as pained as hers must have earlier. "I'm not going to."

Of course not. He had said just two days ago he wouldn't again, and he'd obviously meant it. "Smart."

"Yeah." He lifted their joined hands, turned them, and pressed his lips to her knuckles. When he had first done that nearly two weeks ago, it had healed something inside her. Tonight it broke her to pieces. "We're neither of us naive, Yetta. We both know it's just...wanting."

The pieces broke to pieces. "Mm-hmm."

"Fact is, when all this is over, you'll probably go through a rocky spell. But you're smart and have a solid family, so you'll know how to handle it. In another year or so, I'll pick up the paper and see an announcement that you're marrying some wealthy politician or businessman."

The fractured pieces dug in like splinters. He was ending his courtship before he even started one. "Is that how it will be?"

"Yeah. You'll forget my name in a few years. I'll just be that reformed gambler, the two-bit detective who helped ruin your life."

She might have laughed, if she weren't afraid it would come out a sob. "Right." She would forget.

His fingers traced the contour of her cheek. Funny. As much as his words sounded like one, his touch didn't feel like a goodbye. "Pinkerton will send me north again, I bet. New York or Chicago. Maybe Boston."

She strove to match his tone, easy if a touch regretful. "Where you'll bravely chase down criminals and right society's wrongs."

"Yeah." He twisted one of her curls around his finger. "Just another adventure. I'll look back on this one and..." He swallowed, gripping her hand tighter still. Amusement snapped to life in his eyes. "And wish I had kissed you again tonight."

Marietta smiled because her lips insisted on it. Then, because her heart couldn't handle any more and her head thumped anew in protest of that pain, she backed away. "I had better let you get home." Maybe she meant tonight. Maybe she meant forever. Maybe she just wanted to mean it at all.

Slade didn't release her hand. No, he held it in his, opened her fingers, and this time pressed a kiss to her palm. "I'll have that book back by tomorrow. Just in case."

Right. The book from the cellar. Dev. The Knights. His only purpose here. "Good. And good night."

"Lock the door behind me." He released her fingers and moved to the exit. He cast only one glance at her over his shoulder before he disappeared through it.

Marietta felt as though she trudged through molasses as she followed his path. Leaning into the door, she slid the bolt into place and rested her throbbing head against the panel.

"Miss Mari? You all right?"

Cora's voice was so quiet she couldn't even drum up any alarm.

Marietta pushed herself upright with a sigh that tasted of resignation. "No. I'm a fool." She slogged her way toward the main stairs, picking up the lamp on her way by. When she drew even with where Cora stood at the base of the staircase, she paused. "You didn't need to get up, Cora."

The young woman smiled. "I already was when I heard you pull in. Thought I'd see if I could get ya anything."

"A new past would be appreciated." She shook her head. "Sorry. No, I can manage. Go back to bed."

"If you're sure." Cora's smile had faded to worry. "Miss Mari?"

She stopped on the second step. "Yes?"

"You done the right thing there. Mr. Slade's a fine man, but he ain't from your world. You be savin' yourself a passel o' heartache by not gettin' involved."

Advice obvious to everyone. Barbara alone would disagree, and she could do so solely because of how exceptional Stephen had been, willing to marry for love above all.

But Marietta was no Stephen. They all knew that. She didn't know the first thing about real, uncontainable love. She'd be doing everyone a favor by locking her shifting heart away forever.

"Thank you, Cora. Good night." Feeling as though her whole body were made of aching, weeping lead, she forced herself up the stairs to her room.

Some triumphant debut this had been.

Twenty

Devereaux glanced out the window of his private rail car. The scenery displayed the final stretch into Baltimore, the familiar farms and towns getting closer together. He leaned back into his seat, welcoming the itch to be home. Work waited, both with the business and the Knights. It would be satisfying to report that he had found the perfect hiding place for his cache of Confederate supplies.

Even more satisfying would be his arrival at the house. The last time he had been gone for more than two days in November, his homecoming had been sweet indeed. He had barely made it through the door before Marietta had pulled him into the library and launched herself into his arms. The kiss she'd given him still fueled his dreams.

He hoped his promise to keep his distance until April wouldn't dampen her passions any today. He needed to hold her, to see that longing for him in her eyes. And maybe, once she was hazy eyed from his kiss, he could convince her to shorten this half mourning, to forgive his promise altogether. Two more months. That would be cutting it close. He wanted to have the cache buried by then, and if they found a time to take Lincoln...

Surely he could convince her to marry him sooner.

He shook himself and slid his papers into a neat stack. He must be careful with these. He had needed to draw the map and write down the directions, but he wouldn't keep the documents any longer than necessary. Only until he could come up with the right encryption for Mason to help him leave along the way. The blacksmith had proven himself a willing cohort, praise be to the Almighty. Moving the cache from a small railhead, over the Potomac, and to the cave would require horses, a cart, and two sets of hands.

But at least the cave had been all he remembered and more. As a boy, he hadn't explored it deeply enough to find the small rear exit, but an escape route was always vital. The cave itself was the perfect size, and it was hard enough to find that he could be sure no one would stumble upon it after he and Mason rolled the boulder into place and armed the booby traps.

He slid the papers into his binder and the binder into his satchel. All in all a successful trip. Though he might not be welcome back at the Appalachian Inn on his next journey. His lips pulled up as he set the satchel on the table. He hadn't meant to frighten Ruby, exactly, but after a week of exaggerated flirtation, what did the chit expect him to do?

It had only been a kiss—mostly. More to silence her than out of interest. If his hands had wandered roughly, it had only been to show her what she could expect from such behavior.

Given the tears in her eyes when she pulled away, she had learned her lesson.

No hardship on his part, he admitted. She was no Marietta, but if the promise of having his Helen of Troy forever hadn't been so close at hand, he might have indulged a bit more to stave off the hunger. With more care, of course.

But Helen was at hand, more beautiful than any mythical goddess, and she was all his. He let that thought warm him through the last few minutes of the ride, and it put a bounce in his step as he debarked at one station and hired a carriage to deliver him to the next. His private car would be pulled through the city to await his next pleasure.

When he got down again outside his offices, he spotted Osborne within seconds, talking to one of the guards Devereaux kept on the payroll. He approached the two with long strides.

Osborne looked up as he neared and greeted him with a nod.

"Welcome home, Hughes." The underling moved off, and Osborne held out a hand. He winced when Devereaux gripped it.

"Problem?"

Osborne rolled his eyes and rubbed the hand. "Yeah, with your soon-to-be brothers-in-law. One or the other of them must have bruised something. Or broken it," he added in a surly mumble.

Devereaux lifted his brows. "The Arnauds? What, were you fighting with them?"

Osborne snorted and motioned him to lead the way inside, obviously knowing his habits well. "Shaking their hands. They didn't take too kindly to their grandfather manipulating me into joining the family at the theater last week."

Chuckling, Devereaux hurried toward his office, trusting Osborne to follow. The fellow even thought to close the door behind him. "He's an eccentric sometimes. Why did he insist you come?"

Osborne folded his arms, clearly resentful. "Made me feel that it was my duty to make sure Marietta got there and back safely. Though—"

"Wait." He dropped his bag upon the desk and turned. Slowly, with deliberation. "*Mari* went to the theater while I was gone?"

Osborne shrugged. "She made an appearance, though I had to bring her and Barbara Arnaud home early. Headache."

The anger, quick to flare, was quickly banked. Thad Lane forced his family wherever he willed, and even Mari didn't often withstand him. But it sounded as though she had done what she could to escape.

Still. They'd had an understanding that when she reentered society, it would be with *him*. That was why they had planned... "Blast it." He swept his hat off and tossed it to his desk. "Was she angry with me over canceling our engagement at the Ellicotts?" She hadn't seemed too terribly put out, but she was a woman, after all. They let things fester.

Osborne blinked. "How would I know?"

"She could have said something." Though to Osborne? Unlikely. He gusted out a breath and picked up the stack of post that arrived in his absence. "Never mind. Though I still fail to see why her brothers punished you for being forced to go."

He looked up in time to see the roll of Osborne's black eyes. "Her grandfather introduced me as her 'friend.' I think they got the wrong idea."

The flame licked higher again. "And how many other people heard him say that?"

It was small consolation that the other man looked as put out as Devereaux felt. "At least one too many." He sank into one of the chairs in front of the desk and hooked an ankle over a knee. "I don't know how you tolerate this society nonsense."

Devereaux muttered a curse and slapped an envelope down harder than necessary. "Gossip?"

A snort was his only answer.

He cursed again and flipped quickly through the rest of the post. "Do you have any *good* news?"

"No trouble at the rails while you were gone."

Devereaux ran his hand over his hair. "That is good, though not exactly news. Anything from the brothers?"

"Yeah. I talked to my friend."

Devereaux looked over, but Osborne's expression said no good came of that. "No weaknesses before the inauguration. But Booth and Surratt got wind of a possible review Lincoln will make of the troops a few days afterward, and we all know he's never highly guarded at those."

Devereaux let that roll over in his mind a few times while he sorted the mail into stacks according to importance. At length he nodded. "It's worth pursuing." He shuffled the important correspondence into a neat stack and slid it into his bag. "But for now, home."

At the motion of his hand, Osborne got up and followed him out. All in all, the Yankee made a decent henchman. His only questions were intelligent ones, he followed orders, showed initiative, and knew how to stay out of the way. When all of this was over, Devereaux might have a permanent position for him. He couldn't imagine Osborne would want to remain in Pinkerton's service once he didn't need that cover story anymore.

He considered the idea as they walked to his carriage and measured the man across from him once they had settled. He looked right for the job. No hulking giant to shout his profession, but he always wore that expression that dared anyone to cross him. Devereaux set his bag upon the seat and straightened his gloves. "Do you have plans for the future, Osborne?"

A glimmer of surprise surfaced in his coal-black eyes. At least

Devereaux thought it had, though his usual foul temper swallowed it up in the next second. He shrugged. "Do what I do, I guess."

What lofty goals. Devereaux smiled. "I'd like you to consider doing what you do for me."

For a long moment, Osborne just held his gaze, making no other response. Then he gave a short nod. "I'll consider it. Thanks."

"Good." Considering it would no doubt lead him to the logical conclusion.

For now, the closer they got to home, the more Devereaux's thoughts whirled around the other half of his life. And the tighter his frown pulled. What had she been thinking? He understood the tug of family, but he had specifically told her they would accept an invitation when he got back. *Together*. That most certainly did not mean making a theater appearance with...with an employee. A guard.

He cast a glance at Osborne as they pulled onto Monument Square. Irritation spurted, but he pushed it down. It wasn't his fault he'd been pulled into it. No, that was all Lane. And while Devereaux didn't expect to ever get an apology from the old man, he would get a few answers from Marietta. She should have known better. She must have known better. She must have done it deliberately, which was inexcusable.

By the time he climbed down and strode toward the family home, the fire was a steady burn in his chest. He let himself in the front door, too impatient to wait for doddering old Norris to answer a knock, and nearly bowled into Jess.

"Lawsy!" The old woman splayed a dark hand over her chest. "Mr. Dev, you plumb scared me to death!"

He forced a smile. "Where is Marietta?"

She huffed out a breath and shook her head. "Don't rightly know, sir. Though yo mama's in the drawin' room and looking better 'n I seen her in a year."

Maybe Mother knew where Marietta was. And even if not, he needed to greet her too. "I'll head her way then."

A glance over his shoulder confirmed that Osborne had disappeared, wisely. Devereaux strode into the ground-floor drawing room, a smile ready for his mother to cover the anger simmering below.

"Devereaux!" She rose when he entered, putting aside her mending and not so much as faltering on her way up. That did his heart good, as did the bloom of healthy color in her cheeks as she held out her hands.

He took them in his, noting that her skin no longer felt so fragile and papery, and leaned over to kiss her cheek. "Good day, Mother. Look at you, glowing with health. Have you had a pleasant week?"

"Not as pleasant as this one will be, now that you are home." She gripped his fingers, her smile bright. "How was your trip?"

"Excellent." He urged her back down into her chair but didn't take one of his own. "Is Mari here?"

The usual sour look entered her eyes at mention of Marietta. "I believe so. Probably with that Barbara woman."

Right. *Her.* Surely Marietta would tire of the good deed soon and send the woman away. He didn't like having a Unionist stranger living right above his castle. And he still couldn't figure why Marietta had taken her in to begin with.

It must be some feeling of debt to her so-dubbed saint of a dead brother.

"Don't worry, Mother." Not in the mood to seek all over the grounds for her, he sat after all. His anger would hold. "We've already discussed it. As soon as we wed, that woman leaves."

Mother sighed. "Perhaps you could just buy the house from her. Have you considered that? Then they can both leave."

His fingers curled into the arm of his chair. "I don't just want the house. I want Marietta as my wife."

And he would have both, whatever it took.

Marietta closed the book and made a quick series of signs. "Good job, Elsie." She glanced up at Walker, Cora, and Barbara too, grinning. "And the rest of you. Though not quite as good."

Cora's laugh rang out as she helped the little one from her seat. Blond curls bobbing, the toddler bounced her way to the floor and ran to the window where she'd left her doll.

Watching her, Marietta's heart fisted. Perhaps she had never yearned as much as Paulina and Laura, but looking at Elsie made her wonder. If she had ever conceived, would her child have looked like Elsie? Been so sweet natured?

Probably not. Her children probably would have been doomed to foul tempers and conniving spirits and abounding selfishness. But maybe, just maybe, her blood would have created someone more like Stephen.

Not an issue now. She would never again make the same mistake with a man she had with Dev, and as for marrying again...no. She would count herself blessed beyond measure if she escaped from Dev and wouldn't tempt fate again.

Elsie rose to her toes to look out the window and then turned back to them with familiar curiosity in her eyes. How Marietta loved watching the little one look upon her world these past three weeks, now that she could ask for the names of things. She made the most familiar of her signs, the first two fingers of her right hand tapping against the first two of her left. *Name.*

Marietta joined her at the window and crouched to peer out with her. "What do you see, precious?"

Elsie pointed at the two men descending from the carriage parked across the street and striding for her front door.

Marietta swallowed. Dev was home, and his gait looked none too happy.

Elsie made the sign for *name* again and pointed at him.

They had already introduced her to Slade on Friday when he had shown up for a lesson, claiming Barbara had invited him. Barbara admitted she had, but Marietta suspected it had been pure disbelief that had led him here, not a desire to learn. He had looked utterly bemused when they created a sign for his name for Elsie's use, and he hadn't lingered after the lesson to talk.

He hadn't lingered around her house much at all. That hour was the only time she'd done more than catch a glimpse of him since the theater on Wednesday. Wise. But painful.

Now she cleared her throat and watched Dev storm into her house. Was it cowardly to be glad she was out here, where he would never think to look for her? He would find his mother instead, and seeing her so well would perhaps mollify him.

She drummed up a smile for Elsie. "That's Mr. Dev." She spelled it out, though more to establish habit than anything because the child was too young to understand spelling.

Walker crouched down on the other side of his daughter, formed his hands into a *D* and made the sign for *bad*. "Mr. Dev." He made the sign again.

"Walker." Marietta pressed a cold hand to her forehead. "She knows what that means."

Amusement and challenge winked from his blue-gray eyes. "Can you think of a better way to describe him?"

She sealed her lips as Elsie practiced the sign. Perhaps associating him with the word wasn't such a terrible idea. It would impress on the girl the need to stay away from him. And even if he saw it, he wouldn't know what it meant.

No doubt Walker recognized her sigh as capitulation.

Cora joined them with a muted smile and touched her little girl on the arm to get her attention, and then she pressed her palms together at the side of her face. "Nap time, baby."

Elsie hooked her doll under her arm, popped her thumb into her mouth, and stretched toward her mother. Cora gathered her close and met Marietta's gaze as she stood. "Thank you, Miss Mari."

"Rest well." She kept the smile in place until Cora turned, but then her gaze strayed back out the window, to Slade striding toward the carriage house. Her breath tangled in her chest, and she barely eked out an "Excuse me" before she darted for the door.

Hurrying down the rickety stairs, she touched a hand to the pocket hidden in the folds of her gray satin skirt. The silver chain was where it had been the past five days, still secure inside the muslin pocket she put on each morning under her dress. As if she would really give it to him today any more than she had any other day.

It wasn't done. A woman didn't just make expensive gifts to a man, even if it had cost her nothing. Even if her sister-in-law had taken the matching watch and insisted that, yes, the fob should be put to use by one who needed it.

Marietta couldn't convince herself to put the chain away once she'd realized how closely Stephen's old one matched the one she had seen Slade pull out time and again. But neither could she bring herself to give it to him. She knew well he would refuse it even if she worked up the courage to offer it.

Still. She couldn't shake the feeling that Stephen would have wanted him to have it. Which made absolutely no sense. So it would likely remain in her pocket indefinitely.

She pivoted at the base of the stairs and found Slade a few steps away, frowning.

"Where's your wrap?"

"Hmm? Oh." She clasped her hands to her elbows where the shawl had been earlier, finding only the black cording at the edge of her gray sleeve, the lighter fabric of her undersleeves beneath it. "I must have left it on my chair." She folded her arms around herself, having no idea what else she meant to say to him.

And society had once called her a silver-tongued flirt.

Slade's face slid into one of its usual looks, challenge mixed with cynicism. "In that much of a hurry to see Hughes?"

"No, not him." The words felt at home on her lips, yet the tone came out wrong, uncertain. What was the matter with her? She cleared her throat. "He looked upset."

"Yeah, I...your granddad came to see me yesterday."

Her eyes went wide. He hadn't stopped by to see her. "Why?"

His lips curved into a smile. "To recommend I blame the theater gossip on him, and that I admit it to Hughes first thing."

"Did you?" That would explain the anger.

He nodded. "Lane's a smart man. I'm still alive."

Laughter tickled. Slight and low, but it brought much-needed relief to her chest. "He has instincts like none other. And I am glad they were right."

"Me too." He took a step back. "I wanted to make sure our stories agree. He convinced us both to go and then introduced me as your friend."

Apparently he hadn't assumed she would opt for the truthful explanation. Or perhaps that she hadn't the sense to end it there and let Dev think the gossips had overdone the reports of them being there together.

Would that they had.

Her throat felt tight and dry as she forced a swallow. Relaxing her arms, she squared her shoulders and stepped away from the wooden stairs. "I might as well get this over with. If you'll excuse me, Slade."

Rather than step aside as she moved past him, he fell in beside her. "I'll see you in."

"Not necessary."

"It is." He stayed a step away from her, kept his eyes straight ahead. "We both know he's a violent man."

And so, like the day she brought Barbara home, Slade would hover outside the room, ready to rush to her aid? She shook her head. "I can handle Dev."

Still he didn't so much as glance at her. "Humor me."

He wasn't leaving her much choice, but it grated. If she meant nothing to him, if his feelings were only "wanting," why did he have to concern himself? "I really don't think he would hurt me. He loves me."

Slade snorted and finally glanced her way. For all of a quarter second. "Yeah. That's what my sister says about her husband. While sporting a black eye."

She couldn't help but wince. "I didn't realize you had a sister."

"I do. So humor me."

Marietta tucked her hands under the wide bells of her sleeves. Her fingerless gloves were more for style than warmth. "What's her name?"

"Jane."

Jane. Watching her step to be sure she avoided all the mud from Saturday's rain, she searched her mind. "You've never mentioned her."

This time his snort was a laugh. "Ross was her favorite."

She would have liked to probe deeper, but she couldn't be sure he would answer even were they alone, much less when they were three steps from the entrance she had aimed them at. So she bit her tongue and kept her face neutral as she brushed by him to get through the door he held open.

Mother Hughes's voice came from the drawing room, Dev's baritone joining it, though the words were indistinct. She took a silent step to the side. The allure of getting this reunion over with evaporated.

Maybe she could slip by without being noticed to steal a few minutes in her room.

A fine thought until Slade let the door slam shut, thereby announcing her presence to the entire house. She spun, her eyes wide, expecting to find him looking sheepish and blaming it on the draft.

But no. He was grinning. He even winked at her before his face moved back into its usual lines, eyes going cold and hard. *Winked.*

And gracious, why did she feel like a schoolgirl around him lately, always at sixes and sevens? Desperate to get hold of herself before Dev emerged, she drew in a deep breath and let her own countenance empty of all but the old Marietta and her mask. The one that could dangle keys before Slade's nose with a flirtatious tilt to her lips.

The one who had the man striding from the drawing room with fury in his eyes wrapped around her little finger.

Perhaps she didn't feel it, but her mouth knew the right smile to put on, and her fingers just how to curl as she held out a hand to him and rushed forward. At least, having an audience as they did, he wouldn't expect too warm a welcome.

Slade's plan? She was indebted to him for it.

"Darling! Oh, how I missed you." She stopped a few inches too close as he took her hand and raised it to his lips, a glance over her shoulder at Slade to prove why she didn't do more than rest a hand on his arm. "I didn't expect you until later this afternoon."

"I was eager to be home." He let go her hand and clapped his fingers around her arm like a cuff. The second time he had made such a move in a fortnight, and it infuriated her as much now as it had the first time. He looked over her head to Slade. "Where did you find her?"

"Excuse me?" She pulled her arm free. "Did you sic your bloodhound on me, Devereaux?"

Slade, she hoped, would be amused and not insulted, though she couldn't tell by the quiet huff that could have been either laughter or indignation.

Dev gripped her arm again and tugged her down the hall. "I didn't have to. He knew I wanted to talk to you. And now if you'll excuse us, Mr. Osborne."

Determined not to be forced anywhere, she wrenched her arm free again and stormed into the dining room—the nearest empty chamber. No acting was required to keep her face pulled tight in fury as she turned on him. "I will *not* be spied on in my own home by that—that—"

"At a loss for words, are you, darling?" Though he smiled, it snapped and sparked. He advanced so quickly she retreated by sheer instinct, until the table's edge bit into her hip. Dev rested his arm on the back of the chair beside her, boxing her in. "Get used to it. I intend to keep him around."

Perhaps that too was part of Slade's purpose in announcing her. He had made himself more indispensable. Marietta rested a hand on Dev's chest to keep some space between them. "And what if I don't want him around?"

Dev snorted, gruff and unamused, as he dropped a hand to her waist and yanked her closer. "A strange question, given the rumors flying about the two of you. Really, Mari. Going to the theater with him?"

What could she do but lift her chin and force haughty amusement into her gaze as she would have done before her world shifted? "Marietta Arnaud Hughes on the arm of a—" Casting around for the right words, Slade's own found her tongue. "—two-bit detective? Laughable."

"I'm not laughing." His hand slid up her back, light but unyielding. Each point of contact seeming to brand her, to claim that she was his. And she had no room to argue. She had given him that, given him the right to touch and demand. She had forfeited herself to him. She shuddered, but he either assumed it from pleasure or just didn't care. His nose traced her cheek. "I didn't wait four years to call you my own just to hear your name linked with someone else's."

He knew how she hated it when he did that, referring to her years of marriage to Lucien as nothing but a nuisance to his courtship. "Dev—"

"Why did you do something so foolish? You know how people talk. Were you angry with me, is that it? Because we had to withdraw from the Ellicotts'?"

A shifting shadow in the hallway caught her eye. She could see only the edge of Slade's sleeve, but it was enough to make the anger twist its way into self-loathing. Why did he have to witness her shame? Again?

To Dev's question she shook her head. "Why would I be angry over something to which I am so accustomed? Lucien did the same thing all the—"

"Do *not* compare me to him!"

She saw Slade slide forward even as she drew her head back. No doubt he was ready to spring into action if Dev's hands turned to fists, and for a moment she feared they would. But then she looked in his eyes.

Beneath the anger pulsed pain, strong enough that for a moment she remembered only how she had loved him so recently, and how he loved her still. He had been wrong, so very wrong, to try to lure her away from Lucien, but that did not make his feelings any less real, did it?

"Dev." She rested her palm against his cheek and wished life could be as simple as marrying him and being happy. "I meant only that you have the same responsibilities and I understand them."

He drew in a long breath, and some of the fire went out of his eyes. Then he bent down, trailed his lips down her neck, and held her close.

She dared another glance at the doorway. Her gaze collided with Slade's, but she read no relief in it, certainly no approval. He didn't nod, didn't smile, didn't even smirk. He just blinked once, his nostrils flared. And then he disappeared from view. Gone without a sound.

A tremor started in her stomach and swept its way upward, lodging in her throat.

"Darling." Dev anchored a hand at the base of her neck, under the lace net holding her hair. "Forgive me if I am cross. It is only my impatience making me so." He tilted her head, kissed her jaw. Not so long ago, delight would have raced through her veins instead of ice. "I hate anyone thinking for even a moment that you belong to someone else. You're mine."

His arms were iron bands around her, but she could escape them if she must. The ones around her spirit, though...how was she to break free of those?

His hand moved down her back again and settled at her waist. "Commission yourself a new gown, darling. Something breathtaking and exquisite. We'll find the most well-attended gathering, and you'll wear it there with me. We'll set the wagging tongues aright."

A new gown. A ball. A life that held no shine anymore. But if he would leave it at that, then she would agree to the wasted expense. She pulled away, knowing her smile was tight. "All right."

"Mari." The hand on her neck held her in place and forced her to look up at him. "No doubt you know this, but...if we need to wed sooner. If you are..."

Heat rushed her cheeks, and she made no effort to tamp it down. Some things ought to be blushed over. She shook her head.

When she saw the disappointment shadow his eyes, the sting of heat shifted. She gave him a push, not as forcefully as she would have liked to. "You can't be sorry about that. I would have been ruined."

"Nonsense. There would have been talk for a few days, that is all." Though he retreated a step and let his hands fall, his brow remained in its condescending arch. "You know as well as I that at least half your friends have engaged in affairs. It is hardly a novelty."

Perhaps that was true, but it hardly made it right. "I had never thought to be one of them."

Given the irritation flickering again in his eyes, she expected another retort. Instead, he backed away a step and brought his expression under control. "Your conscience will be assuaged as soon as we are married. In the meantime, pay a visit to your seamstress."

"Certainly." Because the smile felt so false, she curled her fingers tight to her palm. They came to a rest against her skirt, where the silver links were hidden.

"I had best get caught up on correspondence." He measured her a moment, smiled, and then turned to the door.

Somehow she wasn't surprised when he stopped in the threshold, when his gaze went sharp again. "Where were you when I got home? Certainly not on a promenade without a wrap."

Again her hands went to her empty elbows. She must make it a point to keep better track of her shawls. "Making sure Cora is resting. If she doesn't, she can barely move by the end of the day."

He was still for a moment, but his nod looked satisfied. "Very well. But I would prefer you not spend too much time out there. I have never much cared for that half-breed groom."

A defense sprang to her tongue, but she bit it back. She had never had a nice thing to say about Walker in Dev's presence before. She had best not start now.

Dev's gaze went smug. "And I trust you've seen the brat and realize it is Lucien's, from the look of her."

Lucien's? Devereaux knew exactly what he had done to Cora, yet he would try to cast the blame on his brother? Her jaw went tight, but she held the threads of anger tight. "I've seen her."

"And still concern yourself with the mother. You make a fine mistress, darling." With a confident grin in place, he exited the room.

Marietta leaned back into the table, slid her hand into her pocket, and let the warm silver links wrap round her fingers.

Twenty-One

Walker nestled closer to Cora, trying to hold tight to his dream of sunshine and orioles. But an incessant tapping pulled him toward wakefulness.

"You gonna see who's at the door, honey?"

"Hmm?" Walker blinked his eyes open to darkness and groaned. "No. Let 'em come back in the morning."

"Walk."

"I know, I know." He pushed himself up, careful to avoid putting any pressure on the growing mound of babe his hand had been resting upon, pausing only long enough to press a kiss to Cora's sleep-warm cheek. Clumsy fingers fumbling with clothes already set out, he hissed at the unceasing knocking.

Probably Hez. The man was a night owl. Walker didn't know how Paulina tolerated him. Or maybe Mr. Lane, who, the whole family knew, would chase a whim any time of day or night. Or...he wrenched open the door and frowned. "Osborne?"

He'd scarcely seen the detective in the last two weeks since Hughes returned from his trip. Seemed he always had Osborne off on some errand or another, or else he was in the big house where Walker wasn't welcome. He leaned into the doorframe. "This had better be good."

Osborne glanced at the darkened interior of Walker's home. "I need your help."

He grabbed his coat, stepped out, and closed the door behind him. "It can't wait until daylight?"

"Come morning, Hughes will have me busy again." He turned and headed down the stairs, motioning for Walker to follow.

He did, but with a laborious sigh. When they gained the stables, though, the sweet smell of hay wrapped around him and eased his grumpiness. "All right. What is it?"

Osborne stepped close, no doubt so he could pitch his voice low. "The Knights are planning to kidnap Lincoln today."

Well, that woke him up in a hurry. Walker muttered a "Thunder and turf!" and rubbed a hand over his face. "I thought when the inauguration passed without incident..."

"No opportunity opened up beforehand, but today the president is conducting a review of the troops, and he'll be unprotected."

Of all the stupid... "Unprotected? Don't your friends in Washington know he ain't never safe?"

Osborne breathed a nearly silent laugh. "With all the turmoil of the war, I think Pinkerton has spread them thin. They're even using off-duty police officers as guards."

And the Knights were getting desperate, Walker knew. "What do you need me to do?"

"Get a note to my friend. He's the only one who still...who I trust to listen to a warning." In the darkness of the stables, Walker could barely make out Osborne reaching into his pocket and pulling out a thin square that rustled like paper. "I can't risk a telegram, not with the wires originating at Hughes's rail station."

"Encode it." The answer—an obvious one to him, given the Culpers' history with codes—tripped off his tongue before he could think to stop it. Though he wished, when Osborne froze, he could take it back. He shouldn't be allowed to speak before he had a stiff cup of coffee in the morning.

"We haven't established a cipher." At least he didn't sound suspicious, just frustrated. "Should have, but..."

Walker reached out and took the paper. "Is this the message?"

"His address. Will you be able to read it?"

A perfectly valid question for someone to ask a Negro man, even a free one. But Walker couldn't help but snort a laugh. "You *do* realize I was Stephen Arnaud's best friend, right? Owner of all those books you've been reading?"

"Good. I can't risk paying Herschel a visit today, not when I have to meet the others. If you could find him, though, and tell him to change Lincoln's route at the last minute. That's all it will take to foil them."

"I can handle that." Going to Washington hadn't been in his plans for the day, but no doubt Marietta would agree that this was more important than the trip to the hospital the womenfolk had planned. "Gotta ask, though...you really trust me with this?"

Osborne shoved his hands into his pockets. "I'm short on allies, and I can't ask Marietta to help here."

Walker tucked the folded paper into his pocket to examine when he had light. Then he paused. "You trust her these days?"

A beat of silence was the only response he could discern in the low light. "Don't you?"

"Yeah. But we've known each other all our lives." He knew the old Yetta, not just the socialite. The woman so long slumbering under the mask of hurt—and the determination not to feel the hurt.

How much of her did Osborne know? He shouldn't trust the mask... and if she'd lowered it, then they had some talking to do, him and her.

Osborne hummed, low and quick. "One minute I think I have her figured, and then the next..."

"It ain't too hard." He buttoned up his coat and fished thick gloves from his pockets. "The way she seems to be...well, that's my fault."

He could all but hear her screaming at him in his head, telling him he had no business letting Slade in on the secret no one else knew, aside from themselves and Cora. And maybe he didn't. Maybe it was just the lack of sleep forcing the words past his lips.

But he couldn't shake the feeling that this man would respect her the more if he knew all she'd been willing to give up, once, to follow her heart.

"Your fault." The measured, flat tone of caution possessed Osborne's voice. "How so?"

"I hurt her." Walker tugged his gloves on, welcoming the insulation from the cold March air. "We'd been planning to run off together. Go north and get married."

Though shadows cloaked Osborne's face, they sure didn't do anything to mute the surprised inhale.

Walker smiled into the darkness. "I know. Wouldn't think it of her, would you? Fine, rich white girl like her willing to give up everything for a quadroon whose life goal was to work with horses."

"No. I wouldn't have." Osborne's voice was quiet as a thought.

"No one did. Look, I've been judged all my life for my mixed blood and the fact I ain't got a father. Most folks don't know my mama was attacked, and if they did, they wouldn't care." But it was something he'd never been able to get past. Something he sure couldn't let Cora and her unrequested babe go through alone when he found her sobbing in a horse's stall. "Yetta never judged. Never looked at me like I was less."

The breath whispered back out. "What happened, then?"

"I told Stephen. He talked me out of it." Though his companion wouldn't be able to see, he shook his head. "Looking back, I know it was the right decision. But I didn't handle it right. I was going to take off and not tell her, and when she caught me leaving—well, we both said things we shouldn't have. I broke her heart, Oz, plain and simple."

"You're the one she was trying to hurt by marrying a slave owner."

Sounded right, but not coming from him. "She told you that?"

"Yeah." He turned but didn't walk back through the door. "Why are you working here if it ended so badly?"

"Stephen. He made me promise when he signed up that I would watch out for her. He never trusted the Hugheses. He made *her* promise to provide me a job."

"Right." He laughed again, nearly silently. "Marietta and her unexpected good deeds. And here I was surprised she wanted to volunteer at the hospital today with Barbara."

Walker's quiet laugh joined Osborne's. "Me too. Yetta and the sight of blood don't mix, though I doubt she admitted that to Barbara."

Osborne didn't reply to that, but when he went to the door, he paused again, a silhouette against the scrap of moonlight seeping through the clouds. "I could use your prayers today."

Walker aimed his feet toward the tack room, because he certainly wasn't about to take one of Hughes's trains to Washington. "You have them."

A moment later the doorway was empty. Walker shook his head and fetched a saddle. It only took him a few minutes to rouse a horse, get her ready, and slip back upstairs to kiss Elsie's slumbering cheek and whisper to Cora that he would be gone a few hours.

Rather than head straight out of Baltimore Walker headed for the familiar house he always associated with grandfathers—his own and the Arnauds'. Grandpa Henry and Gram Em would be warm in their bed above the Lane carriage house, but somehow he wasn't surprised to see a light burning in the drawing room window of the main house. And he wouldn't have come if he hadn't mostly expected just that.

Thad Lane met him at the kitchen door with a cup of coffee. "I've been up praying. Where are you headed, Walk?"

"Washington, for Osborne. He says the KGC is planning to kidnap Lincoln today if they can." He took a sip of the steaming coffee and breathed a happy inhale. "He wants me to let one of his friends know."

Mr. Lane nodded and took a sip of his own coffee. "Better not linger too long here, then."

Walker shifted from foot to foot. "I just wanted to make sure...do you want me to leave it to Pinkerton's men? Or I could stick around the city for the day."

"No." As usual, Mr. Lane's answer was quick as confidence but soft as wonderment. "This is their job, and they're doing it. Ours is to help where we can quietly. If we get too involved, they'll start asking questions we don't want to answer."

A sigh worked its way up and out. "But we could do more, Mr. Lane."

"We always could do more. That doesn't mean we always should." His smile made wrinkles fan out. "Much as we all like to be the hero, this one isn't for us."

"But—"

"The Culpers saved a president once. We have prevented the Knights from their tasks many times over the last few years. But this..." He took a sip of his coffee, his gaze somewhere past Walker's shoulder. "This one is for Oz to handle."

Walker savored the warmth from the mug, though he was none too sure about the advice. "You've taken to him awful fast."

Mr. Lane chuckled. "Maybe. But I have a feeling he will be around for a while, so why withhold my approval?"

Maybe he wasn't fully awake yet. "How long you think this job will keep him here? I figured a few months at the most."

"I'm not talking about the job." Mr. Lane met his gaze and grinned. "You haven't noticed the way they look at each other? Oz and Mari?"

Walker nearly choked on the sip of coffee he'd just taken. "I noticed how he looks at her. How has she been looking at him?"

Now his host's gaze went soft, yet it focused on him like artillery. "The same way she used to look at you."

He had known? Walker pinched the bridge of his nose. Of course he had known. Thaddeus Lane knew everything that went on in his family. "I guess we oughta pray this isn't as big a mistake as that was, then."

He wasn't about to make a judgment as quickly as Mr. Lane did.

"You have a nice cold ride to fill with prayers." The old man gripped Walker's shoulder. "Take the coffee."

"Thanks." He slipped back outside and onto his horse, willing the sun to come up and warm him. Pointing the mare's nose in the right direction, he set his thoughts toward prayer.

As dawn touched its rose-gold fingers to the horizon, he wished Stephen were here to talk to. If ever he needed his friend's placid eyes and ready laugh, it was...always. Now, yes, but every other now between Gettysburg and today too. Some folks you just never stopped missing. Never stopped needing. Marietta was lucky to be able to call up his face, his words whenever she pleased. Walker's memories were fuzzy around the edges, but still sharp enough to slice.

When the first buildings of Washington appeared in the distance, he took the slip of paper from his pocket and read the direction in the soft morning light. Then he just stared at the hand—quick and efficient, but with the flourish of an educated man. Walker could write like that too, having taken his lessons beside the Arnaud boys, but he never chose to. It didn't make sense for him. He'd learned early on that a man with any black in him had better not put on airs, not in the South. That would get him nowhere but on the kitchen table, his anxious mother patching up his wounds.

Osborne didn't put on airs either. Maybe his clothes were nice, but he only had a couple sets of them. Maybe he dined in the big house, but from what Cora said, he was careful to keep his distance from the masters. He was a hired man. One who lived on his wits, not on his daddy's bank account.

Walker could respect that. It didn't mean the man was right for Marietta, but…it wasn't a mark against him, his common-stock origins. More one in his favor, to Walker's way of thinking. She needed someone who could see beneath the pretty. He wasn't sure Osborne could, but Mr. Lane was usually right about these things.

The streets of Washington soon surrounded him, and he put aside all thoughts but finding the right building. He eventually did, an aging boardinghouse near the Capitol, and by then enough people were out and about that his knock on the back door was quickly answered by a woman who looked as old as the building.

She motioned him into the warm kitchen. "Morning. What brings you here?"

Walker swept his hat off his head with a smile. "I'm looking for Fred Herschel, ma'am."

"He just came down for breakfast. I'll fetch him."

No offer of coffee or food, but that was all right. Walker was grateful for the warmth from the stove and eager to be back on his way. So he was glad when a man sauntered into the kitchen, still wiping his mouth with a napkin. His stopped when he spotted Walker. "What can I do for you?"

He didn't see anyone else lingering about, but wisdom dictated a quiet tone and vague words. "Your friend Oz sent me. Said to tell you to change the route today, and at the last minute. There's trouble afoot."

Herschel measured him for a long moment, though a brief smile at last touched the corner of his mouth. "I suppose I shouldn't worry too much about your being on the other side."

The very thought drew a breath of laughter from Walker's lips.

Even if his mind were twisted enough to want to join the Knights of the Golden Circle, they wouldn't ever take anyone whose blood was part Negro. "No, sir."

"Tell him to consider it done." Without another word, the man pivoted and sauntered back out.

Walker had gotten up at four, in the black of a frigid night, for a thirty-second exchange?

It was easy to see where Herschel and Osborne would get along.

Twenty-Two

I'm so glad you could join me today, Mari."

Marietta summoned a smile that she hoped convinced Barbara she was glad too, though she had a difficult time forcing her gaze from the window of the carriage. "As am I." Mostly. Though her stomach threatened to heave at the mere mention of a hospital. Heaven help them all if they asked her to change a bandage.

But being always in the company of a woman so very good and selfless made her determined to try something other than rolling bandages and stitching sashes. Something to quiet this twisting in her chest she didn't understand.

"Are you all right? You look...perplexed."

"Do I?" Try as she might to laugh that away, it was no doubt true. Part of her was eager to arrive at the hospital at which Stephen had once volunteered, which she had not seen since it was a family home. Part of her recoiled at the imagined sights and smells.

And part of her was none too sure her confusion had a whit to do with that. Sighing, she gave up on the familiar streets leading to the edges of Baltimore and focused on her friend. "I feel strange, Barbara." She splayed a gloved hand over her chest. "An urgency, almost, though I cannot understand why."

"Hmm." Barbara's gaze went unfocused for a moment, and then her usual serene smile touched her lips. "It sounds as though the Spirit may be asking you to pray."

With a long blink and a tongue that seemed unable to wrap itself around words, Marietta shook her head, slowly. Not in rejection but in shock. "But why would the Lord ask *me* to pray?"

Her friend chuckled and reached across the space between them to grasp her hand. "It is all part of your burgeoning relationship with Him."

Was it? She held fast to Barbara's fingers. "I have spent hours lately studying the Scriptures, sermons, dwelling on what Stephen once told me, and still I..." Unable to meet her friend's guileless eyes, she resorted to the window again. "During the day, I feel as though I am finally beginning to understand. Then when Dev shows up for dinner, it is as though chains are cuffed to my wrists and ankles. How does one escape one's past, Barbara? How?"

"Mari." Her tone, gently insistent, bade Marietta look at her again. When she did, she had a feeling Barbara saw everything with her solemn, accepting gaze. All her guilt, all her sin, all her fear. "You have prayed for forgiveness from your sins. Have you prayed for freedom from their bonds?"

"Freedom?" It wasn't a word one could toss around lightly these days. "How am I to pray for freedom when I have slaves under my roof? Would that not make me the biggest hypocrite in the state?"

Barbara chuckled and squeezed her hand. "Not by far. As wretched as I believe physical slavery is, men and women of greater faith than mine are on the opposite side of this war." She drew in a deep breath, her expression as conflicted as Marietta had ever seen it. "Stephen and I spent much time trying to reconcile the differing views with a similar faith. And then at last we realized we didn't have to, because God so very rarely tells us what society should do—rather, He tells us how *we*, as believers, should behave in whatever society to which we belong."

Their eyes met again, and again Barbara's smile shone forth. "Never once in the Bible does God speak either for or against physical slavery. But spiritual slavery—that is a topic He addresses time and again. Over and over Paul pleads with the early church to embrace the freedom of the soul that Christ offers. You must do that, Mari. You must cling, not just to cleansing, but to freedom."

Stephen had said something similar once. *Not just salvation, but redemption.* Redemption again—God had not just taken her sins from her, He had purchased her. And she could not be both God's and Dev's, not when their wills were in opposition.

The carriage rocked to a halt, and she looked out again to see the once-familiar mansion previously called Maryland Square. Her breath stuck in her chest. This was where she had met Lucien, at a ball in the spring of 1860, before the Steuarts' property had been seized because of their Confederate sympathies. Now, rather than rolling acres of gardens, long barrack-like buildings flanked it, row upon row of yellow walls and black roofs. A wooden sign read *Jarvis US General Hospital.*

There would be no music spilling from the windows, no gaiety within the halls. Marietta pulled her cloak tight and reclaimed her hand from Barbara's so she could grip her reticule. So much had changed in their world in the last five years. It was only fitting that this, too, should be so different.

"Do you still get ill at the sight of blood?"

Marietta's head snapped back toward her companion, and she found her grinning. "Stephen mentioned that?"

"It came up when we first met. That is why I never asked you to join me."

She drew in a bracing breath when Pat opened the door and offered her a hand down. "I don't know if it will or not. I have avoided it so long. I suppose we shall see."

Barbara followed her out and patted her arm. "You can begin by helping the men with their correspondence."

"Perfect." Dictation was something she could do all but in her sleep. She would give half her attention to the men laid out upon the rows of cots...and the other half could focus on praying for Slade.

Slade didn't have to feign an anxiousness to match his companion's. As he stroked the nose of his horse, he looked from the street to Booth. The afternoon had ticked away, an hour gone and then two. With each passing minute, the spring wound tighter.

Seven of them had ridden out that afternoon from the boarding house John Surratt's mother owned. They had taken up their positions along Lincoln's route with each detail planned, every contingency explored.

All except this one—that the president didn't come this way at all. *Lord, let that be what happened. Let Hersh have changed the route.*

But he couldn't know, not for sure. He and Booth were stationed at the last point, with the carriage meant to convey Lincoln to Richmond as fast as the horses could fly. They had seen no one all afternoon.

"He must have been delayed setting out for the review, that's all." Booth still held his riding crop, his horse's flank quivering every time he slapped it to his palm.

He'd made the same observation at least fifteen times in the past two hours. Slade had long ago given up responding to it. Instead, he gave his horse one last pat on the nose and turned to the table they had claimed when they first arrived at the tavern on the outskirts of Washington.

Anything could have happened. Maybe Hersh had sent guards instead of changing the route. Maybe Lincoln did come along this road, Surratt and Atzerodt had jumped out at him as planned, and a gunfight had ensued. Mr. Lincoln could be injured or killed. Hersh could be too. Exactly what Slade had hoped to avoid.

Now wasn't the time for violence or to make arrests. Not with Hughes uninvolved in this scheme, and whatever had kept him so busy still tauntingly beyond Slade's understanding. He couldn't make his move yet, and he couldn't risk scaring the whole KGC underground. He had to wait and make sure none of their plans came to fruition before he could determine what, exactly, Hughes was up to.

He took a sip of the coffee that had long ago gone cold and caught Booth's gaze. "It's getting dark."

The actor muttered a curse and dashed the whip to the ground. "I know. He wouldn't wait this long to start out. Something has gone awry."

"Rendezvous, then?"

Booth bent down to snatch his crop, his expression thunderous enough to make Slade wonder if he wouldn't rather snap it in two. "I suppose we must. Blast it! What could have gone wrong? The plan was perfect."

Indeed, it had been. If the first two men failed for some reason, there were another two waiting beyond them. And another pair after that, each with a carriage ready to mask their movements. And finally him and Booth, ready as a final line if all before them failed. Or, if they were successful, to supervise the transportation into Confederate territory.

Slade had spent much of the day praying it wouldn't come to that. If it did, he would have no choice but to show his true loyalties...and that was unlikely to end well.

His only answer to Booth now was to swing up into the saddle. And pray that his relief didn't show in his face. "Maybe the others know more."

"Of course they do." Booth huffed once more but mounted his horse. "'The best laid schemes of mice and men,' I suppose."

Slade's borrowed mare moved of her own volition into a trot and tossed her head when he pulled her back to a walk to await Booth. He would have preferred to let the beast have her head, company be dashed, but he wasn't entirely certain he remembered the way back to the Surratt boarding house given the serpentine route they had taken from it earlier that afternoon.

When Booth drew even with him, curious amusement colored his gaze. "The tavern keeper seemed to be trying to place you earlier. Have you stopped here before?"

"No." But he'd noticed the narrow-eyed stare too. And it made him wonder if maybe Ross had. "He might have met my brother at some point, though."

"Are you and your brother often confused?"

Slade snorted a laugh. Perhaps not as often as one would expect of identical twins, given that Ross had always had his clothes neatly pressed, his hair perfectly combed, and his behavior well under control, whereas Slade had...not. Never once had anyone tried to blame perfect Ross for any of Slade's sins. Why, then, did his brother seem to demand retribution for Slade's very being, and only after he'd changed? Why did it now fall to him to clean up the mess again, when he had already done it once, with his own life?

"More often than either of us liked."

"Hmm." No suspicion entered the actor's eyes, thankfully. "Such things always put me in mind of Shakespeare's comedies of errors. Mistaken identity—a classic device, which the Bard so skillfully put to use. Have you ever seen *Much Ado About Nothing?*"

Slade had a vague recollection of it being performed in a Chicago theater he had visited before a game of cards one evening. A brief nod was sufficient, he knew, to fuel Booth on in his talk of plays.

"I prefer the tragedies and histories, but Shakespeare knew how to write a comedy, to be sure." Booth guided his mount to the left, glancing at Slade as he followed. "Where is he now?"

He couldn't know how the question punched. "Dead."

"My apologies. Must have been hard to lose a brother." Booth's voice went soft, barely discernable over the clop of horse hooves over cobblestones. "I am the ninth of ten children, myself. My brother Edwin and I have always been rivals. He is an actor as well, you know."

"I'd heard."

Booth laughed, tight and short. "And he's a Unionist, of all things. Still, he is my brother. And a dratted fine Hamlet, though perish me if I ever admit it to him."

Slade chuckled because it was necessary, but the sound was a lie. Good humor had no place in him right now. How could it? Even among enemies, sympathy hit whenever he heard of the unseen ravages of this endless war. Loyalties divided, houses divided, families divided.

His father had once preached a sermon on how the End of Days was always at hand. It was hard to deny in this gray world. *When ye shall hear of wars and rumours of wars, be ye not troubled: for such things must needs be; but the end shall not be yet.*

Booth swore under his breath. "I cannot believe we failed again. What do you suppose went awry?"

"Hard to say." But Slade noted that the man's shoulders bunched up, his jaw pulsed. With the Confederacy faltering more each day, with the end in sight, failure would not sit well with any of the Knights. *These are the beginnings of sorrows.*

"We were so thorough. So careful." Booth's fingers went tight on his reins.

But whatsoever shall be given you in that hour, that speak ye: for it is not ye that speak, but the Holy Ghost. Slade drew in a long breath. "We always are." Yet had always failed.

God willing, they always would. Even if it had cost Slade so very dearly already. *Now the brother shall betray the brother to death...*

"I know. Blast it, I know. Perhaps we weren't careful enough. Perhaps there were spies about as we rode into town."

Spies. Though his throat went dry, Slade resisted the urge to swallow. Not a tell he wanted to indulge around an actor schooled at expression. *And ye shall be hated of all men for my name's sake.* He lifted his brows.

Booth huffed out a breath. "Unlikely, I know. But we haven't the leisure for unlikely foils, not anymore. Time is too short."

But he that shall endure unto the end, the same shall be saved.

Had he dared, he would have whispered a prayer that it be so, that the Lord would help him endure until whatever day would be his last. Contenting himself with silence, he made no objection when Booth spurred his horse to a canter. Slade followed suit, shadowing the man through the avenues, around carriages and other horses, until the somewhat familiar facade of the Surratt boarding house came into sight.

As they came to a halt, a Negro man emerged to take their horses. Slade nodded his thanks and leapt up the stairs after Booth, who burst in without so much as a knock, his riding crop still in hand and bellowing, "John!"

Slade closed the door behind him, while Booth strode toward the parlor, from which a steady stream of curses rang out in Surratt's tone. He slid into the room too, just in time to see the usually cool young man gesture with his revolver.

"Ruined! Blighted! I ought to put an end to it all here and now, I might as well—" His self-threat ended in a sputter of unintelligible groans.

Booth paced the room, frantic. Perhaps his own agitation was heightened by his friend's. "Calm yourself, John. We—"

He cut himself off when he turned and spotted what Slade had noticed the moment he stepped inside the room—they weren't alone. In addition to another Knight, one of the boarders sat in the corner, a book in hand and his mouth agape.

The fellow cleared his throat, looking more than a little frightened. "Good evening, Mr. Booth."

Had the actor attempted a smile, it no doubt would have been convincing. But he didn't bother. "I didn't see you there."

Surratt charged from the room, motioning his friends to follow. They did, leaving the boarder staring after them.

Booth scarcely waited until they were all ensconced in a chill, dim back chamber. "What happened? What is it?"

"What happened?" Surratt spun toward the entrance with blazing eyes. "How am I to know? Perhaps one of the others fouled up. Perhaps we were betrayed."

The echo pulsed through the room, leeching out what warmth had been in it. Slade sucked in a breath only because the others did.

Surratt sighed and folded himself onto a couch. "Foolishness, I know. It's merely our usual bad luck asserting itself. His driver took another route."

Praise the Lord.

Booth groaned and sank into a wingback chair. "Why?"

"There was no reason, so far as I could tell. I spotted them coming, was prepared to act, and then they just turned. I tried to rush away, to alert the others or intercept him elsewhere, but..."

But they hadn't scouted all the other roads. They didn't know where else they could set upon him without being noticed. Hence why changing the route had been so sensible a plan. Relief wove through gratitude within Slade.

Lincoln was safe. Herschel was safe. More, Herschel had trusted him. Slade sat too, and rubbed a hand over his face.

Maybe Ross hadn't completely succeeded at ruining everything. Maybe Slade really could put it to rights. Maybe he'd emerge from this with a hope for a future.

Maybe...but doubt still plagued him. And with doubt came the flashing of cat-green eyes in his mind. He hadn't let himself think too much, yet, about what Walker Payne had told him that morning about the unknowns of Marietta Arnaud Hughes. Didn't dare. Because thinking about it made him wonder. A woman willing to run off with a quadroon laborer surely couldn't be so opposed to a two-bit detective on principle, after all.

But principle didn't matter a whit in these things. He was none too sure either of them had anything left to give. Wasn't sure what it would take to overcome the obstacles. She and Payne must have loved each other something fierce to plan such a thing, but that hadn't been enough either.

Maybe nothing would be.

Twenty-Three

Marietta's hand shook as she folded the letter and slid it onto the table beside the soldier's cot. Last week she had made it through her first hospital visit with nary a roll of nausea. Then again, last week an amputation hadn't been underway behind the curtain. She hadn't heard the groans of the patient before they sedated him, the clang of surgical tools.

Hadn't heard the grinding of the saw. No, not just heard it. Felt it in her own bones.

She attempted a smile for the bandaged man, but it wobbled. How pathetic that he had to give her an encouraging pat on the hand. "Are you a new volunteer, ma'am?"

She didn't dare open her mouth right then. If she tried, she couldn't be sure what might come out. She nodded.

The man settled his hand on the cot beside him again and slid his eyes closed. "You get used to it. Amputations happen every few days."

Every few days. How many men, then, would be leaving here—assuming they survived to leave—with missing limbs?

The sawing hitched, and she heard the doctor say, "Bone nippers, Mrs. Arnaud."

Marietta pressed a hand to her mouth. How could Barbara serve in that room day after day? Catching a glimpse of her now beyond the curtain, she saw her friend's once-white apron stained scarlet.

The roll of her stomach brought her to her feet. She muttered what she hoped was a polite farewell to the soldier to whom she'd been reading and made a dizzy dash for the door. Fresh air, she needed fresh air. And an escape from the terrible noises. She left the ward, flew down the hall, and finally drew in another breath when she pushed out into the blustery March sunshine.

It did precious little to steady her. She could not possibly go back in there, not unless the Lord gave a direct command.

For once her shawl was still wrapped around her. She pulled it close and cast her gaze around the bustling estate. What was she to do for the two and a half hours until Barbara was ready to go home? Wandering the grounds was hardly an option, what with the hundreds of men milling about.

And Pat wasn't waiting. She had given him permission to visit a cousin in the city, too far for walking from here.

"Mrs. Hughes."

She turned, her spine going stiff when she saw one of the doctors approaching, still adjusting his hat on his head. He smiled, but if he meant to ask her to come back inside for some reason...

"Your sister-in-law asked me to check on you and see you home if need be."

Marietta relaxed and prayed a blessing upon Barbara. Though how the woman could worry for her in the midst of surgery... "Thank you, Doctor. Are you headed out?"

"I am, yes. I need to call on a patient who lives near Monument Square. You are near there too, are you not?"

"Yes. Thank you, I would be most grateful for a ride." She walked with the doctor to a waiting carriage and accepted his servant's help into it. Once settled, she fully expected a few questions about her quick egress, but her rescuer spoke only of people she was likely to know, and of what a blessing Barbara had been to them at the hospital.

When the carriage neared Monument Square, he paused. "I am headed to Fayette Street. Where shall I drop you?"

"There is fine. I would welcome a short walk." Expecting an argument, she clutched her shawl and prepared to defend her request.

But the doctor merely nodded and smiled. A few moments later the carriage rocked to a halt, and he bade her farewell as if it were no great thing for a woman to walk through the neighborhood alone.

She drew in a grateful breath when her feet touched sidewalk. With a parting wave, she struck out at a confident pace, praying her knees held up. Absent distractions, impressions crowded again. The blood on Barbara's apron, the sounds, the smells.

Shuddering, that grateful breath turned sour and weakness seeped through her legs. Perhaps a walk hadn't been such a grand idea. She should have had him drop her at her door. It would have been only minutes out of his way.

Rather than head back to the square and then down her own street as she would normally have done, Marietta latched her gaze onto an alleyway that would cut her walk in half. In those cloaking shadows she could indulge in a moment of lapsed composure. That promise spurred her faster, until her wobbly legs had propelled her well into the alley and she finally dared to halt, close her eyes, and let her shoulders sag.

In the next second a foul-smelling arm slammed over her throat and shoved her against the brick wall with enough force that her toes dangled off the ground. Eyes flying open again, she scratched at the arm and kicked. In vain, as her feet only managed to tangle in her skirts.

Brown eyes glared at her, malice flashing with the blade the man held up. Under his slouch hat his hair was straggly and unkempt, his beard frazzled. He bared his teeth. "Money. Where be yer money, pretty lady?"

She could only move her mouth and gasp for air, tugging at his arm. No, that was wrong. Brothers. Her brothers had taught her...the face, she should go for the—

As if he heard her broken thoughts, his arm released her, but before she could sag, he slammed her face to the bricks. "Money!"

Pain bit, and it tasted of blood. The smell of it filled her nose, and her vision blurred.

Money. Her reticule. Where was her reticule?

That gruff face. She knew that face.

The images flashed too fast, dizzying. Her bedroom, her drawing room, a table in the library. Under her bed, wrapped in her shawl. Blood. Barbara. The hospital.

Faces, too many faces. Bearded, clean-shaven, leering. Nodding, smiling politely. Hands held out for money. Street corners. Her house. The fence.

There, by the soldier's cot. Pushed underneath.

A paint bucket. A brush in this man's hand.

"Where be it? Ye ain't got no fancy bag, but sure an a fine lass like you don't never go out withou' ye quid."

The images flew too fast, spun and bobbed and wavered. A painter. Where was his name? Somewhere, but she couldn't...

"Hidden on ye, is it?"

"Stop!" The feel of his hands was too much to bear as they slid up her side. Or perhaps just the impetus she needed to replace shock with rage. She spat out the blood and knocked away the roaming hand, at least, though the one with the knife still hovered at her neck. "Please, I–I don't have it. I dropped my bag at the hospital and fled too quickly to remember it. Please."

He sputtered, curses flying from his lips along with the spittle that spattered her face.

She winced and turned her face to the wall again, though that made the pain at her temple and cheekbone throb. "Please. Tell them I sent you to fetch it for me and keep whatever was in there. I believe I had five dollars, perhaps a—"

"Ye think me a fool?"

Doyle. The name materialized in her mind, though she couldn't discern if it was his first or last. And hardly cared. "Doyle. Doyle, stop. Please."

Stop he did, for half a beat before he pressed the blade to her throat. She squeezed her eyes shut. Bad idea, letting him know she knew him. And now that she had the name to put to the face, the rest came flooding in, pushing aside the irrelevant images. She knew where he lived— or had four years ago, when she had hired him to paint her fence and outbuildings the summer after she wed Lucien. She knew he had a sickly wife, and eight children all under the age of ten, at the time.

And when she heard the tap of wood on paving stone, the sick ball dropped lower in her stomach. Risking a glance only proved what the sound had told her. Doyle had only a peg where his foot had been.

"Know me, do ye?" He stroked the blade over her skin. "Then I know ye too. And I might as well kill ye and then rob yer whole house."

Never before had she stared down death—were waves of sorrow supposed to slam her? She was doomed to die the same death her husband had, a victim to a violent town and starving men, and she could think only that she had done nothing with her life. A waste of twenty-three years, with nothing to show for them but a fledgling faith too young to take wing.

Lord…be with Barbara and my family. With Walker and Cora and their children. Slade, be with Slade. Help him in his task when I'm gone. And… at least help me die with the honor with which I failed to live.

She lifted her chin and did her best to calm her frantic breathing. "Make it quick then, I beg of you."

He hissed out a breath. Had he been…bluffing? Dare she hope? Her hand gripped her skirt, detecting something hard within her pocket—the fob. And she still wore Grandmama's necklace too, under her high collar. Either, both may appease this man, but was her life worth the trade of a legacy?

"You there! Unhand her!" Granddad Thad's voice pummeled the shadows, and the deliberate *click* of a cocking gun sent them fleeing.

Doyle muttered and backed away a step. When she opened her eyes, he was edging toward the cover of a large crate. Bracing against the wall to keep herself upright, Marietta turned her face toward her grandfather.

What a menacing picture he made, a giant silhouette at the end of the alley, his pistol extended and trained on her assailant. No shaking in his limbs, no uncertainty, no sorrow. "Drop your knife," he commanded, voice low as a threat, "and stay where you are."

Did he mean to haul the man to the authorities himself? Probably, knowing him. And he would do it, too, despite his eight decades.

The ruffian took off toward the opposite end of the alley, his peg tapping furiously with every other step.

Granddad gave chase, but he stopped first at Marietta and cupped her chin. "Are you hurt, Mari?"

She gripped his arm and clung. "Let him go."

"I could catch him."

"I know." The ghost of a smile felt strange on her lips and made blood ooze into her mouth again. "But that man has eight children and no way to feed them. Please. Let him go."

His gentle fingers turned her face this way and that. "Did he crack you in the nob, sweetheart?" He clucked his tongue. But he stayed where he was.

Relief made her legs go boneless, and she sagged against his familiar chest. "What are you doing here, Granddad?"

"I had a feeling." Of course he did. "I didn't realize it would be you, here like this. And I don't much like seeing you with blood on your face."

Did he have to mention it? She squeezed her eyes shut and held tighter to him.

"What were you doing out alone, Mari? Even in broad daylight, even in this section of town, you ought to know better."

"I know. I'm sorry." She did, and she was. And she was something else, something she couldn't quite put a name to. Something that made her tremble in the deepest depths of her being and want to curl into a ball and disappear to where no one would care if she laughed or cried in hysteria. She tilted her face up. "Will you take me home?"

Granddad uncocked his gun and slid it back into its place at his belt. Then he tucked her close to his side. "As if you need to ask."

Devereaux charged through the front door before Norris could open it for him, letting the wood bang against the wall behind it. Let the slave close it again, or Osborne. He didn't care, not when his mother's note still burned his eyes.

Hurry. It's Mari.

A message uncharacteristically short and vague for Mother, and she had scratched a hole into the paper on "hurry." "Mari" had been shaky and faint. When he had seen that, he had nearly throttled the delivery boy and demanded to know what had happened. But a hired courier would have no answers.

"Mother! Mari!"

"Devereaux!" Mother's voice came from the stairs, and her figure joined it a moment later, rushing down the steps with a speed he hadn't seen of her in years. Tear tracks webbed her cheeks.

He ran to her, gripped her shaking hands. "What is it? What happened?"

"It's just like Lucien." Mother's voice wisped and choked, fresh droplets spilling from her eyes. "She was attacked in our own neighborhood. She was attacked. Just like Lucien."

"Attacked?" What did she mean, just like Lucien? All the blood in his veins seemed to gather, to pulse with too much force. Not like Lucien—it couldn't be like Lucien. "Is she all right?"

She had to be all right. Had to be. He couldn't lose her now, wouldn't. If he had to revive her himself, he would find a way. If he had to bring in the best doctors in America, if he had to give his fortune on medicines. Anything it took, but she *would* be his.

Mother tugged one hand free to wipe at her cheeks. And then, a simple move to shift the world, she nodded. "She is well enough. A few scratches and bruises, and she is shaken. Thad Lane was coming this way and intervened."

A few scratches. His breath eased out, though his pulse still hammered. "Not too injured then."

"No." But still Mother sniffed and blinked back an onslaught of tears. Still she gripped his hand as if the world were ending. "I could have lost her. As quickly as we lost Lucien, she could have been gone, and I...she has always...I have been so ungracious to her, and yet she has always loved me. Simply because of the bonds of family. What if I had lost her, Devereaux? With that over my head?"

For a moment he could only stare, unable to process the words. Lucille Fortier Hughes never changed her mind about anyone. Never indulged in regrets. Could this have actually achieved that impossibility?

A wonder for another time. Now he stepped to the side and headed up the stairs, her hand still in his. "I must see her. Where is she? Her bedroom?"

"No, her drawing room. Mr. Lane just left to fetch Julie."

Wasting no more time on words, he let go of his mother so he could take the stairs two at a time and then run down the hall to the blue-and-green chamber. The moment he stepped in, his gaze flew to the bright-red of her hair...and then fell to the even redder marks on her too-white face.

"Mari." Her name barely made it past the tightening in his throat. His pulse pounded louder. Whoever had dared mark her flawless skin would pay. Oh, how they would pay. He strode to where she sat on the S-shaped conversation sofa he had always hated because he couldn't sit beside her. Dropping to a knee before her, he cupped her cheek and took in every discoloration on her alabaster complexion. None so disturbing as the hollow way she gazed at him.

May whoever did this rot. "Darling." He leaned forward, determined to spark life in her eyes, and took her lips.

She pulled away with a wince. Only then did he notice the swelling of her lower lip, and the crack at its corner.

He bit back a curse. "I'm sorry. Darling, I'm so sorry someone hurt you like this. Tell me what happened."

She averted her face. "There is hardly anything to tell. A man pushed me into a wall and demanded my money, of which I had none. He had a knife."

"Why did you not give him your necklace? Your rings? You know better than to argue with ruffians."

"I...I forgot I was wearing the necklace, and I'd taken off my rings before going to the hospital. But Granddad came just in time, and he had a pistol."

His blood pounded faster, and he took her hand, weaving their fingers together. "Where were you? Near the hospital?"

Her eyelids fluttered down. "I...couldn't stay. A doctor drove me home, but I got out a street over."

"Of all the stupid...what doctor? He ought to be shot for leaving you like that."

That at least brought her gaze up and lit a spark in it, however weak. "It is not his fault."

"You're right. It's the fault of the scoundrel who dared to assault you.

Where is he? Did your grandfather detain him?" A long shot, he knew, no matter how spry the old man claimed to be.

Marietta shrank into the curved back of her seat, a strange flicker in her eyes. She pulled her fingers free of his and reached for the cup of tea steaming on the end table. "He got away."

"No matter." He patted her knee. "You can describe him, and we'll have an artist do a sketch. This man will not go unpunished." And when he got his hands on him, they would see how he liked having a knife pulled on him.

Her teacup shook as she sipped and then lowered it back to the table. "He had my face pressed to the wall. Perhaps to keep me from getting a good look at him."

Devereaux rocked back on his heels. "He no doubt got a good look at you, though, and I imagine your grandfather shouted your name. He could figure out easily enough who you are and where you live, and could very well mean to collect later what he failed to take then."

The green of her eyes snapped with fear. "Surely not."

One never could tell with those base-born, desperate men. "I'll not risk it. We must find him and see he meets justice." The eternal kind, from which he would never awaken. Devereaux lifted her fingers and pressed his lips to them. "I love you too much to lose you."

Maybe, finally she would speak the words he'd wanted for years to hear—but no. She glanced past him and pressed her lips together.

He looked over his shoulder and rose to his feet. Osborne stood in his usual motionless stance just inside the doorway, still as a statue. No, a guard dog. His eyes were, as always, wary and on alert.

Devereaux adjusted his coat, the thrum of his pulse resonating. "I will speak with your grandfather, get his description of the man, and talk with the police. Osborne?"

The detective straightened.

"Forget the rails, forget any other business. Your job now is to protect Mari. Do you understand? Until this scoundrel is found, you're not to let her out of your sight."

Marietta pushed to her feet, swayed. "Dev, this is ridiculous. I am not—"

"I didn't ask your opinion, Marietta." He glanced at his mother, fussing over sandwiches and cakes, and then back to Osborne. "Are we understood?"

Though Osborne's black gaze darted briefly to Marietta, Devereaux read no hesitation in it. Calculation, perhaps, but that was to be expected. He gave one curt nod.

Good enough. With one last kiss upon Marietta's knuckles, he strode for the door, his aim the cellar and the knife stored there.

He had a thief to hunt down.

Twenty-Four

Slade slid further into the room, out of the way of Hughes. Mrs. Hughes murmured something about returning directly and rushed after her son, but Slade paid no attention to the swish of her skirts as she passed. He kept his gaze on Marietta.

The trauma of the day cloaked her, sloping her shoulders, darkening her eyes. He caught her gaze, held it, and waited. The thoughts swirled over her countenance, coming to a rest not on fear or exhaustion, but on regret. She twisted a handkerchief around her fingers and sighed. "I'm sorry, Slade. You don't have to guard me. He's overreacting. But you can use the time to do whatever you must."

He took a few steps until he stood right in front of her. Close enough to see the S.O. on the handkerchief in her hands. Close enough to see the angry red of the scrapes on her cheek. Close enough to see all that churned through her thoughts. "You knew him."

He expected her to look away, perhaps to narrow her eyes in denial. Instead, a spark of amusement flashed in them, and a fraction of a sad smile touched her lips. "Must you be so good at your job, Detective?"

His smile was no bigger, but not so sorrowful. "Why are you protecting him?"

Her breath easing out, she sank onto her seat again. Slade crouched down to avoid towering over her. Her gaze went contemplative. "He did work here some years ago—painting. He had eight children and a sickly wife, and now he is missing a foot. I can only imagine the hardships his family faces."

Two months ago he wouldn't have believed her capable of being so moved by compassion. But then, he had read her wrong in a lot of ways. He settled his hand on top of hers, joined over his handkerchief. "You can't excuse what he did to you."

"Desperation will drive people to lengths they never expected." She looked down and swallowed. "I asked Cora and Walker to put together some necessities and food. I added a bit of cash to see them through."

She intended to feed the family of the man who had attacked her? No, he never would have expected that, even now. Slade pushed to his feet. Moving to the other side of the S-shaped sofa, he sat, leaning back so he could still see her face. "I'll go with Walker when he takes it." Heaven knew the man probably lived in a lousy part of town, one Walker oughtn't to have to venture into alone.

Besides. He'd like to see the man's face when they handed him a gift from his victim. Judge for himself if Marietta was making a wise move or inviting extortion.

Her eyes went wide. "You don't have to do that."

"I want to."

"And you don't have to guard me."

"I want to."

She stared at him, her feline eyes still wide and suspiciously damp. Her "Why?" came out as no more than a wisp.

The wisp echoed through him far longer than it should have.

He pulled in a breath and savored it for a moment. Then let himself reach out and brush away the scarlet curl touching her cheek. "Because you matter."

The sentiment ought not to take her by surprise. Her family would move heaven and earth for her. Hughes would kill for her. Yet disbelief glimmered in her eyes. "Why?"

"Don't." He draped his arm over the curved back between them and found her hands. Took one, lifted it, and held it to his lips. He could handle most things he came across in this life. He could face the gray that had taken over the world. But it shouldn't steal her vibrancy.

She'd still been bright after death and loss, after learning the truth of the Hugheses. This couldn't break her—not a simple mugging, so despicably common in Baltimore. He wouldn't let it. "Don't question that."

She blinked and presented him with her profile. Her fingers slipped from his and tangled again with the square of cotton. "Would you read to me, Slade?"

Another breath filled his lungs and eased back out. "Sure." Given that no book rested nearby to indicate she'd been reading it, he reached into his pocket for the prayer book.

He opened to the ribbon that marked where he'd left off that morning. "'Eternal Father, it is amazing love, that Thou hast sent Thy Son to suffer in my stead, that Thou hast added the Spirit to teach, comfort, guide, that Thou hast allowed the ministry of angels to wall me round...'"

The words of the prayer twined through him, shoring up the places inside that always threatened to topple. The writer obviously knew God with intimacy...yet just as obviously felt like a miserable, hateful worm. Deserving of rejection, but so very aware of the ever-forgiving love of the Father. Slade prayed Marietta would feel the same assurance. That though she was as sinful and proud and unworthy as the rest of humanity, she was also as loved.

By the end of the page, Mrs. Hughes had come back into the room and settled into a chair. Slade glanced her way once or twice. Looking, he admitted, for the lie in her countenance. It had always been there before, no matter how sweet or caring her words to her daughter-in-law.

Not so today. Today, the pain she'd voiced to her son on the stairs seemed genuine and consuming. Today she seemed finally to look on Marietta as a daughter instead of an interloper. What a shame it had taken violence to achieve that. And what a shame it came so late, when their world was about to crumble.

Maybe that was part of God's plan too. His way of knitting them together when they were sure to need the support soon.

A thought that shouldn't pierce so deep, that Slade would only get to be the destroyer here, not the comforter.

He had turned the page twice more when he felt the weight of Marietta's head on his shoulder and became aware of the deep, even cadence of her breathing. Because he had to fight the urge to press his lips to the top of her head, he looked again to Mrs. Hughes, sure she wouldn't approve of the posture. With his luck, she would even guess at his restrained intent.

Her frown shone soft, concerned. "The poor dear. It must have frightened her so, to find herself in the same position that proved to be Lucien's last."

Slade nodded, because it surely had. But his mind went back to the stairs again, when Hughes had heard the words from his mother. *Just like Lucien.* Something had flickered across his face, something of a different shade than fear.

Slade's chest went tight as his gaze tracked back to the red curls spilling over his shoulder. He knew exactly what Hughes had been feeling—a soul-wrenching rejection of the thought of losing her. The same had rendered Slade immobile at the foot of the steps throughout the Hugheses' conversation, too distressed to move. First at the scare, then at the wonder of feeling it so acutely.

Hughes wouldn't wonder at it. No more than he would linger to give comfort when he could instead rush out to find vengeance.

His loss.

"Thank you for agreeing to protect her, Mr. Osborne." Mrs. Hughes brushed a flaxen lock away from her face. "I don't know what we would do if we lost her. Devereaux loves her so."

Did she have any idea how much? Did she know her eldest—and now only—son had killed for her? That he had loved her long before he should have?

Slade forced what he could manage of a smile and told himself not to judge. Was he, after all, any better? He had known very well she and Hughes had an understanding when he came on the scene, but it hadn't stopped him from feeling that intrigue. From kissing her once and wanting to more.

But he never would have touched her had she been married. He was still none too sure Hughes could claim the same...though now the uncertainty clawed. Now he didn't *want* to believe that Marietta would engage in something so base as an affair with one brother while married to the other.

Commotion downstairs made him shift, which in turn made

Marietta's breath catch and her head lift again. He didn't know whether to focus on the plethora of voices drawing nearer or the pained, muted whimper that slipped from the woman beside him.

The woman won out. He turned to see her better as she lifted a hand to touch her cheek, her eyes clouded.

If it weren't for the audience and the couch's curved back between them, he would have wrapped his arms around her. Probably a good thing circumstances didn't permit that. "Are you all right?"

A veil came down over the pain in her eyes, and a smile appeared on her lips. The same imitation of one he'd seen from her when he first arrived, which he now knew was but a dim reflection. "A minor irritation, nothing more."

Mrs. Hughes leapt up to fuss again, fluttering her hands uselessly about Marietta's face. "The bruising is beginning to show, and it will take weeks to fade. I'm afraid you shall have to postpone your plans to attend a ball with Devereaux, dear. And your new gown just arrived! Such a shame."

"Yes. A shame." She darted a glance at Slade, so quick he would have missed it had he not been watching her steadily.

Steadily enough to know there was no regret within her over that.

Well, he wouldn't torture himself by sticking around to be interrogated by the brothers whose voices he now recognized on the stairs. He sent Marietta a small grin as he stood and moved to the edge of the room. With any luck, the Arnauds wouldn't even notice him.

Mrs. Arnaud led the way into the room, a surge of blue satin aimed straight for her daughter. Slade caught the concern on her face, one echoed stormily upon her sons'.

They wouldn't be going anywhere for a while. He edged out the door before either Hezekiah or Isaac could spot him, pivoting into the hall—and nearly smacking into the lanky figure of Thaddeus Lane.

The old man greeted him with a smile and jerked his head toward the stairs. He followed him down, along the hall, and all the way to the side door. Only when they were out in the halfhearted March sunshine did Slade speak. "Did Hughes find you?"

"Briefly." Lane made a face and directed his stride toward the carriage house. "I gave him just enough information to keep him busy. Is Mari still determined to protect the man?"

What could he do but huff? "Yeah."

Her grandfather chuckled. "When that girl decides to change, she doesn't do it by half measures." He charged into the dim interior of the stable. "We had better hurry. Julie and the boys will fuss a good while, but they will eventually notice I'm gone."

Slade didn't have to ask to realize the man intended the same thing he did, to accompany Walker on his errand. And when Walker glanced up from the wagon he was loading, his expression looked about how Slade's felt. They were all of the same mind, and no one wasted time with words. Lane and Slade lent a hand with the last two boxes, and then they loaded themselves in.

The reins fit Walker's hands like a natural extension, and the two horses responded as one to the single click of his tongue. "I had a feeling I would have some company," he said as he directed them toward the alley. "Fool woman."

Lane chuckled. "I admire her for wanting to help."

"But?" Walker sent him a sideways glance.

The old man shrugged. "But I don't know the man. And I don't feel very gracious to anyone who would hurt my granddaughter."

Slade snorted. He wasn't feeling particularly gracious either. But as he settled in among the boxes in the back, he didn't want to err on the side of Hughes. He let his gaze settle on the house as they rumbled away from it. Marietta was safe there, at least when surrounded by family.

Soon the buildings towering around him weren't so hopeful, nor so unravaged by the war. Soot marred them, paint peeled and chipped, mortar crumbled. The pedestrians wore threadbare garments, and some of the children were barefoot despite the fact that winter hadn't completely let go of its hold yet.

Questions churned in Slade's mind. "Say, Lane. Did they ever catch Lucien's murderer?"

The old man turned on the bench. "No. You don't think the same...?" He glanced ahead of them.

"No reason to think so. Just curious. How long did Devereaux search?"

Lane pursed his lips and looked to Walker. "Longer than the police cared to keep looking into another random mugging-gone-awry. A month, maybe."

Walker turned his head enough to catch Slade's gaze, to share his thoughts. "He loves Yetta a whole lot more than he loved his brother, though. He's gonna be a dog with a bone over this."

"He won't have anything to go on unless Mari or I give him a description." Amusement, of all things, lit the old man's yellow-brown eyes. "I wouldn't be surprised if he hired you to find him, Oz."

"Nah. He'll want to do that himself." Half his mouth tugged upward. "He hired me to protect her in the meantime."

"Convenient. And stupid." Lane chuckled as he shook his head. "He honestly doesn't see it? He, who is usually so jealous of anyone who looks twice at her?"

Wariness whipped through him, made him struggle to find a more comfortable position against the rough-hewn wood. "I don't know what you mean."

Lane rolled his eyes. "Thunder and turf, man, what good does it do to lie to yourself about it? When I met my Gwyn, I knew within three weeks she would be my wife."

Wife? When did they start talking about wives? He turned his gaze on Walker. Surely he, who had already given him a talking-to on the subject of Marietta, would pipe up and help him wiggle out of this conversation.

Walker remained mute.

Lane didn't. "Don't look to him for help. He'd only known Cora a week or two before they married. Sometimes you just know."

Yeah, well. "I don't." He didn't know much of anything, not when it came to Marietta.

"No?" Lane leaned over the bench's back, eyes narrowed. "How did you feel when you learned she was attacked?"

That stab of powerlessness came back too fast, too strong. No matter what he did to try to stop a few evil men, more always came, eager to destroy what mattered most.

She could have been killed. He could have lost her, and he wouldn't even have the right to grieve. He wouldn't have anything but another hollow place to carry inside him.

"That's what I thought." Lane turned back around, but Slade had no trouble imagining the smug smile he would be wearing.

Walker sent a glower Slade's way. "You'd better be careful. Real careful. If Hughes realizes his error in assigning you to her, he'll make up for it with a bullet."

This is why he preferred the company of men like Herschel, who knew the value of holding their tongues. "I'll keep her safe. That's all."

"I know you will, otherwise I'd try to convince her again to go home to her mother." Lane turned just enough to reveal the edges of that smile. "That will go a long way with her brothers, you know. Protecting her and eventually getting Dev away from her. And Jack will approve of you, I have no doubt. That will matter to Mari."

Jack...as in, her father? Approve of him? Slade shook his head, but it did nothing to ward off the strange itch in his chest. "You're crazy, old man."

"You're the one who just said you were in love with my granddaughter. I'm merely providing you some hope as to how well you'll fit into the family."

The wagon bed might as well have dropped out from under him. "I did not."

"Not with words. But then..." Lane turned more toward him, revealing his full, frustrating grin. "Since when do you need them?"

Slade folded his arms and focused his eyes on the faded buildings rolling by. There was nothing to do but ignore him.

Twenty-Five

Not since Lucien's death had so many people crowded into Marietta's house. She had attended aid meetings aplenty the past seventeen months, with just as many fluttering females, but never had she wanted to snarl at them as she did today.

So she brightened her smile and made it a point not to touch the scrape on her cheek. It itched, but if she touched it, the bruise would throb. And everyone would look at her. Her mother and Barbara and Mother Hughes with concern—even *that* irritated her today—and her neighbors and so-called friends with an interest bordering on delight. In their eyes, it was merely exciting that she had been mugged. They reveled in the injuries and cajoled her to tell the story.

She nearly wept with relief when the gaggle made their exit.

Mother Hughes arranged a bonnet over her flaxen curls and sent Marietta a look at once so very welcome and so very stifling. Finally, the woman's eyes held no veiled animosity, but in the past forty-three hours, she had scarcely let Marietta out of her sight. "Are you certain you do not mind me visiting with Bulah this afternoon, dear? I hate to leave you alone."

Please, please leave me alone. She felt ungracious even thinking the thoughts, but they wouldn't go away. All she could do was sweeten her smile and pray her heart would match it. "I am hardly alone." She motioned to her mother and Barbara. And beyond them, to the corner in which Slade had taken up residence. She had fully expected him to disappear when the hordes of women arrived, but instead he had become a shadow.

Smart of him, which she realized when an acquaintance who had seen them at the theater looked his way with arched brows, obviously recognizing him. And just as obviously recognizing the stance he now took. Guard, employee. Servant.

The women paid him no more heed, other than an occasional stolen glance. Those, no doubt, were merely because he looked as alluring as ever, scowling at his current book in that way he always did.

Not that Marietta stole any glances.

"If you're certain." Mother Hughes gave her a careful embrace, as if she feared hurting her. "Can I fetch you anything on my way home?"

Some of the resentment faded. "Thank you, but I have all I need. Enjoy your afternoon, Mother Hughes."

Barbara came to her side the moment Mother Hughes left it. "What shall we do this afternoon, Mari? I can set up a game, or read to you, or—"

"Nonsense." Mama, bless her, put her hands to Barbara's elbows and pointed her toward the door. "It is your afternoon at the hospital, and I am accompanying you."

Barbara's horrified expression would have been amusing had it not been so sincere. "But Mari—"

"Needs some quiet." Mama shot her a knowing grin. "She likes coddling for exactly a day after injury or illness, after which she may just bite the hand trying to spoil her. Right, dearest?"

Why had the Lord blessed her with such a family? A father who adored her and a mother who understood her so well, though they were nothing alike. She leaned over to kiss her matron's cheek. "Thank you. For everything."

"I only wish I could take it from you entirely." Mama's arms came around her and held her tight for just long enough. Then she pulled away with a smile and cast a glance over her shoulder. "I daresay I shan't convince Mr. Osborne to leave, though."

"Not a chance," he said without even looking up.

Though Marietta chuckled, the realization that his presence didn't bother her in the least, that she wanted him to stay when she wanted no one else to, made the good humor fade quickly. "I hardly notice him."

Her mother gave her a look that said she didn't believe her for a moment, but she merely wove her arm through Barbara's and headed for the door. "I will see you both at dinner tomorrow."

When they disappeared into the hallway, she breathed in blessed silence with gratitude. It wouldn't last long—she was due at the carriage house within the half hour for Elsie's sign lesson—but she would savor it while it lasted.

Which was all of five seconds before she heard familiar footsteps in the hall and Dev's rumble of greeting. "Mrs. Arnaud, good day."

Mama made a polite reply. And since he, as usual, spared no greeting for the other Mrs. Arnaud, his tread soon sounded again.

The irritation, soothed by Mama's understanding, flared up again as he strode into the room. And blazed into outright anger when he caught Slade's gaze and jerked his head toward the door.

Slade, happy to play the lackey, got up without a word. She knew by now he wouldn't go far, but that wasn't the point.

"Close the door behind you."

His gait hitched, but he obeyed. Marietta sank back to her seat rather than holding out a hand to greet Dev.

He would notice the slight. The edges of his smile strained as he sat beside her. "How was your aid meeting, darling?"

"Inconsequential. You needn't check on me, Dev."

His blue eyes snapped, but he banked the flame. "I want to." He took her hand in his and held it tight despite her keeping it limp. "And I wanted to see if you had remembered anything more about the scoundrel who did this to you. I have questioned all the usual petty thieves, but I do not think any of them our culprit."

For a moment she studied his face. Was it love that made him pursue this so relentlessly when she had given him so little to go on? Or did he merely hate the thought of another daring to mark what he considered his? Finding no answer in his gaze, she shook her head. "I told you all I could." She certainly wouldn't mention that Slade and Walker and Granddad had delivered the goods she sent, and that Granddad had offered the man employment at his warehouse in addition. Doyle, they assured her, would haunt the streets no more. And his nine children, now motherless, would have food on their table.

"I know. But something more could have come to mind." With his free hand, he touched her cheek under the mottled bruise, his frown fierce. "I will find him if I have to question every low-life ruffian in Baltimore. I promise you that."

She turned her face away. "What does it matter? He stole nothing, the scrapes and bruises will fade—"

"He hurt you, and he will pay for it." He said it with such superiority, as if he weren't every bit as guilty of hurting her, and so much more deeply. "He put marks on your skin and shadows in your eyes. He interfered with our plans—and Mother said your new gown is perfect."

Marietta hadn't even looked at it. "A few weeks' delay, that is all."

Simple words, but something must have come through in her tone. Dev dropped her hand and put a few inches between them on the divan. "What is the matter with you lately, Mari?"

She lifted her chin and met his accusing glare. "I don't know what you mean."

"Like blazes you don't. You haven't been acting yourself, not since you brought that *woman* into the house."

"'That *woman*'?" She pushed to her feet, knowing her cheeks had flushed scarlet. "That *woman* is my sister and friend."

He followed her up, where of course he towered over her. "You have changed."

"That has nothing to do with Barbara."

"Ha!" He pivoted away but then spun back on her, a finger leveled at her chest. "Perhaps she isn't the cause, but she is certainly proof of it. My Mari would never, *never* have taken her in. Certainly wouldn't sit around for hours listening to her pious prattle without filling my ears with complaints about it later. What has happened to you?"

She squeezed her eyes shut. Perhaps Barbara was indeed evidence of her change, but the start...the start had come well before. A bit, even, before she learned the full truth. "You know well what happened, Dev. One sin too many finally opened my eyes to them all."

He expelled an angry hiss of breath. A moment later his hands closed around her shoulders, forcing her eyes open again. "That's what all this has been about? Your *guilt*?"

Wrenching free of his hands did nothing to erase the feel of them. "Don't mock me. Perhaps you can do whatever you please without feeling the pangs of your conscience, but I cannot."

His snort might as well have been a slap. "Since when?"

She turned away, unable to face the truth of his accusation. "Not long enough. I admit that. But I have changed, and I will be a better person now."

"Better? You call this *better*?" With a few strides, he stood before her again, fire dancing in his eyes. "Arguing with your intended at every turn, going behind my back to invite guests to stay here of whom you know I would disapprove, disregarding our plans for your debut, stupidly going about the city on your own—this strikes you as an improvement?"

Marietta folded her arms across her chest. "Funny that you name the things I would always have done. I have never suffered a man to dictate my life." Even when listening to her father or brothers would have been wise.

He spat out a curse, gripped her elbow, and yanked her closer. "You have never acted this way with me before, never. We have always understood each other, and now you tell me you want to change? That, what, you do not like the Mari you have always been, knowing well how I love her?"

Her stomach knotted and rose to block her throat. Doyle's image swam before her mind's eye. The hate-filled eyes, the unkempt beard. She could feel again the pressure cutting off her air, taste again the sting of blood.

Dev gave her arm a punctuating shake that bit like brick. "And what if I don't like this new Marietta? Hmm? What if all you've done with your infernal turn to piety is lose what set you apart?"

When he let go of her elbow, she staggered back, hating how her knees shook. "Then I guess you can be grateful nothing is official between us. If you no longer like me, then go find some other, more docile female. One not so afflicted by this 'infernal piety.'"

"Mari." His tone was heavy as lead with warning, but she couldn't look in his eyes. Not now.

She waved him away with an arm no steadier than her knees. "If you don't like me, then get out of my house."

"Marietta."

Now the warning rang of steel. She moved to the door, more a stumble than a stride. "Ah, right. Your house. If that is what you want, I will sign over the deed and show myself out this very day." She wrenched the door open.

"Enough." Somehow he ended up in front of her in the hallway, halting her with hands, gentle now, on her shoulders. "Darling. I'm so sorry. I should have realized how upset you still are by the attack."

"That has nothing—"

"Of course it has. But once we find him, you will feel better, knowing he can hurt you no longer." He leaned over and pressed his lips to her forehead. "We must stop taking our frustrations out on each other. That is no way to begin a life together." He moved his lips to her cheek, feathered a kiss there, and then settled them at her ear. "You know I love you. More than life itself, more than all the world. You can do nothing to change that. Be whoever you must be. You will still be mine, and I will still adore you."

Words that would have sounded so sweet were they not the very threat she most feared. She didn't attempt a smile. He would see right through it anyway.

Dev managed one. It was warm, apologetic...and yet harder than flint. He straightened his arms, urging her back a step.

A second set of hands cupped her elbows, their touch sending a shiver up her spine. Dev looked over her head. "See that she rests."

Rest. That was all anyone had let her do since Tuesday. If Slade thought for a moment she would go mildly up to her room...

His thumbs, hidden in the volume of her sleeves, made small circles against her arms that calmed her more than they should have. "Yes, sir."

"Good." Dev brushed away a curl from her cheek and then turned to stride away, confident his dictates would be obeyed.

Slade didn't move but for that slow circling of his thumbs. By the time the door closed on Dev, she was all too aware of how close they stood. And unable to remember why she shouldn't lean back against him.

His breath caught as she gave in, and his hands slid forward along her arms in welcome. She felt his indrawn breath release, sensed it as his head lowered down beside hers. His nose tickled her ear. "That would have been a far too easy end to things with him. And yet for a moment, I hoped..."

An echo of laughter slipped out, and with it came reason. She stepped away. And wished she hadn't. "I was too irritated to hope."

He wore a lopsided smile when she turned to him. "You should have slugged him. I would have paid good money to see that."

"Slugged?"

"Yeah, you know..." He mimed delivering a blow to a chin.

Marietta blinked, grateful to have a lighthearted distraction. "'Slug' is a synonym for an uppercut?"

"Just a punch in general." But his eyebrows came into their habitual V. "You know what an uppercut is?"

"Isaac enjoys boxing."

He breathed a laugh. "Thanks for the warning. Did he teach you?"

"Enough that I could have slugged Dev, had I thought it wise." Which she couldn't imagine doing. Not when she had done such a poor job defending herself two days ago. What good did recall do if one couldn't think when to apply it?

"Hmm." Slade's eyes sparkled as he swept his gaze down her.

"What?"

"Just imagining you in a boxing ring. Maybe with a pair of those newfangled gloves. Wearing breeches and—"

"And?" She laughed, though her face heated. If most boxers were like Isaac, there *was* no "and." "That is enough imagination from you, I think."

His grin eclipsed the irritation that had snapped at her heels all day. He held out a hand and motioned with his head for the door. "Sign lesson?"

"Sign lesson." Though she shouldn't, she slid her hand into his.

He kissed her knuckles, setting her nerves aflame, and then tucked her fingers into the crook of his elbow to lead her out the side door. March was mild as a lamb today, the sun warm and bright as they stepped out. Maybe she could convince him to take her for a promenade later.

Slade halted them in the first patch of sunlight. "Just so you know...I like this new Marietta."

She tilted her face up to the sunshine so she could blame the suffusing warmth on it. "You didn't know the old one."

"I saw enough of her." His fingers trailed over hers on his arm. "I liked her too. She was intriguing, and that kind of confidence...well. But adding the depth of faith, the light of compassion—that sets you apart more, not less."

For a second the words kissed her spirit as the sun did her face, but then the clouds rolled in again. The only thing that ever set her apart was her uselessness. Her family had always said she was capable of anything, that with her mind she could do great things.

But what things could a woman do? Any options open to her required either the support of a husband or would mean the scorn of society.

No. God should have given her memory to Stephen or Hez or Isaac instead. They could have used it to make a difference. She had never found any purpose in it beyond entertaining her friends. She had never found any purpose at all.

Lowering her face again, she set her gaze on Slade. She had one now, at least. A purpose handed to her from the great-grandmother she'd never met, through the hand of the grandfather she trusted with every ounce of her being. They had given her a reason for the gift, a way to use it...but she had done nothing but play scribe.

She could do more, though. She could. Her fingers tightened on Slade's arm. "Slade...will you show me the entrance to the castle?"

Like lightning, the gleam in his eyes turned to caution. "Pardon?"

Perhaps she should have done her musing out loud so he could see how she arrived at that request. Moistening her lips, she drew in a quick breath. "I want to help. I want to do more than distract Dev so you can sneak about."

She half expected him to retreat, for the wolf to snarl to life. Instead, he sighed. "I appreciate that, but there's no help to be had from the castle. Trust me. I've examined every inch of it."

"But—"

"Yetta." He shook his head, squinting into the sunshine. "You don't want to go down there. There's nothing that would help, just...images you don't need to see. Trust me."

She did...and yet. "It's my house. I want to know what goes on under it. Were Barbara not so often with me, I would have made more of an effort to find the entrance myself. I know it is somewhere over here." She motioned to the side of the house along which they stood, where the hedges always remained too high. Concealing. Where Barbara had heard voices several times now.

"No. It's no place for a lady." He turned her resolutely toward the carriage house.

She let him tug her only two steps before stopping again. Desperation clawed at her throat. "But I want to do more to help. I *have* to. Can't you understand that? That I need to do something that matters with my life?"

"You are." His tone was so sure, so steady. His gaze warm and certain. "I appreciate all you've done for me, all those papers you transcribed. But you know what really matters?"

She tucked in her chin and shook her head.

He motioned toward the city. "You gave a whole family a way to survive." He pointed at the carriage house. "You're giving that little girl a chance for a future. There aren't many who would do that. Especially..." He looked to the window of the little apartment, where Elsie's blond head bobbed.

Marietta sighed. "She isn't Lucien's."

The conclusion, then, was obvious, and he would have no trouble drawing it. He echoed her sigh. "Does that make it easier?"

"No."

"Didn't think so. He forced her?"

To that, she could only nod and try her best not to hear the scream again.

Slade shook his head. Determination cloaked him. "You are definitely not going into that castle. You're not going to do anything more to cross him. Do you understand me?"

Another dictate. Yet this one didn't make the anger flare so hot. "I want to help. I *need* to help."

"And I *need* you to stay safe." He slid a hand onto her neck, under her hair, and anchored her head. "Please. Please stay out of this."

"I'm already in—"

"Then get out of it. I can't have you hurt." His gaze lingered on the discoloration on her cheek. "Please."

There was a day not so many months ago when it would have given her a thrill to reduce a man like Slade Osborne to begging. Not so today. Today she could only curl her fingers around his wrist and wish she could hold on forever. "What about you? You're far more likely to get hurt than I am."

With a thumb tracing her ear, his eyes went soft. "A necessary risk. It's my job. Which means I know how to be careful."

"Really? Coulda fooled me." Walker's voice pounded its way in, unexpected enough that she jumped back. And had to wonder when Slade's other arm had slid around her waist. Walker stood only a few paces away with a ferocious scowl in place as he tugged off his work gloves. "Looks to me like you're trying to get the both of you killed, standing around like that in plain view of the street."

"I wouldn't call it plain view, with the hedge..." When Walker turned fully toward him, Slade cleared his throat, looking, for some bizarre reason, to be fighting a laugh. "Right. You're right. Stupid of me."

Shouldn't he have been making some excuse for having her in his arms at all, rather than where he held her so? Marietta repositioned the shawl still miraculously around her shoulders.

Walker spun on her. "And you, princess." Now the corners of *his* mouth were twitching. "Didn't I teach you how to properly sneak around with a man?"

A blast of heat hit her face, scorched her neck, and tied her tongue. He had never, not once, spoken of those days with anyone else around, yet he would all but shout it now, with Slade standing there grinning?

Grinning! He already knew. Knew and...and...thought it funny.

The blasted heat wouldn't let up. She shook her head. "We were not..." But they were, when it came down to it. They certainly wouldn't have behaved so if Dev or Mother Hughes were around. "And we did not..." But of course that was a blatant lie. She had always been sneaking off to the stable to find him.

And they both had the gall to enjoy her discomposure. She had no choice but to straighten her spine, lift her chin, and sweep past them. "Insufferable jackanapes, the both of you."

Their laughter followed her to the carriage house.

Twenty-Six

Devereaux stepped off the train in Washington City with thunder in his veins. Six days had gone by since the attack on Marietta, and he had nothing to show for it. The imbeciles that passed for police officers in Baltimore had done absolutely nothing, and his own inquiries had led to dead ends.

Granted, it had relieved a certain amount of stress to knock a few ruffians stupid in the process of getting names from them. But none of them had given him any helpful information.

And Marietta, blast her, had barely spoken to him. Even Mother had noticed it and asked him if they had quarreled.

He would not lose her. It was bad enough, the news they kept hearing of the war in the South, of the state of General Lee's troops, of the continued failures of the KGC. He couldn't lose her too.

He had only a cryptic note in his pocket to lead his feet through the streets of Washington, but he needed no more. He told himself to enjoy the warming weather, the perfect sunshine, the promise of a meeting with his brothers.

Somehow, seeing Surratt and one of his cohorts going ahead of him into the Herndon Hotel only set his teeth on edge.

Surratt caught sight of Devereaux in the hotel lobby and held up to await him. "Where is Osborne?"

Devereaux strode by. If he paused, he might just hit the man. Why did he think he had the right to question him? "Attending other business. Where is Booth?"

"New York. He said he told Osborne."

He let a grunt suffice for an answer and headed for the stairs. Osborne had, in fact, said something about it, but Devereaux had been trying to organize a shipment of gold bars and had been distracted.

But the gold was now in place, hidden away in the back of the rail yard. Not far from the crates of rifles and ammunition. His part was coming together nicely. He had only to smuggle another shipment or two into Baltimore, and then he could take the entire lot by rail to the mountains. A month at the most—a fortnight, he hoped. Then, assuming the attacker were found and taken care of, his world would settle again until the time came for the next revolt.

Assuming this other business didn't foul everything up. He let Surratt knock on the correct door and cast a gaze over at the other man. The so-called doctor—nothing but a cover story, that, to excuse his frequent visits to the room—gave him a strained smile.

Devereaux wasn't inspired. Striding through the door the moment the occupant, "Wood," opened it, he turned to face the other Knights with a frown. "I don't intend to stay. I just want to make sure you have your plans well in hand. This will be your last chance, gentlemen."

"We know that." Surratt shifted from foot to foot. "We won't fail. We have our list of those we will seize, and we will snatch them all at once."

Wood studied Devereaux with obvious concern. "I apologize, sir, but we are not acquainted. Who are you?"

Of all the...he glared at Surratt, who cleared his throat. "This is our captain, Mr.—"

"No names." If they weren't telling him theirs, they certainly weren't getting his. "Have you men enough for this?"

"With Booth and Osborne, yes."

"Good. Now, funds. Who will be securing them?"

Surratt lifted a hand. "I have a trip to Canada planned. With our permission from the Confederacy in hand, the agent in Montreal ought to be willing to disburse."

"Excellent." Devereaux pulled out his watch. He still had business to attend in Baltimore, and no desire for it to cut into his evening. "Just remember to use one of the ciphers when communicating by wire, and trust no one outside your own circle."

He looked at them again, these men supposedly as dedicated to the Knights as he himself was. Whether or not they would have the gumption to carry out the tasks with prison or death as a consequence was yet to be seen for some of them. "Be careful. If you get even a strange feeling from someone, keep your distance and seal your lips."

Surratt drew in a long breath. "You can be sure of it, sir."

"Good. My orders from Richmond keep me busy, but if you need my input, do get word to me." He didn't wait for Surratt or one of the others to ask what kept him busy but merely gave them a nod and left the room. The day would certainly come when all the Knights would learn of the existence of the caches, when they would be instructed in how to follow the signs to them.

But not yet. Not until the goods were safely stored and the map to them established. Until then, only a select few of three hundred thousand brothers could know. This, above all, they must guard against the spies.

Perhaps there was little they could do about the present war at this point, but that made protecting their future hopes all the more vital.

Devereaux took his private car back to Baltimore, but the ride did little for his mood. Because the closer he got to home, the more he thought of Marietta. And the more he thought of Marietta...

Denial achieved nothing. She was slipping through his fingers.

Fingers which tightened into a fist as he climbed into his waiting carriage at Camden Station and ordered his driver home. Never would he have thought that her family's religious fervor would grip her. Yes, she had always idolized that do-good brother of hers, especially after Gettysburg. But Devereaux well remembered how ill they had often gotten along when Stephen was alive, how they had argued.

His fingers curled tighter. It was his own fault. He should have known, after her many refusals before, that he would pay for his seduction. That making her his would suffocate her in guilt. But he had hoped that once she had spent a night in his arms, she would forget the morals that had been more rote than belief and be happy as his mistress until they could marry.

A miscalculation. Four years of patience possibly ruined—but he hadn't lost yet. She wanted to embrace her parents' morality? Fine. Let *it* tell her she must marry him to be an honest woman again.

When he climbed from the carriage outside his house, the swish of her lavender skirt caught his eye as she sashayed around the corner of the family home. Osborne, keeping pace beside her, looked up, met Devereaux's gaze from across the street, and nodded a greeting. He must have said something to Marietta, because she then looked up too, at him without meeting his gaze.

No doubt she thought he'd stride directly across the street to her as he always did, dismiss Osborne, and lead her on a walk himself.

Maybe that was part of the problem. He had done nothing but pursue her for years, devoting far too much attention to each look he could gain, each stray brush of a touch, each veiled word. Naturally, she thought she could string him along, knowing he would be waiting when she had worked through her foul humor.

Well, she was about to learn that she wasn't the one setting the terms anymore. Let her, for once, miss him. With a move of his head to tell Osborne he needed to speak with him, he turned and strode into his own house.

Slade had battled off the tension for an hour now. He had bitten his tongue when Barbara left for the hospital, had forced a smile when Marietta insisted she wanted to enjoy the warmth of the day in her small backyard. He had done his best to remain pleasant while she and Elsie and Walker's mother visited in the garden.

But something in the air made him edgy. It was too heavy. Too hot for the last week of March. And the clouds slicking their way across the horizon were too blasted dark for his peace of mind.

"Would you please stop scowling?" Marietta's fingers barely brushed his arm, but it was enough. Enough to pull Slade's gaze from the flash of lightning over the harbor to her smiling face.

By thunder, the tug got worse every day. Much worse in the last few since Hughes had kept his distance. Though he hadn't said a word about it, Slade knew well what he was trying to do—make her miss him. And he sure wasn't going to tell the man her smile grew more brilliant with his absence.

As for how Slade was going to leave her side when all this was over...

He didn't bother summoning up a smile of his own. She knew by now he wasn't one to force them. "I don't like the looks of those clouds."

"Hmm." She turned toward the Chesapeake, standing a bit too close. Not so much that she couldn't cover it up quick enough if someone came along, but enough that he was all too aware of how easy it would be to weave his fingers through hers. To lean over and feather a few kisses over the garish green bruises. That single red curl brushed her shoulder as she surveyed the horizon. "I daresay we are in for a storm."

Worry flickered through her gaze, which made the tension wracking Slade redouble. That greenish cast to the clouds was too similar to the one he'd noted in Chicago five years ago.

The wind, having grown from breezy to steady through the day, loosed a gust strong enough to send Marietta back a step. "I hope Walker and Barbara make it home before it hits."

Another jagged flash of lightning shot down from the heavens. Slade anchored his bowler against the next blast of wind. "If not, they will wait it out at the hospital. We, however, should get inside."

She spun in the opposite direction. "Where are Elsie and Freeda?" Even as she asked, she must have spotted them just inside the stable door, where the girl played with a few stray pieces of hay. "Freeda! You had best hurry home."

The woman looked up from her granddaughter with surprise, her gaze tracking to the black horizon. "Gracious, when did those move in? I had best indeed. I'll just run Elsie into the house to Cora—"

"I'll take her." Her hands trembled as she stretched them toward the girl. "You go. You know how nervous my mother gets in storms, and she'll be watching for you."

Freeda leaned over to kiss Elsie's cheek, and Marietta's too while she was at it. "Thank you, dear." She rushed back into the open, her gaze snapping to Slade's. As she went by, she murmured, "Julie isn't the only one who gets anxious. You keep Mari distracted, hear?"

"Yes, ma'am." He watched her bustle away for another moment and then turned his attention back to Marietta. Afraid of storms? Part of him wanted to smile. He wouldn't have expected so mundane a fear from her. But then, the thunder that ripped through the heavens didn't sound terribly mundane.

She jumped, held Elsie close, and hurried for the house. Slade followed, but not fast enough. The first fat drops of rain hissed down around him. He hoped the torrent he could see in the distance would hold off long enough for Freeda to get home.

Inside, Marietta tossed her bonnet aside and then rubbed a hand over the girl's back, probably for her own comfort. Elsie looked as happy as could be. "I imagine Cora is helping Tandy at this time of day. I'll just...oh." She turned into the hall toward the kitchen but came to an abrupt halt. "Mother Hughes, excuse me."

Slade stepped near enough to be able to see Mrs. Hughes's face. In his two and a half months here, he had never once seen Elsie inside the house, and he wasn't sure if that was by Cora and Walker's choice or a command of the mistress.

Given the blank look upon the older woman's face, the decision belonged to the Paynes. She gave a vague smile. "I was just giving instructions on dessert. Who is this, Mari?"

Marietta cleared her throat. "Cora and Walker's daughter. I thought it prudent to send Freeda home ahead of the storm, so I was bringing her in to her mother."

Though Elsie had buried her face in Marietta's shoulder, Mrs. Hughes couldn't possibly miss the fair locks only a shade off from her own. That no doubt explained the surprise that flashed through her eyes in time to the lightning out the window. "Oh." Her hand fluttered up to her lace collar. "I didn't...why, I suppose I forgot that Walker is a mulatto. A quadroon, even, isn't he?" She reached out as if to touch the golden locks but then pulled back and shook her head. "I always find it so disconcerting when they look like us."

Slade's breath fisted, grateful neither Walker nor Cora were here to hear the horror in her tone.

Marietta edged up her chin, though he didn't miss her shiver at the next mighty heave of thunder. She said nothing at all, though he imagined some choice explanations ran through her mind.

Mrs. Hughes stepped by them. "Well, I was just on my way to lie down. I always enjoy listening to the rain."

"Certainly. Rest well, Mother Hughes." Marietta shifted her hold on Elsie and continued to the kitchen.

Slade grinned when the girl peeked at him and made the sign for his name. He returned the greeting with the sign for hers. He was far behind the others in terms of understanding, but a few of the oft-used signs he had picked up this past week. When he wasn't staring in amazement at how Marietta never once faltered as she taught them.

She faltered now, though, when the kitchen windows shook in their frames as they entered. His instinct was to slip an arm around her waist, but he didn't dare. Tandy, loyal to Mrs. Hughes, certainly couldn't be counted on to not mention it, and he had the impression Cora wasn't all that pleased at his and Marietta's familiarity either, despite Walker's new amusement with it. All he felt safe doing was to briefly touch the small of her back.

Cora stood before a stack of vegetables and within seconds had taken Elsie from Marietta's arms. Rain hammered against the glass, and no one tried to speak above it except to explain Freeda's departure. Within a minute, Marietta left the room.

Slade paused in the doorway and looked from Cora to Tandy to the small, high panes of glass over the work area. "Stay away from the windows."

Marietta must have heard his quiet warning. When he caught up with her in the main hall, she sent him an almost accusing glare. "Why would you tell them that?"

As if in answer, the sound of shattering glass came from the parlor. With a whimper, Marietta took off that direction, and Slade ran to gain the room ahead of her. He stopped her a step inside with an outstretched arm. It wasn't too bad—the topmost pane of the corner window now had a jagged hole, but it was on the protected side of the house, so not much rain should come in. Though it apparently hadn't stopped the piece of slate from hurtling at them from the nearby roof. The broken culprit rested, wet and heavy, on the floor amid shards of glass.

"We can take care of it when the storm passes. It will be all right." But when he turned around, she didn't look all right. Her eyes were wide as a kitten's and her hands shook, though she tried to hide them in the folds of her skirt.

Another peal of thunder shook the remaining panes and looked to nearly undo her. What was he to do but wrap his arms around her and hold her close? "Ah, Yetta." The scent of lilacs drifted from her hair. Which he may not have noticed had he not rested his head on hers. "It's nothing to worry about."

"Says the man who just spent an hour frowning at the clouds." Her arms cinched tight around him.

He wouldn't have, had he realized how much she hated storms. Though to be honest, the howl of the wind didn't set easy with him either. If he saw those clouds twisting, the way they did five years ago... "Come on. There's nothing we can do, so we had better find a distraction."

Giving in, he touched his lips to the bruise on her temple. Unwise on the one hand, though he couldn't regret it when he pulled away and saw that old flirtatious glint in her eyes. Much as he liked the depth of the new Marietta, he did have a certain predilection for the fire of the old one.

Her fear very nearly left her eyes when she batted her lashes at him. "What kind of distraction do you have in mind, Mr. Osborne?"

For the sake of his sanity, he chuckled and stepped away. Then he grabbed her hand and pulled her out of the parlor. "Don't tempt me, Mrs. Hughes."

"Why ever not? I can think of no better distraction than—"

"We're going to have to make due with second-best." He pulled her into the library, to a corner well away from the sweeping glass window, and swung her toward a chair.

She put just enough weight into the movement to land on the couch instead, and then she tugged him down beside her. Heaven help him, he shouldn't smile...but he couldn't help it. "Now there's something worth noting. When you get frightened, you get flirtatious."

Lightning flashed, the thunder all but tripping over it. Her eyes flickered like a lamp in the wind. "You had better provide that second-best distraction soon, Slade, or I will be forced to resort to the first."

"Right." He pushed back to his feet before he could invite the fool move. "If you will light a lamp, I'll grab the book."

It took him a minute to locate it on the shelf. He had picked it up before but had opted as usual for one that would remind him of who he was and what he was doing here. Now, though, they needed an escape, not a sermon.

There. He grabbed the volume of short stories and turned back to the couch. A glowing lamp perched on the table beside Marietta.

She looked unsteady as she stared out the window, and no wonder. The boughs of the trees bent low, and the rain lashed at the glass. Down the street, a piece of fencing ricocheted off one building and then another. His throat went dry.

"Here." He handed Marietta the book and settled beside her again.

She frowned. "Poe? You think to distract me from the storm with Gothic horror?"

"The storm will be nothing but a backdrop. You obviously like his work."

"Hmm?" Confusion cloaked her face for half a moment. "Oh, the parlor game. I glanced through this compilation once. I don't really... but you have a point. It will provide ample distraction."

Slade leaned into his corner of the sofa and studied her as she opened the tome and flipped through it with shaking fingers. The pages seemed determined to stick together. Or maybe her hands just refused to cooperate. After a moment, she slapped the cover shut again and shut her eyes, drawing in a long breath. "Which story would you like?"

"How about 'The Cask of Amontillado'?"

She nodded but made no move to open the book. Didn't even open her eyes.

Slade cleared his throat. "Do you want me to find it?"

"No."

"Or I can read—"

"No. Just..." She shook her head and leaned back. "'The thousand injuries of Fortunato I had borne as best I could; but when he ventured upon insult, I vowed revenge.'"

"Wait." He sat up straight again. "You have it memorized? You just said you had read it once."

Her eyes opened and glowed green-gold in the lamplight. "Do you want to hear it or not? Because if not, I would be more than happy to toss myself into your arms to pass the time."

His lips twitched. That rated as the most interesting threat he had ever received. "Sorry. Go on."

She closed her eyes again. "'You, who so well know the nature of my soul, will not suppose, however, that I gave utterance to a threat...'"

He slid the book from her lap and located the story, reading along with her. She didn't miss a word—or rather, when she did, she quickly corrected her fumble. Nearing the end of the page, he prepared to flip it...and frowned. The pages were still folded together from the press, uncut, making the inner pages inaccessible. He fished out his penknife.

Marietta stumbled over her words, came to a halt, and opened her eyes. A frown marred her brow. "Let me see that." Without waiting for his reply, she took the book back and sighed when she noted the same thing he had.

He leaned over and slid the blade along the crease, separating the pages and revealing the words.

She glanced at one page, the other, and then handed the book back and closed her eyes again. "'We had passed through walls of piled bones, with casks and puncheons intermingling, into the inmost recesses of catacombs.'"

"Yetta." He didn't know whether to stare at the book or her. Obviously, she had never read these pages before.

"'I paused again, and this time I made bold to seize Fortunato by an arm above the elbow.'"

"Yetta." He seized her by the elbow, though hesitatingly. But she opened her eyes, glanced once out the window at the still-raging storm, and then turned her gaze to him, somber. He rested his arm on the back of the couch, his fingers resting against her shoulder. "What are you doing?"

Her smile, for a reason he couldn't discern, looked self-deprecating. "Reading."

"No, you're...what? Reciting?"

"No." Her gaze fell to her hands, which were twisting and untwisting a portion of her skirt. "Recitation, as I understand it, is when you purposely commit something to memory and then deliver it through practice. I am *reading*. From the pages in my memory."

"Reading from..." He blinked, but that did nothing to help. He moistened his lips, but with the same lack of result. "You mean, you have only to glance at a thing once, and you can recall the entire page perfectly?"

So all those times he had seen her sitting in seeming idleness, with her eyes closed just like this...

"Mm-hmm."

"The files from the desk." That was how she had copied them so exactly after she had given him her key. And what was it she had said when he asked her whether she had looked at them? That she had taken a glance—and that a glance was all it took. "The way you flipped through the book in the cellar. Yetta, that's—"

"Interesting, odd, and hard to believe."

He reached for her hands and stilled them. "I was going to say miraculous. But how—so you remember everything you set your eyes to, or do you have to make a point of it?"

"Everything." The way she said it...her tone heavy, her shoulders slumped. "Everything. Always. Not that the images are always there, but they can reemerge without warning. And they can evade me when I am too tired or in distress. Sometimes they flip so quickly before my mind's eye that I can scarcely lay hold of any one memory."

A miracle and a burden both, then. He couldn't imagine. Sure, it would be convenient not to forget the important things. But everything? "Just visual memories, then. Things you read or see or..."

"No." She said it on a half laugh, but this time she looked at him. Exhaustion filled her eyes. "Every word spoken, every event on every day."

Which would mean every harsh word. Every scream, every tear, every fear. "How do you not go mad?"

Again she laughed, more fully this time, with a hint of relief. Her fingers hooked around his. "For years I decided the only way to handle it was to live solely in the moment."

"There's a certain kind of logic to that."

"A foolish kind, but yes." Her breath quavered as she pulled it in, but he didn't think it had anything to do with the newest roar of thunder that shook the house. "My family...they always thought it so amazing. A miracle, as you said. A gift from God. And it is, but they never understood why I sometimes hated it. Why I never wanted anyone to know. It is one thing to amuse a party with a parlor game, but they always thought it some trick."

His hand on her shoulder traced the contour and trailed up her graceful neck. "Easier that way. If they realized, then they would never say an honest word in your company."

"Exactly. And the Hugheses..." She shook her head, turned his palm over between hers, and wove their fingers together. "The thought of them knowing set alarm bells ringing. Perhaps I always knew they protected their ambitions above all, and they might think me a threat to them if they realized."

So they didn't know. Lucien hadn't, and neither did Dev. But Walker would, growing up with her. That was why he had asked her to help with the signs. Why she never fumbled with them.

And she had told him. She made a definite choice to by reading as she had just done. Made him one of a select few who knew the depths of her mind.

And here he was, determined not to kiss her. Why, again, was that the wise course?

She glanced up at him. "But I could help you more. You see that, don't you? If you show me all you're working with, I can help."

If she didn't look so resigned to failure even as she asked it, he may have suspected her motives. He still did, in part. He drew in a long breath. "Is that why you just told me this? To try to get me to bring you into this business?"

The lightning-lit surprise in her eyes couldn't have been feigned. "No. I just...trust you. You've become a..."

"Friend?"

"Not the word I was looking for." She raised their joined hands and kissed his. Who knew such a light touch could make his stomach go so tight? "But I suppose it will do."

Heaven help him. "I can't put you in any more danger, Yetta. I can't. But...Hughes is involved in something important. I think the orders came straight from Richmond. So if you hear anything..."

She nodded, a hint of fresh life sparking in her eyes. "I'll be listening. Though he hasn't been over much."

"Yeah." Hearing footsteps scurrying along the hall, he removed his hands back to his own lap and rested them on the book again. "I can't say I mind his absence."

Especially given her smile as she whispered, "Me neither."

Twenty-Seven

Marietta stood at the library window and watched the merrymakers in the street with a catch in her throat. Church bells tolled all over the city, and even with darkness falling, riotous laughter still drifted in through the open window.

Richmond, the Confederate capital, had fallen. This day, the third of April, marked victory. Triumph for the Union, and part of her thrilled at that. But she had to wonder at the cost.

In the falling darkness, Dev trudged from his carriage. His fortnight of distance would end tonight, she knew. He would want comfort, and he would turn to her. Hence the cloud of dread hovering over her.

"I think I will retire early." Mother Hughes's voice pulled Marietta around to face the room with its other two occupants. Since the news had come earlier that day, her mother-in-law had been nearly silent. Seeing now how she faltered as she rose, Marietta prayed her health wouldn't slip again. "When Devereaux arrives, would you please ask him to visit with me for a few moments?"

"Of course." She hurried over to her Mother Hughes's side and slipped an arm around her waist. "Barbara, could you fetch Jess?"

Barbara smiled and slipped a ribbon into the book of medicine she had been reading. "Certainly. I will be but a moment."

Waiting until her friend had hurried out, Marietta leaned close. "Mother, you needn't pretend for my sake. I know your family will be mourning today as mine celebrates. I know you must mourn with them. I do not begrudge you that."

Tears clouded her sky-blue eyes. "I have had to deny them so long. But today..."

"I understand." Marietta leaned in for a gentle embrace. "Be free to grieve within this house, please. You are safe here."

A sob caught in Mother Hughes's throat and she hugged Marietta back. "It is a wonder, isn't it, that I made it through these years of martial law without being deported across the Potomac?"

Marietta breathed a low laugh. "No, it is no wonder. Not when your sons are president of the most important railroad in the Union."

The matron eased away. "The more I hear of the destruction down South, the more I want to go home. Silly, I know."

"I think I would feel the same way."

Their gazes held for a moment before Mother Hughes looked away. "They are Devereaux's family too. Not that blood determined loyalties for many in this war, but...if he seems conflicted tonight..."

Oh, she didn't think he would be conflicted at all. He would be furious and crushed, plain and simple. But Barbara was returning with Jess, so Marietta said nothing of his loyalties. "You needn't worry. I well understand that too."

Mother Hughes frowned even as Jess lumbered to her side. "It pains me to see you two at odds lately, Mari. Whatever has come between you, he loves you. Please, handle his heart gently."

A nod seemed the wisest answer. She added a strained smile and stepped away to let Jess into her place. Once those two had left the library, she sank onto the couch beside Barbara.

Her friend had shadows under her eyes again. Marietta wished for the hundredth time in the past two hours that Slade hadn't been called away to Washington. She might not dread Dev's arrival quite so much if she knew he lurked outside the door.

She rested her hand on Barbara's arm. "You have been working too hard."

"Nonsense." As always, Barbara's smile beamed warm and peaceful. "There is just too much to do to be idle. So many families suffered from that terrible storm, and the injured soldiers cannot tend themselves."

"That is no reason to neglect your own well-being. And when I think of you going about those neighborhoods—" A shudder cut her off.

Barbara shook her head. "Oh, Mari. The men who may view you as someone to steal from merely ask me to visit their ill children or tend their wives during their lying-in. I am one of them."

More like one of the angels. Marietta stood again and walked to the window. The front door of Dev's house opened. "Perhaps you should retire early as well, Barbara."

At the silence that greeted that suggestion, she turned to find her friend's lips pressed together. "Is something the matter?"

Barbara set aside her book. "I promised Slade I would not leave you alone with him. Not today."

Irritation sputtered to life. Much as she appreciated his concern, surely Slade realized that bringing Barbara into the mix was a terrible idea. "You know well he will simply ask to see me in another room if he wants to be alone with me."

Her friend looked sterner than she had ever seen her. "That doesn't mean you hand him the opportunity. Be wise, Mari."

She was trying. If he demanded to see her alone and Barbara refused to leave... She glanced out the window again. He was on the front walk now, and his expression shouted that he was in no mood to be refused.

Her throat went tight. Barbara might be mild under normal circumstances, but she didn't take promises lightly. And a confrontation between them would not end well.

Her decision made, Marietta ran toward the exit.

"What are you doing?"

She ignored the alarm in Barbara's tone. "I will lead him to the back garden. Walker will be able to see us."

Not waiting to see whether Barbara approved, Marietta pivoted into the hall and made for the door. The first tap had just sounded when she pulled it open.

Surprise cloaked his face. "Mari. You are opening your own doors now?"

She smiled and stepped out into the warm twilight. "I was waiting for you." True enough, if without the happy expectation he would wish. She pulled the door shut. "It is too nice an evening to spend indoors. Will you join me in the garden?"

"Gladly." Pleasure lit his eyes for the first time in weeks as he tucked her hand into the crook of his elbow. She felt his gaze on her face as he led her around the corner. "The bruises are gone, I see."

"Mm-hmm. And I imagine with the victory news, there will be many a ball we can attend together." The very thought made unease spread its wings within her, but what else was she to do?

"I suppose so." No satisfaction laced his tone. It must be eclipsed by the mention of the victory he would deem defeat. "Or...your mourning will be over in another two weeks."

Thirteen days, to be exact. A mark on her mental calendar that at once thrilled and terrified her. She would be free, finally, of the confines of grief. But that meant she would be in the direct path of Dev's expectations.

"You cannot know how I long to see you in full colors again. In that green dress, perhaps. You know the one." Desire made his voice husky and sent a shiver of warning up her spine.

She knew the gown, all right, and saw again the way Dev had looked at her when she wore it to a ball. Heard again the whispered proposal he had made when Lucien left her side to fetch her a lemonade. She had laughed him off as always, but it had been too difficult. She had known then that she must put a halt to the attraction before it led her down a path she didn't want to tread. Had vowed, silly a step as she knew it, never to wear that dress around him again.

It was the last colored gown she had donned. The very next night Lucien had gone out late when he got word there was trouble at the rail station. And an hour after that, it had been not her husband who came home, but the police, with the news of his murder.

"Mari." Dev halted her at the trellis, under the newly blossomed wisteria vine. Its sweet fragrance whispered through the air, lending a mood she didn't want. He slid his hands onto her waist and pulled her close. "I need you tonight."

She couldn't look at him, couldn't bear to see that dark light in his eyes. "Dev, I cannot...I *will* not. Not again."

His hands slid up her back, possessive and undaunted. "Marry me, then. Now. I can call the minister and get whatever license we need within an hour."

Panic brought the images clamoring, nonsensical and pointless. The scores of weddings she had attended, snippets from her own. Lucien laughing, the victory in his summer-green eyes as he spun her into their first waltz. The answering challenge in Dev's as he claimed the next one.

Granddad Thad emerging too somber from Daddy's study, watching her.

Dev leaned down now with obvious intent, fanning the flames of panic hotter. "Be mine, darling. Now and forever."

She tried to twist away, but his arms held her tight. "Dev, you can't be serious. Elopement? You wanted a courtship. To show the world—"

"And how better to do that than with a *fait accompli?*" He claimed her mouth in a fierce kiss that kindled revulsion within her.

God of my end, help me. Show me how to escape him, Father.

Father—a thought she held tight to as she extracted herself from his embrace, careful to keep only sorrow on her face. "Darling, you know how I have longed to marry you, but the war is over, or it will be within days. My father will be home. Please, let's wait for him."

He turned away with a curse vile enough to make her wince and then pivoted back with tight rage on his face. "You don't understand. It has to be now. Things will change with the end of the war, Mari. Things will...happen."

She could feel her pulse thudding in her throat and prayed he couldn't see it in the low light. "Of course things will change, but not for us."

He gripped her by the shoulders, his fingers digging enough that a whimper of pain escaped. They relaxed immediately. Apology lit his eyes. "Don't be a fool. Do you think Lincoln will just release all the power he has seized?" His fingers bit again. "I need you to trust me. I need to know where you stand, Mari."

A shiver slithered up her spine. Granddad Thad's very words two and a half months ago, the morning he brought her into the Culper Ring. Had embracing her loyalties made any difference at all? Had she accomplished anything with her hours of transcription, with the bottles of invisible ink she had used?

She knocked his hands away. "At the moment I stand with a man who is acting the bully. Don't play the tyrant with me, Devereaux."

"Don't push me away. I swear to you, you'll regret it." The look in his eye sent her back a step, though he followed. "At least give me the words. Is that so much to ask?"

She retreated more, though again he pursued her. "What words?"

"The ones you refused Lucien." The flash in his eyes put her in mind of the storm that had left so many houses in ruins. "He thought it a blessing, the fool, that you never asked for words of love. But we know the truth, you and I." He grabbed her arm again, twisting so that she had no choice but to land against his chest or else let him wrench her shoulder out of socket. "We know you never spoke of love to him because your heart was mine."

Words echoed, a crystalline reminder. *God's, not Dev's.*

"Tell me." He pressed her too close, so that she could scarcely breathe. "Tell me you love me. Tell me you're mine."

"You think you can demand those words by force?" She pushed in vain at his chest, her heart thundering when she saw a shadowed figure beyond him. "Let go, Dev. You're hurting me."

"No. You're mine, Marietta. You have already given yourself to me. Why fight me now?"

Oh, Lord, please don't let that be Slade. He already knew plenty of her secrets, but that one... He would no doubt look at her with the same horror Walker had. But if his eyes shone with disappointment instead of the affection that had taken place of the wolf, she wasn't sure she could bear it.

The shadow stepped into a patch of dim light. Walker. *Thank You, Lord.* Though he didn't look nearly so happy as she felt at seeing him. "I believe the lady asked you to take your hands off of her."

Dev let go with one, but only so he could turn around, dragging her with him. The muscle in his jaw pulsed. "You think you can order me around, boy?"

Walker smiled, small and mean. "You think I'm gonna stand here while you ravage her like you did Cora? Give me an excuse, Hughes. Give me an excuse to hurt you."

Pushing her away, Dev reached under his coat and pulled out a dagger that gleamed with menace in the light from the windows.

Not *a* dagger—it was the one from the cellar. Marietta sucked in a breath and jumped between them. Grateful as she was to have a champion, her tainted virtue wasn't worth Walker's life. Her eyes fastened on Dev's too-calm face. "Put that away."

He didn't even glance at her. "Step aside, Marietta. I don't intend to let some half-breed mutt think he can intimidate me."

From behind her came the rustle of fabric. The sound of a gun being cocked, of a revolver's cylinder rotating into place. "Do your worst, Hughes." Walker's voice was a low rumble, sure and steady.

For a moment, she feared Dev would lunge past her, take his chances against a bullet, and plunge the knife into Walker's chest. The way he narrowed his eyes...but then he shifted his gaze to her, and the calculation changed.

His smile was more threat than reassurance, but he lowered the knife. "Not with Mari here. Though if you have the intelligence of a stray dog, you'll know this isn't over."

And no doubt he would have more than a knife next time. She could barely force a swallow down her tight throat. "Dev, please."

He slid the blade back into the sheath on his belt. "Come here, Mari."

Walker's breath hissed out behind her. "Don't, Yetta. Don't go anywhere near him."

The fresh flash of lightning in Dev's eyes spurred her forward before he could draw his weapon again. When he moved his gaze from Walker to her, she expected violence or some show of force.

Instead, he slipped a soft hand behind her head and pressed his lips to hers in a caress of a kiss. Somehow, the contrast made it more terrifying. "Have it your way, Mari," he murmured as he pulled away. "No wedding until your father comes home. Just remember that those were your terms, not mine."

He spun on his heel and headed for the back entrance. No doubt he would go in to see his mother perfectly confident he would have his way at some point.

Marietta wanted nothing more than to let her knees buckle and to sink down into the damp earth. Forcing herself to turn to Walker instead, she slipped a hand into her pocket and twirled the silver fob around her fingers, praying it would anchor her.

Walker was just repositioning his coat over the pistol. Even in the deepening shadows she could see that every line of his face had gone tight. The next tolling of the bells across the square seemed the knell of death rather than victory.

"You have to get out of here, Yetta. Now. You and Barbara. Go to your mother or grandparents. Better still, go to Connecticut."

She squeezed the chain into her palm. Wise advice at this point. If Walker hadn't come out...and to think she had claimed Dev wasn't violent. That he wouldn't hurt her.

But he was. He would. And far more certainly, he would kill Walker without a second thought. She loosed the fob. "I will if you do. You can't stay here."

Frustration huffed from his lips. "Miss Lucy won't let Cora and Elsie go until she has to. You know that."

It was on the tip of her tongue to insist that he go, then, until this had blown over, but why even give voice to such inanity? Cora would have her babe any day, and Walker would never leave his wife and children in the path of a raging Devereaux.

"Then I guess we'll have to keep each other safe until this is all over."

"Are you mad?" He stepped close, pitching his voice low. "Do you realize what he would have done to you?"

Oh, to deny it...but she had seen his eyes, determined and deadly. "I know. But I already let him ruin me by my own choice, so—"

"Don't. You know better. You deserve better than that, princess, no matter what your mistakes were before."

Maybe. But one could also argue that she deserved whatever she got at his hands. She sighed and looked up.

A light appeared in Barbara's window, two feminine silhouettes blurred behind the filmy curtains, one with a rounded belly. Cora and Barbara, and with Mother Hughes already retired too. She didn't dare go back in. Not until Dev left. So she slid over to the cool stone bench and sat. "Elsie?"

"Asleep. I left a window open so I can hear her if she wakes." He sat beside her. Bracing his elbows on his legs, he was silent for a moment. Then he looked over at her with those silver-blue eyes. "You really never told Lucien you loved him?"

Marietta picked at a stray thread in her skirt. A few months ago, she would have denied it, knowing how it would appear to Walker. But that was before he became her friend all over again. "I didn't want to lie about that."

Walker kept his gaze on the silhouettes. A half smile touched his mouth as he watched Cora move in and out of view. "I didn't think I'd ever love anyone else. When Stephen wrote and told me you were marrying Lucien Hughes, I might have charged in to stop it if I weren't so spittin' mad at your choice."

Her chuckle felt like honey, soothing and sweet. "I meant for you to be. Not that I thought to see you again. I certainly didn't expect Stephen to force you to work here...or for you to marry Cora so soon."

"I couldn't let her suffer like my mama did."

"I know. You did right. And look what God has given you." She could smile, seeing the adoration in his eyes. "A woman you love. A beautiful family."

"And I tell her so every day." He looked to Marietta, the pearly light of the rising moon catching in his eyes. "What about you? You gonna tell Oz how you feel?"

Oz? Her lips tugged up. That was one of her grandfather's nicknames if ever she heard one. The man just couldn't call someone he liked by a full name. Though she shook her head at the question. "He intends to leave when this is over."

"So? I don't see any fetters round your ankles. You could go with him, wherever he might end up."

Would the panic ever stop nipping at her heels? Her hand sought her pocket again. "He already told me he has no interest in a relationship."

Walker snorted and leaned back, folding his arms across his chest. "I have a feeling that was some time ago. Have you asked him lately?"

"Of course not." It was one thing to tease a man about a kiss and quite another to demand he love her and seek her hand. How could she? Look what happened the last time she had planned to follow someone.

No, she must face facts. Maybe she inspired the wrong kind of passion in the wrong kind of man, but the ones worthy of her love would never deem her worthy of theirs. Not enough to fight for her.

"Aw, Yetta. Don't go cryin' on me, now. You know how I hate that."

Startled, she lifted a hand to her cheek and felt tears slipping down.

"Thunder and turf." Walker rubbed a hand over his face. "You really do love him."

Had he just been baiting her when he said it a minute ago? She withdrew her hand from her pocket and slapped at his arm. And then slumped. "Maybe I do. But don't worry. I'm sure it'll pass after he leaves."

It always did.

Twenty-Eight

"Y ou sure you're all right, honey?"

Cora took a long moment to answer Walker's question. Her breathing wasn't heavy the way it was when the pains were fully upon her with Elsie, but the discomfort must have been intense enough. She kept her eyes shut, kept on gripping the back of the chair until her knuckles were white.

At length she gave him a weak smile. "Just fine, Walker. No more serious today than they were yesterday. Only, since they kept me up last night..."

Not knowing any words to make it easier, he just settled his hand on her abdomen. The muscles were tense, hard as rock. Might not be today, but his babe was coming soon, and he couldn't decide if he was more excited or terrified. He remembered cradling the tiny, new-born Elsie, holding her to his chest so she could hear his heart beating for her.

Or in her case, feel it.

He looked forward to that again, but fear hovered as big as hope. So many women didn't live through the birthing.

"Don't you worry about me." Easier again, she covered his hand and rubbed it. "I be just fine. Miss Barbara said everything's as it should be, and she's been well trained by all them doctors. If I need anything, she's right there. You go on."

He would rather stay by her side until the baby came, but since the horses wouldn't take a holiday from their business just because he asked nicely, he sighed and took a step away. Though only one. "I think it counts."

She blinked her pretty brown eyes at him. "Ya lost me, honey."

He splayed a hand over her stomach again. "Maybe it won't take effect until December, but the amendment passed. I think that counts. This little one will be born free."

She cupped his face, tenderness in her eyes. "Close enough, I guess. I sure don't feel like runnin' anywhere, anyway."

Relief washed through him as he kissed her. If she had insisted they make a run for it now, he didn't know what he would have done.

A minute later he stepped out into the midday sunshine, feeling that he should have been inside this time of day for a sign lesson. But Cora didn't feel up to them right now, so he went down the stairs, turned, and halted.

Osborne sat on a bench with no Marietta in sight. These days, that was something worth noting. "You get sacked, Oz?"

The detective looked up, but without the amusement Walker had expected, and only for a moment. "Yetta's too blasted curious for me to read this in the house. It's a missive from Booth."

Feeling rather blasted curious himself, Walker came closer. "Bet the Knights were none too happy to hear about Lee's surrender today."

"You could say that." Letting out a gusty exhale, Osborne shoved to his feet. "They're going to act in the next few days. This was my notice to be ready. They've assigned me to capturing Stanton, the Secretary of War."

"Isn't that enough, then? To arrest them?"

Osborne shook his head as he slipped the letter into his pocket. "Right now it's just talk, like their every other attempt. Besides." He stared at the house, probably trying to divine where Marietta was, given his wistful look. "Hughes isn't involved with this. He's been working on something else, and I haven't figured out what. I have a feeling it's big, though."

"So you need to figure out the one and stop the other."

"Yeah. I—" He cut himself off with a frown when the clop of hooves sounded and took a few quick steps to where he could see the street.

Walker bit back a grin when he muttered a few choice words. "Still not on good terms with the Arnaud boys, I take it."

The look Osborne shot him at least had a touch of humor in it this time. "But while they're here with Yetta, are you up for a little excursion to the rail yard?"

Snooping around in broad daylight, while Hughes was there in his office? Walker grinned. "Now you're talking my language."

Osborne headed into the stable, but Walker strode instead for Ize and Hez, who must have caught a glimpse of Osborne, given their scowls in that direction. He chuckled and took the horses' leads in hand. "You two ever gonna let up on him?"

Isaac snarled. "Sure. Once he leaves."

Hez sighed. "I would probably like him well enough if Mari didn't like him so well."

"Hez." Walker shook his head and rubbed the nose of the painted mare.

"Well, one cannot ignore the evidence. She has faulty taste in men. First Lucien, and then Dev."

"Don't overlook the bevy of other objectionable beaux she stringed along until Lucien proposed." Ize scowled in the direction of the house. "Our sister is inconstant and often foolish. If she likes someone, chances are he is too ambitious, too selfish, or of questionable morals."

All amusement faded. He knew Isaac was mule headed, but Hez— he'd have thought Hez would have seen the change in her. Reevaluated, like the scientist he was. He clicked his tongue to urge the horses forward. "She has made her fair share of mistakes, but the real fools here are you for not realizing she's repented of them."

He left them to chew on that, though they probably wouldn't. Deliberately shaking it off, he helped Osborne finish saddling their horses and was grateful for his silence as they mounted up and headed for the station.

The change in the city was palpable as they rode through. Still just as beat-up and run-down as ever, but folks seemed to smile more. Hope had finally come to call this past week. There might yet be a few skirmishes, but the war was over. With Richmond fallen, Lee's surrender, and the Thirteenth Amendment passed, things were finally going to be different.

It took a few minutes for him to realize Osborne kept sending him sidelong glances. Walker lifted his brows. "Something on your mind, Oz?"

The detective pursed his lips and nodded. "Rumor has it Lincoln plans to go to Fort Sumter for the raising of the American flag on the anniversary of the battle."

He waited a moment, but when Osborne said no more, he drew the connecting lines himself. The anniversary was the twelfth of April—just two days away. If Lincoln were to go to South Carolina now, then... well. That might get in the way of the KGC's plan to act in the next little while, mightn't it? "Sounds like we need to pay your friend Herschel another visit."

"Not 'we,' Walker. Not with Cora as she is."

Hence the looks, he supposed. "So you go. I'll keep an eye on Yetta."

Osborne nodded, but he gripped the reins too tightly. No doubt worrying over Hughes being so close to Marietta with him gone. Walker had told him about the scene in the garden the week before. Though when he'd seen the way Osborne's eyes snapped, he'd almost wished he had kept it to himself.

Camden Street Station soon appeared, a hub of activity as always. It should be easy to blend into the crowds. They probably ought to hitch their horses out of sight and walk in. Slip through the crowds of passengers and around to where the workers were. No one would think anything of seeing Osborne around. So long as they could avoid Hughes...

"Osborne!"

Blast.

Osborne no doubt had the same thought, but he covered it well. His fingers relaxed, and his face moved into its usual mask of wary watchfulness. He turned his mount toward where Hughes stood, a hand lifted.

He didn't look concerned at finding Osborne there, though the glare he sent Walker could have set fire to a bucket of water. "Bringing your dog to work now, Osborne?"

Though he shifted in his saddle, Oz made no reply. Just measured Hughes in the way that said *Get to your point.*

He did, his gaze back to welcome when he turned to Osborne. "I didn't expect you so soon. The courier must have been eager for a tip. You didn't leave Mari alone, did you?"

Though Osborne must wonder why Hughes had sent a courier to fetch him, he didn't so much as blink out of turn. "Her brothers are there."

"Ah, good. Well, your friend is waiting in my office." He motioned toward the building but headed in the opposite direction. "Take your time. I have inspections to conduct."

His friend? He no doubt had plenty of them, but the only one Walker had ever heard him mention was Herschel. That would be an answer to an unspoken prayer.

After securing their horses, Walker followed Osborne into the building and down the hall to an office that screamed money with dark woods and soft leather. Osborne strode in with no hesitation, though he came to an abrupt halt only three steps in.

A man stood inside staring at a painting, but it sure wasn't Herschel. And if the lack of response from Oz were any indication, whoever it was wasn't someone he had expected to see.

"Kaplan?"

The stranger turned, but no light entered his eyes. Nothing but animosity. Strange. Why seek him out for a visit if he didn't actually want to see him? "Osborne." His gaze flicked to Walker, but he apparently didn't deem him worth a greeting. "Your new boss seemed real pleased with your work. Told me to pass along to Pinkerton how well he trains us."

Us. Another detective, then. Though the way he and Osborne stared bullets at each other, Hughes obviously hadn't chosen a good word when he called him a "friend."

Osborne didn't say a thing.

Kaplan aimed a stream of tobacco juice at a spittoon and pulled a wrinkled paper from his pocket. "Hersh asked me to deliver this personally. I wouldn't have if I didn't owe him a favor."

A breath of dry laughter puffed from Oz's lips. "And here I thought you came for tea." He reached for the paper and then frowned. "You read it."

"What do I look like, a fool? No way was I going to be party to anything underhanded, if you'd managed to turn him somehow."

Walker leaned into the wall. Turn him? What, did this guy think Osborne was here, working with Hughes and the KGC, because he wanted to be?

Possible. Possible indeed that none of his former friends knew about his cover. The first rule Mr. Lane had taught him as a Culper was that safety lay in anonymity. The fewer who knew what an intelligencer was about, the better.

Kaplan waved a hand. "No secret, though. Pinkerton had a new job for him and sent him away. Don't know where or for how long, and that doesn't say neither. But that last part?" He leaned over, jabbed a finger at the bottom of the page. "About me being the one most likely to listen to any other 'advice' you have? He's dead wrong on that."

Osborne inhaled, the long and deep kind meant to instill patience. "Kap...I don't know what my brother did or said to you. But please, you have to listen."

"No, I don't." As if to prove it, he grabbed the hat sitting on Hughes's desk and shoved it on his head. "I promised Hersh I'd give you the letter, and I gave you the letter. Duty done, favor repaid, that's it."

Osborne slid over a step, between Kaplan and the door. "Just hear me out. The KGC intends to act. Soon. Kidnap the president and all the important cabinet members besides. If you can just make sure he goes to Fort Sumter like they say he might, that would stymie them."

With a grunt of incredulous laughter, Kaplan shoved past him. "If that's what you want, then you can be sure I'll advise the opposite."

"Kap, *please.*" Osborne grabbed at his arm, hopeless fury in his face. "Just look at me. Look me in the eye."

Something shifted in Kaplan's expression too. Went from animosity to resignation. "That's the problem, Osborne. I looked you in the eye every day and never had a clue who I was seeing. I don't know you." He pulled free. "I don't know if I ever did."

Osborne didn't make another attempt to detain him. He just stood there working his jaw and staring after him, crushing the letter in his hand.

Walker cleared his throat. "Interesting friend, Oz."

Smoothing out the paper again, Osborne shook his head. "Did I ever mention I had a twin?"

A twin. All sorts of possibilities rose up then, in light of that conversation. "Nope."

"Apparently I never mentioned it to them either." He slid the letter into his pocket and met Walker's gaze, straight and unwavering. "Thanks to him, I don't have many friends left."

"Well." Funny how brothers could be sometimes. Some were like the Arnauds, sticking together no matter what, through disagreement and distance. Some...weren't. "I guess it's a good thing you've made some new ones here then."

A flare of his nostrils was the only indication of feeling. But it was enough. "It is."

Walker turned to the door, eager to get out of Hughes's lair. He led the way back into the warm spring sunshine without any difficulty, but then he let Osborne take the lead.

They zigzagged around, always with a gait that spoke of purpose. Though if Osborne had a method to his route, Walker couldn't detect it. Maybe they were his usual rounds. He didn't volunteer anything, and Walker didn't ask. No doubt he was still mulling over the confrontation with Kaplan, and a man needed some silence to mull.

Apparently it didn't distract him, though. He came to a halt at the exact moment Walker did, when a familiar top hat came into view. Of one accord, they plastered themselves to the side of a box car before Hughes could spot them.

"That's where he keeps his private car," Osborne murmured. He peeked around the corner and came back with narrowed eyes. "He has a few freight cars there too. Strange."

Walker did a quick survey of the area. "If we can get over to that caboose, we might get a better look."

"My thought too." He peeked out again, holding a hand up. When he motioned with it a moment later, Walker took his cue to follow, stealthy as a shadow, to a better position.

Hughes had opened one of the freight cars, the hefty lock still swaying from the door's slide. He was even then disappearing into the interior, though he reemerged quickly, marking something upon the paper in his hands. Then he shut the door again, fastened the lock, and slid the key into his pocket.

Walker hugged the caboose's wall until the crunch of Hughes's shoes on the gravel faded. He looked over at Osborne. "Did you see what I saw in there?"

"Crates of guns." Osborne exhaled. "Looked like ammunition too. Not good."

"You think he's storing them for use here or means to move them?"

Osborne shook his head. "Surely if he intended some sort of riot here, the Knights would all be involved. But where else would he be taking them?"

"Maybe they were intended for the Confederate troops. Before the surrender."

That made sense, but Oz's head kept on shaking. "It doesn't feel right. They must be tied to whatever else he's been doing. I've read through so much of his stuff at this point, surely the pieces are there. I just can't quite put them together."

Walker held his breath and waited for some other answer, any other answer, to come to mind. None did. "You could ask Yetta for help."

Osborne's eyes went dark as midnight. "No."

"I know you don't want to get her involved. But her memory is... good. She could help."

"If by good you mean perfect, then yeah, I know. But the answer is still no." He pivoted and headed in the direction opposite Hughes's.

"She told you?" Surprise had him lurching to catch up.

Apparently so obvious an observation didn't warrant an answer. Osborne said nothing for a solid minute as they walked. Then he sucked in a deep breath. "I know she could help. I know she would. But I can't ask it. I can't risk her."

Walker understood that. He'd sooner die than bring Cora into any of this mess. But then, Cora wasn't in a position to stop a monster. Marietta was. "What if it comes down to no other way?"

Again silence answered him. But this time, it seemed to say Osborne knew well that it was a decent question. He just didn't like it.

Twenty-Nine

Slade closed the prayer book and returned it to his pocket, but peace still eluded him. He had tossed and turned all night. He had risen before dawn, fallen to his knees, and prayed everything he could think to pray, begging the Lord for answers. But the vise around his chest wouldn't ease.

"Are you all right?" Marietta's delicate fingers rested on his arm, a quiet demand for his attention.

He looked up and wondered when Barbara and Mrs. Hughes had left the room. The fact that he didn't know made his brows knit. His job was to know, to watch, even when doing something else. If he was failing at that today, then something had to change.

His gaze made its way to Marietta's face, and the vise went tighter. "Hmm?"

"You are brooding," she accused. Then she smiled. "More than usual."

Because he couldn't help it, he smiled. And because he had no right to smile, it vanished. She was still too beautiful, too able to use it to her advantage, but if she were still just that, this wouldn't bother him. He wouldn't care, more than in a general sense, how she fared when all this was done.

But he did. Because she was too much more than beautiful, and he was far, far too aware of it.

If only there were another way.

There wasn't. "Yetta." He moved the arm under her fingers, caught them in his, and urged her to sit on the couch beside him. "How good are you at puzzles?"

She sank to the cushion, her green eyes narrowing. "Good, unless they are too complex. When too many memories clamor, it takes time to sort through them all. Why?"

Why indeed? Why was he even considering laying all his cards on the table and asking her to build his hand?

He knew the answer. Because she could help, and he needed it. Because if he didn't figure this out now, he would never make right Ross's wrongs.

Why, then, did he hesitate?

But he knew that answer too. Because he wasn't so sure, anymore, what mattered more to him. Bringing down the Knights of the Golden Circle or protecting Marietta Arnaud Hughes.

He kissed her hand but then released it. At this point, he couldn't do either without her help. "Do you still want to see the castle?"

Her eyes went wide, her lips parted. "You changed your mind?"

He stood and held out a hand to help her up too. "I'm running out of time. I still don't think it's a great idea for your sake, but...I need you."

Her fingers already resting in his, she paused. "Has something happened?"

"Yeah." Once she was on her feet again, he led her from the room and across the hall to Hughes's study. They might as well start where she left off. "Booth says we should be ready to move within the next couple of days."

Her hand went tight around his. "The plan is still to kidnap the president?"

"In theory." He closed the study door behind them, knowing his worry shone in his eyes. "They are so desperate, though, with the news of defeat upon them. I've always feared they may decide on a simpler approach."

"You don't mean..." Her skirts swished to a halt as he fiddled with the hidden latch. "No one has ever assassinated a president. Surely they won't either."

If only he could be sure. But the suspicion had redoubled since he received that note from Booth yesterday. It hadn't just said to be ready for the agreed-upon plan. It had said to be ready for whatever was required. "Pray you're right about that, Yetta. Pray it with every beat of your heart."

The panel popped forward, and he slid it open while Marietta lit the lantern. She handed it to him with solemn eyes. "I will pray. I will ask Barbara and my family to pray without giving them specifics. And I will do anything I can to help you."

"I know." For the first time that day, a zephyr of peace touched his spirit. The last time he stood with her on these stairs, he wasn't convinced she was on his side. Now it was one of the few things he trusted. He led the way down into the cellar. "There are some things here you didn't see last time. After that, we'll head to the castle entrance."

"All right." Her voice strove for confident, but he caught the undertone of nerves.

In silence he set the lamp upon the table and unpacked the crates, laying out papers and books she'd yet to see. Whenever she nodded at one batch, he replaced it with another. Occasionally she would correct him on his ordering as he put it back, but otherwise she didn't speak either.

Within five minutes, they headed back up the stairs, and he couldn't help but note the crease between her brows. Once all was back to rights in the study and they were in the hall, he sighed. "Are you sure—"

"What a long way you've come, Slade, to be wasting words on ridiculous questions to which you already know the answers." When she glared like that, her confidence outshone her anxiety. She looked once more like the dangerous, catty woman who had so confused him three months ago, and less like the genuine, selfless lady he'd spent so many hours with lately.

Somehow, realizing both were within her made him feel better. He led the way to the side stairs.

Marietta's steps slowed behind him. "Where are we going?"

"Ballroom."

"What? I thought the entrance was outside the house." And the outrage in her voice at realizing it wasn't, that the Knights had therefore been coming *inside* her home, made him grin.

He led her past the steps to Barbara's room and down the hall toward the ballroom. The members all used the exterior entrance to the room, through the door partially concealed by the overgrown hedge. Hughes left a key for that door and kept this interior one locked.

Slade knew where he kept this key too, and he used it to let the mistress of the house into the room she probably hadn't seen in nearly two years.

Her breath caught when she glided past him, her gaze latching on the mirrors and windows draped in black. "They never took down the mourning."

"Hughes apparently forbade the servants from entering since the day of Lucien's funeral. When you gave him the keys to the study and, by extension, the castle."

She fingered one of the swags of black crepe. "I told them to close it up. I didn't realize..." Huffing, she planted her hands on her hips and turned to a piano in the corner, its coat of dust thick and white. "He could have at least let them drape the furniture first."

A snort of laughter escaped. He couldn't help it. The things women worried about sometimes.

She spun back to him and smiled. And then went serious again far too fast. "Lead the way, Detective."

"Right." He crossed to the far wall, found the piece in the ornate molding that opened the door not so dissimilar from the one in the study, and swung it wide. Here, a recess in the wall of the staircase held a lantern and a box of matches.

They went down the stairs and then along the corridor to the series of rooms. He took her first to the farthest one, the initiation chamber. So far as he had been able to discern, nothing there would be any help. But he intended to be thorough, so she would have no reason to demand that he bring her down here again.

She poked about, looking at every crack and crevice. He expected questions, but she asked none. Not in that first chamber, nor in the next, nor the next.

She studied every detail of the maps, she flipped through the encoded papers tacked up here and there. She stared too long at the defaced poster of Lincoln. If anything, she became quieter as they went, until at last, when she gazed at the president's faded, smeared face, he had to strain to hear her breathing.

He touched a hand to her arm. "That's all there is to see, Yetta. We might as well go back up so you can read it in comfort."

Marietta made no reply.

"Yetta?" Sliding his fingers around her arm, he gave it a gentle squeeze to get her attention.

Lately, any casual touch would earn him a smile. Or at least she'd lean in to him a little. Now she didn't flinch a muscle.

Her stillness felt wrong. He set the lantern on a rickety end table so that he could see her face. "Yetta."

She didn't look at him. Wasn't, so far as he could tell, looking at anything. Her eyes were opened but unfocused, occasionally flicking back and forth, but obviously unseeing. As though she were dreaming.

Claws dug at the pit of his stomach. He clasped her hands, both of them between his. Squeezed, rubbed. Still nothing. "Come on, kitten. Shake this off. Come back to me."

Shouldn't she have grinned at him for being scared over nothing? Brushed him off like a fly? Done something?

His mind screamed a prayer, though he didn't know what words to use. A plea for help, for inspiration in what to do, for the Lord to touch her and make whatever this was stop. It couldn't be good. Couldn't be healthy, could it, to disappear like this?

He gripped her shoulders and tried a light shake, the type that would rouse a sleeper. Maybe this was some kind of...of trance. Like that hypnosis mumbo-jumbo one of his old gambling pals had told him about. Maybe he just had to wake her up. "Marietta. Talk to me."

Whatever was holding her erect seemed to snap. She slumped and listed to the right. Slade caught her with a hiss and gathered her close. "I've got you. I've got you."

So far as he could tell as he hooked the lantern handle on one finger, she couldn't even hear him. But she had to come out of it soon, didn't she? *Please, Lord. Please.* "We'll just get you back upstairs and you'll be fine. You just need to get away from all this."

He'd known this was a bad idea. Why had he brought her here? The answers weren't worth hurting her. Nothing mattered so much that he should have risked her like this. Even if he couldn't have known that this would happen, he'd known it was too much.

"All right. Okay. Almost there." He kicked the room's door shut and hurried along the corridor and then up the stairs. Pushing the lantern back into place, he blew it out even as he stepped into the ballroom.

The muted light still felt bright after the tunnel, that was why he blinked so much. And the dust, that's what made his nostrils flare. He put her back on her feet, his arms clamped firmly around her. Maybe sunlight, however diffused, would bring her around. Maybe being out of the castle would be enough. Maybe...

"Ah, Yetta." He ventured one hand onto her cheek. Her eyes were still doing that strange, blurred half flicker, and now her lips twitched, as though she whispered to herself.

"Yetta. Yetta, I'm sorry." He pressed his lips to hers, quick and panicked. "I'm so sorry." It felt right to kiss her. Maybe because it stilled the silent muttering, maybe just because. He kissed her again. "I shouldn't have taken you there." Another kiss, soft and pleading. "Come back to me, kitten. Please. I'm so sorry I put you through this."

She drew in a quick breath, the kind one might make when waking. Her hands, resting against his chest, curled in. When she blinked, her lashes fluttered against his cheek. "Stop."

Thank You, Jesus. He pulled his head away.

Her eyes still looked clouded, but they were clearing. Even shone a bit—though too dimly—when the corners of her mouth turned up. She shook her head. "Apologizing. Stop apologizing. Don't stop kissing me."

He breathed a laugh that felt like hope and shook his head too. There she was—shaken, but back. He did the only thing he could possibly do. He leaned down and kissed her.

Marietta closed her eyes against the race of images and focused on Slade. She pushed aside the quick snap and flutter of the pounding parade within her head and didn't let herself ask how she had arrived back at the ballroom when her last memory was of stopping before the ruined election poster.

They still clamored and buzzed, those crashing images. But his lips hushed them. He pulled her back to the here and now—exactly where she wanted to be.

She slid one arm around his neck, rested the other against his chest, and felt a rush of contentment. This, this was what she had been waiting for for so long. This gentle touch of a kiss that somehow both wanted and gave. That touched her heart as well as her lips. When he pulled her close, she wanted to melt into him, to stay just there where all else faded. Where she was safe, protected, cherished.

The kiss took her deeper, and she marveled at how it could while also making her soar. His first embrace, two months ago nearly to the day, hadn't had this effect. Something had changed. Between them, or perhaps in them. It wasn't just wanting anymore.

That terrifying realization may have sent her a step back had he not angled his head and melded his mouth to hers a new way, drawing her back in.

Perhaps she had toyed with the word *love* in connection with him, but she hadn't been thinking of it right. She had been thinking of the quick tumble in and out that she had felt with the Hugheses. The new and innocent kind that had blossomed so slowly over the years with Walker.

This was neither, and both. This was the unfurling of a rose. The summer heat of the sun. The steady rush of a gurgling stream. This was beauty and life and...and surety. How that was possible she couldn't have said. But for the first time in her life, she knew it wasn't a matter of just wanting to be in the arms that held her—it was a matter of belonging there.

As he stroked his thumb over her cheek and eased away, she knew his feelings must have grown too. Did he love her? Did he feel this same stretching of his soul toward hers? This yearning to simply be in the presence of the other? She wanted to believe he did, that he must.

"I don't know what that was down there," he whispered, resting his forehead against hers, "but don't ever do that to me again."

She wasn't even sure what he was talking about. Closing her eyes, she toyed with his lapel and tried to ease back into her mind. But there was just so much. The actual memories of her actions in the castle tangled with the things she had seen. The pictures kept shifting, turning, realigning.

The election poster hovered, Mr. Lincoln's face with that dreadful smear. She remembered looking at it, recalling the first time she had done so from the secondary tunnel. For some reason, that had triggered the whirlwind.

Gripping his coat, she refused to be swept up again. Not now. She clung to Slade, shaking the images away and searching for him in the memories of when she stood before the poster. No images, but his voice was there. Begging, pleading with her.

Marietta opened her eyes, narrowed, at his handsome face. "Did you call me *kitten?*"

His blink was blank, but then a smile tugged a corner of his mouth. "Maybe."

"Maybe?"

She felt his shrug as much as she saw it. The lopsided smile made no attempt to even out. "You have cat eyes."

A soft laugh filled her throat. Her fingers, of their own will, feathered through the hair at the back of his head. "Should I call you 'puppy' then?"

Another blink. "Pardon?"

She grinned. "You have wolf eyes."

And oh, how she loved the glint of amusement in them. "Nice. But no. Don't even think about it."

Another laugh soothed its way through her, but quick on its heels came the press of images. Too many, too fast. She kissed him again to force them back, but even as it worked, she knew it was but a stopgap. A rickety dam that would give way at any moment.

She eased back down from her toes. "I need paper and pen to work through this."

Slade nodded and loosened his arms. The worry took over his eyes again. "Yetta...has that ever happened before?"

"Not to that extent. But as soon as I can bring some order to the thoughts, they will settle." She let her hand trail down his neck and then over his shoulder. She was reluctant to let go but had no choice. "I am sorry to have startled you. Or I would be, had it not inspired you to kiss me again."

Chuckling, he turned her toward the ballroom's exit with a hand upon her back. "You're something else, kitten, that's for sure."

Maybe that shouldn't have felt like the highest compliment she had ever received, but it lit a glow deep inside her. She walked with him toward the closed double doors, wondering if her smile looked as smug as the cat he called her.

He paused with his hand halfway to the knob, turned to her instead, and cupped her cheek. "Just one more," he murmured before he lowered his lips to hers.

He made it count. Where his embrace a minute earlier had soothed and steadied, this one stole her breath and made her head swim. She held tight, praying with every shared beat of their hearts that this moment would be one of many more. Perhaps not today, but surely they could make a way for themselves. He could come back. She could follow him. Something. Because as his touch stilled her memories and his heart lit a new fire in hers, she knew without doubt that she would never get over this man. If he left, she would mourn him the rest of her days.

When he pulled away, she nearly begged him to hold her longer. But the memories crowded again, making her throat go tight.

Paper now. Begging and pleading later.

He must have read the mounting disquiet in her face. His eyes went dark, his mouth set in a firm line, and he pulled her quickly through the doors, locking them behind him. Then she led the way to the main stairs and up to her drawing room.

He pulled out her desk chair for her, and she opened the topmost drawer to take out paper. Then, with the key hidden in that drawer, she opened the bottom one and withdrew a quill.

"Let me know what I can do." Slade leaned onto the edge of her desk, fiddling with the blotter. He must still be nervous, still scared for her, to indulge in idle movement like that.

Hoping her smile reassured him, she turned back to the paper and let her pen take the lead.

The lines forced their way forward first, perhaps because of their oddity. On the backs of papers, many of them, some barely visible in pencil, others strong and bold, but looking like random scratches... when looked at alone.

Puzzles. Slade couldn't have known how right a word he had chosen. That was what each of the pages looked like as they marched through her mind, pieces of a puzzle. She copied a few of them down, but smaller in scale, and let the mental pictures shift and rearrange until she found the ones that matched.

"Maps." Slade leaned over her when several of them were completed. "May I?"

"Please." She needed the work space. Handing them to him, she took out fresh paper, pulled to mind fresh images.

Codes. Not one, like the Culpers used, but many. She had to sift and sort to figure out which key went with which message, and the effort brought a pounding to her head. But they settled, one by one. And one by one, she transcribed the messages.

Scarcely taking the time to read the letters and notes as she wrote them, she handed them off and moved on to the next. Eventually she took a moment to stretch, to loosen her neck.

To smile at Slade, who was poking through her bottom drawer. "Looking for something in particular, Detective?"

He angled an unrepentant grin her way. "A pen, at first. Then I thought I had better liberate my handkerchief. Then I had to wonder what it was wrapped around." He had her vial of lilac water in hand and gave it a swirl.

She snatched the square of white linen back from his fingers and shoved it into her pocket with the links of silver. "Oh no, you don't."

Her nerve endings danced to his laughter. After uncorking the vial, he took a sniff. The smile he wore did strange things to her chest. "Smells like you."

"That is the idea. For my correspondence."

He put that one back and picked up the vial of invisible ink. Pulled out the cork and sniffed at it too. This time his brow furrowed. "This isn't perfume."

It was her turn to smile. "Your skills of observation never cease to amaze me. What was your first clue? Its total lack of odor?"

With an exaggerated glare, he recorked the vial. "What is it? Some serum to make your wit more biting?"

"As if I need the aid." She flexed her cramping hand. To no one else outside the Ring would she ever give the truth about that bottle. But this was Slade. "It's invisible ink."

He froze with the bottle poised over its spot in her drawer. "Pardon?"

"One of Hez's concoctions. The other is the counter liquor, to develop it."

Though she didn't look at him, she heard him switch the bottles out. "You seem to have used a great deal of it."

There was a fine line between suspicion and curiosity, and she wasn't sure which side his tone struck. She picked up her pen again and debated. She would be perfectly comfortable telling him about the Culpers, but that didn't seem to be a decision she ought to make alone. For now, she smiled. "Wouldn't you, if you had some?"

He snorted a laugh. "I guess I would." More shuffling noises followed, though there was nothing else of interest in there. "Ah. Pen."

She let him steal a piece of paper from her stack and kept at her work, pausing now and then to give her hand a rest. The clock in the hall chimed two in the afternoon when she finally set the quill down and stared at the sheet before her.

How many times in a few short months could one un-wish a truth?

Leaning over her again, Slade hissed out a breath. "The task is going to be immense for them. Stockpiling all those weapons and supplies in so many places. And am I reading this right? It sounds as though they expect him to be the one to rouse the leaders of the next rebellion. I guess he is in the best position to do so, being so well respected by Union politicians."

"I read it the same way." She squeezed her eyes shut and took a moment to be thankful when no new images swarmed her. "But it sounds as though the other captains have not even begun yet. Why, then, is he so set on getting his cache in place by Easter?" She splayed her hand on the paper, just below those freshly penned words.

Slade's silence held for only a moment. "Because that isn't the only task this castle has been assigned."

Very true. They had also the task of kidnapping Lincoln, and try as Devereaux might to stay out of it, he was still a part. If caught, the other Knights could implicate him. He would have to be in a position to escape to safety, from which he could still call those secret leaders to arms, his cache already in place.

But Easter was only five days away. That meant he would be leaving within days to take it... She pulled forward the maps Slade had set on the corner of the desk. "Western Maryland, it looks like. Perhaps West Virginia. But what is this?" She indicated a few dark spots on the map of the Appalachians, another that seemed to be little more than random lines.

"Mountainous out there. So perhaps caves?"

It made more sense than anything else. "When he went to Cumberland in February, he must have been finding his location."

Silence greeted that logic, and when she looked up at Slade's profile again, she found his jaw set, his eyes flinty. She settled her fingers on the hand he had braced on the desk. "You cannot stop them all, my love. You are but one man."

"I know." Heavy words that spoke a vast truth into that simple cliché. "I'll get a message to Pinkerton, asking for help. But..."

She waited and then squeezed his hand. "But?"

Shaking his head, he straightened. "They won't come. They don't trust me enough."

"We do." She stood alongside him and kept her fingers clasped in his. "Use us. Walker, Granddad, my brothers. Me, if I can help." He didn't need to know their name to know the Culpers were ready.

Resistance gleamed in his eyes, and she could understand that. He wanted his brothers, the ones he had served beside for years. The ones lost to him through the treachery of the man who shared his blood but not his heart.

Still. "You cannot do this alone, Slade. You need us."

"I need you safe." He pulled her against him, so decisively that it might have been fierce if not for the fear in his eyes. "That's what I need."

She could understand that too. But that need was surely secondary. He would see that when the time came.

Thirty

A knock sounded at the front door.

Slade looked up from the volume of Kierkegaard in his hands. Even with the Danish dictionary he had found, he hadn't made it through the first sentence. He hadn't really expected to, but Marietta had bet him his handkerchief for a kiss that she could translate it before he could, so what was a man to do?

Lose—obviously, what with her unfair advantage. Not that he minded in the least the payment she would demand. But since nothing else he read made any more sense to his preoccupied mind than the Danish, he might as well give it a few hours.

Another knock reminded him that Norris and Tandy had been given the afternoon off to attend a church service. Slade pushed himself up and strode from the library, opened the door to one of Hughes's servants from across the street.

"There you is, Mr. Slade. This just come for you. Boy said it was real impo'tant."

"Thanks, Eli." Slade took the letter and closed the door.

The ladies' voices from the main floor drawing room seeped into the hall, Barbara excusing herself to check on Cora, and then Mrs. Hughes's laborious sigh. "I don't know, dear," the woman said. "It is such a very *long* performance."

Marietta's laughter soothed a few of his rough edges. "That is the idea, Mother Hughes. Bach wanted listeners to leave the St. *Matthew's Passion* emotionally and physically exhausted. How better to contemplate all Christ did for us on this day?"

Slade smiled and carried the missive back into the library, not too upset over the thought of Mrs. Hughes not joining them at the church for the performance that afternoon. Granted, she had been far more palatable since the mugging, but he would already be dealing with the Arnaud brothers. That was quite enough for one Good Friday outing.

Two days from Easter. Something would be happening soon, and that certainty wound his nerves tighter than a spring-loaded coil.

Slade glanced at the envelope, his pulse hammering when he recognized John Booth's hand. He broke the seal and pulled out the paper.

> *We move tonight. I just discovered the tyrant will be attending Our American Cousin at Ford's this evening. Such a stroke of fortune—nay, of fate—must not be ignored. Surratt is still not home from Canada and several of the others are unreachable, so we haven't the men for the original scheme.*
>
> *We must swear instead to assassination. Lewis will strike Seward in his home. Port Tobacco the vice president in his hotel room. You the secretary of war. I will handle the tyrant myself.*
>
> *Our moment is 10:15—timed according to the loudest moment of the play, when a gun's report will be muted by laughter. Then follow the escape route without delay.*

Slade crumpled the sheet in his hand. Perhaps he had known all along, as he saw the hatred in the Knights' eyes, that no one would be content with merely kidnapping Lincoln. Still, he had hoped and prayed.

For just a moment, he squeezed his eyes shut and let the words that had been rattling around in his mind for the past day clang louder in his ears, the ones in the telegram from Pinkerton. *You know I believe you, but I am afraid you are on your own. Use your best judgment, but do not invite defeat if the odds are too much against you.*

The odds. He had made a career of calculating them before he left the gambler's life, had used the lessons learned at the card table time and again as a detective. His gut knew the odds without any input from his head.

Three men, all with pistols loaded and primed. Three men, all bound for different parts of Washington. And only one of him, forced to decide whose life was the most worth saving. Politically, the answer was obvious. He must, at all costs, protect the president.

The families of the other targets would disagree.

Lord, what am I to do? Yetta was right. I can't stop them all. Not on my own.

Instead of an answer, another realization hit. He wouldn't be up against three—he would be up against four. Hughes would have gotten word too. He would even now be coupling his cars full of gold and guns and powder to a train headed into the mountains. He would follow his own plan, one that guaranteed his safety so he could lead the next rebellion.

One that surely included Marietta by his side.

"Slade?"

Had his thoughts summoned her? He blinked, focused on her beautiful, worried frown, and reached for her hand. Pulled her into the room, past his usual chair, and into the alcove. The one where, two and a half months ago, she had collapsed in tears.

That day she had been oblivious to anything but her inner turmoil. Today, her entire focus was upon his face, upon his disquiet.

If it was the last time he saw her, he would have the most compelling of pictures to carry with him to his grave. He brushed away that one curl always dangling at her cheek, savored the silk of it on his fingers, and leaned down. He meant only to touch his lips to hers, but it wasn't enough. Not for forever. Deepening the kiss, he held her tight and prayed she could taste something beyond the goodbye in his embrace.

When he pulled away, the frantic gleam in her eye said otherwise. She gripped his arms and shook her head. "Don't. Don't go."

"I have to." He kissed her once more, just once more, softly if lingering. "So do you. Promise me, kitten. You'll pack now and get out of Baltimore before he comes home. Go to your family. Make them help you get away."

Her rapid blinking didn't disguise the mist in her eyes. "Slade."

"*Promise* me."

Pressing her lips together, she nodded. Her breath came in short, quavering gasps. "I promise."

They would deliver her out of Hughes's reach. He had to believe that. Still, he couldn't convince his arms to release her so she could obey. He rested his forehead on hers. "Yetta...I love you. I didn't mean to. I just couldn't help it."

Her laugh came quick but faded quicker. She pressed a hand to his cheek. "I know the feeling. I didn't mean to love you either. But I do, so much."

Why couldn't that mean forever instead of farewell? "If I live through this, I'll find you. I wish I could promise more than that."

At least he could be sure she would never forget him. Not her.

Her fingers traced over his face. "Don't talk like that. Tomorrow all this will be behind us and..." A shiver coursed through her. "And then you'll need to know I made a mistake. With Dev, before you arrived."

For half a second, it pierced. He had hoped, wanted, prayed he'd been wrong in his first assumptions...but he knew well she wasn't the same person she'd been before he arrived. Knew because his own past always cast a shadow. If anyone knew the value of the Lord's forgiveness, it was him. He locked his gaze with hers. "It doesn't matter."

She looked away, her cat eyes clouded. "I daresay you'll look at it differently when you don't have all these other worries."

"No, I won't. I've made my share of mistakes on that front too."

She didn't meet his gaze again. "It is different for a man. We both know it."

"Not in the eyes of God, and not in the eyes of love." He pressed his lips to hers—one more time, that was all—and then pulled away. "I promise you. All that matters to me is that you love me. Now go. Pack."

"Mari!" Barbara's voice filtered their way from a distance.

Slade pulled away and pulled her out of the alcove. "You'd better take Barbara with you."

Her fingers went tight around his. "Promise me you won't try to stop them all alone. *Promise* me."

The hesitation lasted only a second. He couldn't, could he? He would fail at it all if he tried. He needed friends, needed family. Needed a plan, and he needed one fast.

He felt a warmth against his chest, odd and yet...right. Right where the book of prayers rested. "I'll go to your granddad." If anyone knew who he could trust, it was surely Thaddeus Lane.

"Mari!"

She glanced toward the hall and Barbara's nearing voice, her face filled with worry. "Go. I will follow as soon as I can get us packed."

He stole one more kiss—the last one—and sped for the door.

Marietta stepped into the hall after Slade and jumped as the door closed behind him. It sounded too final. Too hopeless, that slam of wood on wood.

"Mari!" Barbara ran down the hall, her skirts billowing behind her and her cheeks flushed. "The babe is coming at last. I need your help."

Marietta felt the blood leave her face, rush to her middle, and twist into nausea. Little experience as she had with it, she knew childbirth was a bloody business. But this was Cora—she must do what she could.

How, though? She had promised to leave within minutes. To take Barbara with her...impossible if Cora's babe were coming now.

Oh Lord, why all at once? Please, show me what to do.

"Marietta Hughes." Her mother-in-law stalked her way, fury snapping. "Dallying with a hired man? I thought you better bred than that."

Her throat tightened. Mother Hughes must have glimpsed that last kiss.

But Marietta had only to appease her for a few minutes before making her escape. "It isn't what you think." It was so, so much more than any dalliance. "He was merely saying goodbye."

"Where could he possibly be going that he—" Mother Hughes cut herself off, the accusation fading. She knew. She had to know. Why else would her expression veer toward indulgent? Smoothing down her skirt, she cleared her throat. "I will overlook it this time. But if I see any more such behavior, you can be sure I will report it to my son."

"Do what you must." Marietta raised her chin and stormed past her toward Barbara. "Is your satchel in your room?"

Glancing once toward Mother Hughes, Barbara nodded and hurried beside her toward the stairs. "I know you will not want to be present during the birth itself, but if you could lend a hand with Elsie until Walker returns with his mother..."

She dared no response while they climbed the staircase. Only once they were in the sanctuary of Barbara's suite of rooms, the door latched behind her, did she even take a deep breath.

Her friend turned to regard her with somber eyes. "Is something wrong? Slade has so rarely left us lately, and I would not have thought him careless enough to kiss you before an open door."

That deep breath shook on its way out. "Can Cora be moved?"

Barbara went still. "I wouldn't recommend it, but I suppose if it were enough of an emergency—"

"We need to leave here before Dev comes. Now. We haven't any time to lose."

Most people would have asked questions. Barbara just measured her quietly for a moment before the familiar shine of peace settled in her eyes. She nodded. "It will take me a few minutes to gather all we'll need."

God had been smiling on her the day He compelled her to this woman's door. "Thank you. I will meet you at the carriage house."

Footsteps sounded, loud and heavy and fast—a man's, and he was in a hurry. *Please Lord, let it be Walker, home and coming to hurry Barbara along.*

But she knew the sound of Walker's utilitarian work boots, and these struck her as far more like the softer-soled congress boots a gentleman would wear. Slade, perhaps, returned for some reason?

The pounding at the door behind her head suggested otherwise. She reached for the key in the lock but too late. It turned under her hand and the door was pushed open with enough force to knock her backward.

Dev took only one step in. He curled his hand around her arm, his smile far too normal for all she knew must be going through his head. His gaze took in Barbara and the medical satchel in her hands, and then it settled on Marietta's face. "Mother said you came up here. I need to speak with you, darling."

She prayed her smile looked every bit as easy, despite the thundering of her pulse. "Of course, Dev. I'll be just a moment. I'll find you in my drawing room." A few minutes, that was all she needed to escape.

"No. It's urgent." A muscle ticked in his jaw as he glanced at Barbara again. "Is it not her day to be at the hospital?"

Barbara shifted her satchel from one hand to the other. "I was needed here. Cora—"

"Too bad." His lips twitched, as if ready to snarl, and he spun Marietta into the hall. When he twisted the key in the lock and slammed shut the door, Barbara trapped inside, Marietta couldn't contain the squeak of outrage.

"What are you doing? You cannot lock my guest in—"

"I can." He jerked her down the hall, slipping the key into his pocket. "Had she been where she was supposed to be, it would not have been necessary."

Was there a second key in the room? Or the window—she could open a window and hail Walker whenever he came home. That might not be soon enough to save Marietta, but it would guarantee Barbara would be all right and there to help Cora. "I fail to see why it is necessary now. Whatever is so urgent that—"

"For once in your life, Mari, do what you're told."

He increased their pace, and she could scarcely find air enough to breathe. Why had she let Mother Hughes retie her corset this morning in Cora's stead? The woman seemed bent on tight-lacing.

Dev tugged her around the corner and to the stairs leading to the third floor, where only the family bed chambers were. She dug in her heels. "Where are we going?"

She got the feeling his pause would cost her. That shadow in his eyes looked alive and ready to devour her. "Immediately? To your room so you can pack a few things. We are taking a little trip."

The maps flashed. The rails leading to Harper's Ferry and then westward to Cumberland. The caves, that dot marked as an inn. So far away. So many places for him to hide, both the stockpile and himself. And her?

Marietta shook her head. "I cannot travel with you, you know that. We are not yet wed—"

"A predicament I tried to remedy last week, if you recall." He pulled her closer, his hand a steel band on her arm, his eyes flashing danger.

"Let me make this very clear, darling. Choose me. Choose me above whatever else might tie you here—your family, your friends, your dashed new faith—or those things will pay. I will sever every bond holding you back until you are solely, wholly mine. Do you understand?"

Her throat closed off, and her fingers tangled in the muted gray silk of her dress. His eyes churned with a shadowy passion—one she knew too well. One she had been seeing since the nineteenth of December 1860. How had she ever been so foolish as to call it love? Love could have no part in such darkness.

But then, perhaps one couldn't see that truth until one abided in the Light.

She had no choice but to nod and let him pull her up the steps. A plan was called for, but she needed time to devise how to get away without him hurting the people she loved.

Their images flashed before her. Each and every person she held dear. Only this time her imagination got involved and transposed that awful poster overtop them. Mama, Daddy, Granddad, and Grandmama with bloody slashes across their faces. Cora, Walker, Elsie, and Barbara. Her brothers, their wives and children. Slade.

When Dev forced her into the corridor of family bedrooms, his mother stepped into the hall. For a second, one shining second, she hoped some help would come from the woman.

"Are we traveling by coach or train, Devereaux? I need to know what to pack."

Obviously a vain hope.

Dev growled. "What do you think, Mother? Do we own a coach company or a railroad?"

A shiver stole through her. Never, in all the years she'd known him, had he spoken so harshly to his mother.

Mother Hughes seemed just as taken aback. "Devereaux Hughes, there is no call for such impertinence."

"Oh, but there is. You have three minutes, or I leave without you. And you, darling." He gave her a shake and shoved her toward her door. "Three minutes, or you go with nothing."

He released her arm once she was inside. Perhaps he would stride away to attend something else, and she could—but no. He withdrew the pistol on his hip and used it to direct her toward her boudoir. "I believe your trunks and bags are in there?"

When he touched the barrel to her back to keep her moving, she didn't dare wonder how he knew where she kept her bags. "You can remove the gun, darling. And you could have mentioned your mother was coming as chaperone. That would have resolved my objection."

If only her objection were so simple.

As soon as they stepped into the small chamber, he pulled a valise from the shelf and tossed it to the floor. "When you are falling asleep by my side tonight, we can laugh about it. For now, indulge me."

By his side? She turned to face him, gun or no gun. "Pardon?"

He chuckled into her outrage. "Two minutes, darling. Don't bother with dresses—we will purchase you new ones when we get there."

With trembling hands she pulled items at random off shelves and from drawers and stuffed them into the valise. Her hairbrush had no sooner joined the chaos within the case than he slammed it closed, latched it, and nudged her from the room with the pistol again. "Time is up."

He didn't even slow as they passed his mother's room. He just called out, "I'm leaving." Marietta heard harried steps behind her but didn't look around lest she stumble on the stairs.

Two sets of steps, though. Dev must have noted the same thing, for he glared over his shoulder. "I said not to involve the slaves, Mother."

She huffed. "Well, I could hardly pack on my own, and I cannot get along without Jess. She must come with us."

Dev's lips pressed to a thin line. He paused on the second-floor landing and turned to face the two older women. He raised his pistol, probably set to wave it at them as he had at—

Bang.

Screams. Mother Hughes's, Jess's, and given the burning in her throat, her own. The servant crumpled to the stairs, clutching her leg. Crimson soaked through her skirt.

Marietta's stomach heaved upward, and her vision blurred. Voices clamored and clanged, but she couldn't unravel them from each other. Couldn't tell which way was up. Couldn't...couldn't...

A blast of wind blew some of the cobwebs away, but that made her stomach churn more. Dev was putting her on her feet, outside, beside his carriage, and she had no recollection of getting there.

"I am sorry you had to see that, darling." He brushed her hair from her face with one hand and tossed her valise into the coach with the other. "I know how you detest the sight of blood. But she will likely survive, so calm yourself."

Calm herself?

Mother Hughes was crying. Farther away, someone screamed her name. Barbara—she must have heard the gunshot.

Her vision cleared and latched onto a spot of shining gold. It took her a second to realize it was a small head—Elsie's, and the girl stood nearly under Barbara's window, partially concealed by the hedge.

Marietta opened her mouth, but she daren't try to answer Barbara, not with Dev's finger still on the trigger and too many targets about.

Elsie pulled her thumb out of her mouth, pointed both fingers, and then made the letter D and shook it. *Where are you going?*

"Enough, Mother. Mari, up you go."

Lord, let her understand and remember! Discreetly as she could, she made the sign for Dev and two fingers along the matching two from the other hand for train. She managed to add a quick *Tell Daddy* before Dev lifted her into the carriage.

Thirty-One

Slade paced to the window again, worry's teeth gnawing at him. Perhaps a scrap of peace would have been instilled by the steady stroke of Mrs. Lane's pencil over her paper, but her husband's pacing, mirroring Slade's, negated it.

He had detoured to the telegraph office, had sent a wire to Pinkerton. *Can't come tonight*, he had written, their agreed-upon code for when the KGC was acting. *Attending the theater at Ford's with friends*.

Once he arrived at the Lane residence, he had explained the situation to the old man. His promise to help, though, hadn't relieved the anxiety building like a thunderhead.

Marietta should be here by now. "Where is she?"

"Helping Barbara with Cora, no doubt," Mrs. Lane said from her desk.

Slade shot a glance to Lane, who exhaled and shook his head. "I don't know, sweet. I have a bad feeling."

Mrs. Lane's pencil stilled, and she spun on her chair to face them. "Then why are you still here?"

"I thought at first it was unease over the situation in general, but..." The old man slapped his leg and spun to the door, face set. "You're right. Come, Oz. Waiting will accomplish nothing. If she is on her way, we'll pass her along the street."

Unless she took side streets to avoid detection, which was why they hadn't immediately headed back to intercept her. But Slade followed Lane across the room. If they missed her somehow, her grandmother would tell her where they went.

Walker's grandfather had horses waiting and handed them the reins with a grim face. "You need me, you let me know," he said to Lane.

"As always." The old man swung into the saddle with the ease of a youth. "Be praying, Henry."

"As always."

Slade nodded his appreciation and, once mounted, nudged the horse into a trot.

According to Lane, they could count on Walker, Hez, Henry, and the two of them. Isaac could be called upon in a pinch. So they had five or six—certainly better odds than one against four, even with two of them being eighty.

What really struck him was how quickly Lane had rattled that off. As if accustomed to examining his family through such a lens.

It seemed to take forever to make their way to Monument Square, though he recognized there were few others out on this holy day before Easter. Many businesses were closed, school children ran about at play in the spring sunshine, little traffic clogged the roads.

The shouts could be heard from Marietta's house from halfway down the street. Kicking their mounts up to a canter for the remaining distance, Slade ended up swinging down a second before Lane at the carriage house.

Barbara and Walker staggered from the side door of the big house, old Jess carried between them. The woman's head lolled, and a huge patch of red stained her skirt.

"Thunder and turf." Lane took off at a speed that shouldn't have been possible for a man of his age, one Slade had trouble keeping up with. "What happened?"

Barbara, holding Jess's feet, looked up at them with gratitude. "Praise Jesus. I was uncertain I would be able to get her up the stairs. Mr. Hughes shot her. He and his mother and Mari are all gone, and I don't know to where. He locked me in my room. Walker only just freed me."

Every vile word he had ever heard vied for a place on his tongue, but Slade bit them all back. He would follow Barbara's example. "Lord, guide us." He took Jess's legs from her and motioned with his head for her to precede them to the carriage house stairs. "When?"

Barbara looked to Walker. "I am unsure how long I was banging on the door after I heard the gunshot, but Mr. Hughes arrived not five minutes after you left, Slade."

And he had been wasting time pacing the Lanes' drawing room. That truth knifed through him and left him quaking. Where could Hughes have taken her? Surely not the train station yet. He wouldn't risk keeping her around all those crowds too long, and the next train didn't leave for Cumberland until three o'clock.

"She was unconscious when we got to her." Walker started up the stairs backwards, the lines scored deep in his forehead. "This ain't gonna help Cora in her labor."

The door above them opened, and Freeda stepped out with a frown to match her son's. "Where's Elsie? Has anyone seen her?"

A twist to the knife. Surely, surely nothing had happened to the girl.

"She's here in the hedges." Lane's voice carried a smile. "I'll stay with her. She doesn't need to see her gramma hurt like that."

That the little girl was safe was a short-lived relief in light of all else that was so very wrong. Slade and Walker got Jess inside and onto the table, Cora's moans coming from the bedroom. Barbara rushed in behind them and set her black satchel on a chair.

"What…what's goin' on?" Cora panted. "Been so much screamin'…"

Barbara shooed Slade and Walker away and leaned over Jess. "Most of that was me, locked in my room. Your mama's been hurt, Cora, but we'll take care of her. Can you tell me how you're doing? Are the pains still worse each time?"

"Mama? How did she get hurt?"

Slade kept his gaze averted, but he could hear rustling from the bedroom.

Freeda waved her hands at him and Walker. "You menfolk get outta here, now. Ain't no place for you. If we need ya, we'll call."

Though his friend seemed reluctant, Slade obeyed happily. He sped out and down the steps, over to where Lane crouched before Elsie. She had made a nest for herself in a break in the hedge, having dragged a blanket over, her doll, and even a cup of water. She must have been hiding here a good while.

His breath caught. "Elsie." He crouched beside Lane and cleared his face. As Marietta had taught him, he touched the child on her shoulder to get her attention and then made the sign for her name.

She grinned up at him and waved, signing his name back.

She was so young...but he had to try, didn't he? Scrounging in his mind for the few signs he had learned, he pointed to her, his eyes, and then made the sign for Marietta.

Lane hummed. "Good thought. She could have seen them."

Elsie hooked a finger in her mouth as she nodded. She repeated the sign for Marietta, swept her hand around her face. *Marietta is beautiful.*

His smile felt a little more genuine as he signed *yes*. He looked to Lane. "Do you know how to ask if she saw her leave?"

"I do." He made a few quick motions, but Slade kept his eyes on the tot. Did she understand?

He wasn't sure at first. Then she nodded and formed the letter D with her hand, moving it in the word *bad*. "That's their sign for Hughes."

"And that," Lane added as she moved her fingers across her others, "is train. He's taking her with him. We have to stop him, Oz."

Walker appeared and scooped up his daughter. "Someone explain."

Slade let Lane do the honors while he stood and turned away. Why? Why would Hughes have taken them to the station already, if Cumberland were their destination? He had to know Marietta was not with him willingly. He might be conceited and obsessed, but he was no idiot. A man couldn't run a company the size of...

Of course. Slade was the idiot. The man owned the whole rail line. Why would he be bound by the timetables? He could modify the schedule as he pleased.

Which meant the train could already be gone. Or leaving in a matter of minutes. He had no time to lose.

He spun around, mouth open to ask, beg, inform, whatever he had to do.

Lane's gaze was already on him. "Go. Hurry. We'll do what we can in Washington."

That was all the confirmation Slade needed. He ran back to his waiting horse and dug his heels into its flanks. He nearly turned the wrong way at the end of the street, toward Camden Station, until he realized that Hughes would have to have his cars pulled through the city by horse to President Street Station if he were heading west.

Maybe, just maybe, that would have gained him some time.

The city blurred around him, each pound of hooves echoed by his heart. Each beat of his heart a silent cry heavenward.

It shouldn't be this way. He had known the stakes were high, but it should have only been about the Knights. About Lincoln. About Ross's betrayal and Slade's reclaiming of his reputation.

It shouldn't have been about loving, so definitely not about this agonizing fear of losing the one he loved. Had he known this was part of the price...

A whisper moved through him. A solid thought that wouldn't budge.

God knew. God had known all along and had called him here anyway.

A single flame of anger licked through him, but he banked it. He could ask *why* of the Lord forever and never find all the answers, but he knew enough of them. Knew that, even if he failed at his every task today, it would be worth it to have tried.

Worth it to have loved her.

President Street Station came into view, and his heart galloped far ahead of the horse. There, smoke already rolling from the locomotive's stack, was the Hughes car, with three freight cars attached at the rear.

He urged his horse faster over the final stretch of street. *Lord, get me there!*

There was a whoosh of steam, a chug, and the wheels squealed into motion.

"We need to go with him." Mr. Lane stood staring in the direction of the road, though Osborne had disappeared from view long ago.

Walker smoothed a curl from Elsie's sleeping face and straightened. He was surprised she had curled up the way she had on her blanket and drifted off, but he was glad of it. Too much was going on inside for her to be underfoot.

He stepped to Mr. Lane's side, studying the man's profile rather than the road. "You don't think he can handle Hughes?"

His companion turned, sorrow in his eyes. "He'll do all he can. But you can bet Hughes will have help. And he has already proven he isn't opposed to using violence to achieve his ends."

Those concerns made sense, so he nodded. But it was more than that. "And it's Yetta."

Mr. Lane sighed. "Yes. It's Mari. She has always been so special to me. The thought of her in that devil's clutches..." He scrubbed a hand over his face, skewing his hat. "I have had loved ones in danger before and felt the hand of the Lord telling me to be still, to trust Him to care for them. Today I feel only an urgency to get myself on the next train to the mountains."

"Then go."

"But with all that will be happening in Washington—"

"We've hours enough to see to that. Their one agent is a ferry oper-ator out of Port Tobacco, which means Grandpa Henry will know him. I'll try to find Pinkerton or Oz's friend and convince them this is seri-ous. Hez and I will handle the rest." Even as he said it, his heart tugged him back toward the carriage house, where Cora's groans kept com-ing through the windows. Jess's bleeding had stopped, but she hadn't woken up yet.

They would pray. And then pray some more.

Mr. Lane slapped a hand to his leg. "I have to go. I will take Ize with me and send Hez and Henry here. Gwyn and Julie I'll set to praying."

"When the rest of the servants get back from church, I'll get them praying too."

Decision made, Mr. Lane took off for his horse.

After checking on Elsie again, Walker jogged up the stairs to home. He knew Barbara and his mother would only let him in for a few min-utes, but he had to know how Jess and Cora were doing.

He found his mother-in-law still unconscious on the kitchen table. A blanket covered her where her skirt had been cut away, and blood-ied bandages were in the corner.

At the moment Barbara was bent over the stove, and he spotted Mama in the bedroom wiping a cloth over Cora's forehead. He headed for his wife and took the side opposite his mother. "How are you doing, honey?"

Her eyes were clouded with pain, but she managed a smile. "Miss Barbara says everything's real good. I'm just prayin' for Mama." She reached for his hand and gripped it hard. "You gonna help Mr. Slade catch him? You gotta help, honey. You gotta see he pays for what he did."

He covered her fingers with his. "Mr. Lane and Ize are going to help Oz. They asked me..." How much should he tell them? There were worries enough saturating this room. And yet if she were still laboring, if Jess were still struggling when it was time for him to head to Washington, he couldn't very well leave without a word. He sucked in a quick breath. "There's some men planning on killing the president tonight, honey. Oz was trying to stop them too, but he can't do it all. He asked me if I'd help."

"Then what are you doing here?" She propped herself up on her free elbow. Sweat beaded on her forehead. "You gotta save him. You go right now, Walker Payne."

That was his Cora. He leaned over and kissed her head. "Nothing I can do yet, honey. Won't have to leave until dark. So you just have this baby before then so I can leave without that worry, all right?"

Even as he finished speaking, her face contorted again. And his mother, again, shooed him back outside.

Thirty-Two

Devereaux had been glad, at first, for the silence from the females. He had been too busy checking the windows, his lists of supplies, and the timetables, to have any desire to deal with their histrionics.

But an hour had passed with nothing but the *clickety-clack* of the wheels over the iron ribbons, and now their continued petulance grated. His mother's glare drilled him, and Marietta hadn't said a word since he tossed her into his private car. She had remained on the seat he had put her in, not so much as shifting from her landing position. Her gaze had remained fixed on the floor.

She was here. She had not made a fuss, had not cried "Murder!" and brought the police down upon him, but only because she took his threats seriously. She did not want to be at his side.

His veins sizzled with that certainty.

"I will never forgive you," his mother burst out. "I have had Jess since we were girls. She has served me faithfully and loyally all these years, and you shoot her as if she is nothing more than a lame dog?"

"Would you rather I had shot you for insisting on bringing her?" At her wide-mouthed gasp, he rolled his eyes. Were it not for the women, he would slip out again, over the connector, and into the first of the freight cars. "It is your own fault for disobeying. I will get you another maid, so do stop pouting like a child."

"You cannot just replace a lifelong servant, Devereaux."

He tapped his pen against the page, his gaze on Marietta again. He would get a rise out of her one way or another. "I suggest you make better use of your time than fuming at me, Mother. Perhaps you and Mari should plan the wedding. It will have to be small, of course, but you have always liked the house in Cumberland. I imagine you can make it lovely."

Marietta blinked, shifted, and turned on him eyes so cold his blood had to boil to compensate. "You can force me before a minister with a gun to my head," she said, her voice even and passionless, "but you will have to convince him I am mute. I will not say vows to you."

He felt every thud of his heart, every scorching pulse through his body. It resonated, echoed, overcame. "Have it your way, Mari. If you will not be my wife, you can be my mistress. But one way or another, you will be mine."

She sat straighter and fisted her hands. "How can you be such a fool, Devereaux? Do you really think you will get your way through violence and threat? You can ravage me and abuse me, you can take whatever you will from this body, but I will *never* be yours."

He leapt to his feet, fire slicking through him far faster than the train through the countryside. "You will be mine," he said, voice icy and dead in contrast to the raging life within, "or you will be nothing."

Marietta rose too. So small across from him, but her spine stayed straight as the rails, her every curve perfection, the snapping in her eyes at least alive again, as he most loved seeing them. How could she deny what they had both known for years? She was meant to be his. Created solely to please him. No words could change that she belonged to him, nothing she could do would erase the brand he had put upon her.

"Then kill me." Her voice, low and sultry, seethed fury.

The coursing fire exploded. He grabbed the table and sent it flying toward the opposite wall. "By thunder, Marietta, don't think I won't! I killed my brother for you. I won't hesitate to kill again if you are idiot enough to rebel when you should rightfully be mine!"

The dual gasps, his mother's piercing keen, pushed him forward. He was upon Marietta in two steps, grasping her shoulders and pulling her flush against him.

Now her eyes weren't so cold. Now she couldn't doubt of what he was capable. Better the horror on her face than the ice. "You did *what?*"

"It's your own fault. Had you simply consented to an affair—but you refused me, every time you refused me, saying you could be with no one but your husband." The fire shook him, shook her by extension. "What else was I to do? Wait for him to grow old and die, to claim you only when you were too faded to be of use to me? I have waited years, *years* for you!"

She tried to break free, the idiot woman. As if she could ever escape the power of their love, as if denying it would change how it had consumed them both. "Get off me." Her voice shook with the same resonance, proving, even in her anger, that they were built for one another. "Get away from me! How could you? How could you kill your own brother?"

She pushed at his chest, shoved at his arms. Made him smile. That was the Mari he loved, full of passion and vim. "It was the simplest thing in the world, darling. Lure him away, lie in wait, plunge the knife into his stomach, and watch him die. I should have done it sooner. Then you would already be my wife."

She managed to pull one of her arms free. Her eyes narrowed to yellow-green slits, she bared her teeth and pulled the arm back.

His smile faded when her fist slammed into his nose.

He was going to kill her. Marietta saw it flash in his eyes when she struck him. She saw the gleam of murder, pulsing moments before, snap from recollection to promise. And still she couldn't regret embracing the whisper of those long-ago lessons from Isaac.

He had killed him. He had been the one to stab Lucien in that dark alleyway, not some random thief. The knowledge made every muscle quiver and contract.

One of Dev's hands still gripped her upper arm with enough force to bruise her; with the other he dabbed at his nose, cursing when he saw the blood upon it. Fingers digging in still more, he jerked her forward, toward the back end of the car.

Mother Hughes's cry went from animal whimper to sobbing, but he didn't so much as glance at her.

"How could you do this, Dev?" She tried to plant her feet, but he was so much stronger. Every time she dug in, he simply jerked her onward. "You destroyed your family. You have undone us all. He loved you, he—"

"He was a braggart and a tyrant, always flaunting his advantages." With one vicious yank, he opened the rear door.

Her stomach flew to her throat at the ground whizzing by outside. Would he toss her over? The ground was still all but flat around them; the fall might not kill her. But a river snaked just ahead. Would he wait until they were on the bridge?

She knew how to swim, but she would first have to escape her heavy clothing, and that might be impossible.

Despite her challenge to him a few minutes earlier, she had no desire to die. When he tried to pull her out the door, she braced her feet and free hand on the posts. "Let me go, you monster!"

Another nasty curse tripped off his tongue. He took a step onto the rickety, rocking metal grate between the two cars and slid open the door on the second one. Then, as if all her resistance were no more effective than a kitten's, he picked her up and tossed her into the dark tomb of the freight car.

She landed hard on her hip, her ribs striking a crate that robbed her of breath.

Dev filled the whole opening, a black silhouette. "Maybe a few hours in here will calm you."

"Calm me?" Wincing at the strain against what would surely be another set of bruises, she pushed back to her feet. "You killed my husband, and you expect a few hours in the dark will *calm me?*"

She flew his way, screaming when the door slammed shut before she could reach him. Unable to pound at him, she pounded at the door instead, tears mixing with the rage. "He was your brother! He loved you!"

Pain sent her to her knees. Not from the bruises, but from within. She might not have been the one to wield the dagger, but she had encouraged Dev, had made it so clear that the only thing between them was Lucien. Her hand had not held the knife, but his blood still stained her. "Oh God, forgive me."

"Don't you dare take the blame for anything he did."

The unexpectedness of the voice made her jump, but its blessed familiarity brought her back to her feet. Her gaze probed the unrelieved darkness. "Slade?"

She heard the sound of a quiet snap, saw the small whoosh of a match igniting, and then a golden glow illuminated the contours of his face, the neatly trimmed goatee, the black eyes she so loved. She had to climb over crates and boxes, but she reached him just after he touched the flame to the wick of a lamp. His arms closed around her as hers did him.

And with that security, the storm within broke loose, and she clung to him to remain upright. "He killed him, Slade. He killed Lucien. It was Dev, not a mugger. *Dev* stabbed him, and he said it was for me—to be with me." A shudder came over her, so strong she gasped with it. "It is my fault. If I hadn't flirted with him, hadn't thought such wicked things—"

"Shh." He held her close and stroked a hand down her back. "It wasn't your doing, Yetta. Perhaps you did wrong, perhaps the Lord would have judged you for those thoughts had you not asked forgiveness of them, but Dev's actions are his own. Not yours."

She buried her face in his chest and wished she could let the tears rage, that they could wash it all away. But they couldn't. "I thought I loved him. To my shame, when Lucien still lived. I grieved for him, but not enough. Because of Dev. And now to realize...how could I have been so foolish?"

"You didn't know."

"I should have. I should have realized the kind of man he is. He plotted his own brother's murder."

She felt him shift and then saw the way the lantern light flickered through his eyes. The pain and guilt in them. "No." She tightened her hold so he couldn't pull out of her embrace. "You are nothing like him. You defended yourself against Ross. He was the one who plotted murder."

"I still killed my brother." His hand, splayed on the small of her back, flexed with that agony.

Agony so very different from Dev's cold satisfaction. She touched a hand to Slade's cheek and stretched up to kiss him. "You are a good man, Slade Osborne, and I love you. You are doing all you can to undo—wait." Now she pulled away so she could glare at him. "You should be in Washington stopping Booth. What are you doing here?"

The agony faded as his lips turned up. "Nothing out of the ordinary. Just jumping onto moving trains. Stopping a villain. Rescuing the girl."

"Fool." She slapped at his chest and then curled her fingers into his lapel to hold him close. "You cannot be wasting time on the girl, especially when the villain will kill us both if he sees you. You need to get off this train and to Washington."

His eyes glinted black as hardened steel. "Your grandfather promised they could handle that. Hughes has to be stopped too. But you're right about the danger. The next time the train slows, you jump."

Of all the idiotic suggestions. "Absolutely not."

"Soon, before we reach the mountains." As if he actually thought he would talk her into it, he strode over to the large side door, slid the latch, and pulled it open a few feet. The thunder of the mechanical beast rushed in, along with a gust of air. "The ground is still relatively flat here. When we slow for the next town—"

"I said no." She sat defiantly upon a barrel...until she saw that it said *gunpowder*. Then she jumped back off. "We are in this together."

"Yetta." He came back over and framed her face in his hands. "Kitten, listen. I know you feel guilty for what he's done, but this isn't your fight."

But it was. Dev and the KGC were trying to undermine her country. The one her brother had fought and died for. The one her family had risked their lives for throughout the generations. She gripped his wrists. "Yes, it is. Slade...I knew who you were before you arrived. I knew what you were about. I was charged with helping you."

A breath of laughter puffed from his lips, though it faded as he gazed into her eyes. His hands slid down to link with hers. "What do you mean?"

"Granddad. He...he was an intelligencer in the War of 1812. His mother before him in the Revolution. He has kept the group active through the years. We call ourselves the Culper Ring."

"We." Now he sat on the barrel and didn't seem to care that it could explode with a random spark. "Are you trying to tell me that you're a...a spy?"

"A spy too, don't you mean, Detective?" She gave his hands a squeeze. "Why is that so shocking after all I've done to help you?"

He blinked, his gaze on her chin rather than her eyes. "You're talking about an organized group of them."

"They are just my family. Doing what they can for the country they love, as everyone should do."

"Just your family." He freed one hand to pinch the bridge of his nose. When he lowered it again, he revealed a small smile. "You really are something else, kitten. Come here."

She hesitated a moment, but what did it really matter if the gunpowder spontaneously exploded? At least they would go up together, and perhaps take Dev out with them. She perched on his knee and wrapped her arms around his neck.

He anchored her with a strong arm. "Listen, if we live through this..."

She tightened her arms, knowing exactly what he would ask and biting back a *yes*. Yes, of course she would marry him! But she would let him get the question out first.

He grinned and ran his nose down her cheek. "I could put in a good word for you with Pinkerton. Get you a job using these skills of yours."

A job? He was proposing a *job*? The laughter started deep in her stomach and felt like heaven in her throat. She gave it rein and then rewarded him with a sound kiss.

When finally their lips broke apart, he tucked her head to his shoulder and held her close. She felt his sigh building before she heard it ease out. "I don't know what our odds are here, and I hate that. I want to think we can stop him. I have to think that, have to believe it. I just don't know what the cost will be."

The lamp sputtered. Marietta felt for the necklace she had scarcely taken off since Grandmama gave it to her, and found it under the collar of her dress. A legacy, she had called it. *Their* legacy, not just of the Lanes and Arnauds, but of the Culpers. A legacy of secrets and whispers and spies...a legacy of failures and successes. Of faithfully doing what they could, when they were called to do it, no matter the cost.

She closed her eyes against the dying flame. "I believe, my love, that all our chips are already on the table. The hand has been dealt. There is no point in worrying over which cards might be turned up... we have only to play. And to pray."

His hand slid into her hair and pulled loose the lace snood, spilling the curls down her back. "Listen to you, using gambling language. Have I mentioned that I love you?"

She breathed in his citrus scent. "Only twice now, which isn't nearly sufficient. We had better pray hard, because I need to hear it thousands more times."

"Hmm. Guess we had better do this right then, so I have some time for all those words."

She smiled into his collar and turned her head into his hand. "I figure it'll take you years. Decades, even."

"Probably. And that's if we're together more often than we're apart. So I guess we should get married or something."

She chuckled and pulled away enough to look him in the eyes, to see the pure love shining there. "What a romantic you are."

He grinned, though the lamp sputtered again. At his urging, she stood so that he could check its fuel level.

"Is there more?"

"Logically somewhere, but..." He shrugged and headed for the door. When he slid it wide, precious little light came through. Gray clouds blanketed the sky. "Looks like rain in the mountains."

"Good. That should make it more difficult for him to move this to wherever he's going to hide it." She came to his side, gripping his hand as she watched the fields roll into hills. "We could dump it out along the way."

"Tossing all those weapons and powder into the hands of strangers? Not wise."

"Have you a plan, then?"

"Not yet. None of them felt right. But that was when you were in there with him." Turning away from the door, he sat on a crate, pulled out his revolver, and set it beside him. "You know how to use this?"

Able only to nod, she sat too, on the other side of the weapon. "If necessary."

"I'm hoping it won't be, but let's be cautious. He doesn't know I'm here, and he won't expect you to be armed when he comes back for you. Two advantages to us. But right now, let's focus on the most important one."

He extended his hand, palm up, and closed his eyes. Marietta put her fingers in his, bowed her head, and turned her heart to prayer.

Thirty-Three

With the mountains came darkness, more from the moaning clouds than the descent of the sun. Thunder had been rolling for the past twenty minutes, and flashes of lightning danced around the hilltops.

Marietta scooted closer and closer to his side, which Slade accepted with nary a complaint. He might only have another hour with her, so he would savor every moment.

"How long until we get there, do you think?" Her words were muffled against his chest.

Slade smiled and coiled another scarlet strand around his finger. "I'm not sure. We haven't been stopping the way passenger trains do."

He had no idea where they were now. In West Virginia, somewhere—whenever Marietta released him long enough to move near the door again, he could see the Potomac winding its way through the valleys.

They had decided after prayer that they should wait until they were on solid ground before taking any action. Mrs. Hughes could too easily be injured in any fray they took to his private car, and Marietta insisted they spare her whatever fresh pain they could. So when the train slowed, Slade would close the door again and hide. Marietta would go with Hughes when he came for her—with Slade's revolver; he had liberated another from the crates—and pretend to be repentant.

Hughes might believe her for a few minutes, anyway. Long enough for her to get the mother separated from the son. Slade would give himself enough time to see how many cronies the man had recruited and do what was necessary to stop them.

Another tongue of electricity flashed through the sky, and Marietta scooted closer. "That seemed close. What if it strikes us, or sends a tree onto the tracks? What will we do then?"

"Just what we planned, kitten. With a few modifications."

She shuddered when the thunder rolled over them, loud as a cannon. "I'm sorry I'm such a ninny about these stupid storms."

His chuckle disappeared into a gust of wind that sent the sliding door banging. "You can snuggle up to me anytime you want. In fact." He shifted, tilted her face up toward his. "What was the 'best distraction' you had in mind a couple weeks ago?"

"Hmm. I can't recall." She pressed a hand to the back of his head. "Let's see if a kiss refreshes my memory."

Did she use phrases like that just to sound like an ordinary person? Maybe someday, if they had a someday, he would ask her. For now, he touched his lips to hers, intending to keep the kiss sweet and soft. She would remember this forever, and if it were their last embrace, it should tell her always how much he loved her.

Marietta must have had different ideas. Her lips tasted of urgency and moved with purpose over his.

That was all right too.

His eyes slid shut, but he still saw the next flash through the lids, and no thundering pulse could drown out its electric snap. They were in the heart of the storm now. The door crashed again—he would have to secure it in a minute. Rain lashed the floor of the car, and they would do better to stay dry than to have the evening's meager light.

But that would require releasing Marietta, and his arms refused. Better to hold her tight, to meet her kiss for kiss.

There was a roar—human, not heavenly—and then the world shifted. A sturdy boot connected with his ribs, and his eyes flew open to see the devil himself towering over him. Hughes had Marietta by the torso, pinning her left arm to her side and pressing her legs into one of the barrels.

Slade hit a crate, fell to an empty section of floor, and slid through the puddle as the train raced around a curve.

Hughes, shrouded largely by shadow, snarled. "Exactly how many ways have you betrayed me, Osborne?"

"Me?" Guns—he needed one of the guns. "I haven't done any betraying." There, still on the crate. He levered himself up, though the chances of getting to it before Hughes could act were slim.

Where was Marietta's?

"Haven't done any—" Hughes spat out a curse, his voice venomous. He must have made some move, because Marietta whimpered. "You are in my train when you should be in Washington. With your *hands* on my *woman*."

Lightning flashed, and in its light he saw the flash of metal. Her gun—in her right hand. Praise to the Almighty.

His praise turned to silent plea when he saw that Hughes's hand was clasped around hers on the weapon. And that he was forcing her arm up, inch by inch.

She whimpered again, her arm shaking.

Images flashed before his eyes. Fire spitting from the barrel of his revolver, aimed at his heart. The cylinder turning, another bullet sliding into the chamber. Hughes turning the gun—Slade's own gun—on Marietta.

"No!" Whether it was fear, premonition, or prophecy, he didn't know, but he had to stop it one way or another. He had to save her. He tried to take a step, but the wet floor beneath him sent him slipping. He grabbed at anything he could.

Wind whipped his back. His fingers had found purchase, but not until he reached the door.

Marietta's scream blended with the rumble of thunder.

Lord, help me. Help me save her.

Dragging in a breath, he called up the mask he usually wore in Hughes's presence. Slid a step to the side, so the metal door was at his back. "Relax, Hughes. I came along to help, that's all. Booth sent me a note saying Surratt had just returned and they wouldn't need me in Washington."

He prayed it didn't sound as stupid to Hughes's ears as it did to his own. And if it did, then maybe a cocky smile would smooth it over. "As for your woman." He added a shrug. "You know how she gets in storms, I imagine. Just eager for comfort. And after listening for hours to her moan and groan about how much she loves you and how afraid she is you wouldn't believe her, I just wanted to shut her up. Thought I'd have a little fun doing it."

Lord, forgive the lies. Please. Please save her.

Eyes wide, Marietta rubbed together the thumb and forefinger of the arm pinned to her side, over and again. He frowned until he realized it was a sign, one of the ones Elsie used frequently. *What are you doing?*

He hadn't the words, silent or vocal, to answer. *Giving you a chance,* he wanted to say, but his hands didn't know how and his lips didn't dare.

So he had to settle for a command. One simple word, one simple motion of the hand from waist to heart, with his thumb up. *Live.*

She shook her head, though whether in answer to him or Hughes he couldn't tell. The gun was level now, Hughes's finger on the trigger. He knew she would do everything she could to keep the weapon from firing. Everything she could to affect the aim.

He owed it to her to try, one last time. With one final *please, Lord* he lunged for the crate.

Fire spat from the barrel of his revolver. She managed to jerk Hughes's arm, but it didn't matter. The car shifted, his foot slid. Fire kicked him. He reached out, trying to grab something, anything, to halt him. For one moment his fingers caught hold of the edge of the door, but the metal was rain-slick, and his hand would not obey his command to hold tight.

A scream. A curse.

Empty air embraced him. Nothing but air for an eternity, long enough that he saw the scarlet curls fly out the door after him. Saw them jerk back in. Long enough that he could be thankful she didn't follow, that he heard no second shot.

Then earth, rock, tree limbs. Some rushing by, some reaching out greedy claws to grab at him, pummel him, bite him. The mountainside went on forever.

His arms wouldn't obey his orders to reach out and find a hold. His breath wouldn't come. His chest felt as though the locomotive had seared its way through him.

Crashing, snapping. Green filled his vision, then gray. So much gray, no color left in the world. Nothing but that memory of her fiery red hair.

Splash. The cold of the water made him jerk, twist, and blackest night edged out the gray. *To live is Christ…to die is gain.*

Eternity pressed down. He could see only a splinter of the world— the track on the mountain above him, the hillside he had just tumbled down. He could feel only the nothingness of the icy Potomac. He could hear only the din of a cry whose words made no sense.

"Aunt Abigail! Aunt Abigail, hurry!"

A wisp of blue that should have been gray. Of black that should have been red. A face, there one moment and gone the next. Something pressing, pushing eternity away.

More voices, jumbles of words. *What* and *train* and *fall. Shot* and *bridge* and *ran.*

Another face. A woman. "Who did this to you, mister?"

Did he have any breath left? He gathered what he could, expelled it on the name. "Hughes. Dev…" The black grew. The splinter shrank. The fire of pain both consumed and, somehow, numbed. He dragged in one more breath. His last words couldn't, wouldn't be that monster's name. They had to matter. They had to matter as much as she did. "Lord…save…her."

His answer was a bolt of lightning, a crack that rent the very air in two. A treetop rushing toward him.

The black descended.

Time was a dragon set against him, and as Walker ran down the dark streets, he felt it breathing down his back. He didn't need a watch to know too many tocks had ticked. Didn't need the knot in his gut to tell him things were all wrong. Didn't need the cold bite of night air to send a chill down his spine.

Evil walked tonight.

"Lord, go before me. Make clear the way. Protect the family I left at home."

Cora and their tiny son were doing well when he left them at dusk. Jess had woken up. That would have to suffice for now.

He sucked in a breath and turned the corner onto Tenth Street. He prayed that Hez had made it to Secretary Steward's house and convinced them to be on their guard. He knew the family, which was why he'd been the one to go. But then he would try to make his way to the theater too.

Grandpa Henry had gone to the Kirkwood House, where Vice President Johnson and Atzerodt were both staying. His grandfather knew "Port Tobacco" well enough to promise he could get him talking, get him drinking...and that then it would be a simple matter of dissuading him from his role.

That left Walker with the biggest task of them all. Hez should have done it. He knew that as he hurried down the street with all the rich white folk and felt their stares upon him. Hez could have gone into the theater and made sure the president stayed safe. Walker, on the other hand...

But they had decided to obey their own rules and stay undetected. So Hez went to the family who wouldn't ask questions he couldn't answer. And Walker went to find one of Pinkerton's men.

Herschel wasn't back. The other doors he had knocked on had either slammed in his face when he mentioned Osborne or waved him away as a fool. So much time wasted. What choice did he have now but to try to get into the theater himself?

Ford's was just ahead. Cabbies waited outside, drivers hunching into their blankets and horses' ears twitching. He hurried along, trying his best to look like just another servant out on a mission from his master, no one to pay any heed to.

He nearly collided with a sot staggering out of a tavern. Yellow light and tinny music spilled out with him, and Walker hissed out a breath when he saw his face. "Mr. Kaplan?"

The detective leaned against the tavern's filthy brick wall. "Shine my shoes, boy?"

He shook that away. "Mr. Kaplan, thank the Lord. There's a man planning on shooting the president in just a few minutes. You can stop him."

Kaplan straightened and spat. "Not much to be thankin' God for these days, is there, boy? War might be over, but it killed all the good ones. Nothin' left but the sick and the weak and cowards. God musta turned His face away from us long ago."

Sometimes it sure seemed that way. But then, you couldn't see if God had turned His head when you'd already turned yours. "He's still there. Still waiting for us to do the right thing. Will you help me, Mr. Kaplan?"

"Help you?" Kaplan hiccupped and waved a hand toward the theater. "Do I look ready to work to you? Someone else is on guard duty tonight. Let him stop him if there's even a him to stop. It's...it's..." He squinted and then loosed a low, ugly laugh. "It's Parker, that's who. He's watching Lincoln. Assuming he isn't drunk or asleep on the job like he was last week. And last month. And—"

"Thunder and turf!" Walker sidestepped the drunk and darted across the street to the theater.

A black man stepped forward in the uniform of a doorman, his hand up. "Whoa, there. Where do you think you're going, son?"

Walker knew he would stop him, but maybe, just maybe he could get around him. "Please, you have to let me in. I got an important message."

The older man shook his head, though sympathy lit his eyes. "You know I can't let you in this door, not the one the white folks use. You gotta go round the back."

"You don't understand." He stepped closer, praying the man would relent. Would look the other way. "It's urgent. Life-and-death kind of urgent."

"I'm sorry." The doorman shook his head again. "If I let you in, it's real trouble for me. You gotta go round. Right on round there and then through the back entrance. My boy can help get your message to your master."

Briefly, Walker considered force. But if he tried it, he would get shot or beaten within steps of the door. Folks wouldn't take too kindly to a black man bursting into a place like that. He nodded and followed the doorman's outstretched arm.

The theater shared walls with the other buildings on the street, and he had to jog all the way to the corner and around, and then down an alleyway. The moon still shone hazy and dim through the clouds, but it felt darker, as though something had swooped down over the street.

Walker slowed only when he spotted the theater doors, open to the night. Folks loitered around it in the circle of light, smoking and laughing. He pushed through them with an abstract nod of greeting and stepped into an unfamiliar world. Props, curtains, discarded costumes, and rows of what he assumed were backdrops. People were darting this way and that, some with extravagant costumes on, some obviously never to see the stage.

Seeing a boy who had the look of the doorman about him, he stopped him with what he hoped was a casual grin. "Hey there. You know where the president's box is?"

The boy, probably twelve or so, grinned back. "You want a glimpse of him too? Come on. I'll show ya the best view."

He didn't need the best view; he needed the closest one. But at least it would give him an idea of the layout.

The boy waved him down a dark corridor. "You gotta be real quiet," he whispered. He paused at a break in the wall and nodded toward the brightly lit stage. "That there's Miss Keene. Listen—this is the best line of the play."

He could barely see the woman and didn't much care. He edged onward as she said, "I am aware, Mr. Trenchard, that you are not used to the manners of polite society."

Another piece of wall, another break in it. He halted. What were all those banners hanging over on the side there, above the stage? Red, white, and blue ones...the president's box?

A man on stage preened. "Heh, heh. Don't know the manners of good society, eh? Well, I guess I know enough to turn you inside out, old gal—you sockdologizing old man-trap!"

Laughter roared through the audience. Walker strained forward. Was that Lincoln standing in the shadows of the box? Or—

Crack.

Chaos, instant and deafening. Walker tried to rush forward, but the actors were running, screaming, pushing into him.

A figure jumped from the balcony to the stage. Booth, shouting something in Latin. He took off for the back.

Walker took off after him, bowling over the boy and getting caught in the shouting, darting crowd of theater people. But even as he fought his way outside, he knew he was too late.

Booth was gone. Lincoln was shot.

Walker sank to the cool bricks and stared into the thick darkness. Two more minutes, and he could have been there. He could have stopped him. Two more minutes, and the Culpers would have won.

Two more minutes the world had refused him. And now he could only watch them reel.

Thirty-Four

Marietta had gone numb lying on the cold, damp rock. The blindfold made time swim, the gag sucked all the moisture from her mouth, and the rope tying her wrists chafed her raw as she struggled.

Why fight? a voice snarled in her ear. *He's dead. You lost.*

Her eyes burned behind the blindfold, but she couldn't cry, not if she wanted to obey Slade's last instruction. Not if she wanted to live to find him justice.

She wasn't sure she did. She wasn't sure it mattered. Why had Dev stopped her from jumping behind him from the train? She had caught a glimpse of the landscape only in that last second, hadn't known when she managed, too late, to break free that the ground fell away so dramatically. The fall very well could have killed her. And that would have been so much easier on them all.

To live is Christ and to die is gain. Stephen had quoted that as he swung onto his mount before he joined his regiment. Had he thought of Barbara then? Was she what had made his eyes go soft? *I have living left to do—Christ still to show to many. I won't go home until the Lord calls me.*

The Lord must have called on that battlefield in Pennsylvania. But it would seem He hadn't, yet, called Marietta to join her brother. No matter that she could see the gain in dying—she hadn't. And so she must yet live for Christ.

Beside her sounded a sniff, a moan from Mother Hughes. Dev obviously still held affection for his matron. Why else would he have instructed his cohort not to tie her too tightly, not to gag her?

A courtesy not extended to Marietta. He hadn't yet killed her. He wouldn't send her into eternity so quickly. If she didn't get free of these ropes, she would suffer long and painfully at his hands.

Another sniff, a longer moan, and the sound of rustling fabric. From the right came footsteps, two sets, and yet another heavy thud.

Sixty-two. How much more could they possibly have to haul?

"Devereaux." Mother Hughes's voice was faint and scratchy and sounded so heavily of resignation that Marietta's heart twisted for her. "Devereaux. I need water."

Water! The very word made her ache, made her tongue push against the gag. But when she heard the boots pause, pivot, and head their way, she kept her body limp as a rag.

His footsteps paused mere feet away. "Are you finally finished crying?"

His mother sniffed once more. Perhaps she nodded or made some other silent answer, but she said nothing. There came a metallic scrape and then the sound of gurgling. Marietta nearly moaned in jealousy.

"You always loved him best." Dev must have crouched down to assist his mother in drinking.

"No, I didn't." Heartbroken amusement tinted Mother Hughes's voice. "I always loved you best. You should have heard how I fought with your father when he said he intended to train Lucien to take over his role instead of you."

"So Father loved him best."

"Don't be a fool. He loved the railroad best, pure and simple. Lucien stayed to learn it while you went off to make your own way. In his eyes, that meant your brother must love it best too. That was all that mattered."

Something hit the ground with a soft thud. "So you would weep so long for me?"

A moment of silence, another soft moan. "That was for you, Devereaux. For my precious firstborn who has such a fight ahead of him."

He grunted. "Lean forward, Mother. Let me untie you so you can drink."

"May I take off the blindfold?"

A pause. "For now, yes. You will have to put it back on when we leave. For your own safety."

"Thank you."

Though she wanted to writhe and scream, Marietta kept her breathing even and slow, her limbs lax. She didn't even hold her breath when she felt him step nearer to her.

At last his footsteps headed away. More gurgling that made her throat ache in longing as the steps faded to nothing.

Then frantic rustling, padded thuds at her side. "Give me a moment, dear. My hands are tingling."

What? She couldn't mean—but she did. The blindfold slipped away, though precious little light reached them in this rocky alcove. She could just make out Mother Hughes's foot as she reached behind Marietta and worked at the gag.

"There."

Thank You, Lord! Gasping in a long breath, she tried to speak her thanks aloud but managed only a rasp. Mother Hughes helped her sit up and then tilted a canteen to Marietta's mouth. Cool water touched her lips, her tongue, her throat, and made the rest of the world brighten.

The woman's frown didn't agree with that assessment. She lowered the canteen again and scooted behind her. "These knots will take me a moment, I'm afraid. Oh, Mari—your wrists are bloody and raw. Do they hurt?"

Terribly, but Marietta gritted her teeth against the pain. "They have mostly gone numb. Why are you helping me?"

Her fingers didn't slow. "Because you made Lucien happy. Because when I was ill, you cared for me with patience and love. Because every time I slapped at one cheek, you turned the other. You, my dear, are more my daughter than that monster out there is my son. He *killed* my son, my favorite son."

Her head snapped around, though she still couldn't see her mother-in-law's face. "You—you were lying to him?"

"Where do you think Devereaux learned the art?" She grunted and tugged hard at the rope. "You must have loosened it some. I nearly have it...there!"

Her wrists fell to her side. Blood rushed into her hands, making her wounds catch fire. She clenched her teeth and scrambled for the canteen.

Mother Hughes settled before her, her face a decade older than it had been that morning. "You must find a way out. He will kill you, but only after he has made you wish yourself dead a thousand times over."

Nodding, Marietta took another drink and looked around. This must be one of the caves marked on his maps. Would he have selected one with a single entrance? Even if so, she could surely sneak past them. There were only the two of them, and they were gone for long stretches, no doubt as they unloaded more crates from the train and carted them over what had sounded like a small bridge.

Though her legs protested, she pushed herself up and crept to the edge of the rock wall beside her.

A large central cavern stretched out, the pile of crates and barrels small within it. The line of muddy footprints tracked the men's comings and goings. Lanterns revealed other dark, gaping places in the rock. Nine of them, counting the one she and Mother Hughes were in, which extended but ten feet off the main chamber.

"He told me nothing about where we are."

"Rest easy, Mother. I have a few aces yet up my sleeve." One large cavern, nine arms attached. The map surfaced in her mind. His sketch had been surprisingly good, the ratio exact. She hoped that meant she could trust it to have the twists and turns of the second entrance correct too. She turned back to her companion. "There is another way out. I saw a map he had drawn of this. We can—"

"You, dear." Mother Hughes shook her muddied blond tresses. "I would slow you down. But when that other man carried me in, he knocked my head against something, and I've a bump. I will say you freed yourself and that you struck me. It will keep me safe."

"I cannot leave you with him!"

"Mari, what hope have I of outpacing him through the woods?" Her look now bade her to be realistic. "You are young and strong. You must find the authorities and bring help back here."

Another lie? Perhaps...perhaps she meant instead to warn Dev and disappear with him. But since Marietta could hardly drag the woman from the cave, she had no choice but to trust.

She stepped back into the sheltering oblivion of the wall and slid her eyes closed. "Lord, lend me Your strength. Give wings to my feet. Give purpose to my life."

"Amen."

Drawing in a long breath, she turned her back to Mother Hughes. "Would you loosen my corset? And untie the hoop and petticoats, if you would."

"Of course." Her fingers seemed to have regained some agility, for they flew over the row of pearl buttons and then tugged at her stays.

Marietta sucked in a deep breath for the first time all day and, when her heavy petticoats sagged to the floor, stepped over them. Mother Hughes secured the now-too-long skirt for her and then stepped away.

Marietta took a moment to capture the woman's image as it was now. Dirty, bedraggled, broken—yet tall with that stubborn will that had caused Marietta so many headaches over the years. She surged forward and gathered her in a quick embrace. "I will send someone back for you."

"I know. God speed, Mari."

"God keep you." Anticipation tying new knots in her chest, she pulled up the mental image of the map again, strained to be sure she heard no footsteps returning, and then darted along the wall of the cavern. Ten long steps and she could breathe again, back in the cover of darkness.

Trying not to think about what might be creeping and crawling along beside her, she felt her way along the tunnel, nearly panicking when her hair brushed the ceiling, when the sides closed in. Near panic ratcheted to full panic when she heard the men's voices echoing through the main chamber.

But that was good. If they were inside, they wouldn't be outside when she emerged. Drawing in a calming breath and whispering another prayer, she pressed on. The tunnel couldn't get too small, or Dev never would have made it through to realize it was an exit.

No light told her when she reached the end, nothing but rock one moment and then wet leaves in her face. Her toes struck a wall, her hands found a ledge, a hole. Pushing aside the leaves, weak moonlight filtered through the disbursing clouds.

She sifted through the other maps in her mind, finding the one of the area. Assuming this was the dot he had circled, assuming the other markings were accurate, her best bet was the inn a mile away.

If only he had noted every tree root, every undulation in the landscape. If only she had spent more time outside with the boys on Grandpapa Alain's wooded property in Connecticut. If only, when she crawled out into the chilly night, a hand of sorrow didn't press on her heart.

She curled into a ball on the wet ground to catch her breath. Sorrow choked her and made the tears well.

He was gone. Slade was gone, his body probably but a mile or two away—the train had squealed to a halt so soon after he fell. *Let someone find him. Let me take him home to his parents. Let me...let me...*

The sorrow pressed her down into the earth until it threatened to swallow her.

His face swam before her, frozen in that last moment, the one that sealed his fate. When love had pulsed from his midnight eyes, when he had said without a single word that she was all that mattered. When his hand had given that simple, profound command. *Live.*

"Jesus, help me." The words were barely a whisper.

But He was a rushing wind. It swept over her, blew away the sorrow, and lifted her back to her feet. Without another thought, she took off at a run toward that scratch on the map.

Sensations swirled and melded, a cacophony of impressions that made little sense. The light hurt. Why did the light hurt? Heaven should be free of pain.

Daggers attacked his chest when he drew a breath, and Slade's eyes flew open at the agony. The ceiling spun. A little face appeared above him with a cloud of dark hair and a smudge on her cheek. If she was an angel, then she needed to take a swim in the crystal lake.

"Are you waking up?" The cherub bent over him, a sticky hand on his arm. "Aunt Abigail said to holler if you wake up. But you keep opening your eyes and just shutting them again, and that doesn't seem very awake. I do that sometimes when Ruby tries to get me to go to school but I don't wanna."

Abigail...Ruby...faces flashed to match the names, but they wouldn't still long enough to figure out why he knew them. He drew in another breath, more slowly, and blinked.

The girl's halo cleared, and freckles appeared on her nose. She grinned down at him and patted his bare arm with those sticky fingers. "My name's Rose. I usually have to be in bed by nine o'clock, but it's almost eleven now, and I'm still up because you could die any minute, and it ain't right for a man to die alone, but all these guests are flooding in from the train stuck behind the fallen tree up on the mountain."

"Rose Elizabeth Kent, will you stop chattering for five minutes and let the man die in peace?" A boy's voice came from the left, tired and short.

The cherub stuck out her tongue. "His eyes are open."

"What?" Footsteps, and then a boy's face joined Rose's over him. Her brother, from the looks of him. His eyes went wide. "Mister? Mister, can you hear me? Say something if you can hear me."

The girl gave the boy a push. "He's hearing me. I'm the one talking to him. You're just hiding in the hall in a grump."

Slade swallowed and tried flexing his fingers. How was it possible that he was alive? The pain searing his chest proved the bullet had struck, and he remembered falling into nothingness. And then...what?

"Yetta." Her hair, he saw her hair spilling from the freight car's door. Did she fall? Was she here somewhere too? *Oh God, let her be alive. Please, please let her be alive.*

"Who?" Rose squinted at him, head tilted. "Judah? He's right here, though you don't wanna talk to him. He gets cranky when he stays up past his bedtime. Not me, though. Aunt Abigail says if she let me, I'd be up until the rooster crowed. I tried it once, but—"

"Rose, *stop.*" Judah put a hand to the top of her head and pushed her out of Slade's line of sight. "Sorry about her, mister. Are you all right? Do you need a drink or something? Do you have a name?"

"Don't be dumb, Judah. Everyone has a name. Is it in here?" Rose must have jumped onto the bed beside him—the mattress bounced, and the pain doubled with his vision. His breath hissed out. She fluttered the pages of something.

"Rose, be careful! And what did Aunt Abigail say about nosing through his things?"

"It's just a book. Golly, it looks old. Are you Ob...Oba...Obadiah Reeves?"

The name swam in his head with the rest of them, but it settled into place when the room stopped spinning. She had the prayer book, that was all. She was looking at the last page, where the family names had been written, the ink getting rustier as one followed the list upward. He had found them only a month ago but had read them so many times since that he knew each flourish of the various hands.

Obadiah Reeves. Hezekiah Reeves. Winter Reeves. Thaddeus Lane.

"Slade." He moistened his lips. "I'm Slade."

Her face scrunched up. "You're not in here."

No. He hadn't ever meant to leave his mark on that family.

She held up the book and peered through...a hole? "What's this for?"

"Rose." Judah's voice again, longsuffering. "The bullet got it. Didn't you hear Doc say that? You never pay any attention."

What? "No!" Slade lifted a hand before he thought better of it, wincing at the new surge of agony as well as the damage to the tome.

Judah put a restraining hand on the foolish arm. "I wouldn't get too upset about the book if I were you, mister. Doc said it coulda been what kept you from dying then and there. Coulda slowed the bullet down just enough, he said, before it went into you." The boy shrugged. "Didn't seem to do much good to me. You about gave up the ghost on our kitchen table, but maybe I was wrong."

"Besides, it's just the corner. You can still see all the words. Mostly."

Floorboards creaked, and footsteps sounded somewhere nearby. Judah and Rose both snapped to attention and called out "Ruby!"

"How is he?" An older voice, but still young. Slade eased his face toward the door and frowned. Something about the blue dress, the black hair were familiar, though he wasn't sure why. Her eyes went just as wide as Judah's had. "You're awake!"

Another of the Kent siblings, it would seem. Older, more woman than girl. She charged in and pushed her brother aside, gripped his hand, and leaned over him. "Can you speak? You scared a decade off of my life when I saw you falling from the train. Was it really Devereaux Hughes who shot you?"

He had to blink to keep his head from swimming again. These kids sure didn't know the value of quiet.

"I am sorry, sir." Another woman's voice, older, drifted into the room. "Her train must have made it through before the tree came down. I have seen no young woman with red hair today."

"It would have been an unscheduled train." That voice—masculine, familiar, and asking after a young woman with red hair. But it couldn't be Lane. Lane was in Washington, saving Lincoln. He couldn't be here.

He dug his fingers into the mattress under him. Of course he was here, doing the same thing Slade had been doing—trying to save their Marietta from that monster.

Footsteps halted outside his room. "Interesting. An unscheduled train came through just before the lightning strike. I cannot speak to your granddaughter, but a man was shot and fell from one of the cars into the river. We brought him here, though the doctor thinks he cannot hold on much longer. Perhaps you would know him too?"

Ruby leaped from his side. "Aunt Abigail, he's awake!"

A clamor of footsteps followed, and a moment later a trio rushed through the door. A woman whose face seemed as familiar as Ruby's—Abigail, apparently—and two tall men partially visible behind her. Lane, it had to be. No one else was that tall. Sweet relief sang through him at knowing someone was here to help where he couldn't.

"Lane." He tried to sit up and ended up back on the pillow, moaning.

"Oz." The old man was at his side in one step. He shook his head as he took the chair beside the bed. "I knew, even as I prayed, something had gone wrong. What happened, son?"

Isaac came up behind him, looking conflicted.

Slade focused on the grandfather. "I don't know where she is. We were together in the freight car, but Hughes..." His eyes slid closed. Such a blur. He could remember her face, the love and the fear in it, her hand shaking and straining against Hughes's as they raised the gun. "I tried to give her a chance. I tried. I..." He couldn't breathe. It hurt too much, within and without.

She had to be all right. She *had* to be.

"We'll find her." Lane gripped his forearm. Firmly, but there was a quaver in his hand, and his smile lacked its usual confidence. "I daresay when we do, she will settle for nothing less than your full recovery."

He didn't know what to say to that. He didn't know that he could have said anything even if the perfect words rested on his tongue. Lane's face went blurry, Isaac's behind him contorted.

The black approached again.

Did she hear voices behind her or just the night giving chase? Was that a light up ahead, through the budding trees, or a star breaking through the clouds? Not knowing, Marietta could only ignore the cramping in her side and run onward, faster, narrowly dodging trees, slapping at stray limbs, stubbing her toes countless times on roots.

Yes, it was a light, set on the next hillside—half a dozen windows shining out hope, and even lanterns twinkling their way toward it. The inn, it had to be. And it was the most beautiful thing she had ever seen.

A *crack* split the air, and the pound of thunder shook her. She looked first to the heavens, but the clouds were still thinning.

The thunder increased. *Hooves.*

Another *crack*, and this time bark flew off a tree a few paces to her left. "Mari! You might as well give up!"

Dev. Not looking behind her, she prayed God would lift her and set her feet toward the light.

She had to get there. Had to find help. Had to keep her promise to Slade.

She had to live.

A gunshot echoed. A scream rent the air. High, desperate, it struck Slade right in his wound and brought him bolt upright, agony be hanged. "Yetta!"

Lane and Arnaud were already out the door, Judah and Ruby and Abigail behind them. Slade tossed aside the blanket and swung his legs to the floor. He had no shoes, no socks, and the trousers he wore were unfamiliar. Blood stained the bandage wrapped round his torso...a stain that grew as he watched.

Little fingers wove through his. "Mr. Slade, you better lay back down. You're bleeding again, and I don't want you to die."

He dug up a smile for the girl. "I can't lie back down, Rose. My Yetta's out there, and I can't let a bad man hurt her."

Her big eyes solemn, she nodded. "I better help you then. You can lean on me. I'm real strong."

He didn't have time to argue. Marietta's scream tore through the room again, masculine shouts following. He tried to tell himself Lane was there, her brother was there. They would save her.

Not good enough. He accepted the little one's support and staggered up, lurched toward the door, and let her lead him down the hall. Every step felt heavier, and he had to pause halfway along and lean into a doorway.

He was glad he did when he spotted the rifle propped against the wall. Sucking in a deep breath, he reached for it and checked the chamber—loaded. "God of my end," he murmured as he stumbled back into the hall, his vision narrowed upon the door swinging wide in the breeze, "it is my greatest, noblest pleasure to be acquainted with Thee."

Perhaps it was just the wind whistling through the opening—or perhaps it was the touch of the Father, lending him a breath of borrowed life. He released Rose and told her to stay out of sight inside, and then he slid onto the porch and leaned against a post.

He stared at the pure horror in the yard.

A lathered horse quivered, reins dragging the mud. Lane and Arnaud both stood with their backs to him, guns drawn. Abigail had Judah and Ruby clutched to her chest, terror frozen in her eyes. And there, facing him, barely in the circle of light, stood Hughes. He held a thrashing, gnashing Marietta before him as a shield, Slade's revolver pressed to her temple.

The pain in his chest nearly crippled him, but not where the bullet had bit. Somewhere deeper, far deeper. His Yetta—his beautiful, vibrant Yetta, fighting for her life.

"If you hurt her, you'll be dead in a second. Let her go." Lane's voice sounded hard, daring. "Let her go or I will shoot you in the head here and now."

Hughes sneered. "If your aim were that good, old man, you already would have taken the shot. How about you two put down your guns instead and we back away. I swear if either of you twitches a finger, I'll kill her."

Marietta kicked at his shin. "He'll kill me anyway. Just shoot him, Granddad!"

He wouldn't, and Hughes no doubt knew it. He wouldn't risk hitting her, and neither would her brother. They were in a stalemate.

But they weren't counting on Slade. If she stopped flailing for a minute, just a minute to get Hughes to relax a few precious degrees, he could slide forward and raise the rifle. It would have better aim than the pistols. More, she would react when she saw him. He knew she would, knew exactly what she would do—lunge, lurch, as frantic to reach him as he was to reach her. Maybe she'd break free, and even if she didn't, it would move her body away from Hughes's for a second.

Lord? If that's what I'm to do, I need Your help.

Hoofbeats echoed through the night. For a second he feared the intrusion would spur Hughes to act, but the rider didn't seem to be veering their way. His shout, though, resounded through the trees. "Lincoln is shot! It just came over the wire! The president is shot!"

Hughes's laugh slicked like oil, oozing malice and darkness. The rest of them went stock-still, even the wind dying to nothing. His teeth flashed white in the moonlight. "We've won. We've *won*!"

"Not yet, you haven't." Slade had the rifle resting against his shoulder, had Hughes's head in his sights. He had no idea where the strength came from to lift the heavy weapon, were it not straight from the Lord. Every pulse was a new pain, but it made time slow down. Made it so clear, so very clear.

"Slade!" Marietta's cry held the whole world, it seemed. All the love, all the hope, all the fear and pain. More, she jerked out of view.

And oh, the shifting expressions on Hughes's shadowed face. The evil joy melting to shock and then hardening into hatred.

Slade pulled the trigger. The shot rang out, sounding, to his ears, like a second chance. A second chance for her to live, free of those chains. A second chance for the nation to rebuild itself, without the looming threat of another break. When he pulled back, he saw the bullet had found its mark. Hughes lay, unmoving, on the ground.

Slade slid down the post, the gun clattering to the stairs as its kick set up a new throb. So loud. It drowned out the cries, the footsteps, and made them nothing but echoes.

Except for hers. Her voice he heard clearly, saying his name over and over, ever louder. Then her face appeared, streaked with mud and tears, her hair flowing like a flame around her shoulders. "Slade. Slade, my love, hold on. Hold tight to me. Don't let go."

Her fingers encircled his. Cold but solid. Unharmed. *Thank You, Jesus.* Had he the strength, he would have tangled his other hand in her hair.

All he managed was a swallow. His tongue felt swollen and heavy. "You gonna wanna look away, kitten. Bleeding." He could feel it, feel the warmth spreading. Too fast, too hot.

"No." Her gaze latched on his, she gripped his hand tighter. "No, I want to look right here. You keep looking back, Slade. Keep looking at me."

He blinked, barely dragging his lids open again. The words echoed through his mind. Booth had succeeded. He had shot the president.

The circle of light dimmed. "Tried. Tried to stop it all."

Her fingers soothed over his jaw, down his neck, and rested feather light on his chest. "We can never stop it all, my love. Not in this world. We can only do our part, answer our call, and pray the Lord will heal the wounds left behind."

Her voice caught, but her eyes stayed clear. Clear and green and bright, like life itself. She was right. There was too much evil in the world for them to fight it off single-handedly. Battles would be lost, as battles always were.

But the war didn't have to be. Not when they found families to fight beside. He gathered all the strength he could find to strain up that inch, to catch her lips with his.

He wished, oh how he wished he could have saved them all.

And yet, he couldn't regret choosing his family. "I love you, kitten." He sagged down. Though his eyelids felt like lead, he kept them open just one more second. To seize one last picture of her face to take with him into eternity. "Don't mourn for me. I've had enough of black and gray. You need to...bring...the color back."

He focused on the green of her eyes until it all faded away.

Thirty-Five

Marietta Hughes smoothed a hand over the green skirt of her dress and felt a twist in her stomach that never seemed very far away these days. Everywhere she turned was some reminder of all that had passed, of all that had been lost. The black crepe of mourning still covered all the windows, all the mirrors. Not just here in her parents' home, but throughout the city. Throughout the country.

"Hurry, Marietta, or we'll miss the train!"

"Coming, Mama." But it took another second to convince her hand to release the fabric of her new traveling dress and clutch instead the worn maple of her childhood home's main staircase.

When she reached the entryway, the door stood open, spring's sweet breeze wafting in. The coaches waited, already loaded with trunks and valises. Hers, Mama's, Barbara's. Granddad Thad's and Grandmama Gwyn's. Daddy, his telegram had said, would meet them in New York.

A low whistle made her jump and then made her pulse gallop as a figure stepped into the doorway. A smile teased her lips as his gaze swept up and down her.

If only he didn't still have to lean against the doorframe for support.

The fool man—he should have given himself another week to rest, at least. One fortnight was not enough to recover from a gunshot wound to the chest, no matter how stubborn the man. No matter how big the miracle that he survived it at all. "Slade, you said you would wait in the coach."

"And you said you would be right back down." Shadows still ringed his eyes, and he had lost too much weight, but his smile had never been brighter. "I was beginning to think you ran away."

She lifted her chin and sailed toward him with a regal sniff. "Why would I do that?"

He chuckled and held out a hand. "You tell me." She slipped hers into it and eased up against him, not daring to put any weight against his chest.

Her fear nearly sent her running back up the steps. "What if your parents hate me?"

His hand on her waist held her steady. And his eyes sparkled with a decidedly wolfish mirth. "They might."

"Slade!"

"Well, you're not what they would expect of the girl I finally bring home. You're a rich Southerner." He kissed her, slow and promising. "But it won't take them long to see why I love you."

"Humph." They would see soon enough, she supposed. A few hours by rail, and they would be, oddly, back in the place the Culpers had begun—New York City. "Just promise me you will take it easy while we are there. You have been pushing yourself too hard."

"There's been a lot to do." His eyes flickered. His smile dimmed.

She kissed him again and then pulled him out the door. He had insisted on attending the funeral service one short week after the assassination. He had sat in a row with his friends, finally believed only when his warnings proved true.

An irony she suspected they all recognized. One that made all their feet shuffle extra slow as they said farewell to their commander in chief.

"Miss Mari, you forgot your shawl again." Cora's voice preceded her down the stairs, tiny little Freeman strapped to her with a long piece of cloth.

Marietta paused with a smile. When her friend came near with the shawl extended, she took it with a nod of thanks and brushed her fingertips over the infant's smooth head. "He's going to be so big when I get home. A whole month. It seems he's doubled in just these two weeks."

Cora's grin was bright as the sun. "He sure will be. And with a little luck, the house will sell fast and we can cut our ties. We lookin' forward to Connecticut."

She was praying for the same, but not quite so joyfully. There had been some sorrow in shutting up the Hugheses' home. So many memories lived there, not just of Lucien and Dev, but of these past months with Slade and Barbara, Cora and Walker. The months when the world had shifted.

But it was silly to keep the big old place open when they would be happier at her parents'. And Mother Hughes had refused to stay in Baltimore after they buried Dev beside Lucien and their father. Her place, she had said, was Louisiana.

Cora's smile faded too. "Walker still gets so quiet sometimes. Sayin' how if he just had two more minutes, if they hadn't sent him round back..." Her brows drew in, her hand stroked over her sleeping baby. "So much has changed. So much hasn't."

"I know." She sighed and, when Mama waved frantically from the coach, stepped away. "Keep reminding him of their victories of the night. On the other lives they saved." Just as she must rest in the peace that Granddad had taken care of sealing the cave, had charged the family of innkeepers to watch over it. Marietta had been uncertain about trusting them so much, at first, when she realized they were Confederate, but they wanted peace as much as the Culpers. They would do anything they could to keep a new break at bay, and the only other man who knew the location of the cave and its guns and gold had been silenced before Dev came after her.

Perhaps the treasure would be found someday. But not in their generation.

"Yetta." Slade made a show of pulling out his watch and staring pointedly at the face.

Which reminded her. Slipping a hand into her pocket, she shook her head as she took a step toward him. "A watch without a fob. What will your father say, Slade?"

He winced and closed the lid. "I meant to buy a new one before we left, but..."

"Well. Lucky for you, I happen to have one just lying around." She pulled out the silver links, dangled them in front of his nose.

He looked from the fob, obviously worn, to her and lifted a brow.

She smiled. "It was Stephen's. He would have wanted you to have it. He would have been proud to call you a brother."

"Yetta." He took the chain and then leaned down for a kiss. He paused two inches away and chuckled when a chorus of impatience sounded from the two coaches. "Guess I'll save that part for later."

Tucking her hand in the crook of his elbow, she led him down the walk. Soon enough he would be back to normal, back to work, wherever Pinkerton might send him. But not alone anymore.

He shot her a grin as they neared her family. "You know, my father's a minister. Our families will all be together..."

Her pulse thrummed. "And?"

That smirk she loved appeared as he leaned close. "And we could be married by this time tomorrow, once my parents stop hating you."

A laugh tickling her throat, she gathered her skirt in preparation of the step into the carriage. "Tempting."

"Yeah?" He sounded one part surprised and four parts hopeful.

Foregoing the social whirl of an engagement and forging ahead into a lifetime of new memories? She let the laugh bloom full. "Very tempting indeed."

Discussion Questions

1. In the first chapter, Marietta learns devastating secrets about the Hugheses. Have you ever learned something about someone that completely redefined your relationship?

2. Would you ever join a secret society? Why or why not? What type might you consider being a part of?

3. Who is your favorite character and why?

4. Brotherhood is a central theme in the book, represented in many different ways. Have you experienced any of the varieties of sibling relationships—or spiritual brotherhood—that the characters have?

5. Marietta's amazing memory was inspired by true stories I heard of people reading with their eyes closed after glancing at a book's pages. What are some amazing stories of the human mind that you've heard?

6. Slade and Marietta both have what could be called checkered pasts. How do you think the Lord took their flaws and used them to His glory?

7. Several times through the book, Marietta reflects on the truth that forgiveness of sin does not negate the consequences of sin. Have you ever seen an example of this?

8. Walker and Cora and their family will face many changes in the next years, as the nation adjusts to new laws...and in some ways changes very little. What do you think their future will look like? What do you think will become of Elsie?

9. Slade learns by the end of the book that he cannot do anything alone. How have you found that family and friends affect your goals?

10. The secret workings of the Knights of the Golden Circle were really referenced in one of Lincoln's speeches as "the fifth column"—an actual, if invisible, part of the Confederate war machine. Why do you think they had the successes they did? Why do you think they experienced so many failures? How does this relate to the successes and failures of all the characters in *Circle of Spies*?

Author's Note

I hope you enjoyed journeying with the Culpers into the Civil War! In the first two books in the series, espionage and intelligence gathering were considered dirty business best suited to lowlife rabble. By this time spies were everywhere, working on both sides. I had so much fun bringing agents from three different organizations into one clash, even if it made me a bit dizzy at times. ;-)

I loved weaving a few threads through the entire series—the pearl necklace, sign language, and the book of prayers. The prayers were taken from *Valley of Vision: A Collection of Puritan Prayers & Devotions* compiled by Arthur Bennet and used by permission.

I wanted to take a moment to discuss the Hughes's railroad ties. Though I based the facts of the railroad culture and locations upon the B&O line, I in no way wanted to indicate that the president of the Baltimore & Ohio was in any way connected to the KGC. He was, in fact, one of the most valuable assets of the Union. Which is, of course, what made me wonder, "But what if he hadn't been?" And so my fictitious Hughes family was born...and hence why the railroad is never specifically named.

The Pinkertons are another group I have always had fun imagining scenarios for. Despite some of the terrible incidents they were involved in surrounding union strikes, Allan Pinkerton created something new and pretty cool with his team of detectives. They were the Union's primary source of intelligence in the Civil War, and he is known for his investigative techniques of "shadowing" and "assuming a role." These were techniques my Culpers were already using, so I thought it right and proper to have them working together, however unbeknownst to my detective at the time.

And oh, the joys I had in my research! This time in our nation's history resulted in changes we still feel the effect of today. Lincoln seized more control into the hands of the president than anyone before him in history thought possible, and we can't know what he intended to do after peace returned to the land. Though it's often overlooked in the shadow of his assassination, two other targets that night survived. Who's to say the Culpers didn't have a hand in that?

The KGC reportedly hid massive amounts of gold, weapons, ammunition, and medical supplies in hopes of a future uprising. We don't know where most of them are, though many treasure hunters joyfully follow the clues laid out.

What we do know is that from its very foundation, the United States has been a nation of diversity...diversity that can either make it great or fracture it. Through writing this series, I gained new appreciation and love for the country I call home, and new determination to do what I can to keep it on solid footing. It's my prayer that through reading the Culper books, you too might wonder what you can do to carry on the Culper legacy and quietly effect change in your world.

About the Author

Roseanna M. White grew up in the mountains of West Virginia, the beauty of which inspired her to begin writing as soon as she learned to pair subjects with verbs. She spent her middle and high school days penning novels in class, and her love of books took her to a school renowned for them. After graduating from St. John's College in Annapolis, Maryland, she and her husband moved back to the Maryland side of the same mountains they equate with home. Roseanna is the author of two biblical novels as well as several American historical romances. She is the senior reviewer at the Christian Review of Books, which she and her husband founded, the senior editor at WhiteFire Publishing, and a member of ACFW, HisWriters, and Colonial American Christian Writers.

Roseanna loves little more than talking to her readers! You can reach her at:

roseanna@roseannawhite.com

Be sure to visit her blog at
www.RoseannaMWhite.blogspot.com
and her website at www.RoseannaMWhite.com
where you can sign up for her newsletter to receive
news about upcoming books.

**Love Has No Place
in a World of Spies**

1779—Winter Reeves is an aristocratic American Patriot forced to hide her heart amid the British Loyalists of the city of New York. She has learned to keep her ears open so she can pass information on British movements to Robbie Townsend, her childhood friend, and his spy ring. If she's caught, she will be executed for espionage, but she prays the Lord's protection will sustain her, and Robbie has taught her the tools of the trade—the wonders of invisible ink, secret drop locations and, most importantly, a good cover.

Bennet Lane returns to New York from his Yale professorship with one goal: to find General Washington's spy hidden among the ranks of the city's elite. Searching for a wife was supposed to be nothing more than a convenient cover story for his mission, but when he meets Winter, with her too-intelligent eyes in her too-blank face, he finds a mystery that can't be ignored.

Both are determined to prevail at any cost…and each is committed to a separate cause. Will God lead them to a shared destiny or lives lived apart?

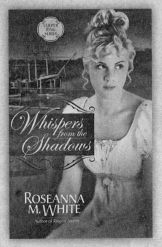

I Love Her...
Can I Trust Her?

I Love Him...Is He Safe?

1814—England and America are again at war. Sudden and implacable treachery causes Gwyneth Fairchild's world to crumble in a moment's time. The daughter of a British general, she barely saves her life by fleeing London aboard a ship bound for America. Her goal is to find refuge with the Lane family in Maryland. Yet after meeting the Lanes' son, Thaddeus, Gwyn wonders how safe she is. For she discovers that this family trades in a dangerous commodity—espionage.

Thad Lane is a prominent citizen in the city of Baltimore. He has the ear of everyone, and he is in a unique position to pass on to leaders of government exactly what he hears. Not long after the beautiful and British Gwyneth Fairchild finds safe haven in his community, he experiences the tug of love, though he fears it may blur lines of loyalty. With family playing the part of enemies and enemies proving themselves friends, a future with Gwyn is more than uncertain—it could be life threatening.

In the end, with the British advancing relentlessly on Baltimore, Thad and Gwyn have to trust in their shared faith in God to be a shield about them. To give them a future and a hope.

Fairchild's Lady

In 1789 General Isaac Fairchild travels across the Channel on a very special assignment. After surviving the American Revolution, he is now gathering information on life at King Louis XVI's court. But he must also locate a countess and her grown daughter and escort them back to England before revolution explodes in France. He knows danger is in the task set before him, but when he meets the beautiful Julienne, a new peril beckons him deeper into the intrigue of Versailles.

A Hero's Promise

January 1835
Baltimore, Maryland

Lenna Lane has already had to postpone her wedding three times. With only two days until their nuptials, Naval Lieutenant Jack Arnaud finally makes it home from a harrowing tour of duty…but something vital has shifted in their world. Can Lenna put Jack's career at risk by sharing the secrets she has kept during his absence? And what is he keeping from her? Jack has never wanted anything to come between him and Lenna, but he cannot bring her into the Culper Ring—and his homecoming is met with a clandestine task of the utmost importance. Will satires and runaways and assassination plots come between them? Or will the promise they made as mere children hold them together still?

To learn more about Harvest House books and
to read sample chapters, visit our website:

www.harvesthousepublishers.com

HARVEST HOUSE PUBLISHERS
EUGENE, OREGON